T0363668

NEW YORK TIMES BESTSELLING AUTHOR

DIANA PALMER

A LONG, TALL TEXANS NOVEL

INVINCIBLE

MILLS & BOON

INVINCIBLE © 2024 by Harlequin Books S.A.

INVINCIBLE
© 2014 by Diana Palmer
Australian Copyright 2014
New Zealand Copyright 2014

First Published 2014
Third Australian Paperback Edition 2024
ISBN 978 1 038 90869 8

SUTTON'S WAY
© 1989 by Diana Palmer
Australian Copyright 1989
New Zealand Copyright 1989

First Published 1989
Third Australian Paperback Edition 2024
ISBN 978 1 038 90869 8

This is a work of fiction. Names, characters, places, and incidents are either the product of the author's imagination or are used fictitiously, and any resemblance to actual persons, living or dead, business establishments, events, or locales is entirely coincidental.

Published by
Mills & Boon
An imprint of Harlequin Enterprises (Australia) Pty Limited (ABN 47 001 180 918), a subsidiary of HarperCollins Publishers Australia Pty Limited (ABN 36 009 913 517)
Level 19, 201 Elizabeth Street
SYDNEY NSW 2000
AUSTRALIA

MIX
Paper | Supporting
responsible forestry
FSC   FSC® C001695
www.fsc.org

® and ™ (apart from those relating to FSC®) are trademarks of Harlequin Enterprises (Australia) Pty Limited or its corporate affiliates. Trademarks indicated with ® are registered in Australia, New Zealand and in other countries. Contact admin_legal@Harlequin.ca for details.

Printed and bound in Australia by McPherson's Printing Group

CONTENTS

In Memoriam

For my friend Verna Jane Clayton: wife of Danny, sister of Nancy, mother of Christina and Daniel, grandmother of Selena Marie and Donovan Kyle.

Your smile burns bright in our memories

Where you will live on, forever young, forever loved.

Never forgotten.

Invincible

Dear Reader,

Carson, the hero of *Invincible*, is one of the Oglala Lakota people. For many years, the Lakota have had a special place in my heart. During World War II, our mother dated a Lakota man and spoke of marrying him. Our father came along before that could happen. But my sister and I grew up hearing stories about the Plains tribes, especially the Lakota (whom most people outside the tribe refer to as Sioux).

I wrote a book once called *Paper Rose*, whose hero had Lakota blood. I thought at the time how nice it would be to do something useful for the nation I held in such esteem. I contacted the Oglala Lakota College in Kyle, South Dakota, and asked about founding a nursing scholarship there in the name of our mother, who was a nurse. So the Eloise Cliatt Spaeth Nursing Scholarship was born.

Over the years, the scholarship has helped a great many people with families afford to go back to school. My friend Marilyn sends me letters from them, which I keep and treasure. I can't tell you how proud I am to be contributing, even in a small way, to such a grand cause. I grew up poor, so I can tell you that education makes all the difference in the world.

One other thing about this book that is special is the dedication. I lost a friend. She was my daughter-in-law's mother, Jane Clayton. Since Christina was seventeen years old, she; her mother, Jane; her father, Danny; and her brother, Daniel, have been part of my family. Of all my memories of Jane, there is this special one: At the kids' wedding rehearsal in Atlanta, she sat with my sister, Dannis; my son, Blayne; her husband, Danny; son, Daniel; daughter, Christina; my niece Maggie; and me, shooting down enemy aircraft in an arcade game. I remember her laughing as if she were a kid. She did have the most beautiful laugh.

Oh, what fun that was! Jane, laughing, with stars in her eyes.

This book is for you, Jane, so that your name will be remembered as long as the book stays in print anywhere in the world. Good night, my friend.

Thank you for reading *Invincible*. As always, I am your fan.

Love,

Diana Palmer

CHAPTER ONE

IT WAS A rainy Friday morning.

Carlie Blair, who was running late for her job as secretary to Jacobsville, Texas police chief Cash Grier, only had time for a piece of toast and a sip of coffee before she rushed out the door to persuade her ten-year-old red pickup truck to start. It had gone on grinding seemingly forever before it finally caught up and started.

Her father, a Methodist minister, was out of town on business for the day. So there was nobody to help her get it running. Luck was with her. It did, at least, start.

She envied her friend Michelle Godfrey, whose guardian and his sister had given her a Jaguar for Christmas. Michelle was away at college now, and she and Carlie still spoke on the phone, but they no longer shared rides to town and the cost of gas on a daily basis.

The old clunker ate gas like candy and Carlie's salary only stretched so far. She wished she had more than a couple pairs of jeans, a few T-shirts, a coat and one good pair of shoes. It must be nice, she thought, not to have to count pennies. But her father was always optimistic about their status. *God loved the poor, because they gave away so much,* he was fond of saying. He was probably right.

Right now, though, her rain-wet jeans were uncomfortable, and she'd stepped in a mud puddle with her only pair of good shoes while she was knocking corrosion off the battery terminals with the hammer she kept under the front seat for that purpose. All this in January weather, which was wet and cold and miserable, even in South Texas.

Consequently, when she parked her car in the small lot next to the chief's office, she looked like a bedraggled rat. Her dark, short, wavy hair was curling like crazy, as it always did in a rainstorm. Her coat was soaked. Her green eyes, full of silent resignation, didn't smile as she opened the office door.

Her worst nightmare was standing just inside.

Carson.

He glared at her. He was so much taller than she that she had to look up at him. There was a lot to look at, although she tried not to show her interest.

He was all muscle, but it wasn't overly obvious. He had a rodeo rider's physique, lean and powerful. Like her, he wore jeans, but his were obviously designer ones, like those hand-tooled leather boots on his big feet and the elaborately scrolled leather holster in which he kept his .45 automatic. He was wearing a jacket that partially concealed the gun, but he was intimidating enough without it.

He was Lakota Sioux. He had jet-black hair that fell to his waist in back, although he wore it in a ponytail usually. He had large black eyes that seemed to see everything with one sweep of his head. He had high cheekbones and a light olive complexion. There were faint scars on the knuckles of his big hands. She noticed because he was holding a file in one of them.

Her file.

Well, really, the chief's file, that had been lying on her desk, waiting to be typed up. It referenced an attack on her father a few weeks earlier that had resulted in Carlie being stabbed. Involuntarily, her hand went to the scar that ran from her shoulder down to the beginning of her small breasts. She flushed when she saw where he was looking.

"Those are confidential files," she said shortly.

He looked around. "There was nobody here to tell me that," he said, his deep voice clear as a bell in the silent room.

She flushed at the implied criticism. "Damned truck wouldn't start and I got soaked trying to start it," she muttered. She slid her weather-beaten old purse under her desk, ran a hand through her wet hair, took off her ratty coat and hung it up before she sat down at her desk. "Did you need something?" she asked with crushing politeness. She even managed a smile. Sort of.

"I need to see the chief," he replied.

She frowned. "There's this thing called a door. He's got one," she said patiently. "You knock on it, and he comes out."

He gave her a look that could have stopped traffic. "There's somebody in there with him," he said with equal patience. "I didn't want to interrupt."

"I see." She moved things around on her desk, muttering to herself.

"Bad sign."

She looked up. "Huh?"

"Talking to yourself."

She glared at him. It had been a bad morning altogether and he wasn't helping. "Don't listen, if it bothers you."

He gave her a long look and laughed hollowly. "Listen, kid, nothing about you bothers me. Or ever will."

There were the sounds of chairs scraping wood, as if the men in Cash's office had stood up and pushed back their seats. She figured it was safe to interrupt him.

Well, safer than listening to Mr. Big Shot here run her down.

She pushed the intercom button. "You have a visitor, sir," she announced.

There was a murmur. "Who is it?"

She looked at Carson. "The gentleman who starts fires with hand grenades," she said sweetly.

Carson stared at her with icy black eyes.

Cash's door opened, and there was Carlie's father, a man in a very expensive suit and Cash.

That explained why her father had left home so early. He was out of town, as he'd said he would be; out of Comanche Wells, where they lived, anyway. Not that Jacobsville was more than a five-minute drive from home.

"Carson," Cash said, nodding. "I think you know Reverend Blair and my brother, Garon?"

"Yes." Carson shook hands with them.

Carlie was doing mental shorthand. Garon Grier was senior special agent in charge of the Jacobsville branch of the FBI. He'd moved to Jacobsville some time ago, but the FBI branch office hadn't been here quite as long. Garon had been with the bureau for a number of years.

Carlie wondered what was going on that involved both the FBI and her father. But she knew that question would go unanswered. Her father was remarkably silent on issues that concerned law enforcement, although he knew quite a few people in that profession.

She recalled with a chill the telephone conversation she'd had recently with someone who called and said, "Tell your father he's next." She couldn't get anybody to tell her what they thought it meant. It was disturbing, like the news she'd overheard that the man who'd put a knife in her, trying to kill her father, had been poisoned and died.

Something big was going on, linked to that Wyoming murder and involving some politician who had ties to a drug cartel. But nobody told Carlie anything.

"WELL, I'LL BE OFF. I have a meeting in San Antonio," Reverend Blair said, taking his leave. He paused at Carlie's desk. "Don't do anything fancy for supper, okay?" he asked, smiling. "I may be very late."

"Okay, Dad." She grinned up at him.

He ruffled her hair and walked out.

Carson was watching the interplay with cynical eyes.

"Doesn't your dad ruffle your hair?" she asked sarcastically.

"No. He did lay a chair across it once." He averted his eyes at once, as if the comment had slipped out against his will and embarrassed him.

Carlie tried not to stare. What in the world sort of background did he come from? The violence struck a chord in her. She had secrets of her own from years past.

"Carson," Garon Grier said, pausing at the door. "We may need you at some point."

Carson nodded. "I'll be around."

"Thanks."

Garon waved at his brother, smiled at Carlie and let himself out the door.

"Something perking?" Carson asked Cash.

"Quite a lot, in fact. Carlie, hold my calls until I tell you," he instructed.

"Sure thing, Boss."

"Come on in." Cash went ahead into his office.

Carson paused by Carlie's desk and glared at her.

She glared back. "If you don't stop scowling at me, I'm going to ask the chief to frisk you for hand grenades," she muttered.

"Frisk me yourself," he dared softly.

The flush deepened, darkened.

His black eyes narrowed, because he knew innocence when he saw it; it was that rare in his world. "Clueless, aren't you?" he chided.

She lifted her chin and glared back. "My father is a minister," she said with quiet pride.

"Really?"

She frowned, cocking her head. "Excuse me?"

"Are you coming in or not?" Cash asked suddenly, and there was a bite in his voice.

Carson seemed faintly surprised. He followed Cash into the

office. The door closed. There were words spoken in a harsh tone, followed by a pause and a suddenly apologetic voice.

Carlie paid little attention. Carson had upset her nerves. She wished her boss would find someone else to talk to. Her job had been wonderful and satisfying until Carson started hanging around the office all the time. Something was going on, something big. It involved local and federal law enforcement—she was fairly certain that the chief's brother didn't just happen by to visit—and somehow, it also involved her father.

She wondered if she could dig any information out of her parent if she went about it in the right way. She'd have to work on that.

Then she recalled that phone call that she'd told her father about, just recently. A male voice had said, simply, "Tell your father, he's next." It had been a chilling experience, one she'd forced to the back of her mind. Now she wondered if all the traffic through her boss's office involved her in some way, as well as her father. The man who'd tried to kill him had died, mysteriously poisoned.

She still wondered why anybody would attack a minister. That remark of Carson's made her curious. She'd said her father was a minister and he'd said, "Really?" in that sarcastic, cold tone of voice. Why?

"I'm a mushroom," she said to herself. "They keep me in the dark and feed me manure." She sighed and went back to work.

SHE WAS ON the phone with the sheriff's office when Carson left. He went by her desk with only a cursory glance at her, and it was, of all things, placid. Almost apologetic. She lowered her eyes and refused to even look at him.

Even if she'd found him irresistible—and she was trying not to—his reputation with women made her wary of him.

Sure, it was a new century, but Carlie was a small-town girl and raised religiously. She didn't share the casual attitude of many of her former classmates about physical passion.

She grimaced. It was hard to be a nice girl when people treated her like a disease on legs. In school, they'd made fun of her, whispered about her. One pretty, popular girl said that she didn't know what she was missing and that she should live it up.

Carlie just stared at her and smiled. She didn't say anything. Apparently the smile wore the other girl down because she shrugged, turned her back and walked off to whisper to the girls in her circle. They all looked at Carlie and laughed.

She was used to it. Her father said that adversity was like grit, it honed metal to a fine edge. She'd have liked to be honed a little less.

They were right about one thing; she really didn't know what she was missing. It seemed appropriate, because she'd read about sensations she was supposed to feel with men around, and she didn't feel any of them.

She chided herself silently. That was a lie. She felt them when she was close to Carson. She knew that he was aware of it, which made it worse. He laughed at her, just the way her classmates had laughed at her in school. She was the odd one out, the misfit. She had a reason for her ironclad morals. Many local people knew them, too. Episodes in her childhood had hardened her.

Well, people tended to be products of their upbringing. That was life. Unless she wanted to throw away her ideals and give up religion, she was pretty much settled in her beliefs. Maybe it wasn't so bad being a misfit. Her late grandfather had said that civilizations rested on the bedrock of faith and law and the arts. Some people had to be conventional to keep the mechanism going.

"What was that?" Sheriff Hayes's receptionist asked.

"Sorry." Carlie cleared her throat. She'd been on hold. "I was just mumbling to myself. What were you saying?"

The woman laughed and gave her the information the chief had asked for, about an upcoming criminal case.

SHE COOKED A light supper, just creamed chicken and rice, with green peas, and made a nice apple pie for dessert.

Her father came in, looking harassed. Then he saw the spread and grinned from ear to ear. "What a nice surprise!"

"I know, something light. But I was hungry," she added.

He made a face. "Shame. Telling lies."

She shrugged. "I went to church Sunday. God won't mind a little lie, in a good cause."

He smiled. "You know, some people have actually asked me how to talk to God."

"I just do it while I'm cooking, or working in the yard," Carlie said. "Just like I'm talking to you."

He laughed. "Me, too. But there are people who make hard work of it."

"Why were you in the chief's office today?" she asked suddenly.

He paused in the act of putting a napkin in his lap. His expression went blank for an instant, then it came back to life. "He wanted me to talk to a prisoner for him," he said finally.

She raised both eyebrows.

"Sorry," he said, smoothing out the napkin. "Some things are confidential."

"Okay."

"Let's say grace," he added.

LATER, HE WATCHED the news while she cleaned up the kitchen. She sat down with him and watched a nature special for a while. Then she excused herself and went upstairs to read. She wasn't really interested in much television programming, except for history specials and anything about mining. She loved rocks.

She sat down on the side of her bed and thumbed through her bookshelf. Most titles were digital as well as physical these days, but she still loved the feel and smell of an actual book in her hands.

She pulled out a well-worn copy of a book on the Little Bighorn fight, one that was written by members of various tribes who'd actually been present. It irritated her that many of the soldiers had said there were no living witnesses to the battle. That was not true. There were plenty of them: Lakota, Cheyenne, Crow and a host of other men from different tribes who were at the battle and saw exactly what happened.

She smiled as she read about how many of them ended up in Buffalo Bill Cody's famous traveling Wild West show. They played before the crowned heads of Europe. They learned high society manners and how to drink tea from fancy china cups. They laughed among themselves at the irony of it. Sitting Bull himself worked for Cody for a time, before he was killed.

She loved most to read about Crazy Horse. Like Carson, he was Lakota, which white people referred to as Sioux. Crazy Horse was Oglala, which was one of the subclasses of the tribe. He was light-skinned and a great tactician. There was only one verified photograph of him, which was disputed by some, accepted by others. It showed a rather handsome man with pigtails, wearing a breastplate. There was also a sketch. He had led a war party against General Crook at the Battle of the Rosebud and won it. He led another party against Custer at the Little Bighorn.

Until his death, by treachery at the hands of a soldier, he was the most famous war leader of the Lakota.

Sitting Bull did not fight; he was not a warrior. He was a holy man who made medicine and had visions of a great battle that was won by the native tribes.

Crazy Horse fascinated Carlie. She bought book after book, looking for all she could find in his history.

She also had books about Alexander the Third, called the Great, who conquered most of the civilized world by the age of thirty. His ability as a strategist was unequaled in the ancient past. Hannibal, who fought the Romans under Scipio Africanus in the Second Punic War at Carthage, was another favorite. Scipio fascinated her, as well.

The ability of some leaders to inspire a small group of men

to conquer much larger armies was what drew her to military history. It was the generals who led from the front, who ate and slept and suffered with their men, who won the greatest battles and the greatest honor.

She knew about battles because her secret vice was an on-line video game, "World of Warcraft." A number of people in Jacobsville and Comanche Wells played. She knew the gamer tags, the names in-game, of only a very few. Probably she'd partnered with some of them in raid groups. But mostly she ran battlegrounds, in player-versus-player matches, but only on weekends, when she had more free time.

Gaming took the place of dates she never got. Even if she'd been less moral, she rarely got asked on dates. She could be attractive when she tried, but she wasn't really pretty and she was painfully shy around people she didn't know. She'd only gone out a couple of times in high school, once with a boy who was getting even with his girlfriend by dating her—although she hadn't known until later—and another with a boy who'd hurt another girl badly and saw Carlie as an easy mark. He got a big surprise.

From time to time she thought about how nice it would be to marry and have children. She loved spending time in the baby section of department stores when she went to San Antonio with her father occasionally. She liked to look at knitted booties and lacy little dresses. Once a saleswoman had asked if she had children. She said no, she wasn't married. The saleswoman had laughed and asked what that had to do with it. It was a new world, indeed.

She put away her book on the Little Bighorn fight, and settled in with her new copy of a book on Alexander the Great. The phone rang. She got up, but she was hesitant to answer it. She recalled the threat from the unknown man and wondered if that was him.

She went to the staircase and hesitated. Her father had answered and was on the phone.

"Yes, I know," he said in a tone he'd never used with her. "If you think you can do better, you're welcome to try." He paused and a huge sigh left his chest. "Listen, she's all I've got in the world. I know I don't deserve her, but I will never let anyone harm her. This place may not look secure, but I assure you, it is…"

He leaned against the wall near the phone table, with the phone in his hand. He looked world-weary. "That's what I thought, too, at first," he said quietly. "I still have enemies. But it isn't me he's after. It's Carlie! It has to have something to do with the man she saw in Grier's office. I know that the man who killed Joey and masqueraded as a DEA agent is dead. But if he put out a contract before he died… Yes, that's what I'm telling you." He shook his head. "I know you don't have the funds. It's okay. I have plenty of people who owe me favors. I'll call in a few. Yes. I do appreciate your help. It's just…it's worrying me, that's all. Sure. I'll call you. Thanks." He hung up.

Carlie moved back into the shadows. Her father looked like a stranger, like someone she'd never seen before. She wondered who he'd been speaking to, and if the conversation was about her. It sounded that way; he'd used her name. What was a contract? A contract to kill someone? She bit her lower lip. Something to do with the man she saw in the chief's office, the man she'd tried to describe for the artist, the DEA agent who wasn't an agent.

She frowned. But he was dead, her father had said. Then he'd mentioned that contract, that the man might have put it out before he died. Of course, if some unknown person had been paid in advance to kill her…

She swallowed down the fear. She could be killed by mistake, by a dead man. How ironic. Her father had said the house was safe. She wondered why he'd said that, what he knew. For the first time in her life, she wondered who her father really was.

SHE FIXED HIM a nice breakfast. While they were eating it she said, "Why do you think that man came to kill me?"

His coffee cup paused halfway to his mouth. "What?"

"The man with the knife."

"We agreed that he was after me, didn't we?" he said, avoiding her face.

She lifted her eyes and stared at him. "I work for the police. It's impossible not to learn a little something about law enforcement in the process. That man wasn't after you at all, was he? The man who was poisoned so he couldn't tell what he knew?"

He let out a breath and put the coffee cup down. "Well, Carlie, you're more perceptive than I gave you credit for." He smiled faintly. "Must be my genes. Your mother, God rest her soul, didn't have that gift. She saw everything in black and white."

"Yes, she did." Talk of her mother made her sad. It had just been Carlie and Mary for a long time, until Mary got sick. Then Mary's mother, and her hophead boyfriend, had shown up and ransacked the place. Carlie had tried to stop them... She shivered.

It had been several days later, after the hospital visit and the arrests, when her father had come back to town, wearing khaki pants and shirt, and carrying a pistol.

There had been no money for doctors, but her father had taken charge and got Mary into treatment. Mary's mother and her boyfriend went to jail. Sadly, it had been hopeless from the start. Mary died within weeks. During those weeks, Carlie got to know her absent father. He became protective of her. She liked him very much. He was gone for a day after the funeral. When he came home, he seemed very different.

Carlie's father spoke to someone on the phone then, too, and when he hung up he'd made a decision. He took Carlie with him to Atlanta, where he enrolled in a seminary and became a Methodist minister. He said it was the hardest and the easiest thing he'd ever done, and that it was a good thing that God forgave people for horrible acts. She asked what they were. Her father said some things were best left buried in the past.

"We're still not sure he didn't come after me," her father said, interrupting her reverie.

"I heard you talking on the phone last night," she said.

He grimaced. "Bad timing on my part," he said, sighing.

"Very bad. So now I know. Tell me what's going on."

"That phone call you had came from a San Antonio number. We traced it, but it led to a throwaway phone," he replied. "That's bad news."

"Why?"

"Because a few people who use those phones are connected to the underworld in some fashion or other, to escape detection by the authorities. They use the phone once to connect with people who might be wiretapped, then they dispose of the phone. Drug lords buy them by the cartload," he added.

"Well, I didn't do anybody in over a drug deal, and the guy I gave the artist the description of died in Wyoming. So why is somebody still after me?" she concluded.

He smiled. "Smart. Very smart. The guy died. That's the bottom line. If he hired somebody to go after you, to keep you from recognizing him in a future lineup, and paid in advance, it's too late to call him off. Get the picture?"

"In living color," she said. She felt very adult, having her father give her the truth instead of a sweet lie to calm her.

"I have a couple of friends watching you," he said. "I don't think it's a big threat, but we'd be insane not to take it seriously, especially after what's already happened."

"That was weeks ago," she began.

"Yes, at the beginning of a long chain of growing evidence." He sipped coffee. "I still can't believe how many people's lives have been impacted by this man and whoever he was working for."

"You have some idea who his boss is...was?"

He nodded. "I can't tell you, so don't ask. I will say that several law enforcement agencies are involved."

"I still don't understand why you're having meetings with my boss and that…that man Carson."

He studied her flushed face. "I've heard about Carson's attitude toward you. If he keeps it up, I'll have a talk with him."

"Don't," she asked softly. "With any luck, he won't be around long. He doesn't strike me as a man who likes small towns or staying in one place for any length of time."

"You never know. He likes working for Cy Parks. And he has a few projects going with locals."

She groaned.

"I can talk to him nicely."

"Sure, Dad, and then he'll accuse me of running to Daddy for protection." She lifted her chin. "I can take whatever he can hand out."

He smiled at her stubbornness. "Okay."

She made a face. "He just doesn't like me, that's all. Maybe I remind him of someone he doesn't care for."

"That's possible." He stared into his coffee cup. "Or it could have something to do with asking him for a grenade to start a fire…"

"Aww, now, I wasn't trying to start anything," she protested.

He chuckled. "Sure." He studied her face. "I just want to mention one thing," he added gently. "He's not housebroken. And he never will be. Just so you know."

"I have never wanted to housebreak a wolf, I assure you."

"There's also his attitude about women. He makes no secret of it." His face hardened. "He likens them to party favors. Disposable. You understand?"

"I understand. But honestly, that's not the sort of man I'd be seriously interested in. You don't have to worry."

"I do worry. You're not street-smart, pumpkin," he added, with the pet name that he almost never used. "You're unworldly. A man like that could be dangerous to you…"

She held up a hand. "I have weapons."

He blinked. "Excuse me?"

"If he starts showing any interest in me, I'll give him my most simpering smile and start talking about how I'd love to move in with him that very day and start having children at once." She wiggled her eyebrows. "Works like a charm. They actually leave skid marks..."

He threw back his head and laughed. "So that's what happened to the visiting police chief...?"

"He was very persistent. The chief offered to punt him through the door, but I had a better idea. It worked very nicely. Now, when he comes to see the chief, he doesn't even look my way."

"Just as well. He has a wife, God help her."

"What a nasty man."

"Exactly." He looked at his watch. "Well, I have a meeting with the church officials. We're working on an outreach program for the poor. Something I really want to do."

She smiled. "You know, you really are the nicest minister I know."

He bent and kissed her forehead before he left. "Thanks, sweetheart. Be sure to check your truck, okay?"

She laughed. "I always do. Don't worry."

He hesitated. He wanted to tell her that he did worry, and the whole reason why. But it was the wrong time.

She was already halfway in love with Carson. He knew things about the man that he'd been told in confidence. He couldn't repeat them. But if Carlie got too close to that prowling wolf, he'd leave scars that would cripple her for life. He had to prevent that, if he could. The thing was, he didn't know how. It was like seeing a wire break and being too far away to fix it.

He could talk to Carson, of course. But that would only make matters worse. He had to wait and hope that Carlie could hang on to her beliefs and ignore the man's practiced charm if he ever used it on her.

Carson seemed to hate her. But it was an act. He knew it, because it was an act he'd put on himself, with Carlie's late mother. Mary had been a saint. He'd tried to coax her into bed, but she'd refused him at every turn. Finally, in desperation, he'd proposed. She'd refused. She wasn't marrying a man because he couldn't have her any other way.

So he'd gone away. And come back. And tried the soft approach. It had backfired. He'd fallen in love for the first time in his life. Mary had tied him to her with strings of icy steel, and leaving her even for a few weeks at a time had been agonizing. He'd only lived to finish the mission and get home, get back to Mary.

But over the years, the missions had come closer together, taken longer, provoked lengthy absences. He'd tried to make sure Mary had enough money to cover her bills and incidentals, but one job had resulted in no pay and during that time, Mary had gotten sick. By the time he knew and came home, it was too late.

He blamed himself for that, and for a lot more. He'd thought an old enemy had targeted him and got Carlie by mistake. But it wasn't a mistake. Someone wanted Carlie dead, apparently because of a face she remembered. There might be another reason. Something they didn't know, something she didn't remember seeing. Even the death of the man hadn't stopped the threat.

But he was going to. Somehow.

CHAPTER TWO

CARLIE LOVED THE WEEKENDS. At work she was just plain old Carlie, dull and boring and not very pretty at all.

But in this video game, on her game server, she was Cadzminea, an Alliance night elf death knight, invincible and deadly with a two-handed great sword. She had top-level gear and a bad attitude, and she was known even in battlegrounds with players from multiple servers. She was a tank, an offensive player who protected less well-geared comrades. She loved it.

Above the sounds of battle, clashing swords and flashing spells thrown by magic-users, she heard her father's voice.

"Just a minute, Dad! I'm in a battleground!"

"Okay. Never mind."

There were footsteps coming up. She laughed as she heard them behind her. Odd, they sounded lighter than her father's....

"Sorry, we're almost through. We're taking out the enemy commander...."

She stopped while she fought, planting her guild's battle flag to increase her strength and pulling up her Army of the Dead spell. "Gosh, the heals in this battleground are great, I've hardly even needed to use a potion... Okay!" she laughed, as the panel came up displaying an Alliance win, that of her faction.

"Sorry about that..." She turned and looked up into a pair of liquid black eyes in a surprised face.

"A gamer," he said in a tone, for once, without sarcasm. "Put up your stats."

She was too startled not to obey. She left the battleground and brought up the character screen.

He shook his head. "Not bad. Why an NE?" he asked, the abbreviation for a night elf.

"They're beautiful," she blurted out.

He laughed deep in his throat. "So they are."

"How do you know about stats?"

He pulled out his iPhone and went to the game's remote app. He pulled up the Armory and showed her a character sheet.

"Level 90 Horde Tauren druid," she read, indicating that the player was from the Alliance's deadly counter faction, the Horde. "Arbiter." She frowned. "Arbiter?" She caught her breath. "He killed me five times in one battleground!" she exclaimed. "He stealthed up to me, hit me from behind, then he just...killed me. I couldn't even fight back."

"Don't you have a medallion that interrupts spells?"

"Yes, but it was on cooldown," she said, glowering. "And you know this guy?" she asked.

He put up the iPhone. "I am this guy."

She was stunned.

"It's a small world, isn't it?" he asked, studying her face.

Too small, she thought, but she didn't say it. She just nodded.

"Your father asked a couple of us to take turns doing a walk-around when he's not here. He had to go out, so I've got first watch."

She frowned. "A what?"

"We're going to patrol around the house."

"Carrying a Horde flag?" she asked, tongue-in-cheek.

He smiled with real amusement. "We'll be concealed. You won't even know we're on the place."

She was disconcerted. "What's going on?"

"Just a tip we got," he replied. "Nothing to worry about."

Her green eyes narrowed. "My father can pull that stunt. You can't. Give it to me straight."

His eyebrows arched.

"If it concerns me, I have the right to know. My father is overprotective. I love him, but it's not fair that I have to be kept in the dark. I'm not a mushroom."

"No. You're Alliance." He seemed really amused.

"Proudly Alliance," she muttered. "Darn the Horde!"

He smiled. "Better rune that two-hander before you fight me again," he advised, referring to a special weapons buff used only by death knights.

"It's brand-new. I haven't had time," she said defensively. "Don't change the subject."

"There may be an attempt. That's all we could find out."

"Why? The guy I recognized is dead!"

"We're pretty sure that he paid the contract out before he died," he replied. "And we don't know who has it. We tried backtracking known associates of the man who made the first attempt, the one who was poisoned awaiting trial. No luck whatsoever. But an informant needed a favor, so he gave up some information. Not much. There's more at stake than just your memory of a counterfeit DEA agent. Much more."

"And that's all I'm getting, right?"

He nodded.

She glared.

"So much frustration," he mused, studying her. "Why don't you go win a few battles for the Alliance? It might help."

"Not unless you're in one of them." Her eyes twinkled. "Better watch your back next time. I'm getting the hang of it."

He shrugged. "I don't want to live forever." He glanced around the room. It was Spartan. No lace anywhere. He eyed the title of a book on the desk next to her computer and frowned. "Hannibal?"

"Learn from the best, I always think."

He looked at her. He didn't look away.

Her eyes met his and she felt her body melting, tingling. There was a sudden ache in the middle of her body, a jolt of pure electricity. She couldn't even manage to look away.

"Wolves bite," he said in a soft, gruff whisper.

She flushed and dragged her eyes back to the computer. Somebody sold her out. She wondered if it was the chief. She'd only called Carson a wolf to two people and her father would never have betrayed her.

He chuckled softly. "Be careful what you say when you think people aren't listening," he added. He turned and left her staring after him.

LATER, SHE ASKED her father if he'd ratted her out.

He chuckled. "No. But the house is bugged like a messy kitchen," he confessed. "Be careful what you say."

"Gee, thanks for telling me after I said all sorts of things about Carson," she murmured.

He laughed. "He's got a thick skin. It won't bother him."

She studied him quietly. "Why are they after me?"

He drew in a long breath. "There are some political maneuvers going on. You have a photographic memory. Maybe you saw someone other than the murder victim, and the man behind the plot is afraid you'll remember who it is."

"Shades of Dalton Kirk," she said, recalling that the Wyoming rancher had been warned by the woman who became his wife about a vision of him being attacked for something he didn't even remember he'd seen.

"Exactly."

She poured them second cups of coffee. "So I guess it's back to checking under the truck every time I drive it."

"Oh, that never stopped," her father said with a chuckle. "I've just been doing it for you."

She smiled at him. "That's my dad, looking out for me," she said with real affection.

His pale blue eyes were sad. "There was a long period of time when I didn't look out for anybody except myself," he said quietly. "Your mother wouldn't even let anybody tell me how sick she was until it was too late." He lowered his gaze to the coffee. "I made a lot of mistakes out of selfishness. I hope that someday I'll be able to make up for a little of it."

She sipped coffee. "You never talk about your life before you went to the seminary," she pointed out.

He smiled sadly. "I'm ashamed to."

"You were overseas a lot."

He nodded. "In a number of dangerous foreign places, where life is dirt cheap."

She pursed her lips and stared at him. "You know, Michelle's guardian, Gabriel Brandon, spent a lot of time overseas also."

He lifted an eyebrow and smiled placidly. "Are you fishing?"

She shrugged. But she didn't look away.

He finished his coffee. "Let's just say that I had connections that aren't obvious ones, and I made my living in a shadow world."

She frowned. "You aren't wanted in some country whose name I can't pronounce?"

He laughed. "Nothing like that."

"Okay."

He stood up. "But I do have enemies who know where I live. In a general sense. So it's smart to take precautions." He smiled gently. "I wasn't always a minister, pumpkin."

She was remembering Carson's sarcastic comment when she'd mentioned that her father was a minister. She hadn't known that he was aware of things about her parent that she wasn't.

"I feel like a mushroom," she muttered.

He bent and kissed her hair. "Believe me, you're better off being one. See you later. I have some phone calls to make."

He locked himself in his study and she went to watch the news on television. It was mostly boring, the same rehashed subjects over and over again, interspersed with more commercials than she could stomach. She turned it off and went upstairs.

"No wonder people stopped watching television," she grumbled as she wandered back to her bedroom. "Why don't you just stop showing any programs and show wall-to-wall commercials, for heaven's sake!"

She pulled up her game and tried to load it when she noticed that the internet wasn't working.

Muttering, she went downstairs to reset the router, which usually solved the problem. Except the router was in the study, and her father was locked in there.

She started to knock, just as she heard her father's raised voice in a tone she'd rarely ever heard.

"I told you," he gritted, "I am not coming back! You can't say anything, threaten anything, that will make me change my mind. And don't you say one more word about my daughter's safety, or I will report you to the obvious people. I understand that," he continued, less belligerently. "Trust me when I say that nobody short of a ghost could get in here after dark. The line is secure and I've scrambled important conversations, like this one. I appreciate the tip, I really do. But I can handle this. I haven't forgotten anything you taught me." He laughed shortly. "Yes, I remember. They were good times."

There was another pause. "No. But we did find out who his enforcer is, and our local law enforcement people are keeping him under covert surveillance. That's right. No, I didn't realize there were two. When did he hire the other? Wait a minute—blond hair, one eye, South African accent?" He burst out laughing. "He hired Rourke as an enforcer?"

There was another pause. "Yes, please, tell him to come see me. I'd enjoy that. Like old times, yes. Okay. Thanks again. I'll be in touch."

Totally confused, Carlie softly retraced her steps, made a

racket coming down the staircase and went directly to the study. She rapped on the door.

"Dad? The internet's out! Can you reset the router?"

There was the sound of a chair scraping the floor, but she never heard his footsteps. The door suddenly opened.

He pursed his lips and studied her flushed face. "Okay. How much did you hear?"

"Nothing, Mr. Gandalf, sir, I swear, except something about the end of the world," she paraphrased Sam from *Lord of the Rings*.

Her father laughed. "Well, it wasn't really anything you didn't already know."

"Who's Rourke?" she wondered.

"A man of many talents. You'll like him." He frowned. "Just don't like him too much, okay? He has a way with women, and you're a little lamb."

She gave him a blithe look. "If I could get around Barry Mathers, I can get around Rourke."

Her father understood the reference. Barry, a classmate, had caused one of Carlie's friends a world of hurt by getting her into bed and bragging about it. The girl had been as innocent as Carlie. He wasn't even punished.

So then he'd bet his friends that he could get Carlie into bed. She heard about it from an acquaintance, led him around by the nose, and when he showed up at her house for the date, she had two girlfriends and their boyfriends all ready to go along. He was stunned. But he couldn't call off the date, or he'd have to face the razzing of his clique.

So he took all of them out to dinner and the movies, dutch treat, and delivered Carlie and the others back to her house where her friends' cars were parked.

She waited until the others left and she was certain that her father was in the living room before she spoke to Barry. She gave him such a tongue-lashing that he literally turned around and walked the other way every time he saw her after that. He never asked her out again. Of course, neither did anybody else, for the rest of her senior year.

Barry, on the other hand, was censured so much that his wealthy parents sent him to a school out of state. He died there soon afterward in a skiing accident.

"You had a hard time in school," her father said gently.

"No harder than most other people with principles do," she replied. "There are more of us than you might think."

"I reset the router," he added. "Go try your game."

"I promised to meet Robin for a quest," she said. "I'd hate to let him down."

Her father just smiled. They knew about Robin's situation. He was in love with a girl whose family hated his family. It was a feud that went back two generations, over a land deal. Even the principals didn't really remember what started it. But when Robin expressed interest in Lucy and tried to date her, the hidden daggers came out.

It was a tragic story in many ways. Two people in love who weren't even allowed to see each other because of their parents. They were grown now, but Lucy still lived at home and was terrified of her father. So even if Robin insisted, Lucy wouldn't go against her kin.

Robin worked in his dad's real estate office, where he wasn't harassed, and he was a whiz with figures. He was going to night classes, studying real estate up in San Antonio, where he hoped to learn enough to eventually become a full-fledged real estate broker. Carlie liked him. So did her father, who respected a parent's rights but also felt sympathy for young people denied the right to love whom they pleased.

CARLIE WENT ONLINE and loaded the game, then looked for Robin, who played a shaman in the virtual world. His was a healing spec, so it went well with Carlie's DK, who couldn't heal.

I have a problem, he whispered to her, a form of typed private communication in-game.

She typed, How can I help?

He made a big smiley face. I need a date for the Valentine's Day dance.

Should I ask why? she typed.

There was a smiley face. Lucy's going to the dance with some rich rancher her father knows from out of town. If you'll go with me, her dad won't suspect anything and I can at least dance with her.

She shook her head. One day the two of them were going to have to decide if the sneaking around was less traumatic than just getting together and daring their parents to say anything. But she just typed, I'll buy a dress.

There was a bigger smiley face. It's so nice to have a friend like you, he replied.

That works both ways.

LATER, SHE TOLD her father she had a date. He asked who, and she explained.

"You're both hiding, Carlie," he said, surprising her. His eyes narrowed. "You need to think about finding someone you can have a good relationship with, someone to marry and have children with. And Robin and Lucy need to stand up and behave like adults."

She smiled sadly. "Chance would be a fine thing," she replied. "You might not have noticed, but men aren't exactly beating a path to my door. And you know why."

"Young men look at what's outside," he said wisely. "When they're more mature, men look for what's inside. You're just at the wrong period of your life. That will change."

She drew in a long breath. "You know, not everybody marries…"

He glared at her.

She held up both hands. "I'm not talking about moving in

with somebody," she said hastily. "I mean, not everybody gets married. Look at Old Man Barlow, he never did."

"He never bathed," he pointed out.

She glowered at him. "Beside the point. How about the Miller brothers? They never married. Their sister was widowed and moved back in with them, and they're all single now. They seem perfectly happy."

He looked down his nose at her. "Who spends half her time in department stores, ogling baby booties and little gowns?"

She flushed and averted her eyes.

"Just what I thought," he added.

"Listen, there really aren't many communities in Texas smaller than Comanche Wells, or even Jacobsville. Most of the men my age are either married or living with somebody."

"I see your point."

"The others are having so much fun partying that they don't want to do either," she continued. "Come on, Dad, I like my life. I really do. I enjoy working for the chief and having lunch at Barbara's Café and playing my game at night and taking care of you." She gave him a close scrutiny. "You know, you might think about marrying somebody."

"Bite your tongue," he said shortly. "There was your mother. I don't want anybody else. Ever."

She stared at him with consternation. "She'd want you to be happy."

"I am happy," he insisted. "I'm married to my church, pumpkin. I love what I do now." He smiled. "You know, in the sixteenth century, all priests were expected to be single. It wasn't until Henry VIII changed the laws that they could even marry, and when his daughter Mary came to the throne, she threw out all the married priests. Then when her half sister Elizabeth became Queen, she permitted them to marry, but she didn't want married ministers preaching before her. She didn't approve of it, either."

"This is the twenty-first century," she pointed out. "And

why are you hanging out with McKuen Kilraven?" she added, naming one of the federal agents who sometimes came to Jacobsville.

He laughed. "Does it show?"

"I don't know of anybody else who can hold forth for an hour on sixteenth-century British politics and never tell the same story twice."

"Guilty," he replied. "He was in your boss's office the last time I was there."

"When was that? I didn't see him."

"You were at lunch."

"Oh."

He didn't volunteer any more information.

"I need to go buy a new dress," she said. "I think I'll drive up to San Antonio after work, since it's Saturday and I get off at 1 p.m."

"Okay. I'll let you borrow the Cobra." He laughed at her astonished look. "I'm not sure your truck would make it even halfway to the city, pumpkin."

She just shook her head.

IT WAS A CONCESSION of some magnitude. Her father loved that car. He washed and waxed it by hand, bought things for it. She was only allowed to drive it on very special occasions, and usually only when she went to the big city.

San Antonio wasn't a huge city, but there was a lot to see. Carlie liked to stop by the Alamo and look at it, but El Mercado was her port of call. It had everything, including unique shops and music and restaurants. She usually spent half a day just walking around it. But today she was in a hurry.

She went from store to store, but she couldn't find exactly what she was looking for. She was ready to give up when she pulled, on impulse, into a small strip mall where a sale sign was out in front of a small boutique.

She found a bargain dress, just her size, in green velvet. It was ankle length, with a discreet rounded neckline and long sleeves. It fit like a glove, but it wasn't overly sensual. And it suited her. It was so beautiful that she carried it like a child as she walked to the counter to pay for it.

"That was the only size we got in this particular design," the saleslady told her as she packaged it on its hanger. "I wish it was my size," she added with a sigh. "You really are lucky."

Carlie laughed. "It's for a dance. I don't go out much."

"Me, either," the saleslady said. "My husband sits and watches the Western Channel on satellite when he gets off work and then he goes to bed." She shook her head. "Not what I thought marriage would be like. But he's good to me and he doesn't cheat. I guess I'm lucky."

"I'd say you are."

CARLIE WAS IN the Jacobs County limits on a long, deserted stretch of road. The Cobra growled as if it had been on the leash too long and wanted off. Badly.

With a big grin on her face, Carlie floored the accelerator. "Okay, Big Red," she said, using her father's affectionate nickname for the car, "let's run!"

The engine cycled, seemed to hesitate, and then the car took off with a growl that would have done a hungry mountain lion proud.

"Woo-hoo!" she exclaimed.

She was going eighty, eighty-five, ninety, ninety-six and then one hundred. She felt an exhilaration she couldn't remember ever feeling before. The road was completely open up ahead, no traffic anywhere. Well, except for that car behind her...

Her heart skipped. At first she thought it was a police car, because she was exceeding the speed limit by double the posted signs. But then she realized that it wasn't a law enforcement car. It was a black sedan, and it was keeping pace with her.

She almost panicked. But she was close to Jacobsville, where she could get help if she needed it. Her father's admonition about checking the truck before she drove it made her heart skip. She knew he'd checked the car, but she hadn't counted on being followed. Someone was after her. She knew that her father's friends were watching her, but that was in Jacobsville.

Nobody was watching her now, and she was being chased. Her cell phone was in her purse on the floor by the passenger seat. She'd have to slow down or stop to get to it. She groaned. Lack of foresight. Why didn't she have it in the console?

Her heart was pumping faster as the car behind gained on her. What if it was the shadowy assassin come for a second try? What was she going to do? She couldn't outrun him, that was obvious, and when she slowed down, he'd catch her.

She saw the city-limit sign up ahead. She couldn't continue at this rate of speed. She'd kill someone at the next crossroads.

Groaning, she slowed down. The black sedan was right on top of her. She turned without a signal into the first side street and headed for the police station. If she was lucky, she just might make it.

Yes! The traffic light stayed green. She shot through it, pulled up in front of the station and jumped out just as the sedan pulled in front of her, braked and cut her off.

"You damned little lunatic, what the hell were you thinking!" Carson raged at her as he slammed out of the black sedan and confronted her. "I clocked you at a hundred miles an hour!"

"Oh, yeah? Well, you were going a hundred, too, because you were right on my bumper. And how was I supposed to know it was you?" she told him, red-faced with embarrassment.

"I called your cell phone half a dozen times, didn't you hear it ring?"

"I had it turned off. And it was on the floor in my purse," she explained.

He put his hands on his slim hips and glared at her. "You shouldn't be allowed out by yourself, and especially not in a car with that sort of horsepower!" he persisted. "I should have the chief arrest you!"

"Go ahead, I'll have him arrest you, too!" she yelled back.

Two patrol officers were standing on the sidelines, spell-bound. The chief came out and stopped, just watching the two antagonists, who hadn't noticed their audience.

"What if you'd hit something lying in the middle of the road? You'd have gone straight off it and into a tree or a power pole, and you'd be dead!"

"Well, I didn't hit anything! I was scared because I saw a car following me. Who wouldn't be paranoid, with people watching you all the time and my father having secret phone calls…!"

"If you'd answered your damned cell phone, you'd have known who was following you!"

"It was in my purse and I was afraid to slow down and try to grab it out of my pocketbook!"

"Of all the stupid assignments I've ever had, this takes the prize," he muttered. "And why you had to go to San Antonio…?"

"I went to buy a dress for the Valentine's Day party!"

He gave her a cold smile. "Going alone, are we?"

"No, I'm not," she shot back. "I have a date!"

He looked oddly surprised. "Do you have to pay him when he takes you home?" he asked in a long, sarcastic drawl.

"I don't have to hire men to take me places!" she raged back. "And this man doesn't notch his bedpost and take in strays to have somebody to sleep with."

He took a quick step forward, and he looked dangerous. "That's enough," he snapped.

Carlie sucked in her breath and her face paled.

"It really is enough," Cash Grier said, interrupting them. He stepped between them and stared at Carson. "The time to tell somebody you're following them is not when you're actually in the car. Especially a nervous young woman whose life has been threatened."

Carson's jaw was set so firmly she wondered if his teeth would break. He was still glaring at Carlie.

"And you need to keep your phone within reach when you're driving," he told Carlie in a gentler tone and with a smile.

"Yes, sir," she said heavily. She let out a long sigh.

"She was doing a hundred miles an hour," Carson said angrily.

"If you could clock her, you had to be doing the same," Cash retorted. "You're both lucky that you weren't in the city limits at the time. Or that Hayes Carson or one of his deputies didn't catch you. Speeding fines are really painful."

"You'd know," Carson mused, relaxing a little as he glanced at the older man.

Cash glowered at him. "Well, I drive a Jaguar," he said defensively. "They don't like slow speeds."

"How many unpaid speeding tickets is it to date? Ten?" Carson persisted. "I hear you can't cross the county border up around Dallas. And you, a chief of police. Shame, shame."

Cash shrugged. "I sent the checks out yesterday," he informed the other man. "All ten."

"Threatening to put you under arrest, were they?"

"Only one of them," Cash chuckled. "And he was in Iraq with me, so he stretched the rules a bit."

"I have to get home," Carlie said. She was still shaking inside over the threat that turned out to be just Carson. And from Carson's sudden move toward her. Very few people knew what nightmares she endured from one very physical confrontation in the past.

"You keep under the speed limit, or I'm telling your father what you did to his car," Carson instructed.

"He wouldn't mind," she lied, glaring at him.

"Let's find out." He jerked out his cell phone and started punching in numbers.

"All right!" she surrendered, holding up both hands. "All right, I'll go under the speed limit." Her eyes narrowed. "I'm taking that sword to a rune forge tonight. So the next time you meet me on a battleground, Hordie, I'm going to wipe the ground with you."

He pursed his lips. "That would be a new experience for me, Alliance elf."

Cash groaned. "Not you, too," he said. "It's bad enough listening to Wofford Patterson brag about his weapons. He even has a dog named Hellscream. And every time Kilraven comes down here, he's got a new game he wants to tell me all about."

"You should play, too, Chief," Carlie said. She glanced at Carson. "It's a great way to work off frustration."

Carson raised an eyebrow. "I know a better one," he said with a mocking smile.

He might not mean what she thought he did. She flushed helplessly and looked away. "I'm leaving."

"Drive carefully. And buckle up," Cash told her.

"Yes, sir, Boss," she said, grinning.

She started the car, pulled it around and eased out of the parking lot.

She really hoped that her father wouldn't find out how she'd been driving his pet car. It would be like Carson to tell him, just for spite.

Odd, though, she thought, how angry he'd been that she'd taken such chances. It was almost as if he was concerned about her. She laughed to herself. Sure. He was nursing a secret yen for her that he couldn't control.

Not that he ever would ask her out or anything, but she had grave misgivings about him. He was known for his success with women, and she was soft where he was concerned. He could push her into something that he'd just brush off as insignificant, but her life would be shattered. She couldn't let her helpless interest in him grow. Not even a little. She had to remember that he had no real respect for women and he didn't seem capable of settling down with just one.

She pulled into her driveway and cut off the engine. It was a relief to be home. Just as she got out of the car she saw the black sedan drive by. He didn't stop or wave. He just kept going. Her heart jumped up into her throat.

In spite of all the yelling, he'd shepherded her home and she hadn't even noticed. She hated the warm feeling it gave her, knowing that.

CHAPTER THREE

CARLIE HAD HOPED that her father wouldn't hear about her adventure. But when she got inside the house, he was waiting for her, his arms crossed over his chest.

"He lied," she blurted out, blushing, the dress in its plastic bag hanging over one arm.

He blinked. "Excuse me?"

She hesitated. He might not know after all. She cocked her head. "Are you...angry about something?"

"Should I be?"

He made her feel guilty. She drew in a breath and moved toward him. "I was speeding. I'm sorry. Big Red can really run..."

"A hundred miles an hour," he said, nodding. "You need special training to drive at those speeds safely, and you don't have it," he added patiently.

"I didn't know it was Carson behind me," she said heavily. "I thought it might be whoever still has me targeted."

"I understand that. I gave him...well, a talking-to," he amended. "It won't happen again. But you keep your cell phone where you can get to it in a hurry, whatever you're driving. Okay?"

"Okay, Dad," she promised.

"Got the dress, did you?" he asked, and smiled.

"Yes! It's beautiful! Green velvet. I'll wear Mama's pearls with it, the ones you brought her from Japan when you first started dating."

He nodded. "They're very special. I bought them in Tokyo," he recalled, smiling. "She had the same skin tone that you inherited from her. Off-white pearls are just right for you."

She frowned. "You buy them for a skin color?"

"I always did. Pearls come in many colors, and many prices. Those are Mikimoto pearls. An armed guard stands in the room with them."

She lost a little color. "Maybe I should wear something else…"

"Nonsense. They need to be worn. That would be like getting a special dress and letting it hang in your closet for fear of spilling something on it. Life is what matters, child. Things are expendable."

"Most things," she agreed.

"I made supper, since I knew you were going to be late," he said.

Her eyebrows arched. "That was sweet of you, Dad," she said.

"It's just a macaroni and cheese casserole. Your mother taught me how to do it when we were first married. I never forgot."

"It's one of my favorite dishes. Let me hang up my dress and I'll be right down."

"Sure."

THE MEAL WAS DELICIOUS, even more so because she hadn't had to cook it. She noticed her father's somber expression.

"I'm really sorry about pushing Big Red," she began.

He leaned back in his chair. "It's not the car I was worried about." His pale eyes were narrow and thoughtful. "It might not be a bad idea to send you over to Eb Scott and let one of his guys teach you the finer points of defensive driving. Just in case."

Her heart jumped. "Dad, maybe there isn't a real threat," she said. "I mean, the guy who was afraid of what I remembered about him is dead."

He nodded. "Yes, but there are things going on that you don't know about."

"You were talking to somebody on the phone who wanted you to come back. Come back where?" she asked bluntly.

He grimaced. "I used to work for the feds. Sort of. It was a long time ago."

"Feds?" she repeated, trying to draw him out.

His chest rose and fell. "When you're young, you think you can do anything, be anything. You don't worry about consequences. You take the training and do the job. Nobody tells you that years down the line, you may have regrets." He studied her oval face. "I was away when your mother got sick. What happened to you, because nobody was at home, was my fault. I should have been there."

She glanced down. "They paid for it."

"Not enough," he said coldly, and his face was suddenly hard and merciless. "I don't wish harm to anyone as a rule, but when your grandmother left the world, I didn't shed a tear."

Carlie managed a smile. "Me, neither. I guess he's still around somewhere."

"No. He died in a prison riot last year."

"You didn't say," she faltered.

"I didn't know. My former boss and I were making connections. We looked for anyone dangerous who knew you in the past. I had someone do some checking. I only found out yesterday."

"It's a relief, sort of," she said heavily. She shook her head. "They were both crazy. She was the worst. My poor mother…"

He put his hand over hers and squeezed. "Mary was such a ray of light that nobody blamed her for what her mother did," he reminded her.

"I know, but people have long memories in small towns."

"You have your own spotless reputation," he said gently. "Don't worry about it."

"I guess you're right." She laughed. "Robin hired a limo for us, can you believe it?"

"I like Robin," he said. "I just wish he had more guts."

"Now, now, we can't all be real-life death knights with great swords."

"You and that game. You do need to get out more." He pursed his lips. "Maybe we need to organize some things for the young, single members of our church."

"All four of us?" she mused.

He rolled his eyes.

"I like my life," she declared. "Maybe it lacks excitement, but I'm happy. That should count for something, Dad."

He laughed softly. "Okay. I see your point."

THE CHIEF WAS UNHAPPY. He didn't come out and say so, but he was on a short fuse and it was difficult to get anything out of him past one-syllable words.

"Sir, what about the new patrolman's gear?" she asked gently. "You were supposed to give me a purchase order for it, weren't you?"

"New patrolman?" He frowned. "Oh, yes. Bartley. Okay. I'll do that today."

She bit her tongue so that she didn't remind him that he'd said the same thing the day before.

He caught her expression and laughed hollowly. "I know. I'm preoccupied. Want to know why?" He shoved a newspaper across his desk. "Read the headline."

It said, Matthew Helm to Fill Unexpired Term of U.S. Senator. She stared at Cash without understanding what he was upset about.

"There were three men in the running for the appointment," he said. "One was found by police in San Antonio, on the street, doped up by an apparent drug habit that nobody knew he had. A tip," he added. "The second withdrew from the nomination because his son was arrested for cocaine possession—a kid who'd never even used drugs, but apparently the glove compartment in his car was stuffed with the stuff. Another tip. The third contender, Helm, got the appointment."

"You think the others were set up," she began.

"Big-time," he replied. He glared at the headline. "If he wins the special election in May, we're in for some hard times in law enforcement. I can't prove it, but the prevailing theory is that Mr. Helm is in bed with Charro Mendez. Remember him?"

She nodded. "The enforcer who worked for the late El Ladrón," she said. "He was a cousin to the Fuentes brothers."

"The very same ones who used to run the distribution hub. He's now head of the drug cartel over the border in Cotillo. In fact, he's the mayor of that lovely little drug center."

"Oh, dear."

"I really wish somebody had furnished Carson with more than three hand grenades," he muttered.

"Shame!" she said.

He chuckled. "Okay. I'll get the purchase order filled out." He leaned forward. "Hell of a thing, to have a politician like this in Washington."

"He'll be a junior senator," she pointed out. "He won't have an important role in anything. He won't chair any important committees and he won't have powerful alliances."

"Yet."

"Surely, he won't win the special election," she ventured.

He looked at her. "Carlie, remember what I just told you about his rivals for the appointment?"

She whistled. "Oh, dear," she said again.

"Exactly."

The phone rang. She excused herself and went out to answer it.

CARSON WAS CONSPICUOUS by his absence for the next few days. Nobody said anything about him, but it was rumored that he was away on some job for Eb Scott. In the meantime, Carlie got her first look at the mysterious Rourke.

He stopped by her office during her lunch hour one day. He was wearing khakis with a sheepskin coat. He grinned at her where she sat at her desk eating hot soup out of a foam cup.

"Bad habit," he said, with a trace of a South African accent. "Eating on the job. You should be having that out of fine china in some exotic restaurant."

She was staring at the attractive man wearing an eye patch, with her spoon suspended halfway between the cup and her mouth. "Excuse me?" she faltered.

"An exotic restaurant," he repeated.

"Listen, the only exotic restaurant I know of is the Chinese place over on Madison, and I think their cook is from New York."

He chuckled. "It's the sentiment, you know, that counts."

"I'll take your word for it." She put down the cup. "How can I help you?"

"Is the boss in?" he asked.

She shook her head. "Sorry. He's at the exotic local café having a thick hamburger and fries with a beautiful ex–motion picture star."

"Ah, the lovely Tippy," he chuckled. "Lucky man, to have a wife who's both kind and beautiful. The combination is rare."

"I'll say."

"So, okay if I leave a message?"

She pushed a pad and pen across the desk and smiled. "Be my guest."

He scribbled a few words and signed with a flourish.

She glanced at it. "You're Rourke?"

He nodded. His one pale brown eye twinkled. "I guess my reputation has preceded me?"

"Something like that," she said with a grin.

"I hope you were told it by your boss and not Carson," he said.

She shook her head. "Nobody told me. I overheard my dad talking about you on the telephone."

"Your dad?"

She nodded. "Reverend Jake Blair."

His face softened. "You're his daughter, then." He nodded. "It came as a shock to know he had a child, let me tell you. Not the sort of guy I ever associated with family."

"Why?" she asked, all innocence.

He saw that innocence and his face closed up. "I spoke out of turn, there."

"I know he did other things before he came home," she said. "I don't know what they were."

"I see."

In that instant, his own past seemed to scroll across his hard face, leaving scars that were visible for a few seconds.

"You need to go to one of those exotic restaurants and have something to cheer you up," she pointed out.

He stared at her for a moment and then chuckled. "How about going with me?" he teased.

She shook her head. "Sorry. I've been warned about you."

"How so?" he asked, and seemed really interested in her answer.

She grinned. "I'm not in your league, Mr. Rourke," she said. "Small-town girl, never been anywhere, never dated much…" He looked puzzled. She gave him her best starstruck expression. "I want to get married and have lots of kids," she said enthusiastically. "In fact, I'm free today after five…!"

He glowered at her. "Damn! And I've got a meeting at five." He snapped his fingers. "What a shame!"

"Just my luck. There, there, I'm sure you'll find someone else who can't wait to marry you," she added.

"No plans to marry, I'm afraid," he replied. Then he seemed

to get it, all at once. His eyebrows arched. "Are you having me on?"

She blinked. "Am I having you on what?"

He stuffed his hands in his pockets. "I can't marry you," he said. "It's against my religion."

"Which religion would that be?"

"I'm not sure," he said. "I'll have to find one that prohibits marriage..." He burst out laughing.

She grinned.

"I get it. I'm a bit slow today. Must stem from missing breakfast." He shook his head. "Damned weird food you Yanks serve for breakfast, let me tell you. Grits? What the hell is a grit?"

"If you have to ask, you shouldn't eat one," she returned, laughing.

"I reckon." He smiled. "Well, it was nice meeting you, Ms. Blair."

"Miss," she said. "I don't run a company and I'm not planning to start my own business."

He blinked. "Come again?"

She frowned. "How can I come again if I haven't left?"

He moved closer to the desk. "Confound it, woman, I need a dictionary to figure out what you're saying."

"You can pin a rose on that," she agreed. "Are you from England?"

He glared at her. "I'm South African."

"Oh! The Boer Wars. You had a very famous general named Christiaan de Wet. He was a genius at guerilla warfare and was never captured by the British, although his brother, Piet, was."

He gaped at her.

She smiled shyly. "I collect famous generals. Sort of. I have books on famous campaigns. My favorites were American, of course, like General Francis Marion of South Carolina, the soldier they called the 'Swamp Fox' because he was so good at escaping from the British in the swamps during the Revolutionary War," she laughed. "Then there was Colonel John Singleton

Mosby, the Gray Ghost of the Confederacy. I also like to read about Crazy Horse," she added shyly. "He was Oglala Lakota, one of the most able of the indigenous leaders. He fought General Crook's troops to a standstill at the Battle of the Rosebud."

He was still gaping.

"But my favorite is Alexander the Great. Of all the great military heroes, he was the most incredible strategist…"

"I don't believe it." He perched himself on the edge of her desk. "I know South Africans who couldn't tell you who de Wet was!"

She shrugged. "I used to spend a lot of time in the library. They had these old newspapers from the turn of the twentieth century. They were full of the Boer Wars and that famous Boer General de Wet," she laughed. "I almost missed class a couple of times because I was so entranced by the microfilm."

He laughed. "Actually, I'm distantly related to one of the de Wets, not really sure if it was Christiaan, though. My people have been in South Africa for three generations. They were originally Dutch, or so my mother said."

"Rourke is not really a Dutch name, is it?" she asked.

He sighed. "No. Her name was Skipper, her maiden name."

"Was your father Irish?"

His face closed up. That one brown eye looked glittery.

"Sorry," she said at once. "That was clumsy. I have things in my past that I don't like to think about, either."

He was surprised at her perception. "I don't speak of my father," he said gently. "Didn't mean to unsettle you."

"No problem," she said, and smiled. "We're sort of the sum total of the tragedies of our lives."

"Well put." He nodded thoughtfully. "I might reconsider about that marriage thing…"

"Sorry. My lunch hour's over."

"Damn."

She laughed.

He studied her with real interest. "There's this do, called a Valentine's Day dance, I think. If you need a partner...?"

"Thanks, but I have a date," she said.

"Just my luck, being at the end of the line, and all," he chuckled.

"If you go, I'll dance with you," she promised.

"Will you, now? In that case, I'll dust off my tux."

"Just one dance, though," she added. "I mean, we wouldn't want to get you gossiped about or anything."

"Got it." He winked and got to his feet. "If you'll pass that note along to the chief, I'll be grateful. See you around, I expect."

"I expect so," she replied.

WHAT A VERY strange man, she thought. He was charming. But she really didn't want to complicate her life. In his way, he seemed far more risky than even Carson, in a romantic sense.

When she got home, she mentioned his visit to her father.

"So now you know who Rourke is," he chuckled.

"He's very nice," she said. "But he's a sad sort of person."

"Rourke?" he asked, and seemed almost shocked.

"Yes. I mean, it doesn't show so much. But you can tell."

"Pumpkin, you really are perceptive."

"He said he'd take me to the Valentine's dance. That was after he reconsidered the wedding, but I told him my lunch hour was over..."

"What?" he blurted out.

"Nothing to worry about, he said he wasn't free today anyway."

"Listen here, you can't marry Rourke," he said firmly.

"Well, not today, at least," she began.

"Not any day," came an angry voice from the general direction of the front door. Carson came in, scowling. "And what did I tell you about keeping that cell phone with you?" he added, pulling it out of his pocket. "You left it on your desk at work!"

She grimaced. "I didn't notice."

"Too busy flirting with Rourke, were you?" Carson added harshly.

"That is none of your business," she said pertly.

"It really isn't," her father interjected, staring at Carson until he backed down. "What's going on?" he added, changing the subject.

Carson looked worn. "Dead ends. Lots of them."

"Were you at least able to ascertain if it was poison?"

He nodded. "A particularly nasty one that took three days to do its work." He glanced at Carlie, who looked pale. "Should you be listening to this?" he asked.

"I work for the police," she pointed out. She swallowed. "Photos of dead people, killed in various ways, are part of the files I have to keep for court appearances by our men and women."

Carson frowned. He hadn't considered that her job would involve things like that. "I thought you just typed reports."

She drew in a breath. "I type reports, I file investigative material, photos, I keep track of court appearances, call people to remind them of meetings, and from time to time I function as a shoulder for people who have to deal with unthinkable things."

Carson knew what she was talking about. His best friend, years ago, had been a reservation policeman. He'd gone with the man on runs a time or two during college vacation. In the service, overseas, he'd seen worse things. He was surprised that Carlie, the innocent, was able to deal with that aspect of police work.

"It's a good job," she added. "And I have the best boss around."

"I have to agree," her father said with a gentle smile. "For a hard case, he does extremely well as a police chief." He sighed. "I do miss seeing Judd Dunn around."

"Who's Judd Dunn?" Carson asked.

"He was a Texas Ranger who served on the force with Cash," Jake said. "He quit to be assistant chief here when he and Christabel had twins. But he was offered a job as police chief over in Centerville. It's still Jacobs County, just several miles away. He took it for the benefits package. And, maybe, to compete with Cash," he chuckled.

"They tell a lot of stories about the chief," Carlie said.

"Most of them are true," Reverend Blair replied. "The man has had a phenomenal life. I don't think there's much he hasn't done."

Carson put Carlie's phone on the table beside her and glanced at his watch with a grimace. "I have to get going. I'm still checking on the other thing," he added to Reverend Blair. "But I... Sorry."

Carson paused to take a call. "Yes, I know, I'm running late." He paused and smiled, gave Carlie a smug look. "It will be worth the wait. I like you in pink. Okay. See you in about thirty minutes. We'll make the curtain, I promise. Sure." He hung up. "I'm taking Lanette to see *The Firebird* in San Antonio. I have to go."

"Lanette?" Reverend Blair asked.

"She's a stewardess. I met her on the plane coming down with Dalton Kirk a few weeks ago." He paused. "There's still the matter of who sent a driver for him, you know. A man was holding a sign with his name on it. I tried to trace him, but I couldn't get any information."

"I'll mention it to Hayes," Reverend Blair said. "He's still hoping to find Joey's computer." Joey was the computer technician who'd been killed trying to recover files from Hayes's computer. The computer itself had disappeared, leading Hayes to reset all the department's sensitive information files and type most of his documentary evidence all over again.

Carson's expression was cold. "Joey didn't deserve to die like that. He was a sweet kid."

"I didn't know him," Reverend Blair said. "Eb said he was one of the finest techs he'd ever employed."

"One day," Carson said, "we'll find the person who killed him."

"Make sure you take a law enforcement officer with you if it's you who finds him," Reverend Blair said shortly. "You're very young to end up in federal prison on a murder charge."

Carson smiled, but his eyes didn't. "I'm not as young as I look. And age has more to do with experience than years," he said, and for a minute, the sadness Carlie had seen on Rourke's face was duplicated on Carson's.

"True," Reverend Blair said quietly.

Carlie was fiddling with her phone, not looking at Carson. She'd heard about the stewardess from one of the sheriff's deputies, who'd heard it from Dalton Kirk. The woman was blond and beautiful and all over Carson during the flight. It made Carlie sad, and she didn't want to be. She didn't want to care that he was going to a concert with the woman.

"Well, I'll be in touch." He glanced at Carlie. There was that smug, taunting smile again. And he was gone.

Her father looked at her with sympathy. "You can't let it matter," he said after a minute. "You know that."

She hesitated for a second. Then she nodded. "I'm going up. Need anything?"

He shook his head. He took her by the shoulders and kissed her forehead. "Life is hard."

"Oh, yes," she said, and tried to smile. "Night, Dad."

"Sleep well."

"You, too."

SHE PLUGGED IN her game and went looking for Robin to run some battlegrounds. It would keep her mind off what Carson was probably doing with that beautiful blond stewardess. She saw her reflection in the computer screen and wished, not for the first time, that she had some claim to beauty and charm.

Robin was waiting for her in the Alliance capital city. They queued for a battleground and practiced with their weapons on the target dummies while they waited.

This is my life, she thought silently. *A computer screen in a dark room. I'm almost twenty-three years old and nobody wants to marry me. Nobody even wants to date me. But I have bright ideals and I'm living the way I want to.*

She made a face at her reflection. "Good girls never made history," she told it. Then she hesitated. Yes, they did. Joan of Arc was considered so holy that her men never approached her in any physical way. They followed her, a simple farm girl, into battle without hesitation. She was armed with nothing except her flag and her faith. She crowned a king and saved a nation. Even today, centuries later, people knew who she was. Joan was a good girl.

Carlie smiled to herself. *So,* she thought. *There's my come-back to that!*

SHE WAS TYPING up a grisly report the next day. A man had been found on the town's railroad tracks. He was a vagabond, apparently. He was carrying no identification and wearing a nice suit. There wasn't a lot left of him. Carlie tried not to glance at the crime scene photos as she dealt with the report.

Carson came in, looking weary and out of sorts.

She stared at him. "Well, it wasn't you, after all," she said enigmatically.

He blinked. "Excuse me?"

"We found a man in a nice suit, carrying no identification. Just for a few minutes, we wondered if it was you," she said, alluding to his habit of going everywhere without ID.

"Tough luck," he returned. He frowned as he glanced at the crime scene photos. He lifted one and looked at it with no apparent reaction. He put it back down. His black eyes narrowed on her face as he tried to reconcile her apparent sweetness with the ability it took to process that information without throwing up.

"Something you needed?" she asked, still typing.

"I want to speak to Grier," he said.

She buzzed the chief and announced the visitor. She went back to her typing without giving Carson the benefit of even a glance. "You can go in," she said, nodding toward the chief's office door.

Carson stared at her without meaning to. She wasn't pretty. She had nothing going for her. She had ironclad ideals and a smart mouth and a body that wasn't going to send any man running toward her. Still, she had grit. She could do a job like that. It would be hard even on a toughened police officer, which she wasn't.

She looked up, finally, intimidated by the silence. He captured her eyes, held them, probed them. The look was intense, biting, sensual. She felt her heart racing. Her hands on the keyboard were cold as ice. She wanted to look away but she couldn't. It was like holding a live electric wire…

"Carson?" the chief called from his open office door.

Carson dragged his gaze away from Carlie. "Coming."

He didn't look at her again. Not even as he left the office scant minutes later. She didn't know whether to be glad or not. The look had kindled a hunger in her that she'd never known until he walked into her life. She knew the danger. But it was like a moth's attraction to the flames.

She forced her mind back on the job at hand and stuffed Carson, bad attitude and blonde and all, into a locked door in the back of her mind.

CHAPTER FOUR

THINGS WERE HEATING UP. Reverend Blair went to San Antonio with Rourke. They seemed close, which fascinated Carlie.

Her dad didn't really have friends. He was a good minister, visiting the sick, officiating at weddings, leading the congregation on Sundays. But he stuck close to home. With Rourke, he was like another person, someone Carlie didn't know. Even the way they talked, in some sort of odd shorthand, stood out.

THE WEATHER WAS COLD. Carlie grimaced as she hung up the tattered coat, which was the only protection she had against the cold. In fact, she was worried about going to the dance with Robin because of the lack of a nice coat. The shoes she was going to wear with the green velvet dress were old and a little scuffed, but nobody would notice, she was sure. People in Jacobs County were kind.

She wondered if Carson might show up there. It was a hope and a worry because she knew it was going to hurt if she had to see him with that elegant, beautiful woman she'd heard about. The way he'd looked at her when he was talking to the woman on the phone was painful, too; his smug expression taunted her with his success with women. If she could keep that in mind, maybe she could avoid some heartbreak.

But her stubborn mind kept going back to that look she'd shared with Carson in her boss's office. It had seemed to her as if he was as powerless to stop it as she was. He hadn't seemed arrogant about the way she reacted to him, that once. But if she couldn't get a grip on her feelings, she knew tragedy would ensue. He was, as her father had said, not tamed or able to be tamed. It really would be like trying to live with a wolf.

On her lunch hour, she drove to the cemetery. She'd bought a small plastic bouquet of flowers to put on her mother's neat grave. A marble vase was built into the headstone, just above the BLAIR name. Underneath it, on one side, was the headstone they'd put for her mother. It just said Mary Carter Blair, with her birth date and the day of her death.

She squatted down and smoothed the gravel near the headstone. She took out the faded plastic poinsettia she'd decorated the grave with at Christmas and put the new, bright red flowers, in their small base, inside the marble vase and arranged them just so.

She patted her mother's tombstone. "It isn't Valentine's Day yet, Mama, but I thought I'd bring these along while I had time," she said, looking around to make sure nobody was nearby to hear her talking to the grave. "Dad's gone to San Antonio with this wild South African man. He's pretty neat." She patted the tombstone again. "I miss you so much, Mama," she said softly. "I wish I could show you my pretty dress and talk to you. Life is just so hard sometimes," she whispered, fighting tears.

Her mother had suffered for a long time before she finally let go. Carlie had nursed her at home, until that last hospital stay, taken care of her, just as her mother had taken care of her when she was a baby.

"I know you blamed yourself for what happened. It was never your fault. You couldn't help it that your mother was a…well, what she was." She drew in a breath. "Daddy says they're both gone now. I shouldn't be glad, but I am."

She brushed away a leaf that had fallen onto the tombstone.

"Things aren't any better with me," she continued quietly. "There's a man I…well, I could care a lot about him. But he isn't like us. He's too different. Besides, he likes beautiful women." She laughed hollowly. "Beautiful women with perfect bodies." Her hand went involuntarily to her coat over her shoulder. "I'm never going to be pretty, and I'm a long way from perfect. One day, though, I might find somebody who'd like me just the way I am. You did. You weren't beautiful or perfect, and you were an angel, and Daddy married you. So there's still hope, right?"

She moved the flowers a little bit so they were more visible, then sat down. "Robin's taking me to the Valentine's Day dance. You remember Robin, I know. He's such a sweet man. I bought this beautiful green velvet dress to wear. And Robin's rented us a limo for the night. Can you imagine, me, riding around in a limousine?" She laughed out loud at the irony. "I don't even have a decent coat to wear over my pretty dress. But I'll be going in style."

She caressed her hand over the smooth marble. "It's hard, not having anybody to talk to," she said after a minute. "I only ever had one real girlfriend, and she moved away years ago. She's married and has kids, and she's happy. I hear from her at Christmas." She sighed. "I know you're around, Mama, even if I can't see you.

"I won't ever forget you," she whispered softly. "And I'll always love you. I'll be back to see you on Mother's Day, with some pretty pink roses, like the ones you used to grow."

She patted the tombstone again, fighting tears. "Well…bye, Mama."

She got to her feet, feeling old and sad. She picked up the faded flowers and carried them back to her truck. As she was putting them on the passenger's side floor, she noticed a note on the seat.

Keep the damned cell phone with you! It does no good sitting in the truck!

It was signed with a big capital *C*.

She glared at it, looking around. She didn't see anybody. But he'd been here, watching her. He'd seen her talking to her mother. Great. Something else for him to hold against her. She started to crumple up the note, but it was the first one he'd ever written her. She liked the way he wrote, very legible, elegant longhand. With a sigh, she folded it and stuck it in the glove compartment.

"Mental illness must be contagious," she muttered to herself. "Maybe I got it from Rourke."

She got in under the wheel and started the engine. It didn't occur to her until much later that it seemed to matter to Carson if something happened to her. Of course, it could have just been pride in his work that she wouldn't get killed on his shift. Still, it felt nice. Unless he'd seen her talking to Mary and thought she needed to be committed.

HER FATHER CAME in with Rourke that night just as she was taking the cornbread out of the oven. She'd made a big pot of homemade chili to go with it.

"What a delightful smell," Rourke said in the kitchen doorway.

She grinned. "Pull up a chair. All you need is some butter for the cornbread. I have real butter. Homemade chili to go with it. There's always plenty."

"By all means," Reverend Blair chuckled. "Carlie always makes extra, in case I bring someone home with me."

"Do you do that often?" Rourke asked.

"Every other day," the reverend confessed. "She never complains."

"He only brings hungry people who like the way I cook," she amended, and laughed. Her face, although she didn't realize it, was very pretty when she smiled.

Rourke studied her with real appreciation. If his heart hadn't been torn, he might have found her fascinating.

He looked around the stove and the cabinets.

"Did I forget something?" she asked.

"I'm looking to see if you cooked a grit."

She and her father both laughed.

"It isn't a grit, it's grits. They're made with corn," she pointed out.

He shook his head. "Foreign fare."

"Yes, well, I expect you know how to cook a springbok, but I'd have no idea," she said as she put the pot of chili on the table.

"And she knows about springboks!" Rourke groaned. He sat down and put his napkin in his lap. "She also knows the history of the Boer Wars," he said.

Her father shook his head. "She's a student of military history. A big fan of Hannibal," he confided.

"So am I. He was from Carthage. Africa," Rourke added.

There was silence while they ate. Rourke seemed fascinated with the simple meal.

"I've had cornbread before, but it's usually so dry that I can't eat it. My mother used to make it like this," he added quietly. "She was from the States. Maryland, I believe."

"How in the world did she end up in Africa?" Carlie exclaimed. She blushed. "I mean, if you don't mind my asking."

He put down his spoon. "I was very rude about my father. I'm sorry," he said, his brown eyes steady on her face. "You see, my birth certificate lists my mother's husband in that capacity. But a covert DNA profile tells a very different story." His face was hard. "I don't speak of it in company because it's painful, even now."

She was really blushing now. She didn't know what to say.

"But I wouldn't have hurt you deliberately just for asking an innocent question," Rourke continued gently. "You don't even know me."

She bit her lower lip. "Thanks," she said shyly.

"Now, if you'd been a *man*..." her father mused, emphasizing the last word.

Carlie looked at him inquisitively.

He exchanged a look with Rourke. "There was a bar in Nassau," her father said. "And a member of the group we were with made a sarcastic remark. Not to add that he did know Rourke, and he certainly knew better, but he'd had one too many Bahama mamas." He pursed his lips and studied Rourke's hard face. "I believe he made a very poetic dive into the swimming pool outside the bar."

"Deliberately?" Carlie asked.

"Well, if it had been deliberate, I don't think he'd have done it through the glass patio door," her father added.

Carlie sucked in a breath. She looked behind her.

"What are you looking for?" her father asked.

"Glass patio doors..."

Rourke chuckled. "It was a while back," he remarked. "I'm less hotheaded now."

"Lies," her father said. "Terrible lies."

"Watch it," Rourke cautioned, pointing his chili spoon at the reverend, "or I'll tell her about the Russian diplomat."

"Please do!" Carlie pleaded.

Her father glowered at Rourke. "It was a long time ago, in another life. Ministers don't hit people," he said firmly.

"Well, you weren't a minister then," Rourke teased, "and your embassy had to call in a lot of favors to keep you out of jail."

"What in the world did you people do in those days?" Carlie asked, shocked.

"Bad things," Reverend Blair said softly. "And it's time to change the subject."

"The things we don't know about our parents," Carlie mused, staring at her father.

"Some things are better not known," was the reply. "And isn't your chili getting cold, pumpkin?"

"Why do you call her 'pumpkin'?" Rourke wanted to know.

"Now that's a really long story..."

"And we can forget to tell it unless we want burned meat for a week," Carlie interjected.

The reverend just smiled.

HER FATHER WENT to answer a phone call while Carlie was clearing the dishes in the kitchen. Rourke sat at the kitchen table with a second cup of black coffee.

"You really don't know a lot about your dad, do you?" he asked her.

"Apparently not," she laughed, glancing at him with mischievous green eyes. "Do you take bribes? I can make almost any sort of pie or cake—"

"I don't like sweets," he interrupted. "And it's worth my life to tell you," he added with a laugh. "So don't ask."

She made a face and went back to the dishes in the sink.

"Don't you have a dishwasher?" he asked, surprised.

She shook her head. "Money is always tight. We get a little extra and there's a pregnant woman who can't afford a car seat, or an elderly man who needs dentures, or a child who needs glasses…" She smiled. "That's life."

He frowned. "You just give it away?"

She turned toward him, curious. "Well, can you take it with you when you go?" she asked.

He paused, sipping coffee.

"The Plains tribes had this philosophy," she began, "that the richest man in the village was the one who had the least because he gave it all away. It denoted a good character, which was far more important than wealth."

"I would ask why the interest in aboriginal culture," he began.

She turned, her hands around a soapy plate. "Oh, my best friend was briefly engaged to a Lakota man," she said. "We were juniors in high school. Her parents thought she was too young, and they made them wait a year."

"From your tone, I gather things didn't go well?"

She shook her head. She turned back to the sink to rinse

the dish, aware of a pang in the region of her heart because the story hit close to home. "His parents talked him into breaking the engagement," she said. "He told her that his religion, his culture, everything was so different from hers that it would be almost impossible to make a life together. She'd have had to live on the reservation with him, and his parents already hated her. Then there was the problem of the children, because they would have been trapped between two cultures, belonging to neither."

"That's very sad," Rouke commented.

She turned to look at him, then lowered her eyes to the sink again. "I didn't realize how much difference there was, until I started reading about it." She smiled sadly. "Crazy Horse, Tashunka Witko in his own tongue—although that's translated different ways in English—was one of my favorite subjects. He was Oglala Lakota. He said that one could not sell the ground upon which the People—what the Lakota called themselves—walked." She glanced at him. "Things never mattered to them. Materialism isn't really compatible with attitudes like that."

"You're one of the least materialistic people I know, Carlie," her father said as he came back into the room. "And I'd still say it even if I wasn't related to you."

"Thanks, Dad," she said with a smile.

"I need to talk to you," he told Rourke. "Bring your coffee into the office. Carlie, that new science fiction movie you wanted to see is playing on the movie channel."

"It's not new, it's four months old," she laughed. "But you're right, I guess, it's new to me. I'll watch it later. I promised Robin I'd help run one of his little toons through a dungeon." She made a face. "I hate dungeons."

"Dungeons?" Rourke asked.

"She plays an online video game," her father explained, naming it.

"Oh, I see. You're Horde, too, huh?" Rourke teased.

She glared at him. "I'm Alliance. Proudly Alliance."

"Sorry," Rourke chuckled. "Everyone I know is in Horde."

She turned away. "It seems like it sometimes, doesn't it?" She sighed. She turned at the staircase and held up her hand as if it contained a sword. "For the Alliance!" she yelled, and took off running upstairs.

Her father and Rourke just laughed.

IT WAS FRIDAY. And not just any Friday. It was the Friday before the Saturday night when the Valentine's Day dance was being held at the Jacobsville Civic Center.

Carlie was all nerves. She was hoping that it would be warmer, so she could manage to go to the dance without wearing a coat, because she didn't have anything nice to go with her pretty dress. She had to search out a file for the chief, which she'd put in the wrong drawer, and then she hung up on a state senator by pushing the wrong button on her desk phone.

The chief just laughed after he'd returned the call. "Is it Robin that's got you in such a tizzy?" he teased.

She flushed. "Well, actually, it's the…"

Before she could finish the sentence and tell him it was her wardrobe that was the worry, the door opened and Carson came in. But he wasn't alone.

There was a beautiful blond woman with him. She was wearing a black suit with a red silk blouse, a black coat with silver fur on the collar, and her purse was the same shade of deep red as the high-heeled shoes she was wearing. Her platinum-blond hair was pulled back into an elegant chignon. She had a flawless complexion, pale blue eyes, and skin like a peach. Carlie felt like a cactus plant by comparison.

But she managed a smile for the woman just the same.

The blonde looked at her with veiled amusement and abruptly looked toward the chief.

"Chief Grier, this is Lanette Harris," Carson said.

"So charmed to meet you," the blonde gushed in an accent that sounded even more Southern than Carlie's Texas accent.

She held out a perfectly manicured hand. "I've heard so much about you!"

Cash shook her hand, but he didn't respond to her flirting tone. He just nodded. His eyes went to Carson, who was giving Carlie a vicious, smug little smile.

"What can I do for you?" he asked Carson.

Carson shrugged. "I was at a loose end. I wondered if you'd heard anything more from your contact?"

Cash shook his head. Just that. He didn't say a thing.

Carson actually looked uncomfortable. "Well, I guess we'll get going. We're having supper in San Antonio."

He was wearing a dark suit with a spotless white shirt and a blue pinstriped tie. His long hair was pulled back into a neat ponytail. He was immaculate. Carlie had to force herself not to look at him too closely.

"That desk is a mess! Don't you know how to file things away?" Lanette asked Carlie with studied humor, moving closer. Her perfume was cloying. "However do you find anything?"

"I know where everything is," Carlie replied pleasantly.

"Sorry," Lanette said when she saw Cash Grier's narrow look. "I can't abide clutter." She smiled flirtatiously.

"Don't let us keep you," Cash replied in a tone that sounded as icy as his expression looked.

"Yes. We'd better go." Carson moved to the door and opened it.

"Nice to have met you, Chief Grier," Lanette purred. "If you ever want a competent secretary, I might be persuaded to come out of retirement. I used to work for a law firm. And I know how to file."

Cash didn't reply.

"Lanette," Carson said shortly.

"I'm coming." She smiled again at Cash. "Bye now." She didn't even look at Carlie.

She went to the door and through it. Carlie didn't look up from her computer screen. She hoped she wasn't going to bite through her tongue. Only when she heard the door close did she lift her eyes again and looked through the window.

Carson was striding along beside the blonde and not with his usual smooth gait. He was almost stomping toward his black sedan.

Carlie started coughing and almost couldn't stop.

"You okay?" Cash asked with concern.

"Got…choked on the air, I guess," she laughed. She could barely stop. "Gosh, do you think she bathes in that perfume?"

"Go outside and take a break. I'll turn the AC on for a few minutes to clear the room," Cash said abruptly. "Go on."

She wasn't about to go out front and risk running into Carson and his beautiful companion. "I'll just step out back," she managed, still coughing.

She got outside and leaned against the door, dragging in deep breaths until she was able to get her breath again. There must be something in that perfume that she was allergic to. Although, come to think of it, she'd almost choked sitting next to a woman in church the week before who'd been wearing a musky sort of perfume. She'd learned long ago that she could only manage the lightest of floral colognes, and not very often. Funny, her lungs giving her so much trouble over scent, and she didn't even smoke.

She went back inside after a couple of minutes. Cash was talking to two patrolmen who'd stopped by with a legal question about a traffic stop.

She went back to her desk and sat down.

"You should see your doctor," Cash said when the patrolmen went out.

She raised both eyebrows. "He's married."

He burst out laughing. "That's not what I meant, Carlie. I think you had a reaction to Ms. Harris's perfume."

"Too much perfume bothers me sometimes, it's just allergies." She shrugged. "I have a problem with pollen, too."

"Okay. If you say so."

"I'll get the files in better order," she offered.

"Don't let some outsider's comment worry you," he said curtly. "Women like that one tear holes in everything they touch."

"She was very beautiful."

"So are some snakes."

He turned and went back into his office. Carlie tried not to mind that Carson's elegant girlfriend had treated her like dirt. She tried to pretend that it didn't bother her, that Carson hadn't brought her into the office deliberately to flaunt her.

If only I was beautiful, she thought to herself. *I'd be twice as pretty as his friend there, and I'd have oodles of money and the best clothes and drive an expensive car. And I'd stick my nose up at him!*

Fine words. Now, if she could only manage to forget the miserable afternoon. She was going to a dance, with a nice man. There might be an eligible man there who'd want to dance with her when he saw her pretty dress.

She smiled. It was a gorgeous dress, and she was going to look very nice. Even if she wasn't blond.

THE LIMOUSINE WASN'T what she expected. It wasn't one of the long, elegant ones she'd seen in movies. It was just a sedan.

"Sorry," Robin said when they were underway, the glass partition raised between them and the driver. "I did order the stretch, but they only had one and somebody got there before I did. Some local guy, too, darn the luck."

"It's okay," she said, smiling. "I'm just happy I didn't have to bring my truck!"

He laughed. Then he frowned. "Carlie, why aren't you wearing a coat?" he asked. He moved quickly to turn up the heat. "It's freezing out!"

"I don't have a nice coat, Robin," she said, apologizing. "I didn't want to embarrass you by wearing something ratty..."

"Oh, for God's sake, Carlie," he muttered. "We've known

each other since first grade. I don't care what the coat looks like, I just don't want you to get sick."

She smiled. "You really are the nicest man I know. Lucky Lucy!"

He laughed. "Well, at least she and I will get to dance together," he said, sighing. "You're so kind to do this for us." He shook his head. "I've tried everything I know to make her folks like me. They just can't get past who my grandfather was. Some grudge, huh?"

"I know." She searched his dark eyes. "You and Lucy should elope."

"Don't I wish." He grimaced. "When I get established in my own business, that's exactly what I have in mind. They're pushing Lucy at the guy who's bringing her tonight. He's old money from up around Fort Worth. She likes him but she doesn't want to marry him."

"They can't make her," she pointed out.

"No, they can't. She's as stubborn as I am."

THEY PULLED UP at the door to the civic center, just behind the stretch limousine that belonged to the same car service Robin had used.

"There's our car. At least, the car I wanted to order for us." He frowned. "Who is that?" he added.

Carlie didn't say, but she knew. It was Carson, resplendent in an immaculate dinner jacket. Getting out of the vehicle beside him was the blond woman, in a saucy black gown that hugged every curve from shoulder to ankle, and left a lot of bare skin in between. Her breasts were almost completely uncovered except for a bit of fabric in strategic places, and her long skirt had a split so far up the thigh that you could almost see her panty line.

"Well, that's going to go over big in conservative Jacobsville," Robin muttered as the driver opened the backseat door for them. "A half-naked woman at a dance benefiting the local church orphanage."

"Maybe she'll get cold and put more clothes on," Carlie mused, only half-jokingly.

"Let's get you inside before you freeze," he added, taking her hand to pull her toward the building.

There was a crowd. Carlie spotted the chief and his beautiful wife, Tippy, over in a corner talking over glasses of punch. Rourke was standing with them. He looked oddly handsome in his formal attire. Tippy was exquisite in a pale green silk gown, decked out in emeralds and diamonds. Her long, red-gold hair was up in a French twist, secured with an emerald and diamond clasp. She looked like the world-class model she'd once been.

Close at hand was Lucy Tims, wearing a long blue gown with a rounded neckline, her black hair hanging down her back like a curtain. She was standing with a tall, lean man who seemed far more interested in talking to two of the local cattlemen than with his date.

She waved to Robin, said something to the tall man, who nodded, and made a beeline for Carlie and Robin.

"You made it!" Lucy enthused. "Oh, Carlie, bless you!" she added, hugging the other woman.

"You may call me Cupid," Carlie whispered into her ear, laughing.

"I certainly will. You don't know how grateful we are."

"Yes, she does because I told her all the way over here," Robin chuckled. "Shall we get some punch?"

"Great idea." Carlie looked down at the spotless green velvet dress. "On second thought, the punch is purple and I'm clumsy. I think I'll just look for a bottle of water!"

They both laughed as she left them.

Well, at least she didn't see Carson and his new appendage, she thought, grateful for small blessings. She walked down the table with a small plate, studying the various delicacies and grateful that food was provided. She'd been too nervous to eat anything.

She was trying to decide between cheese straws and bacon-wrapped sausages when she felt the plate taken from her hand.

She started to protest, but Carson had her by the hand and he was leading her out toward the dance floor.

"You...didn't ask," she blurted out.

He turned her into his arms and slid his fingers into hers. "I didn't have to," he said at her forehead.

Her heart was beating so hard that she knew he had to feel it. He had her wrapped up against him, so close that she could almost taste his skin. He was wearing just a hint of a very masculine cologne. His shirtfront was spotless. His black tie was ruffled. Just above her eyes she could see the smooth tan of his jaw.

He moved with such grace that she felt as if she had two left feet. She was stiff because it disturbed her to be so close to him. Her hand, entwined with his, was cold as ice. She could just barely get enough air to breathe.

"Your boyfriend's dancing with someone else," he observed.

She could have told him that she didn't have a boyfriend, that she was only helping play Cupid, but it wasn't her secret to tell.

"Will you relax?" he said at her ear, shaking her gently. "It's like dancing with a board."

She swallowed. "I was getting something to eat."

"The food will still be there when you go back."

She stopped protesting. But it was impossible to relax. She followed him mechanically, vaguely aware that the song they were playing was from the musical *South Pacific* and that the evening actually did seem enchanted. Now.

"Whose tombstone were you talking to?" he asked after a minute.

She cleared her throat. "Nobody was around."

"I was."

"You weren't supposed to be there."

He shrugged.

She drew in a steadying breath and stared at his shirt. "I

took my mother a bouquet," she said after a minute. "I go by the cemetery and talk to her sometimes." She looked up belligerently. "I know it's not normal."

He searched her soft green eyes. "Normal is subjective. I used to talk to my mother, too, after she was gone."

"Oh." She glanced down again because it was like a jolt of lightning to look into those black eyes.

His fingers became caressing in between her own where they rested on top of his dinner jacket. "I was six when she died," he said.

"I was fourteen."

"How did she die?"

"Of cancer," she said on a long breath. "It took months. At least, until she went into hospital. Then it was so fast…" She hesitated. "How did your mother die?"

He didn't answer.

She groaned inside. She'd done it again. She couldn't seem to stop asking stupid questions…!

His hand contracted. "My father was drunk. She'd burned the bread. She tried to get away. I got in front of him with a chair. He took it away and laid it across my head. When I came to, it was all over."

She stopped dancing and looked up at him, her eyes wide and soft.

"She was very beautiful," he said quietly. "She sang to me when I was little."

"I'm so sorry," she said, and meant every word.

He smoothed his fingers over hers. "They took him away. There was a trial. One of her brothers was in prison, serving a life sentence for murder. He had the bad luck to be sent to the same cell block."

She studied his hard, lean face. She didn't say anything. She didn't have to. Her eyes said it for her.

The hand that was holding hers let go. It went to her face and traced the tear down to the corner of her full, soft mouth.

It lingered there, the knuckle of his forefinger moving lazily over the pretty line of her lips.

She felt on fire. Her legs were like rubber. She could feel her heart beating. She knew he could, because his eyes suddenly went down to the discreet rounded neckline, and lower, watching the fabric jump with every beat of her heart, with her strained breathing.

Her whole body felt tight, swollen. She shivered just a little from the intensity of a feeling she'd never experienced before. She swallowed. Her mouth was so dry…

"You'd be a pushover, little girl," he whispered in a deep, gentle tone as he looked at her soft mouth. "It wouldn't even be a challenge."

"I…know," she managed in a broken tone.

His head bent. She felt his breath on her lips. She felt as if she were vibrating from the sensuous touch of his hand at her waist, pulling her close to the sudden, blunt hardness of his body.

He was burning. Hungry. Aching. On fire to touch her under that soft bodice, to feel her breasts under his lips. He wanted to push her down on the floor here, right here, and press himself full length against her and feel her wanting him. Her heartbeat was shaking them both. She was dying for him. He knew it. He could have her. She wouldn't even try to stop him. He could take her outside, into the night. He could feed on her soft mouth in the darkness, bend her to his will, back her up against the wall and…

"Carson!"

CHAPTER FIVE

"CARSON!" THE STRIDENT voice came again.

The second time, Carson heard it. He steeled himself to look away from Carlie's rapt, shocked face and slowly let her move away from him.

He turned to Lanette. She was glaring at them.

"You promised me the first dance," she accused, pouting.

He managed to look unperturbed. "So I did. If you'll excuse me?" he asked Carlie without actually meeting her eyes.

She nodded. "Of course."

He took Lanette's hand and moved to the other side of the room.

Carlie was almost shaking. She went back to the buffet table mechanically and picked up another plate.

"Might better calm down a little before you try to eat," Rourke murmured. He took the plate away from her, just as Carson had, and pulled her onto the dance floor. "Just as well to escape before complications arise," he added with a chuckle. "You seem to be the subject of some heated disagreement."

She tossed a covert glance toward the other side of the room where Carson and his date appeared to be exchanging terse comments.

"I was just trying to get something to eat," she began.

He studied her. "That's a nice young man you came in with. Very polite. Odd, how he's ignoring you."

She looked up at him. "Private matter," she said.

"Ah. So many things are, yes?"

The way he said it amused her. She laughed.

"That's better," he replied, smiling. "You were looking a bit like the hangman's next victim."

She lowered her eyes to his shirt. It had ruffles, and crimson edging. He had a red carnation in the lapel of the jacket. "You're not quite conventional," she blurted out.

"Never," he agreed. "I like to buck the odds. Our friend over there is Mr. Conservative," he added. "He doesn't like the assumption of ownership, so you can figure the beautiful companion will be gone quite soon."

She tried not to look pleased.

He tilted her face up to his and he wasn't smiling. "That being said, let me give you some sound advice. He's living on heartache and looking for temporary relief. Do you get me?"

She bit her lip. She nodded.

"Good. You remember that. I've seen him walk on hearts wearing hobnailed boots, and he enjoys it. He's getting even."

"But I haven't done anything to him," she began.

"Wrong assumption. He's paying back someone else. Don't ask," he said. "I'm not privy to his past. But I know the signs."

There was such bitterness in his voice that she just stared at him.

"Long story," he said finally. "And no, I won't share it. You just watch your step. Carson's big trouble for a little innocent like you."

"I'm the only one of my kind," she said a little sadly. "Everybody says I'm out of step with the world."

"Would you enjoy being used like a cocktail napkin and tossed in the bin after?" he asked bluntly.

She caught her breath at the imagery.

"I thought not." He drew her back into the dance. "That platinum-armored blond tank he's with doesn't care what she's asked to do if the price is right," he said with icy disdain. "She's for sale and she doesn't care who knows it."

"How do you know...?"

He looked down at her with weary cynicism. "This isn't my first walk round the park," he replied. "She's the sort to go on the attack if anything gets between her and something she wants."

"Well, he doesn't want me," she said, "but thanks for the warning."

He chuckled. "Not to worry, I'll be around."

"Thanks, Rourke."

"Stanton."

She pulled back and looked up at him with real interest. "Stanton?"

He smiled. "It's my first name. I only share it with friends."

She smiled back, shyly. "Thanks."

"And *Carlie?* Is it your name or a nickname?"

She looked around to make sure nobody was close enough to hear. "Carlotta," she whispered. "My mother thought it sounded elegant."

"Carlotta." He smiled gently. "It suits you."

"Just don't tell anyone," she pleaded.

"Your secret's safe with me," he promised.

She was remembering Lanette's nasty comment about her desk, right in front of her boss. She imagined the other woman was furious that she'd even danced with Carson. She just hoped there wouldn't be a price to pay.

APPARENTLY CARSON DIDN'T like possessive women, because Carlie had no sooner finished her small plate of canapés than he was back again. He stopped by the bandleader and made a request. Then he went straight to Carlie, took the punch out of her hand and led her to the dance floor.

"That's a tango," she protested. "I can't even do a two-step…!"

"I lead, you follow," he said quietly. He shot a look of pure malice at the blonde, who was standing across the room with an angry expression.

"You're getting even," she accused as the band began to play again.

"Count on it," he snarled.

He pulled her close and began to move with exquisite grace. He stopped abruptly, turned, and in a series of intricate steps, wound his legs around hers.

It shocked her that he was so easy to follow in such a hard dance. She laughed self-consciously. "This doesn't look like tangos in movies," she began.

"That's Hollywood," he mused. "This is how they do it in Argentina. People go to dance halls and do it with strangers. It's considered part of the culture. Strangers passing in the night."

"I see."

He pulled her close again, enjoying the soft feel of her slender young body in his arms. She smelled just faintly of roses. "Have you ever been to South America?"

"You're kidding, right?" She gasped as he pulled her suddenly closer and made a sharp turn, holding her so that she didn't stumble.

"Why would I be kidding?" he asked.

"I've never been any place in my life except San Antonio."

He frowned. "Never?"

"Never." She sighed. "I went up with Tommy Tyler once in his airplane when he bought it. It was one of those little Cessna planes. I threw up. I was so embarrassed that I never wanted to get on an airplane again."

He chuckled deeply. "I imagine he was unsettled, as well."

"He was so nice. That just made it worse. I apologized until we landed. He got somebody to come and clean it up. To his credit, he even offered me another ride. But I wouldn't go."

"Were you serious about him?"

"Oh, not that way. He was in his fifties, with grown children," she chuckled. "His wife and my mother were great friends."

"People around here are clannish."

"Yes. Most of us have been here for several generations. I had a teacher in grammar school who taught my grandfather and my mother."

He looked down at her curiously as he did another series of intricate steps, drawing her along with him. The close contact was very disturbing. He loved it. He glanced at the blonde, who was steaming. He enjoyed that. He didn't like possessive women.

Carlie followed his glance. "She'll be out for blood soon," she murmured.

"Which is none of your business." He said it gently, but his tone didn't invite comment.

She clenched her teeth and tried not to give away how hungry the contact was making her. She was astonished at how easy a partner he was. The tango was one of the hardest dances to master, she'd heard. She'd always wanted to try it, but she'd never had a date who could actually dance.

Carson could. He was light on his feet for such a big man, and very skilled. She didn't let herself think about how many partners he must have had to be so good on the dance floor. She drew in a quick breath. She was getting winded already. It irritated her that she couldn't run or even walk fast for long without needing to stop and catch her breath.

She'd never have admitted it to Carson. The feel of his body against hers was intoxicating. She felt his hand firm at her waist, his fingers curled around hers, as he led her around the dance floor.

She was vaguely aware that they were being watched by more people than just the angry blonde, and that the police chief and his wife had taken the dance floor with them.

Cash was a master at the tango. He and Tippy moved like

one person. He danced closer to them, and winked. "You're outclassed, kid," he told Carson. "But not bad. Not bad at all."

Carson laughed. "Don't rest on your laurels. I'm practicing."

"I noticed," Cash said with a grin at Carlie, and he danced Tippy, who also smiled at them, to the other part of the dance floor.

Several other couples came out, trying to keep up with the two accomplished couples on the floor. Their attempts ranged from amusing to disastrous.

Carson's chest rose and fell with deep, soft laughter. "I think square dancing has a larger following in this vicinity than the tango," he pointed out.

"Well, not many men can dance. Even square-dance," she added shyly.

He slowed his movements, and held her even closer, his head bent to hers so that she could feel his breath, smell its minty tang, on her mouth. "My mother danced," he whispered. "She was like a fairy on her feet. She usually won the women's dances at powwows."

She looked up into liquid black eyes. "The Lakota have pow-wows?"

He nodded. "It's what we call them. The first in is the drum. Several men sit around it and play, but it's always called the drum. There are men's dances and women's dances. They're very old."

She nodded. "I went to a powwow up near San Antonio once," she recalled. "There were Comanche people there."

His fingers moved sensuously against hers. "I have Coman-che cousins."

"Your people are clannish, too," she remarked.

"Very. Both sides."

"Both sides?"

"One of my great-great-grandmothers was blond and blue-eyed," he said. "She married a Lakota man. He was a rather famous detective in Chicago at the turn of the twentieth century. He was at Wounded Knee. She nursed him back to health. Later, he was with Buffalo Bill's Wild West show for a time."

She wouldn't have mentioned it, but his skin was a light olive shade. She'd guessed that his blood was mixed.

"That must have been one interesting courtship," she said.

He chuckled. "So I'm told." He searched over her face. "Your father has Norwegian ancestors somewhere."

"Yes, from someplace with a name I can't even pronounce. I never met any of his people. He didn't come back here until I was thirteen…" Her voice trailed away. She didn't like thinking about that. "Mama had pictures of him, but I only saw him a few times when I was growing up. He'd stay for a day or two and go away again, and Mama would cry for weeks after."

He scowled. "Why didn't he stay with her?"

She stared at his shirtfront as the music began to wind down. "They argued once. I heard. He said that she trapped him into marrying her because I was on the way. I wouldn't speak to him after that when he came home. I never told him why. It wasn't until she was dying that he came home. He's…different now."

"That's what I've heard from other people who knew him. He seems to enjoy the life he has now."

"He says he has to do a lot of good to make up for the bad things he used to do," she replied. "He won't talk about them. At least, he wouldn't. Rourke had supper with us and he and Daddy talked about old times. It was fascinating."

"Rourke?"

She smiled. "He's really nice. He likes my cooking, too."

His hand on her waist contracted as if he were angry. "Rourke's more of a lobo wolf than I am. You'll break your heart on him."

She looked up at him with wide, shocked eyes. "What?"

He pulled her closer, bent her against his body in such a sensual way that she gasped. His head lowered until his mouth was almost touching hers as he twirled her around to the deepening throb of the music. "But better him than me, baby," he whispered at her soft mouth. "I don't do forever. Even a child on the way wouldn't change that."

She was barely hearing him. He'd called her "baby." No man had ever called her that, and certainly not in such a sexy, hungry sort of tone. She felt herself shiver as his hand smoothed up her rib cage, stopping just under her breast on the soft fabric. And she couldn't even protest.

She felt as if her body was going to explode from the tension he raised in it. She bit off a soft moan as she felt him drag her even closer, so that she was pressed against him from breasts to hips.

In all her life, she'd never felt a man become aroused, but he wanted her, and he couldn't hide it. She shivered again, her heart beating so hard that she thought it might break out of her chest.

"You...shouldn't," she choked.

His cheek rasped against hers. "You'd be the sweetest honey I ever had," he breathed at her ear. "I'd go so hard into you that you'd go up like a rocket."

She moaned and hid her face, shocked, embarrassed...excited. Her nails bit into his jacket. Her body moved against his helplessly as his long leg moved in and out between hers as the dance slowly wound down.

He arched her against him as it ended, positioning her so that her head was down and leaning back, his mouth poised just over hers.

She held on for dear life. Her eyes were locked into his, imprisoned, helpless. He pulled her up with exquisite slowness, held her against him while people clapped. Neither of them noticed.

He let her go, his cheeks ruddy, as if he were angry and unsettled by what had happened. He had to recite math problems in his mind to force his body to relax before he let her go. She wouldn't realize what was going on, but that blonde would see it immediately.

"You dance well," he said stiffly. "All you need is practice."

She swallowed. "Thanks. You're...amazing."

His eyes, narrow and wise, searched hers. "You have no idea how amazing, in the right circumstances," he whispered huskily, his eyes falling to her mouth. "And if you're very lucky, you won't find out."

She felt her heart shaking her. She knew he must be able to feel it, too. She could barely get her breath. Funny, it felt as if air could get in but couldn't get back out. She coughed slightly.

He frowned. "What's wrong?"

"Perfume," she faltered. "It bothers me sometimes."

He arched an eyebrow. "I don't wear perfume."

"Not you," she muttered. "Other women."

He sniffed the air and smiled. "Florals, musk, woodsy tones," he said. His eyes smoothed over her face. "You smell of roses."

"I love roses," she told him.

"Do you?"

She nodded. "I grow them at home. Antique roses. My mother used to plant them."

"My mother was an herbalist," he replied. "She could cure anything."

"The music has stopped," the blonde pointed out coldly.

Carlie and Carson turned and looked at her blankly.

"And I'd like some punch, if you please?" Lanette added icily.

Carson let Carlie go. He hadn't realized that the music had stopped, or that he and Carlie were standing so close together... alone on the dance floor.

"I'll be back in a minute," he told Lanette. He let go of Carlie's hand and moved toward the restrooms.

Carlie, left alone with the overperfumed blond wildcat, braced herself for what she knew to expect.

"WELL, THAT WAS an exhibition if I ever saw one!" Her pale blue eyes were like ice. "Don't you get any ideas about Carson, you little hick secretary. He's mine. Hands off. Do you understand me?"

Carlie just stared at her with equally cold green eyes. She was still shaking inside from Carson's sensual dance and the things he'd said to her. But she wasn't going to let the other woman cow her. "That's his choice."

"Well, he's not choosing you. I'm not kidding," the other woman persisted. She smiled coldly. "You think you're something, don't you?" She looked Carlie up and down. "Did your dress come from some bargain basement up in San Antonio?" she asked sarcastically. "Marked down 75 percent, perhaps?" she added and laughed when Carlie blushed. "And those shoes. My God, they must be ten years old! I'm surprised he wasn't embarrassed to be seen dancing with you in that dress...!"

"Got yours at a consignment sale, darling?" came a soft, purring voice from beside Carlie.

Tippy Grier moved closer, cradling a cup of punch in her hands. She looked elegant in her green silk gown, dripping diamonds and emeralds. She smiled at the blonde. "That particular dress was in a collection of only five gowns. I recognize it because I know the designer," she added, watching the blonde's eyes widen. "It isn't to my taste," she added, "because I don't sell myself."

"How dare you... I was on the runway!" Lanette almost spat at her, reddening.

"Honey, the only runway you've been on is at the airport," Tippy drawled. She looked down. "Those shoes are two seasons out of date, too, but I suppose you thought nobody would notice." She pursed her bow lips in a mock pout. "Shame."

Lanette's hands were clenched at her sides.

"Run along now, kitty cat," Tippy dismissed her. "Your saucer of cream's waiting outside the door." She smiled. "Do have a lovely evening."

Lanette was almost sputtering. She turned and went storming off toward Carson, who was just returning. She ran into his arms, making a big production of crying, wiping at her eyes, and gesturing toward Tippy and Carlie. The look Carson gave Carlie was livid before he took Lanette's arm and walked her toward the front door.

"WOW," CARLIE SAID to Tippy. She shook her head. "You're just incredible! I didn't even have a comeback."

Tippy laughed. It sounded like silver bells. Her reddish-gold hair burned like fire in the lights from overhead. Her green eyes, lighter than Carlie's, twinkled. "I've seen her kind in modeling. They think they're so superior." Her smile was mischievous. "When I was new to the runway, there was this terrible woman from upstate New York who made fun of everything from my big feet to my accent. I cried a lot. Then I got tough." She pursed her lips. "You know, if you time it just right, you can trip someone on the runway and make it look like a terrible accident!"

"You wicked woman," Carlie gasped, laughing.

"She really did have it coming." She shook her head. "I almost felt sorry for her. She lost her contract with the designer. She didn't work for six months. When she finally got another job, she was a different person." Her green eyes glittered. "I hate people like that woman. I know what it is to be poor."

"Thanks," Carlie said. "I couldn't think of a thing to say. It is a sale dress, and my shoes are really old."

"Carlie, you look lovely," Tippy told her solemnly. "It doesn't matter how much the dress cost if it flatters you. And it does." She smiled. "I hope she tells Carson what I said to her."

"If she does, he might have something to say to you."

Tippy laughed again. "He can take it up with my husband," she replied, and raised her cup of punch to her lips.

"HOW WAS THE DANCE?" Reverend Blair asked when Carlie came in the front door.

"It was very nice," she said.

He moved closer, his eyes probing. "What happened?"

She drew in a breath. "Carson danced with me and his girlfriend got really angry. She said some really unpleasant things to me."

His pale blue eyes took on a glitter. "Perhaps I should speak to her."

She smiled. "Tippy Grier spoke to her."

"Say no more. I've heard about Mrs. Grier's temper."

"She was eloquent," Carlie said. She shook her head. "And she never said a single bad word the whole time."

"Good for her. You don't have to use bad words to express yourself. Well, unless you're trying to start a lawnmower," he amended.

She pursed her lips. "Daddy, you think 'horsefeathers' is a bad word."

He frowned. "It is!"

She laughed. "Well, I did enjoy the dancing. Rourke is really light on his feet."

"Yes." He gave her a concerned look.

She waved a hand at him. "No way I'd take on that South African wildcat," she said. "I have a good head on my shoulders."

He seemed relieved.

"I'm going on up. You sleep well, Daddy."

"You, too, pumpkin," he replied with a smile.

SHE WAS HALF-ASLEEP when her cell phone rang. She picked it up and punched the button. "Hello?" she asked drowsily.

There was a pause. "It will come when you least expect it," came an odd-sounding masculine voice. "And your father won't walk away." The connection was broken.

"Right." She turned off the phone and closed her eyes. She'd remember to tell her father in the morning, but the last threat about her father had never materialized, nor had any threat against herself. She was beginning to think that it was a campaign of terror. If so, it wasn't going to work. She refused to live her life afraid.

But she did say an extra prayer at church the next day. Just to be on the safe side.

HER FATHER WASN'T at the breakfast table Monday morning. She had a cup of coffee and two pieces of toast and paused to check the truck over before she started it. She wasn't afraid, but caution wasn't too high a price to pay for safety.

She got into the office, put her coat away and shoved her purse under the desk. She pushed her hair back. It was a damp morning, so her naturally wavy hair was curling like crazy because of the humidity.

She turned the mail out of its bag onto the desk. She'd stopped by the post office, as she did every morning on her way to work. There was a lot of it to go through before the chief came in. She made coffee and shared it with one of the patrolmen. He went out, leaving the office empty.

She sat down at her desk and picked up a letter opener. She'd just started on the first letter when the door opened and a cold wind came in.

Carson was furious. His black eyes were snapping like flames. He stopped in front of the desk.

"What the hell did you say to Lanette Saturday night?" he demanded.

She blinked. "I didn't—"

"She was so upset she couldn't even talk," he said angrily. "She cried all the way home. Then she phoned me this morning, still in tears, and said she was having to go to the doctor for anxiety meds because of the upset."

"I didn't say anything to her," she repeated.

His eyes narrowed. "Don't get ideas."

"Excuse me?"

"It was only two dances," he said in a mocking tone. "Not a

marriage proposal. I've told you before, you're not the sort of woman who appeals to me. In any way."

She stood up. "Thank God."

He just stared at her. He didn't speak.

"Your girlfriend was showing more skin than a bikini model," she pointed out. "Obviously that's the sort of woman you like, one who advertises everything she's got in the front window, right? You know why you like her? Because she's temporary. She's a throwaway. She's not the sort of woman who'd want anything to do with a permanent relationship or children..."

His face went hard. His black eyes glittered. "That's enough."

She bit her lip. "You're right, it's none of my business. But just for the record," she added angrily, "you're the sort of man I'd run from as fast as my legs would carry me. You think you're irresistible? You, with your notched bedpost and years of one-night stands? God only knows what sorts of diseases you've exposed yourself to...!"

The insult put a fire under him. He started toward her with blood in his eye, bent on intimidation. The movement was quick, threatening, dangerous. The shock of it took her stumbling backward toward the wall. On the way, she grabbed a chair and held it, trembling, legs out, toward him while she cursed herself for her stupid runaway tongue.

He stopped suddenly. He realized, belatedly, that she was afraid of him. Her face was chalk-white. The chair she'd suspended in midair was shaking, like her slender young body. She was gasping for breath. Wheezing. Coughing.

He frowned.

"Don't...!" she choked, swallowing, coughing again.

The door opened. "What in the hell...?"

"Stay with her," Carson said curtly, running past Cash. He made a dash to his car, grabbed his medical kit and burst back in the door just as Cash was taking the chair from Carlie and putting her firmly down in it.

"Grab her driver's license," he ordered Cash as he unzipped

the kit. He pulled a cell phone out of his slacks. "Who's her doctor?"

"Lou Coltrain," Cash replied.

Carlie couldn't speak. She couldn't even breathe.

She heard Carson talking to someone on the other end of the phone. She heard her boss relaying statistics. Why did they need her weight? She couldn't breathe. It felt as if the air was stuck inside her lungs and couldn't get out. She heard a weird whistling sound. Was that her?

Carson tore open packages. He swabbed the bend of her elbow and pulled up a liquid from a small bottle into a syringe. He squirted out a drop.

"This may hurt. I'm sorry." He drove the needle into her arm. His face was like stone. He was almost as pale as she was.

Her breathing began to ease, just a little. Tears sprung from her eyes and ran, hot, down her cheeks.

"Call the emergency room," Carson told Cash. "Tell them I'm bringing her in. She needs to be checked by a physician."

"All right," Cash said tightly. "Then we'll have a talk."

Carson nodded curtly. He handed Carlie her purse, picked her up in his arms and carried her out the door.

CHAPTER SIX

OUTSIDE, A PATROL car was waiting, its lights flashing like mad.

"Chief said for me to lead you to the emergency room," the patrolman called to Carson.

"Thanks," he said. He put Carlie in the passenger seat, strapped her in and threw himself behind the steering wheel.

He ran two red lights, right behind the police car. It was only a short drive to the hospital, but he wanted to get Carlie there as quickly as he could. Her color was still bad, although she was breathing a little easier.

"Damn...you," she cursed, sobbing.

"Yes," he rasped. He glanced at her as he pulled up at the emergency entrance. "God, I'm sorry!"

He got out, unfastened her seat belt and carried her right past the waiting gurney with its attendant, past the clerk, back into a waiting room, trailing irritated people.

"Dr. Coltrain is ready for her, we called ahead," he said over his shoulder.

"Is that Carlie?" the clerk exclaimed. "Is she all right?"

"Not really," Carson said in a rough tone. He carried her into a treatment room. Seconds later, a blond woman in a white lab coat came in, a stethoscope around her neck.

"Are you the one who called me from her office?" she asked,

glancing at Carson. "You said that she was upset and having trouble breathing."

"Yes," Carson said quietly. "I'd bet my left arm on asthma."

"Asthma?" Dr. Lou Coltrain frowned at him.

She turned to Carlie, who was still gasping. "Epinephrine. You said on the phone that you were giving her epinephrine."

"Yes," Carson replied tersely. He reminded her of the dosage. "I checked her weight on her driver's license first."

She nodded. "Fran, bring me an inhaler," she said to a nurse nearby. She gave the name brand and the dosage. "Hurry."

"Yes, Doctor," the woman said, and went to get it.

Lou examined Carlie, aware that she was glaring at the man who'd brought her in. He had his hands shoved deep in his pockets and he looked as if somebody had cut the life out of him. She didn't have to guess what had prompted Carlie's attack. Guilt was written all over him.

"She has no history of asthma," Lou said.

"Allergies to perfume, difficulty breathing after exertion, coughing fits," Carson said.

Lou frowned as she glanced at him. "Sporadic?"

"Very. Difficult to diagnose without proper equipment. I'd recommend an allergist."

"Yes. So would I."

She finished her examination. Fran was back with the inhaler. Lou instructed her in its use and waited until she'd taken several puffs.

"You're lucky that you had no underlying heart conditions, like a sinus node issue," Lou said as she watched Carlie suck in the meds. "Epinephrine can kill someone with a serious arrhythmia." She glanced at Carson. "You knew that."

He nodded. His face was solemn, still. He didn't add anything to the nod.

"One more puff, and then I want you to lie there and rest. I'll be back to check on you in a minute. Feeling better?" Lou asked Carlie, and smiled as she smoothed the ruffled wavy dark hair.

"Much. Thanks, Lou."

Lou turned to Carson. "Can I speak with you?"

He glanced at Carlie. She averted her eyes. He sighed and followed Lou into an empty treatment room nearby.

Lou turned, pinning him with pale eyes. "You know too much for a layman."

"Field medic in the military," he replied.

She pursed her lips. "Try again."

He drew in a breath. She was quick. Nobody else had ever questioned his skills. "I finished medical school and got my degree. I'd have gone into an internship after, but I quit."

"I thought so. Why did you quit?"

His face closed up. "Personal issues. Serious ones. I went off the deep end for a few years."

"I think you're still there," Lou replied. "Off the deep end, I mean." She jerked her head toward Carlie. "What do you know about her?"

"A hell of a lot more than I thought I did, after the past few minutes," he said flatly. "We had an argument. My fault. I'm hotheaded and I was…frustrated. I started toward her…" He held up a hand when she looked ready to explode. "I've never hit a woman in my life," he interrupted, his black eyes flashing. "My father beat my mother to death in a drunken fit. He went to prison and he was killed by one of her relatives who was serving life on a murder charge. I know more about violence than you have time to hear."

Her face relaxed, just a little. "I'm sorry."

"I would never have struck her. I just went closer." He drew in a breath and leaned back against the block wall, his arms crossed over his chest, his eyes sad. "She backed away and picked up a chair to hold me at bay. That's when I noticed that she was barely able to breathe. I frightened her. I don't know why. Unless there's some violence in her past that I'm not aware of."

"There is," Lou said quietly. "But I don't discuss patients." She smiled to soften the words.

"I understand."

"You reacted very quickly. You may have saved her life." She studied him from across the cubicle. "You also treated Sheriff Hayes Carson when you rescued him and Minette, across the border. You know, doctors are getting thin on the ground. Except for specialists, there's just me and Copper," she added, referring to her husband, also a physician, "and Micah Steele."

His face tautened. "I'm doing a job I like."

"Really?"

He averted his eyes.

"I'm no psychologist," she said after a minute, "but even I can see through the anger. You're hiding, inside yourself."

"Don't we all do that?" he asked.

"To some extent, yes." She smiled. "I'll stop. I just hate to see waste. You surely don't want to spend the rest of your life feeding people to crocodiles?" she added.

He groaned. "Does everybody know everything in this town?"

"Pretty much," she agreed. "We don't have secrets from each other. We're family," she explained. "We come from all backgrounds, all cultures, all religions. But there are so few of us in Jacobsville and Comanche Wells that we think of ourselves as just one big family."

"Not what I connected with small towns," he confessed. "And I don't share my secrets."

"You never carry ID with you," she began. "You work for Cy Parks, but Eb Scott sends you on assignments periodically. You have a very bad reputation for being a womanizer. You don't drink or smoke, you keep to yourself, and you and Rourke are friends."

"Damn," he muttered.

"See?" she added smugly. "Family."

He shouldered away from the wall. "Not for long. I'm moving on soon."

"Because of Carlie." She laughed softly.

He glared at her. "Because I don't stay in one place long. Ever."

She crossed her arms with a sigh. "You can't run away from the past," she said gently. "It's portable. No matter how far you go, it travels with you. Until you come to grips with it, face what you're running away from, you'll never be satisfied."

"Well, if it catches up with me, it had better be wearing track shoes," he replied. He stood erect. "I need to get Carlie home."

"She's more fragile than she looks," Lou said surprisingly. "Try not to hurt her too much."

He didn't say a word. He just walked by her.

CARLIE REFUSED TO be carried. She walked out the front door beside him, slowly, although her breathing was easier.

"I have to go to the pharmacy," she began.

"I'll drive you. Don't argue," he said heavily. "It's the least I can do."

She shrugged. "Okay. Thanks."

She got in and fastened her seat belt so that he wouldn't have to do it for her. She didn't want him any closer than necessary. He affected her too much, and her nerves were raw after what had happened.

HE DROVE HER to the pharmacy and went inside with her. Bonnie, at the counter, smiled at Carlie.

"How's it going?" she asked as Carlie handed her the prescription. She read it and grimaced. "Oh. I see how it's going."

"Can you fill it while I wait?" Carlie asked in a subdued tone.

"Sure. Let me see if we have this in stock." She went to talk to the pharmacist Nancy, who waved and smiled. Bonnie gave Carlie a thumbs-up and went to fill the order.

One of the other clerks, a new girl, who was returning from

lunch, stopped by Carson and smiled. "Can I help you?" she asked in a very sweet tone.

He didn't even look at her. "I'm with her." He nodded toward Carlie.

"Oh. Okay." She gave him a hopeful look. He didn't even glance her way.

She went on to the pharmacy, smiling at Carlie.

Carlie was breathing much better, but the experience had shaken her badly. She hated showing weakness in front of the enemy. Because that's what Carson was, however much she tried to convince herself otherwise.

Filling the prescription didn't take long. Bonnie motioned her to the counter and smiled as Carlie handed her a debit card.

"Directions are on the box," Bonnie said. "I hope you feel better."

"Me, too." Carlie sighed. "Asthma. Bummer. I never even guessed I had it. Dr. Lou's sending me to an allergist, too."

"It will probably be Dr. Heinrich," Bonnie said. "He comes here every Friday to see patients. He's from San Antonio. It will save you that long drive." She looked at Carlie over her glasses as she finished ringing up the purchase, returned the card and handed Carlie the medicine in its white bag. "Especially after you were doing a hundred on the straightaway in your dad's Cobra," she added with pursed lips.

Carlie flushed. "Don't you start."

"I like you," Bonnie replied. "And I hate funerals."

"Same here!" Nancy called across the counter.

"Okay. I'll drive like an old lady," she muttered.

"Mrs. Allen is an old lady, and she pushes that Jaguar of hers over a hundred and twenty when the sheriff's deputies aren't looking," Nancy reminded her.

"I'll drive like a conventional old lady," Carlie corrected.

"Senior citizen," Bonnie whispered. "It's more politically correct!"

Carlie laughed, for the first time since the ordeal began.

THEY WERE BACK in the car. Carlie glanced at Carson, who still looked like a locked and boarded-up house. "Thanks for taking me to the pharmacy," she began.

He ignored her. He wasn't driving toward her house. He went down the highway until he spotted a roadside park by the Jacobs River. He stopped at a convenience store and parked the car.

"Come on," he said gently, helping her out.

"Where are we going?" she asked.

"Lunch." He led the way inside. She picked out a packaged ham and cheese sandwich, a bag of chips, and a soft drink. He got a roast beef sandwich and a soft drink. He paid for all of it and led her behind the store to a picnic area beside the river, complete with concrete table and benches.

The sound of the river, even in winter, was soothing. It was February, and her ratty old coat felt good, but she could have taken it off. It was warmer in the sun.

They ate in silence for several minutes. She liked being outside. When she was at home, she did all the yard work, planted a garden, tended flowers, raked leaves, did all the things she could to keep her out of the house. She loved the seasons, the rain and the rare snowfall. She was an outdoor girl at heart.

When they finished eating, he took the waste paper and put it in a container. There was a recycling bin for the soft drink cans, and he put them in it.

She started toward the car, but he caught her hand gently in his and led her down to the river. He leaned against a tree, still holding her hand.

"Your Dr. Coltrain said that I'm hiding from the past. She's right." He drew in a long breath. "I was married."

Carlie caught her breath. His hand tightened around her fingers.

"She was younger than me. Pretty, bright, full of fun. She teased me and provoked me. I loved her more than my life. We grew up together on the Wapiti Ridge Sioux Reservation in South Dakota. Our people had known each other for generations. She was several grades behind me, but we were always friends. I was in my final year of…graduate school—" he didn't want to say "medical school" "—when we went to a dance together and fell in love. Her parents thought she was too young, but we wouldn't listen. We were married by the local priest."

He hesitated, then went on. "It was a long commute for me, and expensive because I had to fly there. And I had to stay in the dorm during the week. I had a scholarship, or I could never have managed it. My people were poor." He watched the river, his eyes sad and quiet. "She got tired of staying in the little house all alone. She liked to party. She thought I was a real stick-in-the-mud because I didn't drink or smoke." He laughed hollowly. "I guess she understood the drinking part because my father was a drunkard. Everybody on the rez knew about him."

She swallowed. "They say that alcoholism is a problem in some Native American cultures…"

"My father was white," he said, and his voice was cold as ice. "He sold seed and fertilizer for a living. He met my mother at a feed store when he was restocking there. He flattered her, took her places, bought her flowers. She was crazy about him. They got married and he moved onto the rez to live with her. She didn't know he was an alcoholic until she was pregnant with me. He started beating her then, when he lost his temper." His eyes closed. "When I was six, and he was beating my mother, I tried to block him with a kitchen chair. He picked it up and laid it across my head. When I came to, she was lying on the floor, still and quiet, and he was gone. I ran for help. It was too late."

She held her breath, listening. He'd told her some of this before, but not in such detail. She could only imagine the terror he'd felt.

"He went to prison and I went to live with my mother's uncles, aunts and cousins in a small community on the rez. One of my uncles was a reservation cop. He formally adopted me in a tribal ceremony, so I call him Dad, even though he isn't really. He's great with livestock. He and my other relatives were good to me, but they were poor and we didn't have much. I wanted more. I knew the only way to get out was to get an education. So I studied like crazy. I worked at anything I could get paid for, on ranches, in stores, on the land, and I saved every penny. When I graduated from high school, I was second in my class. I got scholarships and commuted back and forth. I graduated with honors and went on to grad school. But then, suddenly, there was Jessie. I couldn't really afford to get married, but I was conventional in those days. My people were religious." He let go of Carlie's hand and folded his arms across his broad chest. His eyes had a lost, faraway look. "Things were good the first two years. But we were drifting apart. I still had a long way to go to a profession and I was away a good deal of the time. There was a man on the rez who wanted her. He bought her stuff, took her to dances, while I was at school or working after classes to help pay for the tuition. I came home one weekend, just after finals, and she was gone. She'd moved in with him."

He drew in a breath. "I tried to get her to come home, but she said she loved him and she was carrying his child. She wasn't coming back. I was sick at heart, but I couldn't force her to leave him. I went back to school and gave up the house. No reason to keep renting it just for weekends, anyway.

"I was getting ready for the graduation exercises when one of my cousins came to see me at school. Another relative back home told him that she'd lied. The child she was carrying was mine. The man she was living with couldn't have children. And worse, he was beating her. She'd just come back from the hospital. He'd beaten her so badly that she had a concussion."

His face hardened. "So I went home. I had a beat-up old car parked in Rapid City that would hardly make the trips back and forth from my house to the airport, and there were heavy floods, but I made it home. I went to see her. I told her that I knew about the child and that if she wouldn't come back to me, I'd have her boyfriend put in jail for beating her. She looked ancient," he said, his face twisting. "What she'd endured was written all over her. But she loved him, she told me. She was very sorry, but she loved him. I could see the child when it came, but she wasn't leaving him, even if I refused to give her a divorce."

He swallowed. "He drove up. We exchanged words. He said no way was she leaving him. He grabbed her by the hand and dragged her out to his car. I tried to stop him, but he was a big guy and I had no combat skills at the time. He wiped the floor with me. He threw her into his car and took off. I picked myself up, got in my own car and chased after him."

He shook his head. "I don't know what I thought I could do. She wanted to stay with him and he wasn't going to give her up. But I knew if she stayed he'd kill her one day, just as my father had killed my mother. And my child would die with her.

"He speeded up and so did I. His car was all over the road." His eyes closed. "If I'd had any sense, I'd have stopped, right then, but I didn't. He went onto a bridge that was unsafe. There was even a sign, but he didn't pay it any attention." He looked away, hesitated. "The bridge collapsed. They fell down in the car, into the river below. It was deep and in full flood." His eyes closed. He shuddered. "They found the bodies almost two days later. If they'd been found sooner, the child might have lived." He bit his lower lip. "It was a boy…"

"I'm so sorry," she whispered. Her eyes were wet. "So sorry."

He turned, pulled her to him and held her. Just held her. Rocked her. "I've never spoken of it, except once. Dalton Kirk's wife, in Wyoming, sat at a table with me and told me all about it, and she'd never met me or heard anything about me. It was a shock."

"I heard about her." She savored the feel of his jacket. It was leather, but soft and warm from his body, fringed and beaded. She'd never seen anything so beautiful. She closed her eyes. He'd frightened her earlier. Now she began to understand him, just a little.

He smoothed over her dark, wavy hair. "I would never have

hit you," he whispered at her ear. "I know too much about brutality and its result."

"You move so quickly," she faltered.

"And for all the wrong reasons sometimes." He sighed. "Dalton Kirk's wife told me that my wife's boyfriend was drinking at the time. I didn't really notice, but if you drink something like vodka, others may not be able to smell it on your breath. She said that was why he went off the bridge, not because of me. I checked the police report. She was right. But it didn't help much. Nothing does. I still feel like a murderer."

"It isn't fair, to blame yourself for something like that." She drew back and looked up at him. "You aren't a person of faith."

"No," he said stiffly. "I don't believe in anything anymore."

"I believe that things happen the way they're meant to," she said softly. "That sometimes God uses people to say things or do things that hurt us, so that we learn lessons from it. My dad says that we should always remember that events in our lives have a purpose. It's all lessons. We learn from adversity."

He searched her green eyes quietly. "You're such an innocent, Carlie," he said gently, and her heart leaped because it was the first time he'd ever called her by name. "You know nothing about the world, about life."

"And you know everything," she murmured with a flash of laughter.

"I do." He traced a line down her cheek. "We're total opposites."

"What happened," she asked. "After?"

He looked over her head. "I went to my own graduation, alone, and enlisted in the military the same week. I learned how to fight, how to kill. I took the most dangerous assignments I could find. For a long time, I avoided women like the plague. Then it became second nature to take what was offered and walk away." That wasn't quite true, but he'd shared enough secrets for one day. "I never got serious about anyone again. I met Cy Parks overseas. He and his group were doing a stint as private contractors for the military, teaching tactics to locals. I fell in with them and came back here to work for Cy and, occasionally, for Eb Scott. It's an interesting life. Dangerous. Unpredictable."

"Sort of like you," Carlie mused.

He looked down into her eyes. "Sort of like me," he agreed.

She drew in a breath. It was much easier to do that now.

"I am truly sorry for what happened this morning," he said, searching her eyes. "I had no right to frighten you."

"You're scary when you lose your temper," she replied.

"Sheltered little violet, under a stair," he said softly.

"Not so much," she replied. "It just seems that way." Her own eyes were sad and quiet.

"You know my secrets. Tell me yours."

She swallowed. "When I was thirteen, my mother was diagnosed with cancer. She was in and out of hospitals for a year. During one of those times, her mother showed up." Her face hardened. "My grandmother was a pig, and that's putting it mildly. She had a reputation locally for sleeping with anything in pants. She had a boyfriend with her, a man who used drugs and supplied them to her. I had the misfortune to come home while they were ransacking my mother's bedroom, looking for things they could sell. I'd hidden Mama's expensive pearls that Daddy brought her from Japan, just in case, but they were trashing the house. I tried to stop them."

She shivered.

He pulled her closer. "Keep talking," he said over her head.

Her small hand clenched on his jacket. "Her boyfriend picked up a beer bottle and started hitting me with it." She shivered again. "He kept on and on and on until I was on the floor. I fought until I was so numb that I just gave up." She laughed. "You think you can fight back, that you can save yourself in a desperate situation. But that's not how it works. You feel such… despair, such hopelessness. After a while, it seems more sensible to just lie down and die…"

"Go on."

"Our next-door neighbor heard me scream and called the police. They got there just in time to keep him from killing me. As it was, I had a concussion and broken ribs. I spent several days in the hospital. They took my grandmother and her boyfriend to jail. She testified against him and got off, but our police chief—one of the ones before Cash Grier—had a nice talk with her and she left town very quickly. She didn't even apologize or come to see me. I heard later that she died from a drug overdose. He was killed in a prison riot just recently." She shook her head. "I've been terrified of violent behavior ever since."

"I can see why."

"One of our patrolmen brought a man in handcuffs in the office once to ask the chief a question. The man grabbed a nightstick off the counter and came at me with it. I fainted." She sighed. "The chief turned that man upside down, they said, and shook him like a rat until he dropped the nightstick. Then he threw him into the patrol car and told the officer to get him to the county detention center right then. He took me to the emergency room himself. I had to tell him why I fainted." She shrugged. "He isn't what he seems, is he?" she asked, looking up. "I mean, criminals are terrified of him. Even some local men say he's dangerous. But he was like a big brother with me. He still is."

"I respect him more than any other man I know, with the possible exception of Cy Parks."

"Mr. Parks is pretty scary, too," she added.

He smiled. "Not when you get to know him. He's had a hard life. Really hard."

"I know a little about him. It's a sad story. But he and his wife seem to be very happy."

"They are."

She searched his serious eyes. "I didn't say anything to your…date," she said quietly. "She was making fun of my dress and my old shoes." She lowered her eyes. "I didn't have a comeback. It was a bargain dress, and my shoes are really old. I didn't wear a coat because this is the only one I have—" she fingered the frayed collar "—and I didn't want to embarrass Robin by showing up in it."

He was very still. "She said that you insulted her."

"Tippy Grier did," she replied. She tried not to smile at the memory. "She was eloquent. She said that my dress looked nice on me and it didn't matter where it came from."

He let out a long breath. "Damn."

"It's all right. You didn't know."

His hand smoothed over her dark hair as he stared down at the river below. For a minute, there was only the sound of the water running heavily over the rocks. "She didn't mention Tippy."

"I just stood there," she said. "I guess she was mad that I danced with you."

His hand caught her hair at her nape and turned her face up to his. Black eyes captured hers and held them. "She was mad that I wanted you," he said curtly.

"Wa…wanted me?" She hesitated.

He let out a rough breath. "God in heaven, can't you even tell when a man wants you?" he burst out.

"Well, I don't know a lot about men," she stammered.

His hand slid down her back and plastered her hips to his. His smile was smug and worldly as he let her feel the sudden hardness of his body. "Now you do."

She flushed and pulled away from him. "Stop that."

He actually laughed. "My God," he said heavily. "I'm dying and you're running for cover." He shook his head. "Just my luck."

She swallowed. It was embarrassing. She tried to draw away completely but he held her, gently but firmly.

"Doesn't your friend Robin ever touch you?" he asked sarcastically. "Or are you having a cerebral relationship with him?"

She wasn't about to admit the truth to him. Robin felt like protection right now, and she needed some.

"He reads poetry to me," she choked. Actually, he wrote poetry about Lucy and read it to Carlie, but that was beside the point.

"Does he now?" He brushed his nose against hers and began to quote. "When I am dead, and above me bright April shakes out her rain-drenched hair, though you should lean above me broken-hearted, I shall not care. I shall have peace, as leafy trees are peaceful when rain bends down the bough; and I shall be more silent and cold-hearted than you are now," he whispered deeply, reciting lines from a poem called "I Shall Not Care," by Sara Teasdale. "It was written in 1919," he added. "Long before either of us was born."

Her heart jumped, stopped and ran away. His voice was like velvet, deep and sexy and overwhelmingly sensual. Her nails curled against the soft leather of his jacket.

"Yes, I read poetry," he whispered, his mouth hovering just above hers. "That was one of my favorites. I learned it by heart just before Jessie died."

Her mouth felt swollen. Her whole body felt swollen. "D... did you?" she asked in a voice that wasn't quite steady.

His lips brushed like a whisper over hers. "Are you sure you don't know what desire is, Carlie?" he whispered huskily.

She was almost moaning. His mouth teased hers, without coming to rest on it. His body was close, warm, powerful. She felt the heat of it all the way down. She couldn't get her breath, and this time it wasn't because of the asthma. She knew he could feel her heartbeat. She could hear it.

"Your father is going to kill me," he said roughly.

"For...what?"

"For this." And his mouth went down against hers, hard enough to bruise, hard enough to possess.

CHAPTER SEVEN

CARLIE WAS DYING. Her whole body was pressing toward Carson's, pleading for something she didn't quite understand. She shivered as his mouth pressed harder against hers, insistent, parting her lips so that he could possess them.

Her arms reached up, around his neck. He lifted her, riveted her body to his, as the kiss went on and on and on. She moaned under his mouth, shivering, wanting something more, something to end the torment, to ease the tension that seemed bent on pulling her young body apart.

"Carlie," he whispered roughly as his fingers tightened in her hair and he paused to catch his breath. "This is not going to end well," he rasped.

She looked up at him, breathless, wordless, shivering with needs she hadn't even known she could feel.

"Oh, what the hell," he muttered. "I'm damned already!"

He kissed her as if he'd never felt a woman's mouth under his own, as if he'd never felt desire, never known hunger. He kissed her with utter desperation. She was an innocent. He couldn't have her. He wasn't going to marry her, and he couldn't seduce her. It was one hell of a dead end. But he couldn't stop kissing her.

Her mouth was soft and warm and sweetly innocent, accept-

ing his, submitting, but not really responding. It occurred to
him somewhere in the middle of it that she didn't even know
how to kiss.

He lifted his mouth and searched her wide, soft, dreamy eyes.
"You don't even know how," he whispered huskily.

Her lips were as swollen as her body. "Know how to what?"
she began dazedly.

The sound of a car horn intruded just as he started to bend
his head to her again. She jumped. He caught his breath and
moved back from her just as Cash Grier got out of his patrol car
and started down to the river where they were standing, now
apart from each other.

"Dum dum de dum dum de dum da da de dum." Carson
hummed Gounod's "Funeral March of a Marionette" as Cash
approached. He smiled wryly, through the piercing agony of
his unsatisfied need.

Carlie chuckled.

"Your father was concerned," Cash told Carlie. "He asked
me to look for you."

"I'm okay," Carlie said, trying to disguise the signs that she'd
been violently kissed. She pushed back her disheveled hair. "He
bought me lunch." She nodded at Carson.

"Did you have it tested for various poisons first?" Cash asked
blandly.

She laughed again.

"I was apologizing," Carson said heavily. "I jumped on her
for something she didn't even do."

"Which was?" Cash asked, and he wasn't smiling.

"Lanette said that Carlie insulted her and made her cry," he
returned.

"That wasn't Carlie. That was my wife." Cash smiled coldly.
"I understand that she was eloquent."

"Quite," Carlie confirmed.

"Your friend has a rap sheet," he told Carson. He smiled
again. This time it was even colder.

Carson scowled. "A rap sheet?"

"It appears that she wasn't always a stewardess. In fact, I don't know how she got to be accepted in that type of job. Probably her lawyer helped her out more than once," he said.

"What was she arrested for?" Carson asked.

"Assault with a deadly weapon. A smart lawyer got her off by pleading temporary insanity, acting in a fit of jealousy." He pursed his lips, enjoying Carson's discomfiture. "She went after another woman with a knife. Accused her of trying to steal her boyfriend."

Carson didn't show it, but he felt uneasy. Lanette had made some threats about Carlie, and he hadn't taken them seriously.

Carlie's face fell at the realization that the blonde might be more dangerous than she'd realized already.

"I'd watch my back if I were you," Carson told Carlie somberly. "The rest of us will help. It seems you've got more trouble than we realized."

"There was another phone call the other night, too," she said, suddenly recalling the cryptic message. "It was a male voice. He said to tell Dad he was coming soon. It didn't make sense."

"A male voice?" Cash asked at once.

"Yes." She frowned. "Odd-sounding voice. If I ever heard it again, I think I'd remember it. Why is somebody after Dad?"

"I don't know," Cash said tersely.

"Rourke and I are trying to dig that out," Carson said abruptly. "We have contacts in, shall we say, unusual places."

"So do I," Cash reminded him. "But mine were a dead end."

"One of my cousins is a U.S. senator," Carson said, surprisingly. "He's using some of his own sources for me."

"A senator." Cash grinned. "Not bad."

"Well, not quite in the same class with having a vice president or a state attorney general for a relative," Carson retorted, smiling back.

Cash shrugged. "We all have our little secrets." He glanced

at Carlie, who'd reddened when he said "secrets." His eyes narrowed. "You told him?"

She nodded.

He looked at Carson and the smile was gone. "I'll tell you once. Don't ever do that again."

"I can promise you that I never will."

Cash jerked his head in a nod.

Carson glanced at Carlie. "I tried to take him once, in a fight." He grimaced. "It wasn't pretty."

"I was a master trainer in Tae Kwon Do," Cash explained. "Black belt."

Carson rubbed one arm. "Very black."

Cash laughed.

"I was going to take her home, but we hadn't had lunch," Carson explained.

"Or dessert," Carlie mused.

Carson glanced at her with warm, hungry eyes. "Oh, yes, we had dessert."

She blushed further, and he laughed.

"Come on," Cash told them. "It isn't wise to be out in the woods alone with crazy people on the loose."

"Did somebody escape from jail?"

"Nothing like that," Cash said. "I was remembering Carlie's phone call and your girlfriend's rap sheet."

"Oh." Carson didn't say another word. He helped Carlie into the passenger seat of his car and made sure her seat belt was fastened before he closed the door.

Cash drew him over to the patrol car, and he was somber. "You need to do something about that temper."

"I had anger management classes," Carson said quietly. "They helped, for a while." He shook his head. "It's the past. I can't deal with it. I can't live with what I did. I'm at war with myself and the world."

Cash put a heavy hand on the younger man's shoulder. He knew about Carson's past. The two were close. "I'll tell you again that it was her time. Nothing could have stopped it. Somewhere inside, you know that. You just won't accept it. Until you do, you're a walking time bomb."

"I would never hurt her," he assured Cash, nodding toward the car. "I've never hit a woman."

"The threat of force is as bad as the actual thing," Cash replied. "She hasn't gotten over what happened to her, either. We carry the past around like extra luggage, and it gets heavy from time to time."

"You'd know," Carson said gently.

Cash nodded. "I've killed men. I have to live with it. It's not easy, even now."

"For me, either." He shoved his hands into his pockets. "I didn't realize Lanette had started the trouble. She was so upset that it really got to me. She's just someone to take around. Something pretty to show off." He shrugged. "Maybe a little more than that. But nothing permanent."

"Your past in that respect isn't going to win you points with certain people around here," Cash said.

"I'm just beginning to realize that. When I was in Wyoming, Dalton Kirk's wife told me that my past was going to have a terrible impact on my future, that it was going to stand between me and something I want desperately."

"It wouldn't matter so much if you didn't flaunt it, son," Cash replied.

Carson drew in a breath. "I don't know why I taunt her," he said, and they both knew he meant Carlie. "She's a kind, generous woman. Innocent and sweet."

"Something to keep in mind," Cash added. "You'd walk away and forget about it. She'd throw herself off a cliff. You know what I'm talking about."

Carson seemed to pale. "Nothing so drastic…"

"You don't know anything about people of faith, do you?" he asked. "I didn't, until I came here and had to face living my life with what I'd done hanging over me like a cloud. I came to faith kicking and screaming, but it gave me the first peace I've ever known. Until that happened, I didn't understand the mindset of people like Carlie." His face tautened. "I'm not joking. Her faith teaches her that people get married, then they become intimate, then children come along. It doesn't matter if you agree, if you disagree, if you think she's living in prehistoric times. That's how she thinks."

"It's radical," Carson began. "She's totally out of step with the times. Everybody does it—"

"She doesn't," Cash interrupted. "And everybody around here knows it. It's why she doesn't date. Her grandmother was the town joke. She had sex with a department store manager in a closet and they got caught. He was married with three kids. She thought it was hilarious when his wife left him. In fact, that's why she did it. She was angry at the woman for making a remark about her morals."

"Good grief," Carson exclaimed.

"She was caught with men in back rooms, in parked cars, even once in a long-haul truck in the front seat at a truck stop with people walking by." He shook his head. "It was before I came here, but I heard about it. Carlie's mother was a saint, an absolutely good woman, who had to live with her mother's reputation. Carlie's had to live it down, as well. It's why she won't play around."

"I didn't realize that people knew about it."

"We know everything," Cash said simply. "If you don't care about gossip, it doesn't affect you. But Carlie's always going to care. And if something happens to her, it will show like a neon sign. Everybody will know. She won't be able to hide it or live with it in a small community like this."

"I get your point." He grimaced. "Life is never easy. I don't want to make it even harder for her," he added, glancing toward Carlie, who was watching them curiously.

"No." Cash studied the younger man. "The world is full of women like your pretty blonde, and they work for scale. Don't try to class Carlie with them." He smiled coldly. "Or you'll have more trouble than you can handle. You do not want to make an enemy of Reverend Blair."

"I do have some idea about her father's past," Carson confessed.

"No, you don't," Cash replied. "Just take my word that you don't ever want to see him lose his temper. And you work on controlling yours."

"I'm reformed." Carson took his hands out of his pockets. "I suppose we all have memories that torment us."

"Count on it. Just try not to make more bad ones for Carlie."

"I'll drive her home." He hesitated. "Is her father there?"

Cash nodded.

Carson sighed. "There are a few unmarked places on me," he commented wryly. "I guess I can handle some more. Time to face the music."

Cash laughed. "Well, you've got guts, I'll give you that."

"Not going to arrest me?" he added.

"Not this time," Cash said.

"Just as well. You can't prove I'm me."

"Why in the hell don't you carry identification?" Cash asked. "Don't you realize that if you were ever injured, nobody would know anything about you, right down to your weight or your medical history?"

Carson smiled wryly. "When I was doing wet work overseas, it would have been fatal to carry any. I just got into the habit of leaving it behind."

"I know, but you're not in the same line of work now," Cash said.

"Certain of that, are you?" he asked with a vague smile.

"Yes."

Carson made a face. "All right," he said after a minute. "I'll think about it."

"Good man."

Carson went around the car and got in under the steering wheel. Cash drove off as Carson was starting up the car.

"Look in the glove compartment and hand me my wallet, will you?" he asked Carlie.

She rummaged around through the papers and produced it. "Do you have a last name?" she wondered aloud.

"Look at the license."

Curious, she opened the wallet. His driver's license read "Carson Allen Farwalker."

She handed it to him. He shoved it into his jacket while they were at a stoplight.

"No comment?" he asked.

"I'd be embarrassed," she replied softly.

He laughed. "On the morning I was born, a man came into our small rural community, walking. It was driving snow, almost a blizzard. He said he'd come from Rapid City, all the way on foot in his mukluks and heavy coat, hitching rides, to see a sick friend who lived near us. It was a far walk. So my mother named me Far Walker." He glanced at her. "Our names don't translate well into English sometimes, but this one did." His face tautened. "I refused to take my father's name, even as a child. So I was known on the rez as Far Walker. When I got my first driver's license, that's what I put on it, Anglicized into one word. It's my legal name now."

"It suits you," she said. "You walk like an outdoorsman."

He smiled.

"I read about how native people get their names. We tend to distort them. Like Crazy Horse. That wasn't his Lakota name, but it was what he was called by Wasichu—by white people," she said, and then flushed. She hadn't meant to give away her interest in his culture.

"Well," he said and chuckled. "Hannibal and Crazy Horse. You have wide interests. Do you know his Lakota name?" he added.

"Yes. It was Tashunka Witko." She laughed. "Although I've seen that spelled about four different ways."

"And do you know what it really means, in my tongue?" he asked.

She grinned. "'His horse is crazy,'" she replied. "I read somewhere that the day he was born, a man on a restless horse rode by and his people named him Crazy Horse."

"Close enough." He smiled gently as he met her eyes. "You're an eternal student, aren't you?"

"Oh, yes. I might have gone to college, but I didn't make high grades and we were always poor. I take free classes on the internet, though, sometimes. When I'm not grinding Horde into the ground," she added without looking at him.

"Runed that sword, did you? We'll find out how well it works on the next battleground we fight."

"I can't wait," she said smugly. "I've been practicing." She glanced at him. "What's a mukluk?"

"Heavy boots that come up to the knee, made of fur. I have some at home. I bought them in Alaska. They're made with beaver fur, with wolf fur trim and beadwork."

"Your jacket is beautiful," she remarked, glancing at it. "I've never even seen one that looks like that before."

"You never will. A cousin made it for me." He smiled. "He makes these from scratch, right down to the elk he hunts for them. He eats the meat and cures the hides. Not the wolves, however. It's illegal to kill them in the States, so he buys the fur from traders in Canada."

"I saw this movie with Steven Seagal, about Alaska. He was on a talk show wearing a jacket a lot like yours. He said the native people he worked with on the movie made it for him."

"Not a bad martial artist. I like Chuck Norris best, however, for that spinning heel kick. The chief does one just like it. Ask him sometime how he learned it," he teased.

"I already know," she laughed. "He says it's his claim to fame locally."

"Feeling better?"

She nodded. "I never dreamed it was asthma," she said heavily. She frowned and glanced at him. "But you knew right away," she said. "You even knew what to give me…"

"I was a field medic in the army," he said easily. "Emergencies were my specialty."

"You must have been very good at it," she said.

"I did what the job called for."

He pulled up in front of her house. Reverend Blair was waiting on the porch, wearing a leather bomber jacket and a black scowl.

He came down the steps and opened Carlie's door. He hugged her close. "You okay?" he asked tersely.

"I'm fine. Honest. I just overreacted."

He didn't reply. He was glaring at Carson, who came around the car to join them.

"It was my fault," Carson said bluntly. "I accused her of something she didn't do and I was overly aggressive."

The reverend seemed to relax, just a little. "You take it on the chin, don't you?" he asked half-admiringly.

"Always." He sighed. "If you want to hit me, I'll just stand here. I deserve it."

The reverend cocked his head. His blue eyes were glittery and dangerous, hinting at the man he might once have been.

"He treated me in the office, took me to the emergency room, then the pharmacy and bought me lunch after," Carlie said.

The reverend lifted an eyebrow and glanced at Carson. "Treated her?"

"I was a field medic in the army," Carson replied. "I recognized the symptoms. But if you're thinking I acted without a doctor's orders, you're wrong. I had her doctor on the phone before I opened my medical kit."

The reverend relaxed even more. "Okay."

"I was more aggressive than I meant to be, but I would never have raised a hand to her," he added. "Violence is very rarely the answer to any problem."

"Rarely?"

Carson shrugged. "Well, there was this guy over in South America, in Carrera. Rourke and I sort of fed him to a crocodile."

The reverend glowered at him. "You're not helping your case."

"The guy cut up a young woman with his knife and left her scarred for life," Carson added. His black eyes glittered. "He bragged about it."

"I see."

"It was an act of mercy, anyway," Carson added doggedly. "The crocodile was plainly starving."

Reverend Blair couldn't suppress a laugh, although he tried. "I begin to see why you get along so well with Grier."

"Why, does he feed people to reptiles, too?"

"He's done things most men never dream of," the reverend said solemnly. "Lived when he should have died. He took lives, but he saved them, as well. A hard man with a hard past." The man's pale blue eyes pinned Carson's. "Like you."

Carson scowled. "How do you know anything about me?"

"You might be surprised," was the bland reply. He shook a finger at Carson. "You stop upsetting my daughter."

"Yes, sir," he said on a sigh.

"I'd invite you to supper but she might have some poisonous mushrooms concealed in the cupboard."

"I won't poison him," Carlie promised. She smiled. "You can come to supper if you like. I'll make beef Stroganoff."

Carson looked torn, as if he really wanted to do it. "Sorry," he said. "I promised to take Lanette out to eat. I need to talk to her."

"That's okay," Carlie said, hiding the pain it caused her to hear that. "Rain check."

"Count on it," he said softly, and his eyes said more than his lips did. "You okay?"

She nodded. "I'll be fine."

"I'm really sorry," he said again.

"Stop apologizing, will you? You'll hurt your image," she said, grinning.

"I'll see you."

She nodded. He nodded to the reverend, got in the car and left.

"I HAVE TO see an allergist," Carlie said miserably. "Asthma, can you believe it? I couldn't get my breath, I felt like I was suffocating. Carson knew what it was, and what to do for it. He was amazing."

"He needs to work on his self-control," her father said tersely, sipping coffee while she dished up pound cake for dessert.

For just an instant she thought of Carson out of control at the river, hungry for her, and she flushed. Then she realized that he was talking about another sort of self-control.

The reverend wasn't slow. He had a good idea why she was blushing.

"Carlie," he said gently, "he goes through women like hungry people go through food."

"I know that, Dad."

"He isn't a person of faith. He works in a profession that thrives on the lack of it, in fact, and he's in almost constant danger." He hesitated. "What I'm trying to say is that he isn't going to settle down in a small town and become a family man."

"I know that, too," she replied. She put his cake down in front of him on the table and refilled his coffee cup.

"Knowing and walking away are two different things," he said curtly. "Your mother was like you, sweet and innocent, out of touch with the real world. I hurt her very badly because we married for the wrong reasons. I wasn't ready. Before I knew it, I was a father." He looked down at the uneaten cake. "I felt trapped, hog-tied, and I resented it. I made her pay for it." His lips made a grim line. "I stayed away, out of that resentment. She didn't deserve the life I gave her."

She was shocked to hear him say such things. She knew that they'd had to get married. She'd heard him say it. But even so, she'd thought her parents married for love, that her father was away because he was making a living for them.

He didn't seem to notice Carlie's surprise. He wasn't looking at her. "I didn't know she was sick. One of my friends had a cousin here, who told him, and he told me that she was in the hospital. I got back just after her mother and her drug-crazed boyfriend did a number on you." His teeth ground together. "That was when I realized what a mess I'd made of all our lives. I walked away from the old life that same day and never looked back. I only wish I'd been where I was supposed to be so that you'd have been spared what happened to you."

"You're the one who's always saying that things happen to test us," she reminded him.

"I guess I am. But for someone who'd never hurt anybody in her life, you paid a high price," he added.

"Mama said that if she'd been a different sort of person, you would have been happy with her," she recalled. "She said her way of thinking ruined your life." She frowned. "I didn't understand what that meant at the time. But I think I'm beginning to." She did, because Carson was the same sort of person her father must have been.

"No. I ruined hers," he said. "I knew I couldn't settle down. I let my heart rule my head." He smiled sadly. "You see, pumpkin, despite how it must sound, I really loved your mother. Loved her desperately. But I loved my way of life, too, loved being on my own, working in a profession that gave me so much freedom. I was greedy and tried to have it all. In the process, I lost your mother. I will never get over what happened to her because of me. If I'd been here, taking care of her…"

"She would still have died," Carlie finished for him. "It was an aggressive cancer. They tried chemo and radiation, but it only made her sicker. Nothing you could have done would have stopped that, or changed a thing."

He studied her soft eyes. "You always make excuses for me." He shook his head. "Now you're making them for the wild man from South Dakota."

"He's wild for a reason," she said quietly.

"And you're not sharing it, right?"

"I'm not," she agreed. "It's his business."

"Nice to know you can keep a secret."

"For all the good it does me. You won't share any of yours," she pointed out.

"Why give you nightmares over a past I can't change?" he asked philosophically. He glanced at his watch and grimaced. "I'm late for a prayer meeting. You'll be okay here, right? Got the inhaler Lou prescribed?"

She pulled it out of her pocket and showed it to him.

"Okay." He shook his head. "I should have recognized the symptoms. My father had it."

"Your father? I never met him."

"He was dead by the time I married your mother," he said. He smiled. "You'd have liked him. He was a career officer in the navy, a chief petty officer."

"Wow."

"I've got photographs of him somewhere. I'll have to look them up."

"What was your mother like?"

"Fire," he chuckled. "She left trails of fire behind her when she lost her temper. She had red hair and an attitude. Tippy Grier reminds me of her, except that my mother wasn't really beautiful. She was a clerk in a hotel until she retired. She died of a stroke." He shook his head. "Dad was never the same after. He only outlived her by about two years."

"I'm sorry."

"Me, too."

"Mama said my grandfather was a kind man. He died when

she was very small. He worked for the sheriff's department. His wife was my crazy grandmother who couldn't control herself."

"I remember Mary speaking of him." He cocked his head. "Your family goes back generations in this community. I envy you that continuity. My folks moved a lot, since Dad was in the service. I've lived everywhere."

"And I've never been anywhere," she mused. "Except to San Antonio."

"Next time you go there, I'm driving," he said flatly.

She made a face at him.

"I'll be home soon."

"Please be careful. Check your car before you start it."

"Cash and Carson told me about the phone call," he replied. "Apparently I'm the target."

"I don't know why," she said. "I was the one who could identify the man who was killed in Wyoming. You never saw him."

"Pumpkin, you're not the only one with enemies," he said softly.

"Would this be connected with that past you won't tell me about?"

"Dead right." He bent and kissed her forehead. "Keep the door locked."

"I will. Drive safely."

He chuckled as he went out the door.

Carlie cleaned up the kitchen, played her video game with Robin for an hour and went to bed. Her dreams were vivid and vaguely embarrassing. And of Carson.

CHAPTER EIGHT

ROURKE WAS SITTING with a worried politician in one of the best restaurants in San Antonio. Unknown to the man, Rourke was working with the feds. Rourke had managed to wiggle himself into the man's employ.

This particular politician, Matthew Helm, had been named the acting U.S. senator, and was hoping to be elected to a full term at the special election in a few months. Rourke was equally determined to find a way to connect him with the murder of a local assistant district attorney. All the evidence had been destroyed. But there were other ways to prove collusion.

Rourke had been in touch with Lieutenant Rick Marquez of the San Antonio Police Department and was keeping him informed through Cash Grier. This politician had also been responsible for the attempt on Dalton Kirk's life, and the one on Carlie Blair's father—or Carlie herself—the intended victim had never been determined—in Jacobsville.

His murdering henchman, Richard Martin, had been killed in Wyoming, but the man's evil deeds persisted. Word was that before he'd died, he'd hired someone to kill Carlie. Nobody knew who had the contract.

Rourke was hoping against hope that this man might provide answers to many questions. But Helm was secretive. So far he hadn't said one incriminating word. Rourke would have known. He was wearing a wire, courtesy of Rick Marquez.

"There are too many loose ends," Matthew Helm said after a minute. He glanced at his other enforcer, Fred Baldwin, and glared at him. "You take care of that problem up in Wyoming?"

"Oh, yes, sir," the big, brawny man assured him. "You can stop worrying."

"I always worry." Helm then glared at Rourke. "What have you found out about my competition for the job?"

"Both men are clean as a whistle," Rourke replied easily. "No past issues we can use against them."

Helm smiled secretly. "So far," he murmured.

"You thinking of planting some?" Rourke asked conversationally.

Helm just stared at him. "What the hell does that mean?"

"Just a comment."

"Well, keep your comments to yourself," Helm said angrily. "I don't fix elections, in case you wondered."

"Sorry. I'm new here," Rourke apologized.

"Too new," Helm said suspiciously. "I can't dig out any information on you. Any at all."

"I'm from South Africa, what do you expect?" he added.

"Well, that last name you gave, Stanton," Helm began, "is a dead end."

"I like to keep my past in the past," Rourke returned. "I'm a wanted man in some places."

"Is that it?" Helm studied him for a long moment. "Then maybe you're not as suspicious as you seem, huh?" He snickered. "Just don't expect instant trust. I don't trust anybody."

"That's a good way to be," Rourke agreed.

Helm drew in a long breath. "Well, we need to get back to the office and work up some more ads and a few handouts for the campaign office. Not much time to bring this all together."

"Okay, Boss," Rourke said. "I'll see you there." He got up, nodded to both men, paid for his coffee and pie, and left.

Helm studied his other enforcer. "I don't trust him," he told the man. "You keep a close eye on him, hire extra men if you have to. See where he goes, who he associates with. I don't want any complications."

"Yes, Boss."

"And start checking out our sources. We'll need some more drugs planted. I can't afford competition for the job," he added. His face firmed. "You don't share that information with Rourke, got it? You don't tell him anything unless you clear it with me."

"I got it, Boss."

"You destroyed the watch, right?"

The other man nodded vigorously. "Oh, yeah, Boss, I smashed it into bits and tossed it into a trash bin."

"Good. Good."

The other man was hoping his uneasiness didn't show. He couldn't destroy the watch, he just couldn't. It was the most beautiful timepiece he'd ever seen, and it played that song he liked.

Fred Baldwin had envied Richard Martin, wearing that watch that cost as much as a sports car. He'd tried to borrow it once, but Martin had looked at him like he was a worm.

Well, Martin was dead now, and Baldwin had the watch. It was warm against his fingers, warm in his pocket where he kept it. He'd set the alarm so it wouldn't go off accidentally. Nobody was crazy enough to throw away a watch that cost so much money! Who knew, one day he might be desperate enough to pawn it. A man had to live, after all, and what Mr. Helm paid him was barely enough to afford his keep. His criminal record made him vulnerable. He couldn't get another job and Mr. Helm warned him that if he even tried to leave, he'd make sure Fred never worked again. It wasn't a threat. It was a promise. Fred knew better than to try to quit, although he hated the job.

Of course, that watch had a history, and Fred knew it. He might be desperate enough one day to talk to somebody in law enforcement about it. The watch could tie Mr. Helm to a murder.

So, no, Fred wasn't about to throw it away. That didn't mean he didn't have to keep it hidden, of course. And he did.

ROURKE STOPPED BY Carlie's house that evening to talk to Reverend Blair. He was amused that Helm's men had tried to follow him. He'd had Carson take his car to San Antonio and park it at a bar. The trackers were sitting out in the parking lot in the freezing cold, waiting for Rourke to come out. He laughed. It was going to be a long night for them.

"Well, you look happy," Carlie remarked when she let him in.

"I've discovered that misdirection is one of my greater talents," he mused, grinning. "Got any more of that wonderful cornbread?"

She shook her head. "But I just took a nice enchilada casserole out of the oven, and I have sour cream and tortilla chips to top it with," she said.

"Be still my heart," Rourke enthused. "Listen, are you sure you wouldn't like to marry me tomorrow?"

"Sorry," she said, "I'm having my truck waxed."

"Ah, well," he sighed in mock sorrow.

"Stop trying to marry my daughter," Jake Blair muttered, his ice-blue eyes penetrating, as Rourke joined him at the kitchen table. "You are definitely not son-in-law material."

"Spoilsport," Rourke told him. "It's hard to find a nice woman who can also cook and play video games."

"You don't play video games," Jake pointed out.

"A lot you know! The police chief is teaching me."

"Cash Grier?" Carlie exclaimed. "My boss doesn't play."

"Apparently that's why he thinks it's a good idea if he does the teaching. His young brother-in-law has forced him into it," he laughed, "because he can't get any friends to play with him. Cash is always up for anything new and exciting."

Jake shook his head. "I just don't get it. Running around a cartoon world on dragons and fighting people with two-handed swords. It's…medieval."

"Teaches combat skills, strategy, social interaction and how to deal with trolls," Carlie retorted, pouring coffee for all of them.

"Trolls?" Rourke asked. "Those great Norwegian things...?"

"Internet trolls," she clarified with a glower. "People who start fights and stand back and watch. They're really a pain sometimes, especially if somebody new to the game makes the mistake of asking for help on trade chat." She started laughing.

"What's so funny?" her father asked.

"Well, this guy wanted a mage port—that's a portal they can make to the major cities. He didn't know what class could do ports, so he asked if anybody could send him to the capital. This warlock comes on and offers to port him for fifty gold." She was laughing heartily. "Warlocks can't port, you see. They can summon, but that's a whole other thing." She shook her head. "I've spent months wondering how that came out."

"Probably about like the death knight your boss told me about, who offered to heal for a dungeon group," Rourke replied, tongue-in-cheek.

Carlie looked shocked. "DKs can't heal!"

"I'm sure the dungeon group knows that now," he quipped, and he was rakishly handsome when he smiled.

"I guess I'm missing a lot," Jake Blair said.

"You should come and play with us," Carlie said.

He shook his head. "I'm too old to play, pumpkin."

"You're kidding, right? One of the best raid leaders on our server is seventy-three years old."

His eyebrows arched. "Say what?"

"Not only that, there's a whole guild that plays from a nursing home."

"I met them," Rourke said. "Cash and I were in a dungeon with several of them. Along with a ten-year-old Paladin who kicked butt, and a sixty-eight-year-old grandmother who was almost able to kill the big boss single-handed."

"I suppose my whole concept of gaming is wrong," Jake laughed. "I had no idea so many age groups played together."

"That's what makes it so much fun," Carlie replied. "You meet people from all over the world in-game, and you learn that even total strangers can work together with a little patience."

"Maybe I'll get online one of these days and try it," Jake conceded.

"That would be great, Dad!" Carlie exclaimed. "You can be in our guild. Robin and I have one of our own," she explained. "We'll gear you and teach you."

"Maybe in the summer, when things are a little less hectic," Jake suggested.

"Oh. The building committee again," Carlie recalled.

"One group wants brick. The other wants wood. We have a carpenter in our congregation who wants the contract and doesn't understand that it has to be bid. The choir wants a loft, but the organist doesn't like heights. Some people don't want carpet, others think padded benches are a total sellout… Why are you laughing?" he asked, because Rourke was almost rolling on the floor.

"Church," Rourke choked. "It's where people get along and never argue…?"

"Not in my town," Reverend Blair said, sighing. He smiled. "We'll get it together. And we argue nicely." He frowned. "Except for Old Man Barlow. He uses some pretty colorful language."

"I only used one colorful word," Carlie remarked as she served up the casserole, "and he—" she pointed at her father "—grounded me for a month and took away my library card."

He shrugged. "It was a very bad word." He glowered at her. "And Robin should never have taught it to you without explaining what it meant!"

"Robin got in trouble, too," she told Rourke. "But his parents took away his computer for two weeks." She shook her head. "I thought withdrawal was going to kill him."

"He uses drugs?" Rourke asked curiously.

"No, withdrawal from the video game we play together," she chuckled. She glanced at her father. "So I had to do battle-grounds in pugs for those two weeks. It was awful."

"What's a pug?" Reverend Blair asked.

"A pickup group," Rourke replied. "Cash taught me." He glared. "There was a tank in the last one that had a real attitude problem. Cash had him for lunch."

"Our police chief is awesome when he gets going," Carlie laughed. "We had one guy up for speeding, and when he came in to pay the ticket he was almost shaking. He just wanted to give me the fine and get out before he had to see the chief. He said he'd never speed in our town again!"

"What did Cash do?" Jake asked.

"I asked. He didn't really do anything. He just glared at the man while he wrote out the ticket."

"I know that glare." Rourke shook his head. "Having been on the receiving end of it, I can tell you truly that I'd rather he hit me."

"No, you wouldn't," Carlie mused. "I wasn't working for him then, but I heard about it. He and Judd Dunn were briefly inter-ested in the same woman, Christabel, who eventually married Judd. But it came to blows in the chief's office at lunch one day. They said it was such a close match that both men came out with matching bruises and cuts, and nobody declared victory. You see, the chief taught Judd Dunn to fight Tae Kwon Do–style."

"Wasn't he going to teach you and Michelle Godfrey how to do that?" Jake asked suddenly.

"He was, but it was sort of embarrassing, if you recall, Dad," she replied. She glanced at Rourke, who was watching her curi-ously. "I tripped over my own feet, slid under another student, knocked him into another student on the mat, and they had to go to the emergency room for pulled tendons." She grimaced. "I was too ashamed to try it again, and Michelle wouldn't go without me. The chief wanted us to try again, but I'm just too clumsy for martial arts."

Rourke's eyes twinkled. "I can sympathize. On my first foray into martial arts, I put my instructor through a window."

"What?" she exclaimed.

"We were standing near it. He threw a kick, I caught his foot and flipped him. The momentum took him right into a backward summersault, right out the window. Fortunately for him it was a low one, raised, and very close to the ground."

"Well!" she laughed.

"I've improved since then." He shared an amused look with Jake.

"Shall we say grace?" Jake replied, bowing his head.

"YOU DIDN'T TELL me that it was the police chief's wife, not Carlie, who insulted you," Carson said as they shared coffee during intermission at the theater in San Antonio.

Lanette looked at him under her long lashes. "I was very upset," she remarked. "Perhaps I was confused. Honestly, that girl is so naïve. And she isn't even pretty! I don't understand why you were dancing with her in the first place!"

He studied her covertly. She was getting more possessive by the day, and she was full of questions about Carlie. It bothered him. He kept thinking of her rap sheet, too.

"Several of us are watching her," he said after a minute. "There was an attempt on her father's life, and she was injured. We think there may be another one."

"On a minister?" she exclaimed, laughing loudly. "Who'd want to kill a preacher?"

His black eyes narrowed. "I don't recall telling you that her father was a man of the cloth," he said.

Her face was blank for just an instant and then she smiled prettily. "I was asking about her at the dance. Someone told me who her father was."

"I see."

"She's just a backward little hick," she muttered irritably. "Let's talk about something else. Are we going to see the symphony Friday night? I bought a new dress, specially!"

He was thoughtful. He didn't like the way Lanette had started to assume that he was always available to take her out. She was beautiful to look at, to show off in public. The poor reservation kid in him enjoyed the envious looks he got from other men when he escorted his striking blond companion in the evenings. But she was shallow and mean-spirited. He forgave a lot because she eased the ache in him that Carlie provoked.

Funny thing, though. Although he enjoyed the physical aspects of their relationship, he couldn't quite manage to go all the way with his gorgeous blonde. It unsettled him, and irritated and insulted her, but expensive presents seemed to pacify her.

He didn't understand his reticence. Lanette was eager and accomplished, but her talents were wasted on him. Deep down, he knew why. It didn't help the situation. Carlie was never going to fall into bed with him. And if she did, her father would kill him and Cash Grier would help.

"I'll be very happy when you're finished with this dumb assignment and you don't have to be around that little hick," Lanette was saying. She brushed back her long, thick, blond hair.

"People in Jacobs County are very protective of her," was all he said.

"She's probably not even in trouble," she muttered. "I expect people are just overreacting because of that attack on her father. For goodness sake, maybe whoever's after her isn't even after her, maybe it's her father!" She glanced at him. "Isn't that what you said about that knife attack, that he was trying to kill her father and she tried to stop him?"

"That's what they said."

She shook her head. "Well, it was a really stupid job," she murmured. "Imagine a man going to the victim's house in the middle of the day, in broad daylight, and attacking a minister in his own house!"

Carson frowned as he listened. "I didn't know it was in broad daylight."

"Everybody knows," she said quickly. "They were even talking about it at that silly dance you took me to."

"Oh."

She glanced away, smiling to herself. "They also said that the man who tried to kill the preacher ended up dead himself."

"Yes, poisoned. A very nasty, slow poison. Something the late Mr. Martin was quite well-known for in intelligence circles."

"I hate poison," she said under her breath. "So unpredictable."

"Have you been poisoning people, then?" he mused.

She laughed. "No. I like to watch true crime shows on television. I know all about poisons and stuff." She moved very close to him. "Not to worry, handsome, I'd never want to hurt you!" she added, and lifted her arms toward his neck.

He raised an eyebrow and stepped back.

"Oh, you and your hang-ups," she muttered. "What's wrong with a hug in public?"

"It would take too long to tell you," he said, not offering the information that in his culture, such public displays were considered taboo by the elders.

"All right," she said with mock despair. "Are we going to the theater Friday?"

"Yes," he said. It would keep his mind off Carlie.

"Wonderful!" She smiled secretly to herself. "I'm sure we'll have a lovely time." She paused. "That mad South African man you know, he isn't coming to the theater, is he?"

"Rourke?" He laughed to himself. "Not likely on a Friday night."

"Why not on a Friday?" she asked.

He almost bit his tongue. Rourke played poker with Cash Grier. He didn't dare let that slip, just in case Lanette knew anyone who had contact with Matthew Helm. "Rourke drinks on weekends," he lied.

"I see." She thought for a minute. "What about your friend

the police chief?" she asked, laughing. "I'll bet he takes that prissy wife of his to the theater."

"Not on a Friday night," he chuckled. "The police chief and several other men get together at the chief's house and play poker after supper."

"Exciting game, poker. Especially the strip kind," she purred. He sighed. "I don't gamble. Sorry."

"Your loss, sweetie," she said with pursed red lips. "Your loss."

FRIDAY NIGHT, REVEREND BLAIR had a call from a visitor to the community who was staying in a local motel outside town.

"I just want to die," the man wailed. Jake couldn't quite place the accent, but it definitely wasn't local. "I hate my life! They said you were a kind man who would try to help people. They gave me your number, here at this motel—" he named it "—so I said I'd call you. Before I did it, you know. Will God forgive me for killing myself? I got some rat poison…"

"Wait," Jake Blair said softly. "Just wait. I'll come to see you. We'll talk."

"You'd come all this way, just to talk to me?" The man sounded shocked.

"I know the motel you mentioned you were staying at," Jake said. "It's just a few minutes from here. I'll be on my way in a jiffy. What's your room number?"

The man told him. "Thank you. Thank you!" he sobbed. "I just don't want to live no more!" He hung up.

"Pumpkin, I have to go out," he informed his daughter as he shrugged into his bomber jacket. "I've been contacted by a suicidal man in a motel. I'm going to try and talk him down before he does something desperate."

She smiled. "That's my dad, saving the world."

He shrugged. "Trying to, anyway. You stay inside and keep the doors locked," he added. "And keep that cell phone close, you hear me?"

"I'll put it in my pocket, I swear."

"Good girl." He kissed her forehead. "Don't wait up. This may take a while."

"Good luck," she called after him.

He waved at her, left and closed the door behind him.

Carlie finished cleaning up the kitchen and went upstairs to play her game. On the kitchen table, forgotten, was the cell phone she'd promised to keep with her. The only other phone in the house was a fixed one, in her father's office...

"GOODNESS, COFFEE JUST goes right through me," Lanette whispered into Carson's ear. "Be right back."

He just nodded, aware of irritated glances from other theatergoers nearby. He wasn't really thrilled with the play. It was modern and witty, but not his sort of entertainment at all, despite the evident skill of the actors.

His mind went back to Carlie on the riverbank, standing so close that he could feel every soft line of her body, kissing him so hungrily that his mind spun like a top. Carlie, who was as innocent as a newborn, completely clueless about the hungers that drove men.

He wanted her until he couldn't sleep for wanting her. And he knew he could never have her. He wasn't going to settle down, as Cash Grier had, with a wife and child and a job in a small town. He liked adventure, excitement. He wasn't willing to give those up for some sort of middle-class dream life in a cottage or a condo, mowing the grass on weekends. The thought of it turned his stomach.

He brushed away a spec on his immaculate trousers and frowned. He didn't understand why Carlie appealed to his senses so strongly. She wasn't really pretty, although her mouth was soft and beautiful and tasted as sweet as honey. Her body was slender and she was small-breasted. But she had long, elegant legs and her waist was tiny. He could feel her small breasts swelling against his hard chest when he kissed her, feel the tips biting into his flesh even through layers of fabric.

He groaned silently. His adventures with women had always been with beautiful, practiced, elegant women. He'd never been with an innocent. And he wasn't about to break that record now, he assured himself firmly.

He'd been vulnerable with Carlie because he felt guilty about sending her to the hospital when he lost his temper. That was all. It was a physical reaction, prompted only by guilt. He was never going to forgive himself for frightening her like that. Her white face haunted him still. He'd only moved closer to make his point, it hadn't been a true aggression. But it must have seemed that way to a young girl who'd been beaten, and then later stabbed by an assassin.

But he hadn't hurt her at the dance, when they'd moved together like one person, when he'd felt the hunger so deeply that he could have laid her down on the dance floor right then. What the hell was he going to do? It was impossible. Impossible!

While he was brooding, Lanette returned. She slid her hand into his and just smiled at him, without saying a word. He glanced at her. She really was beautiful. He'd never seen a woman who was quite this exquisite. If it hadn't been for her attitude, and her other flaws, she might have seemed the perfect woman. That made it all the more inexplicable that he couldn't force himself to sleep with her; not even to relieve the ache Carlie gave him.

CARLIE WAS FIGHTING two Horde in the battleground. Sadly, neither of them was Carson. She flailed away with her two-handed sword, pulled out her minions, used every trick she could think of to vanquish them, but they killed her. She grimaced. She had the best gear honor points could buy, but there were these things called conquest points that only came from doing arenas. Carlie couldn't do arena. She was too slow and too clumsy.

So there were people far better geared than she was. Which

was just an excuse, because the playing field was level in battlegrounds, regardless of how good your armor was.

The painful truth was that there were a lot of players who
were much better at it than Carlie was. She comforted herself
with the knowledge that there was always somebody better at
the game, and eventually everybody got killed once or twice
during a battle. She was just glad that she didn't have to do it
in real life.

"Ah, well," she said, and sighed.

She resurrected at the battleground cemetery, got on her
mount and rode back off to war. Before she got to either her
home base or the enemy's, the end screen came up. The Alliance had lost to the Horde. But it had been an epic battle, the
sort that you really didn't mind losing so much because it was
fought by great players on both sides.

"Next time," she told the screen. "Next time, we'll own you,
Hordies!"

She was about to queue for the battleground again when she
heard a knock at the door downstairs.

She logged out of her character, although not out of the game,
mildly irritated by the interruption, and went down the staircase. She wondered if maybe her father had forgotten to take
his house key with him. He was so forgetful sometimes, it was
funny. Twice now, he'd had to wake Carlie up when he came
back from a committee meeting that lasted longer than expected, or when he returned from visiting and comforting congregation members at hospitals.

She peered through the safety window and frowned. There
was a big man in a suit outside. He looked uneasy.

"Is there something you want?" she asked through the door.

"Yeah," he said after a minute. "I need help."

"What sort of help?" she answered.

He paused for a minute. He looked through the small window
at the suspicious young woman who was obviously not about
to open that door to a man she didn't know.

He thought for a minute. He was slow when it came to improvisation. Maybe he could fool her if he was smart. Yeah. Smart. Who would she open the door for?

"I, uh, came to tell you about your dad," he called through the door. "There's been an accident. I was passing by and stopped. He asked me to come and get you and drive you to the hospital where they're taking him."

"Dad's been in a wreck?" she exclaimed. "Why didn't the police come?"

What did she mean? Did police notify people about wrecks here? He supposed they did. He'd done that once, long ago. He paused.

"Well, they were coming, but I told them your dad wanted me to bring you, and they said it was okay."

She still hesitated. Perhaps it was one of the new patrolmen, and her father had been impatient about getting word to her. A kind stranger might have been imposed upon to fetch Carlie.

"He's hurt pretty bad, Miss," he called again. "We should go."

She couldn't bear to think of her father injured. She had to go to him. She grabbed her coat off the rack near the door. Her pocketbook was upstairs, but she couldn't think why she'd need it. Her father would have money in his wallet and a house key.

"Okay, I'm coming," she said, and opened the door.

He smiled. "I'll take you to him," he promised.

She closed and locked the door behind her. Too late, she remembered her cell phone lying on the kitchen table.

"Have you got a cell phone?" she asked abruptly.

"Yeah, I got one," he said, leading the way to his late model sedan. "Why?"

"In case we have to call somebody," she explained.

"You can call anybody you like, Miss," he said. "Just get right in."

She bent down to slide into the open passenger side when she felt a cloth pressed against her mouth and pressure behind it. She took a breath. The whole world went black.

THE BIG MAN cuffed her hands together behind her before he
slid her onto the backseat. She was breathing sort of funny, so
he didn't gag her. He hoped that would be okay with the boss.
After all, where they were going, nobody was likely to hear her.

Before he got into the car, he dropped a piece of paper on
the ground deliberately. Then he got in the car, started it and
drove away.

CHAPTER NINE

REVEREND JAKE BLAIR knocked at the motel door, but there was no answer. He immediately thought the worst, that the man had actually attempted suicide before his arrival. He might be inside, fatally wounded.

He ran to the motel office, explained the situation, showed his ID and pleaded with the man to open the door.

The manager ran with him to the room, slid home the key and threw open the door.

"Is this some sort of joke?" the manager asked.

Jake shook his head. "He phoned me at home and begged me to come and speak with him. He said that someone locally had recommended that he call me and gave him the number. He said he was suicidal, that he was going to take poison." He turned to the man. "Did you rent this room tonight?"

"Yes. To some big guy with a Northern accent," he replied. "He didn't have any luggage, though, and he didn't look suicidal to me." He glowered. "He just left without paying the bill or handing back the key," he muttered.

"Isn't that the key?" Jake asked, nodding toward the bedside table.

It was. There was a fifty-dollar bill under it.

"Well," the manager chuckled drily. "A man with a sense of honor, at least. Sort of."

"Sort of." Jake shook his head. "I can't imagine why he'd fake something like this." Then he remembered. Carson had a date. Rourke was playing poker with Cash Grier. Jake was here. Carlie was alone. At home.

He bit off a bad word, chided himself for the slip and ran for his car. On the way he dialed Carlie's cell phone, but there was no answer. He was referred to her voice mail. He'd told her to keep that phone with her. She never remembered. He dialed the home phone. The answering machine picked up after four rings. Now, that was unusual. Carlie would hear it, even if she was playing, and she'd pick it up before the message finished playing.

He was very concerned. He wasn't certain that someone was after him because of his past, despite the threatening phone call Carlie had taken. The man with the knife went for Carlie deliberately, it had seemed to Jake. He groaned as he pictured it, recalled her pain and terror. She'd had so much misery in her short life, so much violence. He hated what she'd gone through. Some of it was his fault.

He burned rubber getting home. He ran up the porch steps, put his key in the lock and went in like a storming army. But the house was empty. Carlie's computer was still on. And, although she'd logged out temporarily, her character screen was still up and the game was still running. That meant she'd been interrupted while she was playing. He checked every room. In the kitchen he found her cell phone, lying on the table.

He backtracked out the front door and, with a flashlight in addition to the porch light, searched around. He noticed tire tracks that weren't his. He also noted a piece of paper. It was a rough drawing, a map of sorts. It was a clue that the police would want undisturbed. He had no idea what the map depicted. But he knew what to do at once. He pulled out his cell phone and called Cash Grier.

"I HAD TO call Hayes," Cash apologized when he was on the scene. "You don't live in the city limits."

"That's okay." Jake clapped him on the back. "You're forgiven."

"Don't worry. Hayes has an investigator who dines out on forensics. He even has membership in several professional societies that do nothing else except discuss new techniques. Zack's good at his job."

"Okay." Jake shoved his hands into his pockets. He felt as if it was the end of the world. "I should have realized it was a ruse. Why didn't I think?"

"We'll find her," Cash promised.

"I know that. It's what condition we'll find her in that concerns me," Jake said tautly.

"I don't think they'll harm her," Cash said. "They want something. Maybe it's you."

"They can have me, if they'll let my daughter go," he rasped.

"I phoned my brother," Cash added. "It's a kidnapping. That makes it a federal crime. He'll be over as soon as he gets dressed."

Cash's brother, Garon Grier, was the senior special agent at the Jacobsville FBI office. He was formerly with the FBI's Hostage Rescue Team, and one of the best people to call in on the case. But Jake was concerned that the police presence might cause the kidnapper to panic and kill Carlie in order to get away.

"Where's Rourke?" Jake asked. "Was he playing poker with you?"

"He was, but he had a call from the politician he's supposedly the enforcer for," came the reply. "It seems the other enforcer was indisposed and he needed Rourke to run an errand for him."

"Interesting timing," Jake said.

Cash knew that. He could only imagine how he'd feel if it was his little girl, his Tris, who was missing. He drew in a breath and patted Jake on the back. "Don't worry," he said again. "It's going to be all right."

"Yes," Jake said and managed a smile. "I know that."

JAKE BLAIR EXCUSED himself in the early hours of the morning by saying that he had to visit a sick member of his congregation at the hospital. He left his cell phone number with Cash and asked him to please call if there was any word from the kidnapper.

He went inside and put on jeans and a pair of high-topped moccasins with no soles and his bomber jacket, along with a concealed knife in a scabbard, a .45 magnum in a Velcro holster and a pair of handcuffs.

With his equipment carefully hidden under the roomy bomber jacket, he waved to local law enforcement and spun out of the yard in the Cobra.

Unknown to the others, he'd had time to process the crude drawing on that map. He didn't for a moment think it had been dropped accidentally. No, this was a setup. They wanted Jake to come after Carlie. Which meant that, in his opinion, Jake was the real target.

He assumed that someone in his past was out to get him. He didn't know why. But there were plenty of reasons. His former life had been one of violence. He'd never expected that he would ever revisit it. Until now. His old skills were still sharp. Nobody was hurting Carlie. And as the Good Book said, God helps those who help themselves.

Probably, he amended, God didn't mean with guns. But then, he rationalized, they hadn't had guns in Biblical days, either. He was winging it. He wouldn't kill anybody. Unless it came to a choice between that and watching Carlie die. He couldn't do that. He couldn't live with it.

He followed the highway to a dirt road leading off to a deserted area with just the beginnings of scrubland, with cactus and sand. He parked the car, got out, checked his weapon, stuck it back in the holster and belted it around his waist. He strapped the bottom of the holster to his thigh with the Velcro tabs. He pulled out his knife in its sheath from under the jacket and fixed it on the other side of the belt buckle. Then he started off, with uncanny stealth, down the road.

CARLIE REGAINED CONSCIOUSNESS slowly. Her mind felt as if it was encased in molasses. She couldn't imagine why she was so sluggish, or why it was so hard to breathe.

She tried to move and realized, quite suddenly, that it was because her hands were tied behind her. She was lying on her side on a makeshift pallet. A big, worried man was standing nearby, wearing a business suit and a big gun. He wasn't holding it on her. It was on his belt, inside his open jacket.

"You okay?" he asked. "You was breathing awful jerkylike."

"I'm okay." She tried to take small breaths. She was scared to death, but she was trying not to let it show. "What am I doing here?" She swallowed. "Are you going to kill me?"

"No!" he said, and looked shocked. "Look, I don't do women. Ever." He blinked. "Well, there was one, once, but she shot me first." He flushed a little.

He was the oddest sort of kidnapper she'd ever seen. He was as big as a house and he seemed oddly sympathetic for a man who meant her harm.

"Then why did you bring me here? You said my father was hurt...!" she remembered, almost hysterical.

"Not yet," he said. "We had to get him out of the house so we could get to you," he explained. "It takes time to do these things right, you know. First we get you. Then he comes out here, all alone, and we get him. Real easy."

"Why do you want my father?" she asked, relieved that her dad was all right, but nervous because the man was making threats.

"Not me," he said with a shrug. "Somebody else."

"Why?"

"Lady, I don't know," he muttered. "Nobody tells me nothing. They just say go do something and I go do it. I don't get paid to ask questions."

"Please don't hurt my dad," she said plaintively.

He made a face. "Look, I'm not going to do anything to him," he promised. "Honest. I don't kill people for money. I just had to get him out here. There's two guys outside…they'll do it."

Her heart jumped up into her throat. Her father would be lured here because she was under threat. He'd walk right up to the door and they'd kill him. She felt sick all over. "Couldn't you stop them?" she asked. "Don't you have a father? Would you like to see that done to him?"

His face closed up. "Yeah, I had a father. He put me in the hospital twice. I wouldn't care if somebody did it to him. No way."

Her eyes were soft with sadness. "I'm so sorry," she said gently.

He looked uncomfortable. "Maybe you should try to sleep, huh?"

"My wrists hurt."

"I can do something about that." He went around behind her and fiddled with the handcuffs. They were less tight. "So funny, I got kicked off the force five years ago, and here I am using cuffs again," he mused.

"The force?"

"I was a cop. I knocked this guy down a staircase. Big guy, like me. He was trying to kill his kid. They said I used excessive force. There was a review and all, but I got canned anyway." He didn't add that it was really because he'd ruffled his partner's feathers when he wouldn't take bribes or kickbacks. That was sort of blowing his own horn. He'd been set up, but that was ancient history now. The bad thing was that it had given Mr. Helm a stick to hit him with, because he'd been honest about losing his job. He hadn't known at the time that Mr. Helm was even more crooked than his old partner.

"I work for the police chief, here," she said. "He'd use excessive force with a guy who was trying to kill his kid, too, but nobody would fire him for it."

He moved back around in front of her. He smiled faintly. He had dark eyes and a broad face with scars all over it. He had thick black wavy hair. He was an odd sort of gangster, she thought.

"Maybe he knows the right people," he told her. "I didn't."

She studied him curiously. "You aren't from Texas," she said.

He shrugged. "From Italy, way back," he said.

Her eyes widened. "Are you in the Mafia?" she asked.

He burst out laughing. He had perfect white teeth. "If I was, they'd kill me for telling people about it."

"Oh. I get it."

"Your wrists okay now? That feel better?"

"Yes. Thanks." She made a face. "What did you do to me?"

"Chloroform," he said. "Put it on a handkerchief, see, and it works quick."

She drew in another breath. Her chest felt tight.

"You ain't breathing good," he remarked, frowning.

"I have asthma."

"You got something to use for it?"

"Sure. It's back at my house. Want to take me there to pick it up?" she asked. She wasn't really afraid of him. Odd, because he looked frightening.

He smiled back. "Not really, no. I'd get fired."

"Not a bad idea, you could do something honest for a living before your bosses get you locked up for life," she returned.

He seemed disturbed by that. He checked his watch. It was an oddly expensive-looking one, she thought. He'd said they didn't pay well, but if he could afford a timepiece like that, perhaps he'd just been joking about his salary.

He drew in a long breath. "I have to make a phone call," he said. "You just stay there and be quiet so I don't have to gag you, okay?"

"I can't let them kill my father," she said. "If I hear him coming, I'm going to warn him."

"You're an honest kid, ain't you?" he asked admiringly. "Okay. I'll try not to make it too tight, so you can breathe."

He took out a clean handkerchief and rolled it up, tied it around her mouth. "That okay?" he asked.

She groaned.

"Come on, don't make me feel no worse than I do. You're just a kid. I wouldn't hurt you. Not even if they told me to."

She made a face under the gag. Reluctantly, she nodded.

"Okay. I won't be long."

She heard him go to the door. Just as he started to open it, she thought she must be hallucinating, because she heard a chiming rock song. It went away almost at once, followed by a mild curse. The door opened and closed. She heard voices outside.

What could she possibly do that would save her father? She squirmed her way to the edge of the bed and wiggled so that her feet made it to the floor. She was still a little dizzy, but she managed to get to her feet.

She moved to the door and listened. She heard distant voices. She looked around. The room had no windows. There was a pallet on the floor, nothing else. There wasn't even a table, much less anything she could try to use to untie herself.

Well, she could at least listen and try to hear her father's voice. She might be able to warn him before they shot him. She groaned inwardly. It was going to be on her conscience forever if he died because she'd opened the door to a stranger. When she recalled what the big man had told her, it was so obviously a ruse that she couldn't imagine why she hadn't questioned his story. He'd said her father was hurt. After that, her brain had gone into panic mode. That was why she'd agreed to leave with him.

But it was going to make a really lousy epitaph for her father. If she was lucky, the FBI would involve itself because it was a kidnapping. There was also her boss, who'd come looking for her. Maybe Carson would, too. Her heart jumped. Sure he would. He was probably up in San Antonio with that gorgeous blonde, out on a date. He wouldn't even know she was missing and probably wouldn't mind unless somebody asked him to help find her. That made her even more depressed.

But how would they ever find her in time to save her father? She hoped he had no idea where to find her, that they hadn't left some sort of clue that would lead him here. But there were armed guards at the door, and they were waiting for him, her kidnapper had said. That meant they had to have left some clue to help him find this place.

She closed her eyes and began to pray silently, the last hope of the doomed…

CARSON HAD JUST walked back into his apartment, after insistently leaving Lanette at hers, when his cell phone went off.

He locked himself in and answered it, tired and out of sorts. "Carson," he said shortly.

"It's Cash. I thought you might want to know that we've had some developments down here."

He grimaced as he went into the kitchen to make coffee. "Somebody confessed to trying to off the preacher?"

There was a pause. "Someone's kidnapped Carlie…"

"What the hell! Who? When?"

Cash wanted to tell him to calm down, but he had some idea about Carson's feelings for the woman, so he bit his tongue. "We don't know who. Her father was hoaxed into going to a motel to counsel a suicidal man, who conveniently disappeared before he showed up. Rourke and I were playing poker. We had no idea Carlie was going to be home alone. Somehow she was lured out. Her father said that he found her telephone on the kitchen table and her purse upstairs."

"That damned phone…"

"I know, she's always forgetting it," Cash replied heavily. "It seems that Carlie was the target all along. There was one clue, a crude drawing of a building in the area, but nobody knows where it is. The map isn't very helpful."

"Where's her father?"

"Funny thing," Cash mused. "He says he has to visit a sick member of his congregation at the hospital. The timing strikes me as a bit odd."

"I'll be there in fifteen minutes."

"You won't help her if you die on the way."

"Thanks for the tip." He hung up.

"JAKE BLAIR'S ONLY been gone a few minutes," Cash told Carson when he arrived.

Carson glanced past him. "Crime scene guys at work already, I gather."

"Yes."

Carson went inside and looked at the map lying on the table in a protective cover. It had already been dusted for prints—none found—and cataloged in position. He also saw Carlie's cell phone.

"May I?" he asked.

"It's been dusted. Only prints are hers," Zack, Sheriff Hayes Carson's chief investigator, told him with a smile. "We checked her calls, too. Nothing." He went back to work.

Carson's fingers smoothed over the phone absently. It might have been one of the last things she touched. It was comforting, in some odd way. He thought of her being held, terrified, maybe smothering because the asthma would be worsened by the fear and confusion. His face mirrored his own fear.

He stuck the phone in his pocket absentmindedly as he studied the map once more. His black eyes narrowed. The drawing was amateurish, but he recognized two features on that map because they were on the way to Cy Parks's ranch. He drove the road almost every day. There was a ranch house that had burned down some time back, leaving only a ramshackle barn standing. It had to be where they had Carlie.

He was careful not to let his recognition show, because if

the gangbusters here went shoving in, they'd probably shock the kidnappers into killing her quickly so they could escape. He couldn't risk that.

"Any idea where this place is?" he asked Cash with a convincing frown.

"Not a clue," Cash said tautly, "and I've been here for years."

"It's a pretty bad map," Carson replied.

"Yes."

"You said her father just left?" Carson asked in a low voice, incredulous. "His daughter's been kidnapped, and he's visiting the sick?"

Cash motioned him aside, away from his brother and the sheriff's department. "He was carrying a .45 magnum in his belt. Nicely hidden, but I got a glimpse of it." He pursed his lips. "Can you still track?"

"Not on pavement," he returned.

"He drives a red Cobra," he pointed out. "Not the easiest ride to conceal. And this is a small community."

"I'll have a look around."

"I'd go with you, but I can't leave." He hesitated. "Don't try to sneak up on him," he advised tersely, lowering his voice. "He's a minister now, but you don't ever lose survival instincts."

"What do you know that I don't?" Carson asked.

"Things I can't tell. Go find him."

"I'll do my best." He glanced past Cash at the other law enforcement people. "Why aren't they looking?"

"Forensics first, then action," Cash explained. His face hardened. "I know. I never really got the hang of it, either." His dark eyes met Carson's. "Her father knows where she is, I'm sure of it. Find him, you find her. Try to keep them both alive."

Carson nodded. He turned and went out the door.

JAKE SLOWED AS he neared the turnoff that led, eventually, to Cy Parks's ranch. Carlie, if the map was accurate, was being held at an old cattle ranch. The ranch house was long since burned down and deserted, but there was a barn still standing. He got around to the back of the building without being detected and observed two men standing guard in front of the door.

They were obviously armed, judging from the bulges under their cheap jackets. Apparently whoever hired them didn't pay much.

Jake had spent years perfecting his craft as a mercenary. He could move in shadow, in light, in snow or sleet, without leaving a trace of himself. He was going to have to take down two men at once. He would also have to do it with exquisite care, so as not to alert what might be a third man inside the structure holding Carlie.

It would seem impossible to survive a frontal assault against armed men. He only smiled.

He was able to get very close before he moved out into the open with both arms up. He approached the men who belatedly drew their weapons and pointed them at him. The element of surprise had confused them just enough, he hoped.

"Stop there," one of them said.

He kept walking until he was close to them.

"I said stop!" the other threatened.

"Here?" Jake asked, looking down at his feet. "Next to this snake?"

They looked down at his feet immediately. Big mistake. He ducked under them, hit one in the diaphragm to momentarily paralyze him while he put pressure to the carotid artery of the other man and watched him go down, unconscious. The second one, with his gun drawn, bent over, was easy to knock out with the .45.

Very quiet. Very precise. Not a sound came after. And he hadn't had to kill them. He drew out two lengths of rawhide from his bomber jacket and got busy trussing up the gunmen.

He knew he'd have to work fast. If someone had Carlie at

gunpoint inside, they might have heard the men ordering him to stop. It was a long shot, though. He wasn't that close to the barn.

He secured them by their thumbs, on their bellies with their hands behind them, and moved quickly toward the shed.

On the way, he had company, quite suddenly, but not from ambush. The man, moving quickly, seemed to deliberately make a sound. He'd been warned, Jake thought and smiled. He turned to the newcomer with the knife still in his hand. When he recognized the man, he slid it quickly into its sheath.

The action wasn't lost on Carson, who was remembering what Cash had told him about this enigmatic man.

"Good thing you came with a little noise," the minister said softly. His glittering blue eyes were those of a different person altogether. "I wouldn't have hesitated, under the circumstances."

Carson stared at him with open curiosity. "I've never seen an action carried out more efficiently."

"Son, you haven't seen anything yet," Jake told him. "You get behind me. And you don't move unless I tell you to. Got it?"

Carson just nodded.

They got to the door. Jake pulled a device out of his pocket and pressed it to the old wood. His jaw tautened.

He drew back and kicked the door in, an action that is much easier in movies with balsa wood props than in real life with real wood. It flung back on its hinges. Jake had the automatic leveled before it even moved, and he walked in professionally, checking corners and dark places on his way to an inner room.

Carlie was, fortunately, on her feet about a yard away from the door her father had just broken down. She cried out through the gag as she saw him.

"Dear God," Jake whispered, holstering the gun as he ran to her. "Honey, are you okay?"

"Dad!" she managed through the gag. She hugged him with her cuffed hands around his neck, sobbing. She was breathing roughly.

Carson dug an inhaler out of his pocket and handed it to

her while he took off the gag. "Two puffs, separated," he instructed. He touched her hair. "What did they do to you?" he asked angrily.

"Nothing," she choked. "I mean, he brought me in here and tied me up, but he promised he wouldn't hurt me and he didn't. Except for keeping me tied up all night, I mean," she stammered between puffs of the inhaler. "Thanks," she told Carson. "I forgot mine."

"And your damned phone," Carson muttered, digging it out of his jacket pocket. He handed it to her.

"They had armed men at the door," she exclaimed, gaping at her father. "He said the idea of taking me was to lure you here. He wasn't going to hurt you. But he said the two men, they were going to do it! They were supposed to kill you…!"

He shrugged. "They're not a threat anymore, pumpkin." He pulled a tool from his pocket and very efficiently unlocked her cuffs, touching only the chain. He turned to Carson. "You wouldn't happen to have an evidence bag on you?" he mused.

Carson pursed his lips, produced one from his jacket pocket and handed it to Jake. "I had a feeling," he replied.

Carlie watched her father slide the cuffs, gently and still without touching the parts that had locked her wrists, into the evidence bag. He laid them on the table and took a quick shot with his smartphone's camera. "Just in case," he told them.

"Someday, you have to tell me about your past," Carlie said.

"I don't, pumpkin. There are things that should never be spoken of." He smoothed over her hair. "Let's get out of here."

"I couldn't agree more," she said.

Carson took her arm. "Can you walk?" he asked softly, his eyes darker with concern.

"Sure," she said, moving a little stiffly. "I'm fine. Honest." It delighted her that he'd come with her father to rescue her. She hadn't expected it. She imagined his girlfriend was livid.

Her father led the way out. He had the automatic in his hand and he didn't apologize or explain why.

Carson let him lead, Carlie moving stiffly at his side.

The two previously armed men were still lying on the ground where Jake had left them. "Did one of these guys kidnap you?" her father asked.

She was staring almost openmouthed at them. Two automatic weapons lay in the dirt near them. They weren't moving. But they were certainly vocal.

"No," she said. "I didn't see these ones. Just the man who tied me up."

"You'll pay for this!" one of the captives raged.

"Damned straight!" the other one agreed. "The boss will get you!"

"Well, not if he's as efficient as you two," Jake replied blithely. "And I expect you're going to have a little trouble with the feds. Kidnapping is a felony."

"Hey, we didn't kidnap nobody! We was just guarding her!" the small man protested.

"Yeah. Just guarding her. So she didn't get hurt or nothing," the other man agreed.

As he spoke, several cars came into view along the road. Two of them had flashing blue lights.

Jake turned to Carson with a sigh. They'd figured out the map and now he was going to be in the soup for jumping the gun and leaving them out of the loop. He just shook his head. "You can bring Carlie to visit me in the local jail tonight. I hope they have somebody who can cook."

For the first time, Carson grinned.

BUT JAKE WASN'T ARRESTED. Cash Grier had already briefed his brother, who was in charge of the operation. A man with Jake's background couldn't convincingly be excluded from a mission that involved saving his child from kidnappers. So no charges were pressed. It would have been unlikely anyway, since Jake knew one of the top men at the agency and several government cabinet members, as well. Carlie hadn't known that, until she overheard her dad talking to Garon Grier.

"How did you get past the men with guns?" Carlie asked Carson while she was being checked out at the emergency room. Her father had insisted that Carson take her there, just in case, while he tried to explain his part in her liberation.

"I didn't," he mused. "Your father took them down." He shook his head. "I never saw it coming, and I was watching."

She signed herself out, smiled at the clerk and followed Carson out the front door. "My father is a mystery."

"He's very accomplished," he remarked.

"I noticed."

He stopped at his car and turned to her on the passenger side. "Are you sure you're all right?" he asked.

"Don't you start," she muttered. "I'm fine. Just a little bruised."

He caught her face in his big, warm hands and tilted it up to his eyes. "I thought they might kill you," he said with involuntary concern.

"And you'd miss killing me in battlegrounds online?" she asked, trying to lighten the tension, which was growing exponentially.

"Yes. I'd miss that. And other…things," he whispered as he bent and kissed her with a tenderness that was overwhelming. Then, just as suddenly, he whipped her body completely against his and kissed her with almost bruising intensity. He jerked his mouth away before she could even respond. "Next time, if there is a next time, don't open the door to anybody you don't know!"

"He said Daddy was in a wreck," she faltered. The kiss had shaken her.

"Next time, call Daddy and see if he answers," he retorted.

She searched his angry eyes. "Okay," she whispered softly.

"And for the last time, keep that damned cell phone with you!"

She nodded. "Okay," she said again, without an argument.

The tenderness in her face, the soft, involuntary hunger, the unexpected obedience almost brought him to his knees.

He'd been out of his mind when he'd heard she'd been taken; he couldn't rest until he'd got to her. After Cash had called him, he'd gone crazy on the way down from San Antonio as his mind haunted him with all the things that could have happened to her. The thought of a world without Carlie was frightening to him. He was only just beginning to realize what an impact she had on him. He didn't like it, either.

He fought for self-control. People were walking around nearby, going to and from cars. He let her go and moved away. He felt as if he were vibrating with feeling. "I need to get you home," he said stiffly.

"Okay," she said.

He helped her inside the car, started it and drove her home. He didn't say a word the whole way.

When he let her out at the front door, she ran to her father and hugged him tightly.

"I'm okay," she promised.

He smoothed her hair, looking over her head at Carson. "Thanks."

Carson shrugged. "No problem. Lock her in a closet and lose the key, will you?" he added, not completely facetiously.

Jake chuckled. "She'd just bang on the door until I let her out," he said, giving her an affectionate smile.

"Where's local law enforcement?" Carson asked.

"Packed up all the vital clues and left. They were just a little late backtracking the kidnapper to a lonely barn over near your boss's house," Jake said with biting criticism.

"You did that quite neatly yourself," Carson replied. "I'm reliably informed that local law enforcement followed you there after being tipped off."

"Did you tip them off?" Jake asked with a knowing smile.

Carson sighed. "Yes. I didn't want to have to bury both of you."

Jake became less hostile. "Carson," he said softly, "I wasn't always a minister. I can handle myself."

"And now I know that." Carson managed a smile, glanced at Carlie with painfully mixed feelings and left.

LATER, IN THE corner table at the local café, Carson cornered Rourke. "Okay, let's have it," he demanded.

"Have what?" Rourke asked with a smile.

"That mild-mannered minister—" he meant Jake Blair "—took down two armed men with a speed I've never seen in my life. I didn't even hear him walk toward them, and I was out of my car and heading that way at the time."

"Oh, Jake was always something special," Rourke replied with a smile of remembrance. "He could move so silently that the enemy never knew he was around. They called him 'Snake,' because he could get in and out of places that an army couldn't. He had a rare talent with a knife. Sort of like you," he added, indicating the big bowie knife that Carson was never without. "He'd go in, do every fourth man in a camp, get out without even being heard. The next morning, when the enemy awoke, there would be pandemonium." He hesitated. "Don't you ever tell her," he added coldly, "or you'll find out a few more things about the reverend Blair."

"I never would," Carson assured. "There are things in my past just as unsavory."

Rourke nodded. "His specialty was covert assassination, but he didn't work with a spotter or use a sniper kit. He went in alone, with just a knife, at night." He shook his head. "We tried one night to hear him leave. None of us, not even those with sensitive hearing, could ever spot him. The government begged him to come back when he left for the seminary. He told them he was through with the old life and he was never doing it again. Carlie's his life, now. Her, and his church." He glanced at Carson. "He says she's the only reason he didn't commit suicide after her mother died. You know, I don't really understand religion, but I guess it has its place."

"I guess it does," Carson replied thoughtfully.

"How was your date?" Rourke asked.

Carson made a face. "Tedious."

"She's a looker."

Carson stared at him with cool, cynical eyes. "They all look alike, smell alike, sound alike," he said. "And they don't last long. I don't like possession."

Rourke toyed with his coffee cup. "I don't, either," he said slowly, thinking of Tat. The last he'd heard, she went into a small, war-torn African nation, named Ngawa in Swahili, for a species of civet cat found there, to cover the agony of the survivors. She wouldn't answer his phone calls. She wouldn't return his messages. She might as well have vanished off the face of the earth. He had…feelings for her, that he could never, ever express. He, like Carson, had placated the ache with other women. Nothing did much good.

Carson finished his coffee. "I have to get back up to San Antonio. I may have an offer soon."

Rourke studied him. "Tired of working for Cy?"

Carson's lips made a thin line. "Tired of aching for something I can never have."

"Boy, do I understand that feeling," Rourke said tersely.

Carson laughed, but it had a hollow sound.

He was supposed to take Lanette dancing tonight. He wasn't looking forward to it, but he'd given his word, so he'd go. The job offer would involve travel to some South American nation for a covert op with some ex-military people, on the QT. They needed a field medic, and Carson's reputation had gotten around.

It was a good job, paid well, and it would get him away from Carlie. Suddenly that had become of earthshaking importance. He didn't want to pursue that line of thought, so he called Lanette before he left Jacobsville and told her he'd pick her up at six.

CHAPTER TEN

CARLIE DESCRIBED THE kidnapper to Zack the next day, with her boss and the FBI special agent in charge, Garon Grier, listening in Cash's office.

"He sounded just like one of those gangsters in the old black-and-white movies," she said. "He was big as a house and a little clumsy. He was kind to me. He didn't say a thing out of the way or even threaten me."

"Except by kidnapping you," Garon Grier mused.

"Well, yes, there was that," she agreed. "But he didn't hurt me. He said he was supposed to take me out there to lure my dad to come get me. I suppose that meant they wanted to get him out of town to someplace deserted. I was so scared," she recalled. "I managed to get to my feet, to the door. I listened really hard, so if I heard Dad's voice, I might have time to warn him."

"You weren't afraid for yourself?" Cash asked.

"Not really. He didn't want to hurt me. I was just afraid for Dad. He's absentminded and he forgets things, like his house keys," she said with a smile. Then the smile faded. "But he took down these two huge guys. They had guns, too." She frowned worriedly. "I don't know how he did it. He even kicked in the door! I only just managed to get out of the way in time! And Dad had a gun..."

"He didn't use it," Cash reminded her.

"No. Of course not." She rubbed her wrists. "The kidnapper apologized for the handcuffs. He knew how to loosen them. He said he was a cop once. He knocked a man down a staircase for roughing up a child and they fired him." She looked up. They were all staring at her.

"What else did he say?" Garon asked. He was taking notes on his cell phone.

"I asked why he wanted my dad hurt and he said his bosses didn't pay him to ask questions," she recalled. She was going to add that he was wearing an expensive watch, and about that funny chiming sound she thought she'd heard, but she wasn't certain that she hadn't been confused by the chloroform the kidnapper had used on her. No use making wild statements. She needed to stick to the facts.

"That's not much to go on, but it's more than we had," Garon said a few minutes later. "Thanks, Carlie."

"You're very welcome." She got up. "I'll just get the mail caught up," she told her boss, rolling her eyes. "I expect that will last me a few hours."

Cash chuckled. "No doubt. Hey," he added when she reached the door. She turned. "I'm glad you're okay, kid," he said gently.

She grinned. "Me, too, Chief. Where would you ever get another secretary who didn't hide in the closet every time you lost your temper?"

She went out before he could come back with a reply.

"Isn't this lovely?" Lanette asked Carson as they did a lazy two-step on the dance floor.

"Lovely," he said without feeling it.

"You're very distracted tonight," she said. She moved a little away so that he could see how nicely her red sequined cocktail dress suited her, exposing most of her breasts and a lot of her thigh in a side split. Her exquisite hair was put up in a nice French twist with a jeweled clasp that matched the dress and her shoes. She looked beautiful and very expensive. He wondered vaguely how she managed to afford clothes like that on a stewardess salary. And she never seemed to go on any trips.

"Do you work?" he asked, curious.

"I work very hard," she said. She smiled secretively. "I was a stewardess, but I have a new job now. I work in…personnel," she concluded. "For a big corporation."

"I see."

"What do you do?" she asked.

He smiled enigmatically. "I work for a rancher in Jacobsville mostly, but I'm also a field medic."

"A medic? Really?" she exclaimed. "That's such a…well, I know it's noble and all that, but it sounds just really boring."

Boring. He was recalling several incidents, trying to treat men under fire and get them evacuated by helicopter or ambulance in trouble spots all over the world. Saving lives. "Maybe not as boring as it sounds," he concluded.

She shrugged. "If you say so." She looked up at him as they danced. "I heard on the news that there was a kidnapping in that town where your rancher boss lives. Was anybody hurt?"

"Carlie was frightened, but they didn't hurt her."

"Shame."

He stopped dancing. "Excuse me?"

"Well, she's a little prude, isn't she?" she said cattily. "Doesn't know how to dance properly, wears cheap clothes. My God, I'll bet she's still a virgin." She laughed heartily at the other woman's stupidity. This woman was annoying. He was beginning, just beginning, to understand how Carlie saw the world. She was blunt and unassuming, never coy, never shallow like this beautiful hothouse flower. Carlie was like a sunflower, open and honest and pretty. The fact that she didn't sleep around was suddenly appealing to him. He hated the implication of that thought. He wasn't going to get trapped. Not by some small-town girl with hang-ups.

"They say her father rescued her," Lanette purred.

"Yes. That's what I heard, too," he said, without adding that he'd been in on the rescue. Not that he'd had much work to do. Jake Blair had done it all.

"One guy against two armed men," she said, almost to herself. "It sounds…incredible. I mean, they were really tough guys. That's what I heard, anyway."

"Not so tough," Carson corrected her. "Blair had them trussed up like holiday turkeys."

She let out a rough breath. "Idiots," she murmured. She saw Carson's sudden scrutiny and laughed. "I mean, whoever planned that kidnapping was obviously not intended for a life of crime. Wouldn't you say?"

"I'd say they'd better be on a plane out of the country pretty soon," he replied. "The FBI got called in."

She stopped dancing. "The FBI? That's no threat. Those people are always in the news for doing dumb things—"

"The local FBI," he interrupted. "Garon Grier. He was formerly with the Hostage Rescue Team. His brother is Jacobsville's police chief Cash Grier. You met him at the dance."

She nodded slowly. "I see."

"So the kidnapper will not be sleeping well anytime soon," he concluded.

"Maybe he'll just have to step up his plans while the local FBI get their marbles together," she laughed.

"That's what bothers me," he replied. "What nobody understands is why someone would try to kill a minister."

"Loads of reasons," she said. "Maybe he's one of those radicals who wants everybody to take vows of chastity or something."

"A political opinion shouldn't result in murder," he pointed out.

"Well, no, but maybe the people who want him dead aren't interested in his opinions. Maybe it's just a job to them. Somebody big calling the shots, you know?"

Somebody big. Big. Like the politician who was finishing

out the Texas U.S. senator's term and was campaigning for the May special election to earn his own term.

"What are you thinking so hard about?" Lanette asked.

"Work," he said.

"Oh, work." She threw a hand up. "We're here to have fun. We could dance some more," she said, sliding close to him. "Or we could go back to my apartment…?"

He felt like a stone wall. The thought of sleeping with her had once appealed, but now he felt uncomfortable even discussing it. He thought of all the men Lanette had bragged to him about, the men she'd had. Of course men bragged about their conquests. It was just…when she did that, he thought of Carlie. Carlie!

"Ow," Lanette complained softly. "That's my hand you're crushing, honey."

He loosened his hold. "Sorry," he snapped.

"You are really tense. Please. Let me soothe that ache," she whispered sensually.

"I want to dance." He pulled her back onto the dance floor.

THE NEXT MORNING, just before daylight, he drove back down to Cy Parks's place. He couldn't sleep. He and Lanette had argued, again, about his coldness to her and about Carlie. She was venomous about the small-town girl.

Carson was angry and couldn't hide it. He didn't like hearing her bad-mouth Carlie. He was tired of the city anyway. He just wanted to get back to work.

Cy was working on a broken hoof on one of the big Santa Gertrudis bulls. He filed the broken part down while a tall African-American cowboy gently held the animal in place, soothing it with an uncanny gift.

"That's good, Diamond," the other cowboy murmured softly, using part of the pedigree bull's full name, which was Parks's Red Diamond. "Good old fellow."

Cy grinned. "I don't know what I'd do without you, Eddie,"

he chuckled. "That bull's just like a dog when you talk to him. He follows you around like one, anyway. Nice of Luke to let me borrow you." He glanced up at Carson. "You've been AWOL," he accused. "Couldn't find anybody to hold Diamond while I filed the hoof down, so I had to call Luke Craig and ask him to lend a hand. He sent Eddie Kells here. Eddie, this is Carson."

Carson nodded politely.

Kells just grinned.

"Kells came down here to a summer camp some years ago that Luke Craig's wife, Belinda, started for city kids in trouble with the law. Didn't know one end of a horse from another. Now he's bossing cowboys over at Luke's place," Cy chuckled.

"Yeah, Mr. Parks here saved my life," Kells replied. "I was in trouble with the law in Houston when I was younger," he said honestly. "I was on Mr. Parks's place trying to learn roping with his cattle, trespassing, and he caught me." He let out a whistle. "Thought I was a goner. But when he saw how crazy I was about cattle, he didn't press charges and Mr. Craig hired me on as a cowboy when I graduated from high school." He smiled. "I got no plans to ever leave, either. This is a good place to live. Fine people."

Carson studied the tall young man. He'd have thought that a place like this would have a lot of prejudice. It didn't seem to be the case at all, not if Kells wanted to stay here.

"You Indian?" Kells asked, and held up a hand when Carson bristled. "No, man, it's cool, I got this friend, Juanito, he's Apache. Some of his ancestors ran with Geronimo. He's hired on at Mr. Scott's place. He's been trying to teach me to speak his language. Man, it's hard!"

Carson relaxed a little. "I'm Oglala Lakota."

"I guess you couldn't speak to Juanito and have him understand you, huh?"

Carson smiled. "No. The languages are completely different."

"Only thing I can manage is enough Spanish to talk to some

of the new cowboys. But I guess that's what I need to be studying, anyway."

"You do very well, too," Cy told the young man, clapping him on the shoulder. "That's it, then. You go down to the hardware and get yourself a new pocketknife, and put it on my account," he told Kells. "I'll call and okay it before you get there. Don't argue. I know Luke sent you, but you should have something. That knife's pretty old, you know," he added. Kells was using it to clean under his fingernails.

"Only one I had," Kells said, smiling. "Okay, then, I'll do it. Thanks, Mr. Parks."

They shook hands.

"Nice to meet you," Kells told Carson before he left.

"I had a different concept of life here," Carson told Cy quietly.

Cy chuckled. "So did I. Blew all my notions of it when I moved here. You will never find a place with kinder, more tolerant people, anywhere in the world."

Carson was thinking of some of the places he had been which were far less than that.

"Sorry I didn't get back in time to help," he told Cy. "There's a new complication. I need to talk to Jake Blair. I think I've made a connection, of sorts. I just want to sound him out on it."

"If you dig anything out, tell Garon Grier," Cy replied.

"Certainly." He hesitated. "I'm going to be moving on, soon," he said. "I've enjoyed my time here."

"I've enjoyed having you around." Cy gave him a cynical smile. "I was like you, you know," he said. "Same fire for action, same distaste for marriage, kids. I went all over the world with a gun. Killed a lot of people. But in the end, it was the loneliness that got me. It will eat you up like acid."

"I like my own company."

Cy put a hand on his shoulder. His green eyes narrowed. "Son," he said gently, "there's a difference between being alone and being lonely."

"I'm not lonely," Carson said doggedly.

Cy just chuckled. "Go see Jake. He'll be up. He never was a late sleeper."

"You knew him before?" he asked slowly.

Cy nodded. "He was on special duty, assigned to support troops. We ended up in the same black ops group." He shook his head. "The only person I've ever known who comes close to him is Cash Grier. Jake was…gifted. And not in a way you'd ever share with civilians."

"I heard that from Rourke."

Cy pursed his lips. "Make sure you never share that information with Carlie," he cautioned. "You do not want to see Jake Blair lose his temper. Ever."

"I'm getting that impression," Carson said with a mild chuckle.

It was barely daylight. Carson knew it was early to be visiting, but he was certain Jake would be up, and he needed to tell him what he thought might be going on. Lanette had, without realizing it, pointed him in a new direction on the attempted kidnapping.

When he got to Reverend Blair's house, he was surprised to find Carlie there alone. She seemed equally surprised to find him at her door.

She was wearing a T-shirt and jeans. It was late February and still cold outside. In fact, it was cold in the house. Heat was expensive, and Carlie was always trying to save money. The cold had become familiar, so that she hardly noticed it now.

"What can I do for you?" she asked quietly.

He shrugged. "I came to see your father," he told her.

Her eyebrows arched over wide green eyes. "He didn't mention anything…"

"He doesn't know." He smiled slowly, liking the way her face flushed when he did that. "Is he here?"

"No, but he'll be back…soon," she faltered. She bit her lower lip. "You can come in and wait for him, if you like."

The invitation was reluctant, but at least she made one.

"Okay. Thanks."

She opened the door and let him in. Why did she feel as if she were walking into quicksand?

He closed the door behind him and followed her into the living room. On the sofa was a mass of yarn. Apparently she was making some sort of afghan in soft shades of blue and purple.

"You crochet?" he asked, surprised.

"Yes," she replied. She sat down beside the skeins of yarn and moved them aside. Carson dropped into the armchair just to her left.

"My mother used to do handwork," he murmured. He could remember her sewing quilts when he was very small. She did it to keep her hands busy. Maybe she did it to stop thinking about how violent and angry his father was when he drank. And he never seemed to stop drinking...

Carlie toyed with the yarn, but her hands were nervous. The silence grew more tense by the minute. He didn't speak. He just looked at her.

"Would you mind...not doing that, please?" she asked in a haunted tone.

"Doing what exactly?" he asked with a slow, sensuous smile.

"Staring at me," she blurted out. "I know you think I'm ugly. Couldn't you stare at the— Oh!"

He was sitting beside her the next minute, his hands on her face, cupping it while he looked straight into her eyes. "I don't think you're ugly," he said huskily. He looked at her mouth.

She was confused and nervous. "You said once that you liked your women more...physically perfect," she accused in a throaty voice.

He drew in a breath. "Yes. But I didn't mean it."

His thumb rubbed gently over her bow mouth, liking the way it felt. It was swollen and very soft. She caught his wrist, but not to pull his hand away.

She hadn't felt such sensations. It was new and exciting. He was exciting. She wanted to hide her reaction from him, but he knew too much about women. She felt like a rabbit walking into a snare.

She should get up right now and go into the kitchen. She should…

His mouth lowered to her lips. He touched them softly, tenderly, smoothing her lips apart so that he could feel the softness underneath the top one. He traced it delicately with his tongue. His hands on her face were big and warm. His thumbs stroked her cheekbones while he toyed with her lips in a silence that accentuated her quick breathing.

He hadn't expected his own reaction to her. This was explosive. Sweet. Dangerous. He opened his mouth and pushed her lips apart. He let go of her face and lifted her across his lap while he kissed her as if her mouth was the source of such sweetness that he couldn't bear to let it go.

Helplessly, her arms went around his neck and she kissed him back, with more enthusiasm than expertise.

He could feel that lack of experience. It made him feel taller, stronger. She had nothing to compare this with, he could tell. He nibbled her lower lip while one big hand shifted down to her T-shirt and teased under the sleeve.

She caught his wrist and stayed it. "No," she protested weakly.

But it was too late. His long fingers were under the sleeve, and he could feel the scars.

She bit her lip. "Don't," she pleaded, turning her face away.

He drew in a harsh breath. "Do you think a scar matters?" he asked roughly. He turned her face up to his. "It doesn't."

Her eyes were eloquent, stinging with tears.

"Trust me," he whispered as his mouth lowered to hers again. "I won't hurt you. I promise."

His mouth became slowly insistent, so hungry and demanding that she forgot to protest, and let go of his wrist. He slid it under the hem of her T-shirt while he kissed her and lifted it, sliding his hand possessively over her small breast and up to the scar.

"You mustn't!" she whispered frantically.

He nibbled her upper lip. "Shh," he whispered back, and quickly lifted the shirt over her head and tossed it aside.

She was wearing a delicate little white lacy bra that fastened in front. Just above the lacy cup was a scar, a long one running from her collarbone down just to the beginning of the swell of her breast.

Tears stung her eyes. She hadn't shown the wound to anyone except the doctor and a woman police officer. She tried to cover it with her hand, but he lifted it gently away and unfastened the bra.

"Beautiful," he whispered when he saw the delicate pink and mauve mound that he'd uncovered.

"Wh…what?" she stammered.

His hand smoothed boldly over her delicate flesh, teasing the nipple so that it became immediately hard. "Your breasts are beautiful," he said softly, bending. "I wonder if I can fit one into my mouth…?"

As he spoke, he did it. His tongue rubbed abrasively over the sensitive nipple while his mouth covered and possessed the pert little mound.

Her reaction was unexpected and violent. She shivered and cried out, and then suddenly arched up toward his lips as he made a slow suction that caused unspeakable responses in her untried body.

"No…nooooo!" she groaned as she felt the tension grow to almost painful depths and then, suddenly, snap. The pleasure was unlike anything she'd ever known in her life. She shivered and shivered, her short nails digging into his shoulders as she held on and convulsed with ecstasy.

He felt her body contort, felt the shudders run through her as he satisfied her with nothing more than his mouth on her breast. His hand went to her hip and ground it into his while he continued the warm pressure of his mouth on her damp flesh. He wanted her. He'd never wanted anything so much!

She was lost. She couldn't even protest. The pleasure swept over her in waves, like breakers on the ocean, on the beach. She arched her back and shuddered as her body gave in to him, hungered for him, ached to have more than this, something more, anything....

Finally, he lifted his head and looked down at her. She lay shivering in the aftermath, tears running down her cheeks. She wept silently, her eyes wide and wet and accusing.

"It's all right," he whispered. He kissed away the tears. "There's no reason to be embarrassed."

She sobbed. She felt as if she'd betrayed everything she believed in. If he hadn't stopped, she wouldn't have been able to. She was embarrassed and humiliated by her own easy acceptance of his ardor. He was a womanizer. God only knew how many women he'd had. And she was so easy...

She pushed gently at his chest.

He let her go, very slowly, his eyes riveted to her taut breasts, to the red marks on the one he'd suckled so hard.

She tried to pull the bra over them, but he prevented her with a gentle movement of his hand. He wasn't looking at her breasts. He was looking at the scar. He traced it, noting the ridge that was forming.

She drew in a sharp breath.

"It was deep, wasn't it?" he asked softly.

She swallowed. He didn't seem repulsed. "Yes."

He traced it tenderly. His finger moved down over her breast to the hard nipple and caressed it. He loved touching her. It was surprising.

"I've never had a virgin," he whispered. "I didn't realize how exciting it would be."

She flushed. "I'm...not perfect physically," she choked, remembering the hurtful things he'd said in her boss's office.

He looked into her eyes with regret darkening his own. "Here," he said quietly. "Show-and-tell."

He unbuttoned his shirt and pulled it away from his broad, muscular chest. He pulled her up into a sitting position on his lap and drew her fingers to the worst scar, where a long, deep wound went just below his rib cage on the side near his heart.

"This was deep, too," she said softly, tracing it.

He nodded. "He came at me with a sword, of all things. I drew him in and guided the blade where it would do the least damage, before I killed him." His eyes were narrow and cold.

She shivered. She could never kill anyone.

"He'd just raped a young woman. A pregnant woman," he said quietly.

Her expression changed. Her eyes went back to the scars. "These are…strange," she said, tracing several small round scars below his collarbone.

"Cigarette burns," he said with a faint smile. "I was captured once. They tortured me for information." He chuckled. "They got my name, rank and serial number. Eventually they got tired of listening to it, but my squad came and rescued me before they killed me."

"Wow," she whispered.

He cocked his head and studied her. "You are…unexpected."

Her eyebrows lifted. "I am?"

His eyes went down to her bare breasts. He drew her against him, very gently, and moved her breasts against his bare chest. She moaned. He bent and kissed her, hungrily, urgently.

"I want you," he murmured.

His hands were on her breasts again, and she was dying for him. She wanted that pleasure again, that he'd given her so easily, so sensually, with just his mouth. But with a harsh moan, she dragged herself away from him and pulled her T-shirt across her bare breasts like a shield.

"Please," she whispered when he started to draw her back into his arms. "Please. I'm sorry. I can't. I just…can't!"

She looked as if he'd asked her to go through the entire catalog of sins at once. Probably she felt that way. She was a person of faith. She didn't believe in quick rolls in the hay. She
was innocent.

He felt oddly ashamed. He buttoned his shirt while she fumbled her bra closed and put her shirt back on with tattered pride.
As cold reality set in, she was horrified by what she'd let him
do. All her principles had flown out the window the minute he
touched her.

"I see," he said quietly. "You believe it's the road to hell. And
I don't believe in anything," he added coldly.

She met his eyes. "You don't really even like women, do
you?" she asked perceptively.

His smile was icy. "She said she loved me," he replied. "We
were married for all of a year when she became pregnant. But
by then there was another man." His eyes closed, and his brows
drew together in pain at the memory while Carlie listened.

"It was almost two days after the wreck before they found
the bodies. They thought they could have saved the child, a boy,
if they'd found them just a little sooner." His face contorted. "I
killed them all..."

"No, you didn't," she said. "You couldn't hurt a woman if
you tried."

He looked at her with narrow, intent eyes. "Really? I scared
you to death in your boss's office," he reminded her tautly.

"Yes, but you wouldn't have hurt me. It was the association
with the past that frightened me, not you," she repeated softly.
She touched his cheek, drew her soft fingers down it. "Some
things are meant to be. We don't make those decisions. We can't.
God takes people away sometimes for reasons we can't understand. But there's a reason, even if we don't know what it was."

His face hardened. "God," he scoffed.

She smiled gently. "You don't believe in anything."

"I used to. Before she destroyed my life." His eyes were dark
with confusion and pain.

"You have to accept the fact that you can't control the world, or the people in it," she continued quietly. "Control is just an illusion."

"Like love?" he laughed coldly.

"Love is everywhere," she countered. "You aren't looking. You're living inside yourself, in the past, locked up in pain and loss and guilt. You can't forgive anything until you can forgive yourself."

He glared at her.

"The key to it all is faith," she said gently.

"Faith." He nodded. His eyes were hostile. "Yours took a hike when I started kissing your breasts, didn't it? All those shiny ideals, that proud innocence, would have been gone in a flash if I'd insisted."

She blushed. Her hand left his face. "Yes. That's true. I never realized how easy it would be to fall from grace." Her wide, soft eyes, wounded and wet, met his. "Is that why you did it? To show me how vulnerable I am?"

He wanted to say yes, to hurt her again. But suddenly it gave him no pleasure. No woman had ever reacted to him that way, been so tender with him, so patient, so willing to listen.

"No," he confessed curtly.

That one word took the pain away. She just looked at him.

He drew her hand to his mouth and kissed the palm hungrily. "I've never told anyone about my wife, except Grier and you, and one other person."

"I never tell anything I know," she replied huskily. She searched his dark eyes. "Ever."

He managed a smile. "You have a gift for listening."

"I learned it from my father. He's very patient."

He touched her soft mouth. "The angle of that wound is odd," he said after a minute, staring at the T-shirt. "Was the attacker very tall?"

"Not really," she confessed. "He reached around my father to do it." She shivered. She could still feel the pain of the knife.

"He'll never do it to anyone else," he assured her.

"I know. He died. They said it took a long time." She touched the scar involuntarily. "I'm sorry that his life took such a turn that he felt he was justified in killing people."

"He was an addict and they offered him product," Carson said coldly. "It works, most of the time."

"I'm sorry for him, for the way it happened. But I'm not sorry he's gone." She grimaced. "My dad wouldn't like hearing me say that."

"I won't tell him," he said gently. He looked down at her with faint possession. "Don't beat your conscience to death over what happened," he said quietly. "Any experienced man can overcome an innocent woman's scruples if he tries hard enough. And if she's attracted to him," he added gently.

She colored even more. "Yes, well, I... I didn't mean... I don't..."

He put a finger across her mouth. "It's an intimate memory. For the two of us. No one else will ever know. All right?"

She nodded. "All right."

He brought her hand to his mouth and kissed the palm. "Keep your doors locked when your father isn't here," he said.

The tone of his voice was disturbing. "Why?"

"I can't tell you."

She just sighed. As she started to speak, there was a terrible rapping sound against the side of the house.

Carson was on his feet at once, his hand on the hilt of the big bowie knife.

"That's just George."

He scowled. "Who?"

"George. He's my red-bellied woodpecker." She grimaced. "I put nuts out for him at daylight every day. He's telling me he's hungry and I'm late." She laughed. "Listen." There was another sound, like something small bounding across the roof. "That's one of the squirrels. They let George do the reminding, and then they queue for the nuts." She listened again. There was a loud cacophony of bird calls. "And those are the blue jays. They fight George for the nuts…"

"You know them by sound?" he asked, surprised.

"Of course." She got up, frowning slightly. "Can't everybody identify them from the songs they sing?"

He shook his head. "I don't believe this."

"You can help me feed them if you want to. I mean, if you don't have something else to do," she added quickly, not wanting him to feel pressured.

But he wasn't looking for a way out. He just smiled. "Put on a coat," he said.

She pulled her ratty one out of the closet and grimaced. "This is what it's best for," she sighed. "Feeding birds."

"You should buy a new one."

She gave him a world-weary glance. "With what?" she asked. "We just had to fill up the propane tank again because winter doesn't appear to be leaving anytime soon. New things are a luxury around here."

He was estimating the age of her shoes and jeans. The T-shirt appeared new. He cocked his head. It was black with writing—it had a picture of a big black bird on it. Underneath it read, "Hey, you in the house, bring more birdseed!"

He chuckled. "Cool shirt."

"You like it? I designed it. There's this website. It has nice T-shirts for a reasonable price and you can design your own. This is one of the grackles that come every spring. I haven't seen one just yet."

She led the way, picking up a container of birdseed and one of shelled nuts on the way.

"The pecans came from our own trees," she said. "The farm produce store that sells them has a sheller you can run them through. I did enough to last several weeks."

"Back home, we have ravens," he told her, his hands in his jeans as he followed her out to the big backyard. Towering trees gave way to a small pasture beyond. "And crows." He pursed his lips and grinned. "Did you know that crows used to be white?"

"White?"

He nodded. "It's a Brulé Lakota legend. The crow was white, and he was brother to the buffalo. So he would warn the buffalo when the people came to hunt it. The warriors grew angry that they couldn't get close to the buffalo, so one of them put on a buffalo skin and waited for the crow to come and give its warning. When it did, he caught it by the feet. Another warrior, very angry, took it from him and dashed it into the fire in revenge. The crow escaped, but its feathers were burned. So now the crow is black."

She laughed with pure delight. "I love stories."

"Our legends fill books," he mused. "That's one of my favorites."

That he'd shared something from his culture with her made her feel warm, welcome. She turned to look for the woodpecker. He was clinging to a nearby tree trunk making his usual lilting cry. "Okay, George, I'm here," she called. She went to a ledge on the fence and spread the nuts along it. She filled the bird feeder. Then she motioned to Carson and they moved away from the feeder.

A flash of striped feathers later, George was carting off the first pecan. He was followed by blue jays and cardinals, a tufted titmouse and a wren.

She identified them to Carson as they came in. Then she laughed suddenly as a new birdcall was heard, and started looking around. "That's a red-winged blackbird," she said. "I don't see him."

"I do know that call," he replied. He shook his head, smiling. "I've never known anyone who could listen to a birdsong and identify the bird without seeing it first."

"Oh, I can't do them all," she assured him. "Just a few. Listen. That one's a grackle!" she exclaimed. "Hear it? It sounds like a rusty hinge being moved… There he is!"

She indicated a point high in the bare limbs above. "They're so beautiful. They're so black that they have a faint purple tinge, sort of like your hair," she added, looking at it in its neat ponytail. Her eyes lingered there. He was so handsome that she thought she'd never tire of watching him.

He smiled knowingly and she flushed and averted her eyes. He was wearing that incredible fringed jacket that suited him so. Its paleness brought out the smooth olive tan of his complexion, made him look wild and free. She thought back to what her father had said, that Carson was a lobo wolf who could never be domesticated. The better she got to know him, the more certain she was of that. He'd never be able to stop picking up beautiful women, or looking for the next fight. Her heart felt sick.

She tossed seed onto the ground while the last of the nuts vanished from the fence. Carson reached into the bucket and pulled out a handful of his own and tossed it.

They stood very close, in the cold light of the morning, feeding the birds. Carlie thought it was a time she'd never forget, whatever came after. Just her and Carson, all alone in the world, without a word being spoken.

It felt…like coming home.

Carson was feeling something similar. He didn't want to think about it too much. His life was what it was. He wasn't going to get married again, settle down and have children. It was too tame for him, for his spirit. He'd lived wild for too long.

He knew she must have hopes. Her physical response to him was purely headlong. She would probably give in to him if he pushed her. He thought about doing that. He wanted her very badly. But no form of birth control was surefire. Carlie was an innocent, and she had strong beliefs. She'd never give up a child she conceived, especially his. It would lead to terrible complications…

He scowled. He was remembering some tidbit of gossip he'd heard. He glanced down at Carlie. She looked up, her eyes full of soft memory.

"Your father married your mother because you were on the way," he said gently. "True?"

She swallowed. "Well, yes. She was like me," she said, lowering her eyes to his chest. "She'd never put a foot out of line, never been…with a man. My father was dashing and exciting, well-traveled and smart. She just went in headfirst. She told me once," she recalled sadly, "that she'd ruined both their lives because she couldn't say no, the one time it really counted. She loved me," she added quickly. "She said I made everything worthwhile. But her love for my father, and his for her, never made up for the fact that he'd been pressured into marrying her."

"This isn't Victorian times," he pointed out.

"This is Jacobsville, Texas," she returned. "Or, in my case, Comanche Wells. I live among people who have known my people since the Civil War, when my family first came here from Georgia and settled on this land." She swept a hand toward it. "Generations of us know each other like family. And like family, there are some social pressures on people in terms of behavior."

"Prehistoric ones," he scoffed.

She looked up at him. "Is the world really a better place now that nothing is considered bad? People just do what they want, with anyone. How is that different from what animals do in the wild?"

He was lost for words.

"Everything goes. But the one thing that separates human beings from animals is a nobility of spirit, a sense of self-worth. I have ideals. I think they're what holds civilization together, and that if you cheapen yourself with careless encounters, you lose sight of the things that truly matter."

"Which would be…?" he prompted, stung by her reply.

"Family," she said simply. "Continuity. People get married, have children, raise children to be good people, give them a happy home life so that they grow up to be responsible and independent. Then the next generation comes along and does the same thing."

"Permissive people still have kids," he said drolly.

"They have them out of wedlock a lot, though," she pointed out. "So it's a one-parent family trying to raise the kids. I saw the result in school, with boys who had no fathers around to discipline them and teach them the things men need to know to get along in the world."

He averted his eyes. "Maybe my life would have been happier in a single-parent family."

She recalled what he'd told her, about his father's drinking problem, that he'd beat Carson's mother to death, and she grimaced. "I am so sorry for what happened to you," she said softly. "Except for my grandmother's evil boyfriend, nobody ever hurt me in my life, least of all my parents."

He drew in a long breath. His eyes were solemn as he stared off into the distance. "We attach the same importance to family that you do," he said quietly. "We live in small communities, people know each other for generations. Children are brought up not only by their parents, but by other parents, as well. It's a good way."

"But it isn't your style," she said without looking at him. "You have to be free."

He scowled and looked down at her, but she wouldn't meet his eyes.

"Here, spread the seeds over there, would you?" she asked, indicating another feeder. "I forgot to put up a seed cake for them." She pulled it out of her pocket and took the wrapper off.

In the house, unseen, Jake Blair was watching them with wide, shocked eyes. He turned. "Come here," he told Rourke. "You're not going to believe this."

Rourke followed his gaze out the window and let out a hoot of laughter. "You're having me on," he chuckled. "That can't be Carson, feeding the birds!"

"Oh, yes, it can." He pursed his lips. "I wonder…"

"I wouldn't even think it. Not yet. He's got a lot to work

through before he's fit for any young woman, especially your daughter."

"Men can change. I did," Jake said quietly. "And in my day, I was a harder case than he is."

"You did change," Rourke agreed. "But you don't have the scars he's carrying."

"Tell me," Jake said.

Rourke shook his head and smiled sadly. "I won't do that. It's his story, his pain. He'll have to be the one to tell it."

Jake just nodded. He watched his daughter lead Carson around the yard, saw them laughing together as the birds came very close and they paused, very still, so that they came right up almost to their feet.

That jacket Carson wore was really gorgeous, he thought. Then he compared it to Carlie's old coat and he winced. He'd tried to give her all the necessities. He hadn't realized how difficult it was going to be, living on a minister's small salary in an equally small community. The days of big money were long gone. His conscience wouldn't let him go back to it. He did love his work, anyway.

He turned away from the window, leading Rourke back into his office.

CHAPTER ELEVEN

CARLIE WENT AHEAD of Carson into the house through the back door. Rourke and her father were just having coffee.

Jake held up the pot and raised his eyebrows.

"Please," Carson said. "I haven't had a cup this morning. Withdrawal symptoms are setting in," he added, deliberately making his hand shake.

The other men laughed.

"Breakfast?" Carlie asked, but she was looking at Carson. "I can make biscuits with scrambled eggs and sausage. Fresh sausage. One of our congregation brought it over yesterday."

"Sounds good to me, pumpkin," Jake said easily. "Make enough for everybody."

"You bet." She could almost float. It was one of the best days of her life so far. She had to make sure she didn't linger over Carson when she looked his way. She didn't want to embarrass him.

"Did you come over to help feed the local wildlife?" Rourke asked with a grin.

Carson chuckled. "No. I made a connection. Actually, I made it from something Lanette said. That whoever planned the kidnapping was sloppy, but that it must be somebody big. So I thought of the politician who's connected to the Cotillo drug cartel across the border."

"Why would he be after you, though?" Rourke asked Jake, frowning. "Have you had any contact with people who know things about the cartel?"

"None," Jake said. He sipped coffee and shook his head. "I have no idea at all why I've been targeted, or by whom." He smiled faintly. "Someone from the old life, possibly, after revenge. But if that's the case, they've waited a long time for it."

"I don't think it's that," Carson said quietly. "It just feels... I don't know, jagged."

The other two men stared at him.

"Jagged?" Rourke prompted.

"A man with a drug habit comes after Carlie, but tries to make it look like he was after you," Carson told Jake. "Now, a kidnapping attempt on Carlie to bring you into the line of fire so they could take you out. Why?"

"Jagged," Jake agreed. "Like someone jumped from one victim to another."

"It's just a thought," Carson continued, "but the man who hired the first assassin was on drugs."

"The man who died in the fire up in Wyoming, who was trying to kill Dalton Kirk for something he remembered," Rourke told Jake. "I mentioned it to you. The man, Richard Martin by name, was a former DEA agent, a mole who fed information to the drug cartel over in Cotillo. I'm pretty sure he hired the man who came after Carlie, to stop her from remembering what he looked like. With her photographic memory, she was giving out exact information about him. He didn't want that."

"Because he worked for Matthew Helm, a crooked politician who's just been named to the unexpired U.S. Senate seat in Texas," Carson concluded. "We know now why our computer expert Joey was killed and the computer was trashed, and why Carlie was targeted. You see, the killer had murdered an assistant D.A. in San Antonio who was investigating Helm for

embezzlement and drug trafficking. He had files that mysteriously disappeared. Every bit of the evidence that could have
been used against him is gone, and Lieutenant Rick Marquez
of San Antonio PD told Cash Grier that two witnesses in the
case have refused to testify. One just left the country, in fact."

"How convenient for Helm," Rourke commented.

"This is pretty big," Jake said, listening intently. "He didn't
want his link to Helm to get out, obviously, but why kill a computer tech and try to kill Carlie?"

"Because of the watch and the shirt," Rourke said.

"Excuse me?" Jake asked, wide-eyed.

"The assistant D.A.'s wife was loaded," Carson said. "She'd
just bought her husband a very expensive watch that played a
song and chimed on the hour. She also bought him an exclusive,
equally expensive, designer paisley shirt. Martin took a shine
to both, so he stole them. He didn't want anyone to remember
what he was wearing, because it linked his boss to the assistant D.A.'s murder."

Jake exchanged glances with his daughter. "You told me
about this."

"Yes," Carlie said. She was deep in thought.

"What happened to the watch and the shirt?" Jake asked
Carson.

"I assume whoever ransacked the room Richard Martin was
occupying at the local motel took both and destroyed them."
Rourke sighed. "It would be insane to keep something so dangerous."

"The watch played a song, but nobody ever told me which
song," Carlie said. She looked at Rourke.

He sang it, "I Love Rock 'n' Roll," and grinned because he
was totally off-key. "It was a Joan Jett song from—"

"That's it," Carly cried. "I thought I was just reacting to the
stuff he knocked me out with, so I didn't say anything. The
kidnapper was wearing a cheap suit, but he had this expensive

watch on his wrist. It was sort of like the one Calhoun Ballenger wears. You know, that Rolex."

"I know," Jake mused. "I told him once that he could feed a whole third-world country on the proceeds if he sold that thing. He just laughed and said it was two generations old and a family heirloom. He wouldn't sell it for the world." He glanced at Rourke. "He's going to run for that U.S. Senate seat against Helm. He told me yesterday. I ran into him in town."

"He'd be a wonderful senator," Carlie mused. "His brother Justin is dealing with the feedlot and the ranch anyway, since Calhoun's been a state senator for the past few years. He's done so much for our state..."

"He'll be a target, too," Jake said heavily.

"Yes," Carson said. "The other candidates for the temporary appointment ended up arrested on various drug charges. They swore the drugs were planted. I believe them."

"That politician needs to be taken down," Jake said shortly. "Once he has real power, he'll cause untold misery."

"I'm game," Rourke volunteered. "And since I'm officially his gofer, I have the inside track on what he's up to."

"You be careful," Jake told him.

"You know me," Rourke chuckled.

"I do. That's why I made the remark."

Carson was quiet. He was just remembering something. He didn't want to share it with the others. Lanette had excused herself at the theater the night Carlie had been kidnapped. It was a small, insignificant thing in itself and might be quite innocent. But Lanette hated Carlie. She wore expensive clothes, not the sort she could pay for on a meager salary working personnel for a company. A lot of things about her didn't quite add up.

"You're very quiet," Rourke prompted him.

"Sorry." He smiled faintly. "I was thinking about patterns." He glanced at Carlie. "The man who used the chloroform on you, he was wearing the watch?"

She nodded. "I thought I was hallucinating when it chimed. I mean, I've heard musical watches, but that was totally different."

"I'm reliably informed that the price of a new Jaguar convertible is in the same price range," Rourke commented wryly.

"The kidnapper is the connection," Carson said, frowning thoughtfully. "He can link Helm to the assistant D.A.'s murder."

"The watch by itself won't help a lot," Jake commented.

"Yes, but don't you see, the kidnapper has to be working for Matthew Helm. The fact that he has the watch connects him to Helm, through Helm's man, Richard Martin, who killed the assistant D.A.," Carson emphasized. "It's a pattern, a chain of evidence."

"You're right!" Rourke said, drawing in a breath. "I didn't make the connection."

Carson gazed at Carlie quietly, his eyes dark and concerned. "You don't leave the house without the phone in the console of the truck, and not until it's been checked for devices," he told her.

She just nodded.

Jake hid a smile.

"Promise me," Carson added, staring her down.

She grimaced. "Okay. I promise."

Carson's gaze turned to Jake and became amused. "I've learned already that if she gives her word, she'll keep it. You just have to make sure she gives it."

Jake ruffled Carlie's hair. "That's my girl, all right." Carlie grinned.

"One of us needs to go up to San Antonio and talk to Rick Marquez," Rourke said, getting out of his chair. "This is a development he'll enjoy pursuing."

"If he needs to talk to me, I'll go up there, too," Carlie said.

"Not in the Cobra, you won't."

Jake and Carson stared at each other. They'd both said exactly the same thing at the same time, and they burst out laughing.

"Okay, okay," Carlie muttered. "If you're ganging up on me,

I'll take the truck if I have to go. Just expect a call for help half-way there because my truck barely makes it to work every day. It won't make it to San Antonio without major engine failure!"

"I'll drive you," Jake told his daughter with a smile. "How's that?"

She grinned. "That's great, Dad."

"Carson, you're the best person to talk to Marquez," Rourke told the other man. "I can't be seen near anyone in law enforcement right now. You can ask if he needs a statement from Carlie," Rourke added. "But he lives in Jacobsville, you know. He could probably take a statement down here."

"I forgot. His mother is Barbara, who runs Barbara's Café," she told Carson, who looked puzzled.

"And his father-in-law runs the CIA," Jake added with a chuckle.

"Nice connections," Rourke said. He glanced at his watch. "I have to get back before Helm misses me. I'll be off, then."

"See you," Jake replied.

Rourke punched Carson on the shoulder and grinned as he walked out.

CARSON FINISHED HIS COFFEE. Carlie was clearing away break-fast. She glanced at Carson with her heart in her eyes. He looked at her as if she were a juicy steak and he was a starving man.

Jake turned his attention suddenly to Carson and jerked his head toward the office. Carson nodded.

"Breakfast was very good," Carson told her. "You have a way with food."

She smiled brightly. "Thanks!"

Carson followed her father into his study. "No calls for a few minutes, Carlie," Jake called before he shut the door. As an afterthought, he locked it.

Carson drew in a long breath as he studied the man across from him. Jake had been personable over breakfast, but at the moment he'd never looked less like a minister. His long, fit body was almost coiled. His pale blue eyes glittered with some inner fire.

"You're me, twenty-two years ago," Jake said without preamble. "And that child in there is my whole life. I'm seeing connections of my own," he added in a low tone. "I destroyed her mother. I'm not going to stand by and let you destroy her. She deserves better than a womanizing mercenary."

Carson sighed. He slid into a chair beside the desk where Jake sat down, and crossed his legs. "People are not what they seem to be," he began heavily. "You're thinking about the reputation I have with women. Carlie's already thrown it at me. It's why we argued the day I had to take her to the emergency room with the asthma attack."

"I thought as much," Jake replied.

"Six years ago," Carson began, "I was in the last two years of graduate school when I fell in love with a brash, outgoing, beautiful girl at a powwow on the reservation in South Dakota where I grew up. Her name was Jessica and I'd known her for years. I loved her insanely, so she married me. The first year was perfect. I thought it would never end. But my last year in college, she got tired of having me away so much at school. She took a lover. He was one of the most militant men on the reservation," he continued, his eyes cold and haunted. "He had a rap sheet, and the rez police knew him on sight. I tried to get her to come home, but she said she loved him, she wasn't coming back to a boring life as the wife of a college student. She didn't think much of higher education in the first place. So I let her go."

He shifted in the chair. "But I wouldn't give her a divorce. I knew he was beating her. I heard it from my cousins. I talked to her on the phone, and tried to get her to press charges. She said he didn't mean it, he loved her, he'd never do it again." He met Jake's world-weary eyes. "My father gave my mother the same spiel after he beat her up, over and over again," he said coldly. "I was six years old when he hit her too hard and ran. He was prosecuted for murder and ended up in the same prison with one of my mother's brothers. He died not long after that. My uncle had nothing to lose, you see, and he loved my mother."

Jake's face was relaxing, just a little. He didn't interrupt.

"I went to live with cousins. One of my uncles, a rez cop, adopted me as his son since he had no children of his own. I was given all the necessities, but there's no substitute for loving, real parents. I missed my mother." He paused, took a breath and plowed ahead. "Jessie was pregnant and near her due date. She was living with her lover and she swore the child was his. But I had a visitor who knew one of my cousins. He said it was my child, that Jessie lied about it because she didn't want me to drag her into court for paternity tests."

He leaned forward, his eyes downcast. "I finished my last final and flew back to the rez to see her. She was alone at her house. She was afraid of me." He laughed coldly. "She said okay, it was my child, and I could see it when it was born, but she was staying with Jeff no matter what I did. I was about to tell her I'd let her get the divorce, when Jeff drove up. He stormed into the house and accused her of two-timing him. I tried to restrain him, but he blindsided me. While I was getting back up, he dragged Jessie out the door with him. I managed to get outside in time to watch him throw her into the passenger seat. She was screaming. She thought he was going to kill her. So did I."

Jake's pale eyes were riveted to him.

"So I got in my car and went after them. He saw me in the rearview mirror, I guess, because he sped up and started weaving all over the road. I didn't have a cell phone with me or I'd have called the police on the rez and had them pick him up. I followed them around the dirt roads. He started across a bridge that had been condemned. There were spring floods, huge ones, water coming right up over the wooden bridge."

He closed his eyes. "He went through the rotten boards on the side and right into the river. The car, with both of them inside, washed away." He lifted his head. His eyes were cold, dead. "They found the bodies almost two days later. The child was almost full-term, but they couldn't save him." He closed his eyes. "I graduated, joined the military, asked for combat because I wanted to die. That was almost eight years ago."

He felt a hand on his shoulder. He opened his eyes and looked into pale blue ones. "Listen, son," Jake said quietly, "you were trying to save her. In the process, a madman miscalculated his driving skills and wrecked his car. If it hadn't been that, he might have shot her and then shot himself. He might have died in a fight. She might have died from complications of child-birth. But, it would still have happened. When a life is meant to be over, it's over. That's God's business. You can't control life, Carson," he concluded. "It's a fool's game to think you can even try. You're tormenting yourself over something that no-body could have prevented."

Carson averted his eyes. "Thanks," he said huskily.

"How did you end up with Cy?"

His eyes had a faraway look as he recalled that meeting. "I was doing black ops overseas," Carson said. "Political assas-sination, like Grier used to do." He drew in a long breath. "Cy and Eb Scott and Micah Steele were attached to the unit I was with as independent contractors. We went on missions together, discovered that we worked very well as a group. So I mustered out and signed on with them. It's been...interesting," he con-cluded with a mild laugh.

"I worked with mercs a time or two," Jake replied. He hesi-tated. "I also worked in covert assassination."

"I heard some gossip about that," Carson replied, without blowing the whistle on Rourke.

"She can't ever know," he said, nodding toward the other part of the house where Carlie was. "I gave it up for her. I had a crisis of conscience when her mother died. It took me to a bad place. A minister gave me the strength I needed to turn my life around, to do something productive with it." He leaned back with a sigh and a smile. "Of course, I'll starve doing it," he chuckled. "We're always broke, and there's always somebody who wants me fired because I say something offensive in a sermon. But I belong here now. Odd feeling, belonging. I never wanted it in the old days."

"Your wife," Carson said hesitantly. "Was she like Carlie?"

Jake's eyes narrowed with sorrow. "Exactly like Carlie. I didn't believe in a damned thing. I had no faith, no understanding of how people lived in small towns. I wanted her. I took her. She got pregnant." His face was like stone. "I married her to stop gossip. Her mother was a slut. I mean, a real slut. She even tried to seduce me! So everybody locally would have said, 'like mother like daughter,' you know?" He leaned forward on his forearms. "I refused to stay here and be a tamed animal. I provided for her and the child when Carlie was born. I gave them everything except love. It wasn't until Mary was dying that I realized how much I had loved her, how much I had cost her with my indifference. You think you killed your wife? I know I killed mine. I've been trying ever since to find a way to live with it, to make up for some of the terrible things I've done. I'm still trying."

Carson was speechless. He just stared at the older man, with honest compassion.

"If you're wondering," Jake added softly, "this is a moral tale. I'm telling you about what happened to me so that you won't repeat it with my daughter. I think you have some idea of her feelings already."

Carson nodded solemnly. "I don't want to hurt her."

"That makes two of us. You've lived the way I used to. Women were like party favors to me, and I had my share…"

Carson held up a hand. "Slight misconception."

"About…?"

Carson let out a breath and laughed softly. "I pick up women. Beautiful women. I take them to the theater, the opera, out dancing, sailing on the lake, that sort of thing." He hesitated. "Then I take them home and leave them at the door," he said with a rueful smile.

Jake's confusion was evident.

"My wife was my first woman," Carson said with blunt honesty. "After she died, every woman I took out had her face, her body. I…couldn't," he choked out.

Jake put a firm hand on his shoulder, the only comfort he could offer.

"So other guys think I score every night, that I'm Don Juan." Carson laughed coolly. "I'm a counterfeit one. It makes me look heartless, so that honest women won't waste their time on me. But it backfired." He jerked his head toward the kitchen. "She thinks I'm dirty, because of my reputation. Funny thing, a visionary woman up in Wyoming told me that my past would threaten my future. She was very wise."

"Some obstacles can be overcome," Jake commented.

"So, you want me to go out and involve myself intimately with women…?"

"Shut up, or I'll put you down," Jake said in a mock growl. He laughed. "I could do it, too."

"I believe you," Carson said, with true admiration. "You haven't lost your edge."

"Where do you go from here?" Jake continued.

"When we wrap up this mess with Carlie's kidnapper, I don't know," Carson said honestly. "If I stay here, things will happen that will destroy her life, and maybe mine, too. I have to leave."

"For now, or for good?" Jake asked.

Carson drew in a breath. "I…don't know."

"If you graduated, then you got a degree, I take it?" Jake asked.

Carson pursed his lips. "Yes."

"You couldn't go into a normal profession?"

"It would mean a commitment I'm not sure I can make. I need time."

"Most life-changing decisions require it," Jake agreed. "What degree program were you pursuing?"

Carson smiled. "Medicine. I have my medical degree and I

keep up my license. I just can't practice without doing the internship." He sighed. "I was going to specialize in internal medicine. I see so many heart patients with no resources, no money."

"On the reservation, you mean?"

"No. Here, in Jacobs County. I was talking to Lou Coltrain. She said they're short on physicians, not to mention physicians who specialize."

Jake searched the other man's face. He jerked his head toward the kitchen. "Going to tell her?"

Carson shook his head. "Not until I'm sure."

Jake smiled. "I knew I liked you."

Carson just laughed.

CARLIE WALKED HIM to the door. "Was Dad intimidating you?" she asked when they were outside on the front porch, with the door closed.

"No. He was listening. That's such a rare gift. Most people want to talk about themselves."

She nodded. "He's talked several people out of suicide over the years."

"He's a good man."

"He wasn't always," she replied. "I've heard a little about his old life, although he won't tell me a thing himself." She looked up at him with raised eyebrows.

"It would be the end of my life to say a single word about it," he said firmly.

"Okay," she said, sighing.

He tilted her chin up and searched her green eyes. "What color were your mother's eyes?" he asked.

"They were brown," she said. "Like the center of a sunflower."

He traced her mouth with a long forefinger. "You're very like a sunflower yourself," he said softly. "Bright and cheerful, shining through storms."

Her lips parted on a surprised breath.

"I'm leaving, Carlie," he said softly.

She started to speak, but he put his fingers across her lips.

"You know how it is between us," he said bluntly. "I want you. If I stay here, I'll take you. And you'll let me," he said huskily.

She couldn't deny it.

"We'll be like your parents, one brokenhearted, one running away until tragedy strikes. I don't want to be the cause of that."

Her hand went up to his hard cheek. She stroked it gently, fighting tears. "You can't live a tame life. I understand."

It sounded harsh. Selfish. He scowled at the look on her face, dignity and courage mixed with heartbreak. It hurt him.

He drew her into his arms and held her, rocked her, in a tight embrace. "It wouldn't work. You know that."

She nodded against his chest.

He drew back finally and tilted her face up to his. It was streaked with hot tears that she couldn't help. He bent and kissed them away.

"I'll be around for a while," he promised. "Until we make sure we have the kidnapper in custody."

"Can they catch him, you think?"

"I believe so," he replied. "Just be careful."

She smiled. "I usually am."

"And if someone shows up and says your dad's been in a wreck…" he began.

She pulled her cell phone out of her jeans. "I'll call him up first."

He grinned. "That's my girl." He bent and brushed his mouth softly over hers, savoring the smile she couldn't help.

He left her on the porch and drove away. She stood there until she couldn't see the car anymore.

ROURKE HAD FINALLY convinced Matthew Helm that it was safe to trust him. He did a few discreet jobs—mostly by warning the people he was supposed to muscle first, and having them cooperate—and was finally handed something useful. Useful for the case against Helm, at least.

"I want you to go talk to Charro," Helm told Rourke. He pursed his lips, deep in thought. "That Ballenger man who's running against me has a following. He's local. People know him and like him. He's got three sons. One of them, Terry, is still in high school. I want you two to find a way to plant some cocaine on him. Put it in his locker at school, in his car and tip off the cops, whatever. I don't care what you do, just make sure you do it. I'll handle the press. I'll have one of my campaign workers release the collar, to make sure it doesn't come directly from me and seem like I'm slinging mud. Got it?"

"Oh, yeah, Boss, I got it," Rourke said with a nod.

"Get going, then."

"You bet."

Rourke was too old a hand to go straight to Calhoun Ballenger or even to Cash Grier's office, much less up to San Antonio to see Rick Marquez. He wasn't trusting his cell phone, either, because Helm could very easily find out who he'd talked to recently.

So he went to Cotillo.

Charro Mendez gave him a careful scrutiny. "So Helm trusts you, does he?" he asked.

"He doesn't really trust anybody," Rourke replied. "Neither do I," he added, hands in his jeans pockets. "It doesn't pay, in this line of work. But he trusts me enough to relay messages, I believe."

"And what message does he wish you to bring me?" Mendez asked, propping his booted feet on his own desk in the mayor's office.

"He wants some product planted in a particular place," he replied, leaning back against the wall.

"Ah. Something to do with a rival in the political arena, *si?*"

"Exactly."

"This is not a problem. Who does he expect to perform this task, *señor*, you or me?"

"He didn't say," Rourke replied. "He told me you'd supply the product. I assume that means I'll have to plant it."

"I see." The man grinned, displaying gold-filled teeth. "I would assume that he would not expect a man in my position to perform such a menial chore, however."

"Exactly," Rourke said, nodding.

"Excellent! I will have the…product," he said, "delivered to you across the border. When?"

"He didn't tell me that, either. But it would be convenient to do two Saturdays from now," Rourke continued. "There's going to be a dance at the high school. I can sneak it into the glove compartment of the boy's vehicle while he's inside the building."

"I could almost feel sorry for his father. I also have sons." His face darkened. "I would kill someone who did that to me. But these rich men in Texas—" he waved a hand "—they can buy justice. I have no doubt the politician can have the charges dropped. The publicity, however, will be very damaging, I think."

"I agree."

"Give me a cell phone number where my man can reach you," Charro said.

Rourke handed him a slip of paper. "It's a throwaway phone," he told the other man. "I'll answer it this once and then toss it in a trash bin somewhere. It will never be found or traced to me."

"A wise precaution."

"I try to be wise, always," Rourke replied.

"Then we agree. I will have my man contact you within the week."

"I'm certain my boss will express his appreciation for your help."

"Indeed he will," Charro returned thoughtfully. "Many, many

times, whenever I ask." He smiled coldly. "I will have him, how do you say? Over a barrel."

"A big one," Rourke chuckled.

"Very big. Yes."

CHAPTER TWELVE

ROURKE COULDN'T RISK being seen with any law enforcement official, or overheard talking to one, not with things at this critical juncture. He called Carson.

"Have you been to see Marquez yet?" he asked quickly.

"Well, no," Carson replied. "Something came up over at Cy's ranch…"

"This is urgent. I want you to go see Marquez right now. I've got some news."

So Carson drove up to San Antonio to relay the information Rourke had transferred over to another throwaway phone, a pair he and Carson had arranged at an earlier time.

Rick Marquez did a double take when he saw Carson. The other man was almost his age, with the same olive complexion and long, black hair in a ponytail.

"Lieutenant Marquez?" Carson greeted the other man when the clerk showed him in.

"That would be me. Amazing," Rick mused. "We could almost be twins."

Carson smiled faintly. "Only if you turned out to be from South Dakota."

He shrugged. "Sorry. Mexico. Well, that's where my father

was born. He's now president of a small Latin American nation. Sit down." He offered his visitor a chair.

"I assume you have regular checks for bugs in here?" Carson asked, glancing around.

"My father-in-law runs the CIA," Rick told him as he dropped into his aging desk chair. "He might bug us, but nobody else would dare. What can I do for you?"

"There have been some new developments that you might not have heard about," Carson began.

"Jake Blair's daughter was kidnapped, you and her father freed her and took out two guards, the kidnapper got away," Rick rattled off. "I know everything."

"Not quite," Carson replied. He pursed his lips. "How about coffee?"

"We've got a pot right over there…"

Carson shook his head. "Real coffee. Come on."

Rick was puzzled, but he caught on pretty quickly that Carson didn't trust telling him in the office.

They drove to a specialty coffee shop and moved to a corner table.

"Sorry, I know you think it's secure in your office, but this information could get Rourke killed if it slips out somehow. He's working for Matthew Helm and there's a plot underway. But let me tell you this first. Carlie Blair's kidnapper was wearing a watch. An expensive watch that chimed an old Joan Jett rock tune—"

"You're kidding!" Rick exploded. "We thought the watch burned up with the man who was wearing it, in Wyoming!"

"No," Carson replied. "I was there when he died. There was no watch on him. The local police were trying to backtrack him to any motels he'd stayed at. I assume his boss's men got to the room first."

"What a stroke of luck," Rick said with a short laugh. "That watch, if we can get our hands on it, is the key to a murder and perhaps the end of a truly evil political career."

"The problem is that we don't know where the watch is. The kidnapper has vanished into thin air."

"We have to find him."

"I agree. Rourke's working on it. He's wormed his way into the political process. That's why I'm here."

"Okay. Shoot."

"Helm sent Rourke over the border today to arrange for the delivery of some cocaine. Enough to charge someone with intent to distribute. The idea is for Rourke to plant it in the glove compartment of Calhoun Ballenger's youngest son, Terry, at a school dance in two weeks."

Rick's face hardened. "What a low-down, dirty, mean..."

"All of the above," Carson agreed grimly. "But we know it's going down, and when, and where. Believe me, this is going to send Helm up the river. All we have to do is set a trap and spring it."

"Why isn't Rourke here?" Rick asked.

"Because he's being watched, and probably listened to, as well. We used throwaway phones to communicate, just to exchange this much information."

"And you think my own office isn't secure?" Rick sounded a little belligerent.

"This man has ex-cops working for him," Carson explained. "They'll know all the tricks. It isn't far-fetched to assume he has a pipeline into your office. The missing evidence the assistant D.A. had on Helm, for example, that was destroyed right here in impound?"

Rick let out a heavy sigh. "I get your point. I've been careless."

"Don't sell yourself short. Helm has some pros on his team. His main enforcer is gone, but he's got others. One is an ex-cop who got fired for using excessive violence. Carlie's kidnapper. He knocked a perp down the stairs when he caught him beating a child."

"Know where?" Rick asked suddenly.

"Carlie said the kidnapper had an accent, like you hear in those old gangster movies of the '30s and '40s."

"Chicago, maybe, New Jersey, New York..." Rick's eyes were thoughtful. "I can send out some feelers to people I know in departments there, ask around. Some of the veterans might remember something."

"Good idea. Meanwhile, Rourke's on the job."

"Should we warn Calhoun Ballenger?" Rick wondered aloud.

"If he knows, he'll warn his son, and his son might mention it to a classmate," Carson replied. "It's better to keep him in the dark. We'll make sure his son is watched and protected."

"Don't toss any hand grenades around," Rick warned.

Carson sighed as he stood up. "My past will haunt me."

"Actually, if it was up to me, you'd get a medal," Rick said. "So many dead kids because rich men want to make a profit off illegal drugs." He shook his head. "Crazy world."

"Getting crazier all the time."

"Thanks for the heads-up," Rick said, shaking hands with the other man. "By the way," he added, "nice hairstyle." He grinned. Carson grinned back.

FRED BALDWIN WAS WORRIED. Mr. Helm had promised that he was going to protect him, that he was in no danger of getting arrested for kidnapping Carlie Blair. But he knew from painful experience that Mr. Helm didn't keep many of the promises he made. That was, unless he promised to get you for crossing him. He kept all those promises.

He fingered the expensive watch that he still had, that Mr. Helm didn't know about. He knew why the watch was important. It had belonged to Richard Martin, who burned up in Wyoming after trying to kill two women. He'd killed an assistant prosecutor for that watch. But Martin was dead. And Fred had the watch.

Mr. Helm didn't know that he hadn't destroyed it. He liked the watch. That chime it sounded wasn't a song he knew, but it was okay. It was the two-tone gold on the timepiece, very expensive, and that made him feel good. His father had been a low-level worker at an automobile plant in Detroit. His mother had kept a day care in their home. There were four kids and never enough money. His father drank it up as fast as he got paid.

Two of his brothers were in jail. His oldest brother had died last year. His mother had finally left his father, and went to live with a sister in California. He hadn't heard from her in a long time. She'd loved her oldest child best, the one who died. She hadn't wanted the others. She thought they were too stupid to be her kids. She said so, often.

The only time she'd liked Fred was when he became a policeman. Finally, one of her kids besides her favorite might actually amount to something.

Then he got arrested and fired and she turned her back on him. Well, it was no surprise.

Fred didn't like women much. His mother was cold as ice, heartless. Maybe his father had made her that way. Maybe she was that way to begin with.

He liked that little woman he'd kidnapped, though. She should have hated him. He'd terrified her. But she'd been sorry for him when he told her about his father beating him up. He felt bad that he'd scared her. He was glad to know she'd escaped, that her father hadn't been killed.

Luckily for him, the two would-be assassins got blamed for the screwup. Mr. Helm hadn't hired them in person, so he wouldn't be connected with them.

On the other hand, Fred had hired them for the person who was contracted by Richard Martin to kill Reverend Blair, on Mr. Helm's orders. If they talked, Fred was going to be the one who'd go to prison.

Well, that little woman knew what he looked like, and he had no reason to believe she wouldn't have told the law about him. He knew from something Mr. Helm had let slip once that Carlie Blair had a photographic memory. Mr. Helm said not to worry about it, that he'd make sure Fred was okay. But Fred had seen what had happened to the man Richard Martin had hired to kill Carlie Blair, the same woman he'd kidnapped. Martin had poisoned the would-be killer, right under the cops' noses, and apparently on Mr. Helm's orders.

Funny, that he'd been ordered to kidnap Carlie, when Richard Martin had been ordered to hire somebody to kill her. Not only that, when the first killer failed, Martin had hired someone else to finish the job. But the person he was taking orders from had sent him to kidnap Carlie to draw the reverend out to be killed.

Why did Mr. Helm want the preacher dead? As far as Fred knew, the preacher didn't have anything on Mr. Helm at all. And what Carlie knew didn't matter before, because she remembered Richard Martin and he was dead.

She'd remember Fred now, though. That would be a motive. But they were trying to kill her father!

Well, his opinion was that Richard Martin had been so high on drugs that he hadn't made it clear who was supposed to be the victim. And his hire, to put it politely, was as crazy a person as Fred had ever met. He'd been sent to kidnap Carlie on that person's orders, to strike at a time when she was unprotected at her home. He shook his head. It was nuts. Worse, he was the one who was being set up to take the fall.

He looked at the watch again. He'd never been tempted to talk about it. But after what he'd just overheard Mr. Helm say to his new enforcer, that South African guy, he had to do something. The South African man was going to plant drugs on the son of a politician who was the only serious contender for the U.S. Senate seat. If the man had been a stranger, he might not have cared. But Fred knew Calhoun Ballenger.

He'd seen the cattleman a few months ago, coming out of a downtown hotel where some cattlemen's conference was being held. Two men were waiting in the shadows. One of them was armed. When Mr. Ballenger started down the street, they jumped him.

He was a big man, and he handled himself well, but the man with the gun struck him in the head.

Fred didn't like bullies. He'd never been one, for all his size, and he hated seeing anybody pick on an unarmed man. It was why he'd become a cop in the first place years ago. So without really thinking about it, he jumped in, subdued the man with the pistol and knocked out his accomplice.

He'd left them in the alley and dropped a dime on them while he took Mr. Ballenger down the street to the emergency room of a local hospital.

He didn't dare tell the cattleman who he was, but Mr. Ballenger had wanted to do something for him, to pay him back for the kindness. He'd looked at Fred with admiration, with respect. Those were things sadly lacking in his life. It had made him feel good about himself for the first time in years. He'd waved away the older man's thanks and left the hospital without identifying himself.

Mr. Ballenger's son was going to be targeted by Matthew Helm, and Fred didn't want to be any part of it. But how was he going to warn the man without incriminating himself and his boss? Mr. Helm would turn on him, make sure he went to prison for the kidnapping if he lifted a finger.

He couldn't go to the law, as much as he'd have liked to. But there was one other possibility. This watch was important. The right people could do good things with it. And suddenly, right in front of him, was the very girl he'd kidnapped...

CARLIE WAS PUTTING her groceries into the back of the pickup truck when she came face-to-face with the man who'd kidnapped her.

"Don't scream," Fred said gruffly, but he didn't threaten her. He was wearing a raincoat and a hat, looking around cautiously. "You got to help me."

"Help you? You kidnapped me!" she blurted out.

"Yeah, I'm sorry," he said heavily. "I got in over my head and

I can't get out. I can't go to the law. They're always watching.
Mr. Helm is going to plant drugs on Mr. Ballenger's youngest
son," he said hastily, peering over the truck bed to make sure
nobody was nearby. "He's going to try to get him out of that
Senate race."

"Terry?" she exclaimed. "He's going to try to set Terry Ballenger up?"

"Yeah. That South African guy who works for him, he's
going to plant the evidence," he said quickly. "You got to tell
your boss."

She was absolutely dumbfounded. She couldn't even find
words. He didn't know that Rourke was working with the authorities and she didn't dare tell him. But he was risking his
very life to try and save Calhoun's son from prosecution. It really touched her.

His dark eyes narrowed. "I'm so sorry for what I done," he
said, grimacing. "You're a nice girl."

Her face softened. "Why do you work for that rat?" she wondered.

"He's got stuff on me," he explained. "I can't ever get another job. But I can help you." He took off the watch, looked at
it admiringly for just a few seconds and grimaced. "Never had
nothing so fancy in my whole life," he said, putting it in her
hands. "He told me to bust it up and throw it away. I couldn't.
It was so special. Anyway, that watch belonged to some prosecutor that had evidence on Mr. Helm. Richard Martin killed
him. It was his watch. Martin took the watch and then killed
people who remembered he had it."

"He tried to have me killed," she told him.

"Yeah, and then he hired somebody to kill your dad." He
shook his head. "See, Martin was high on drugs, out of his
mind. I think he got confused, gave the contract out on the
wrong person. I think it was supposed to be you, again, but we
got sent after your dad."

"You know who's behind it," she said, surprised.

He nodded solemnly. "Mr. Helm's behind it. But the contract was given out by Martin."

"Who's got it?" Carlie asked. "Please?"

He searched her eyes. "Some pretty blond woman up in San Antonio. I didn't know until a day ago. Funny, she didn't even know about my connection to Mr. Helm. She asked around for some muscle to help with a hit, and the other guys got hired. One of them was a man I knew, he said I could do it on the side and Mr. Helm would never have to know." He laughed coldly. "Well, Mr. Helm knew already. He just didn't tell us."

"Blond woman…?"

"Yeah. She used to work for Mr. Helm, years ago, when he started out in the local rackets."

Blond woman. Hit woman. Contract killer. Somebody who knew that Carlie would be home alone on that Friday night. Somebody with ties to Jacobsville.

"Do you know her name?" Carlie asked.

He frowned. "Funny name. La… La…something."

Carlie's blood froze. "Lanette?"

"Yeah. That's it. How'd you know?"

Now wasn't the time to fill him in on personal information. But it meant that Carson could be in real danger if Lanette suspected that he might blow her cover. She'd be in jeopardy if her link to the kidnapper here was ever found out.

She slid the watch into her pocket, gnawed her lower lip. She looked up into his broad, swarthy face. "They'll kill you if they find out you gave me the watch."

His dark eyes were quiet and sad. "I don't care," he said. "I never done anything good in my whole life except for being a cop, and I even fouled that up. You were nice to me." He forced a smile. "Nobody ever liked me."

She put a small hand on his arm. "How do you feel about small towns?"

He frowned. "What do you mean?"

"You have to trust me," she said quickly.

"Why?"

"Because I'm going to do something that will seem crazy."

"Really? What?"

She threw back her head and screamed.

"JUST RELAX," CASH GRIER told his prisoner under his breath. "This isn't what it seems. You may think she sold you out, but we're trying to save you. Your boss will think you're being arrested for assault."

Fred Baldwin went along, stunned but willing to cooperate on the off chance that he might not have to spend his whole life in federal prison. "Okay, Boss," he said. "It's your play."

Cash marched him out to the police car, put Carlie in front beside him, and left a patrolman to take her truck home and explain things to her father.

ONCE THEY WERE in the police station, Cash took Fred into his office and removed the handcuffs. He put Fred's automatic in his desk drawer and locked it. Carlie produced the watch out of her pocket.

"And I've got you filing," Cash said, shaking his head at her. "You should be wearing a badge, kid."

"No, no," she protested. "He—" she pointed at Fred "—just turned state's evidence. So to speak. He can make the connections. But we have to get word to Carson," she added quickly. "His girlfriend is the woman who hired Fred and the other two guys to kidnap me and kill my dad."

"Why did you give Carlie the watch?" Cash asked Fred. "You had everything to lose!"

"She was nice to me," he murmured, glancing at Carlie. "They tried to kill her dad, with my help. And now they're trying to frame Mr. Ballenger's son. I took down two hoods who jumped him in San Antonio. Never seen a rich man so grateful for just a little help. I liked him. It's not right, to punish a man's son because the father's just doing something good for the community. I got tired of being on the wrong side of the law, I guess. I thought if I gave her the watch, she'd give it to you and maybe you could stop Mr. Helm before he hurts somebody else."

"I'll stop it, all right," Cash said. He frowned. "But it's suicide on your part. You think Helm wouldn't know who gave us the watch?"

Fred smiled sadly. "I ain't got no place to go, nobody who cares about me. I thought, maybe I could do one good thing before he took me out."

"You're not going anywhere," Cash told him firmly.

"And you do have somebody who cares about you," Carlie said firmly. She took the big man's hand in her own and held it. "Right here."

Incredibly, tears ran down his wide cheeks.

"Now, don't do that, you'll have me doing it, too," Carlie muttered. She pulled a tissue out of her pocket and wiped his eyes and then wiped her own.

"I'm Italian," Fred muttered, embarrassed. "We don't hide what we feel."

"You'd better let me get this on paper," Cash said, smiling. "Coffee?"

"Thanks."

"I'll make a pot," Carlie said. She glanced at Cash. "Carson..." she began.

"I'm two steps ahead of you," Cash promised, picking up the telephone.

CARSON HAD HIS phone turned off, which was a pity. Lanette had already heard from an informant that Fred Baldwin was in custody down in Jacobsville, Texas, for apparently confronting that pitiful little secretary that Carson was so crazy about.

She was livid. Fred was stupid. It was why she'd hired him, because he was expendable and too dumb to realize she was setting him up to take the fall for her when she killed Jake Blair.

But somewhere along the line, he'd had a flash of genius. He was probably spilling his guts. They'd be after her in a heart-beat. That little secretary would be gloating, laughing, feeling so superior to the beautiful woman who was obviously her su-perior in every single department.

Fred had flubbed his assignment. His cohorts were in jail. Now he'd been arrested, too. She'd been paid for a job that she hadn't completed. Word would get around that she was incom-petent. She'd never get another contract. Worse, Fred would implicate her to save himself. She'd be running from the law for the rest of her life. The perks of her profession, all that nice money, her spectacular wardrobe, everything would be lost be-cause her own plan had backfired on her.

Even Matthew Helm had refused to help her. Oh, he made promises, but his back was to the wall right now, and he was trying to save his own skin. He had to know that Fred would rat on him.

Well, she reasoned, at least she was going to have one bit of satisfaction on the run. That stupid little hick in Jacobsville wasn't going to get to gloat. Her feelings for Carson were so apparent that a blind woman could see them. Carlie loved Car-son. So Lanette would go to prison for kidnapping and assault and conspiracy, and little Carlie would end up with Carson.

No way. If she lost Carson, for whom she had a real unre-quited passion, Carlie wasn't going to have him. She'd make sure of it.

She reached into the purse she carried to make sure the au-tomatic was where it was supposed to be.

"I can't stay long," she told Carson, who was impatient to be gone and seemed surprised and irritated to have found her at his apartment door when he arrived.

"Just as well," he said curtly, "because I have someplace to go and I'm already late."

"Couldn't we have just one cup of coffee first?" she asked, smiling softly. "I found out something about that attempt on the preacher."

"You did? How?" he asked, instantly suspicious.

"Well, let's just sit down and talk, and I'll tell you what I know," she purred.

CASH PHONED ROURKE, using the number Rourke had sent him. "Carson's in danger," he told the other man. "His blond girlfriend is the contract killer Richard Martin hired to take out Reverend Blair."

"What!" Rourke exploded.

"I don't have time to go into the particulars," Cash said. "Suffice it to say I have a witness," he glanced at Fred, who was smiling as Carlie handed him a mug of black coffee, "and no time to discuss it. Do you know where he is?"

"At the apartment he rented," Rourke said, shell-shocked. "In San Antonio."

"Can you get in touch with him?"

Rourke let out a breath. "No. Not unless I do it in the open."

"Rourke will have to blow his cover to call Carson, they're monitoring his phone," Cash said aloud.

"I'll do it," Carlie said urgently. "Give me the number."

"Rourke, give me the number," Cash said.

He did. Cash scribbled it down and handed it to Carlie.

"What's this written in, Sanskrit?" she exclaimed.

Cash glared at her, took it back and made modifications. "It's just numbers, for God's sake," he said irritably.

"Sir, your handwriting is hands-down, without a doubt, the worst I ever saw in my life," she muttered as she pushed numbers into her cell phone.

"Hear, hear!" Rourke said over the phone. "I have to go. I'll let you know about Ballenger's son as soon as I have word." He hung up.

Carlie held her breath as the phone rang once, twice, three times...

"Hello?"

Carlie recognized the voice. It wasn't Carson's. It was hers. Lanette's.

She swallowed, hard. "I want to speak to Carson," she said.

"Oh, do you? I'm sorry," Lanette said in a silky sweet tone. "I'm afraid he's indisposed at the moment. Really indisposed." She laughed out loud. "I can't have him. But, now, neither can you, you little backward country hick! And you can spend hours, days, just watching him die!" She cut off the connection.

"She's with him," Carlie said with an economy of words. "You have to get someone to him, quick!"

Cash was already punching in numbers.

While her boss worked to get a medical team to Carson, Carlie hovered, tears running down her cheeks.

"You sit down," Fred said softly. "They'll get there in time. It will be all right. Everything will be all right."

She just looked at him, her face that of a terrified child. It hit him in the heart so hard that he let out a breath, as if it had been a blow to his stomach.

He put down his coffee, got up, picked her up and sat down with her in his lap, wrapped up in his big arms, sobbing her heart out on his broad shoulder. He patted her back as if she were five years old, smiling. "It's okay, honey," he said softly. "It's okay."

Cash watched them and mentally shook his head. What a waste. That man had a heart as big as the world, and he was going to take the fall for that crooked politician unless Cash could find him a way out. That might just be possible. But first he had to save Carson. And that mission had a less hopeful outcome.

THE PARAMEDICS HAD to wait while San Antonio PD broke down a door to get inside, on Lieutenant Marquez's orders. Once the way was clear, they rushed in with a gurney. They found Carson in the kitchen, facedown on the floor. He was unconscious and bleeding from a wound in his chest. There was a lump on his head, as well.

One paramedic looked at the other and winced. This was not going to be an easy run. He keyed his mike and started relaying medical information. It was complicated by the fact that the victim apparently had no ID on him.

BECAUSE FRED BALDWIN could make all the right connections to Matthew Helm, and because they knew about the fate of the former failed hit man, Cash Grier refused to turn him over to the authorities in San Antonio, where Helm would have to be arrested and tried.

"You'll get him over my dead body," Cash assured Rick Marquez on the telephone. "I'm not risking his life. He's too valuable. You come down here and take a deposition, bring all the suits you need and add your district attorney to the list. I'll give you free access. But he is not, under any circumstances, leaving Jacobsville!"

Rick drew in a breath. "Cash, you're putting me in a tough spot."

"No, I'm not. My cousin is still the state attorney general. He'll pull some strings for me if I ask him," Cash added. "Besides that," he said with a whimsical smile, "I have a few important connections that I don't talk about."

"You and my father-in-law would get along," Marquez chuckled. "All right. I'll get the process started. But I'm going to need that watch."

"No way in hell," Cash said pleasantly.

"It's state's evidence!"

"Yes, it is. And evidence doesn't walk out of *my* property room," he added, emphasizing the "my."

"Rub it in," Rick muttered. "Carson already did, in fact." He sobered. "They have him in intensive care."

"I know. My secretary is up there with him. Or as close as she can get," Cash said heavily.

"So I heard. She's parked in the corridor next to the emergency room surgical suite and won't move."

"Stubborn."

"Yes, and very much in love, apparently," Rick replied solemnly. "It won't end well. I know the type, and so do you. Even if he makes it out of the hospital, he'll never settle down."

"Are you a betting man?" Cash mused.

"Why?"

"Because several years ago, you'd have laid better odds that I'd never marry and live in a small Texas town. Wouldn't you?"

Rick laughed. "Point taken." He hesitated. "Well, can we at least see the watch and photograph it?"

"Mi casa es su casa," Cash said smugly. "My house is your house."

"I'll bring an SUV full of people down. May I assume that the state crime lab has already dusted the watch for prints?"

"Our own Alice Jones Fowler did the job herself. She does still work as an investigator for state crime," Cash reminded him, "although she lives here with her husband, Harley, on their ranch. She's not only good, she's unforgettable."

"Nobody who ever met Alice would forget her," Rick agreed. "She even makes autopsies bearable."

"No argument there. Anyway, the watch is adequately documented, even for a rabid prosecutor. And you're going to need the best you've got for Helm," he added quietly. "The man is a maniac, and I don't mean that kindly. He'll sacrifice anybody to save himself. Even assistant district attorneys."

"You don't know how much I'd love to tie him to that murder," Rick said. "The watch is the key to it all. Good luck for us that it wasn't destroyed."

"Even better luck that the man wearing it decided to also turn state's evidence. He can put Helm away for life."

"You've got him in the county jail, I hope?"

Cash hesitated. "Someplace a little safer."

"Safer than the lockup?" Rick burst out laughing. "What, is he living with you and Tippy and Tris?"

"Let's just say that he's got unique company. I'll give you access with the D.A. when you get down here."

"This is going to be an interesting trip," Rick predicted. "See you soon."

"Copy that."

THE HOSPITAL WAS very clean. Carlie noted that the floors must be mopped frequently, because when she got up to use the ladies' room, the back of her jeans didn't even have dust. She knew she was irritating the staff. Security had talked to her once. But she refused to move. They could throw her out, but that was the only way she was leaving. Her heart was in that intensive care emergency surgery unit, strapped to machines and tubes, fighting for his life. They could put her in jail, after, she didn't care. But she wasn't moving until they could assure her that Carson would live. And she told them so.

CHAPTER THIRTEEN

THE NEUROLOGIST ON Carson's case, Dr. Howard Deneth, paused at the nurses' station in ICU, where they'd taken Carson an hour ago, and glanced toward the cubicle where Carson was placed.

"She's still there?" he mused.

The nurse nodded. "She won't leave. The nurses called security, but she said they'd have to drag her out. She wasn't belligerent. She just stared them down, with tears rolling down her cheeks the whole time."

"Unusual in these days, devotion like that," the doctor remarked. "Are they married?"

"Not that we know. Of course, we don't know much, except what she was able to tell us. He doesn't carry identification."

"I noticed. Some sort of covert work, I imagine, classified stuff."

"That's what we thought."

Dr. Deneth looked down at the nurse over his glasses. "He's deteriorating," he said heavily. "The wound was superficial. There was minor head trauma, but really not enough to account for his condition. However, head injuries are tricky. Sometimes even minor ones can end fatally." He pursed his lips. "Let her in the room."

"Sir?"

"On my authority," he added. "I'll write it on the chart, in case you have any flak from upper echelons. They can talk to me if they don't like it."

The nurse didn't speak. She just smiled.

CARLIE HELD HIS HAND. She'd been shocked when the nurse came to tell her that she could have a comfortable chair beside Carson's bed. One of the other nurses had been curt to the point of rudeness when she tried to make Carlie leave the hall.

She guessed that nurses were like policemen. Some were kindhearted and personable, and some were rigorously by-the-book. She worked for a policeman who'd thrown the book away when he took the job. He believed in the rule of law, but he wasn't a fanatic for the letter of it. Case in point was big Fred Baldwin, who was now living in a safe but undisclosed location, so that he didn't end up dead before he could testify against his former boss.

No arrests had been made yet, that she was aware of. She did know that they had an all points bulletin out for the blond woman who'd left Carson in this condition. She really hoped the woman resisted arrest, and then she bit her tongue and said a silent apology. That wasn't really a wish that a religious person should make.

Her father had come to see Carson a few minutes ago. The nurses had at least let him into the room. But when he came out he was somber and although he tried to get Carlie to come home, he understood why she wouldn't. He'd done the same when her mother was in the hospital dying. He'd refused to leave, too.

Carlie supposed he'd seen cases like Carson's many times. Judging by the look on his face, the results had been fatal. He reminded Carlie that God's will had precedence over man's desires. He wanted to stay with his daughter, but she reminded him that having two people in the corridor to trip over would probably be the straw that broke the camel's back for the nursing staff. He went home, leaving Carlie's cell phone—which she'd forgotten—with her so that she could keep him posted.

Unknown to her, one of Rourke's buddies was nearby, posing as a family member in the intensive care waiting room. Just in case Helm had any ideas about hurting Carlie. It was a long shot, but nobody wanted to leave anything to chance.

Meanwhile, the forces of good were coalescing against Matthew Helm. He knew they had Baldwin in custody, and the man was probably spilling his guts. But his attorney could take Baldwin apart on the stand. The man had a criminal record, which is how he was pressured into taking Helm's jobs in the first place. He had a conviction for assault when he was a cop in Chicago. That could be used against his testimony.

After all, Helm's hands were clean. He'd never broken the law. They might have Baldwin and a lot of hearsay evidence, but there was nothing that could connect him to the murder of the assistant D.A. He'd made sure of it.

So now he was free of that worry, and he could concentrate on the Senate race. He was in Washington, D.C., of course, learning his way around, making contacts, making use of all the connections that Charro Mendez had in the country's capital. He liked the power. He liked the privilege. He liked bumping elbows at cocktail parties with famous people. Yes, he was going to enjoy this job, and nobody was taking it away from him in that special election in May!

What he didn't know was that Fred, like Carlie, had an excellent memory for dates and places. With it, the authorities could check telephone records, check stubs, gas receipts, restaurant tickets, even motel logs to see where Helm was at particular times and with particular people. They could now connect him directly to the assistant district attorney's murder through Richard Martin because of the theft of the watch. It went from the assistant D.A.'s body to Richard Martin, who worked for Helm, to Fred Baldwin whom Helm had sent to retrieve it, right back to Helm himself.

The San Antonio D.A.'s office put together a network, a framework, that they were going to use to hang Matthew Helm from. The watch was going to put Helm away for a very long time. Added to Baldwin's testimony, it would be the trial of the century. It had all the elements: intrigue, murder, politics, kidnapping—it was almost a catalog of the deadly sins. And now, with Rourke ordered to set up Calhoun Ballenger's youngest son—with cocaine provided by Charro Mendez—a concrete link between the two men had been formed. The trap was about to spring shut.

Fred had been kept in the dark about Rourke's true allegiance. What he didn't know, he couldn't accidentally let slip.

"TONIGHT'S THE NIGHT," Rourke told Cash Grier on a secure line. "Seven o'clock. Helm himself ordered the plant and I have it on tape."

"Sheer genius," Cash announced. "We're going to catch you in the act." He groaned. "Calhoun Ballenger is going to use me for a mop when he finds out that his son was the bait."

"I'll save you," Rourke promised. "But it's what we need to make the case."

"Good thing we spoke to Blake Kemp about this before you agreed to do it," Cash added.

"Yes, the Jacobs County D.A. should be in on such matters. Just to keep yours truly out of the slammer," Rourke chuckled. "Don't be late, okay? I'm not absolutely sure that Helm won't assign backup in case I get cold feet or he suspects I'm not reliable."

"No worries. We've got one of Eb Scott's men watching you, and one with Carlie up in San Antonio."

"How is he?" Rourke asked.

"No change," Cash said heavily. "Well, one change. They finally let Carlie into the room with him."

"Probably because they got tired of tripping over her in the hall," Rourke remarked. "Stubborn girl."

"Very." Cash's voice lowered. "It doesn't look good. Head injuries...well, you know."

"Any luck turning up that deadly blonde?" Rourke added coldly.

"Not yet, but I'm told they have a lead. She ordered the kidnapping. That's a federal offense. It means my brother gets involved." There was real pride in his tone. "Nobody gets away from Garon."

"Maybe they'll hit her over the head and shoot her while she's lying helpless," Rourke said icily.

"In real life, it doesn't go down like that." Cash sighed. "Pity."

"Yeah. Okay, I'll see you later."

"Be careful," Cash cautioned.

"Always."

CARLIE HELD CARSON'S hand tightly in both of her small ones. He had beautiful hands, the skin smooth and firm, the nails immaculately clean and neatly trimmed. No jewelry. No marks where jewelry might ever have been. She remembered the feel of his hands on her skin, the tenderness, the strength of them. It seemed like an age ago.

The neurosurgeon had come in to check Carson's eyes, and how his pupils reacted to light. He was kind to Carlie, telling her that sometimes it took a little time for a patient to regain consciousness after a blow like the one Carson had sustained. If they were lucky, there wouldn't be too much impairment afterward. He didn't add that the head trauma didn't seem damaging enough to account for the continued unconsciousness. That bothered him.

The head trauma being the predominant condition, Carson was in the ICU on the neurological ward. The gunshot injury, by comparison, was far less dangerous and had a better prognosis. That damage had been quickly repaired by the trauma surgeon.

She only half heard him. She wanted him to tell her that Carson would wake up and get up and be all right. The doctor couldn't do that. Even he, with his long experience, had no guarantees. At the moment, they weren't certain why he was still unconscious.

Carson had been in shock when they transported him, but now he was still breathing well on his own, his levels were good, BP was satisfactory. In fact, he should be awake and aware. But he wasn't. They'd done a CT scan in the emergency room. It did not show extensive brain injury. There was some minor bruising, but nothing that should account for the continued unconsciousness.

Blood had been sent to the lab for analysis, but it was a busy day and a few patients in far worse shape were in the queue ahead of him.

The doctor asked, again, if Carson had any next of kin in the area. She shook her head. Carson was from the Wapiti Ridge Sioux Reservation in South Dakota, but she didn't know anything about that part of his life. Neither did anybody else locally.

He suggested that it might be wise to contact the authorities there and inquire about relatives who might know more about his health history. So Carlie phoned Cash Grier and asked him to do it. She was too upset to talk to anyone. His medical history would certainly be useful, but he was fighting for his life from a set of circumstances other than illness. She prayed and prayed. Please let him live, she asked reverently, even if he married some pretty sweet young woman from his hometown and Carlie never saw him again.

She whispered it while she was holding Carson's hand. Whispered it over and over again while tears ran hot and salty down her pale cheeks.

"You just can't die," she choked, squeezing his hand very hard. "Not like this. Not because of that sick, stupid, beautiful blond female pit viper!" She swallowed, wiping tears away with the tips of her fingers. "Listen, you can go home and marry some nice, experienced girl who'll be everything you want, and it will be all right. I want you to be happy. I want you to live!"

She sniffed. "I know I'm not what you need. I've always known it. I'm not asking for anything at all. I just want you to live until you're old and gray-headed and have a houseful of kids and grandkids." She managed a smile. "You can tell them stories about now, about all the exotic places you went, the things you saw and did. You'll be a local legend."

He shifted. Her heart jumped. For an instant she thought he might be regaining consciousness. But he made a soft sound and began to breathe more deeply. Her hands tightened around his. "You just have to live," she whispered. "You have to."

While she was whispering to him, the door opened and a woman with jet-black hair and black eyes came into the room. She was wearing a white jacket and had a stethoscope around her neck. She glanced at Carlie and smiled gently.

"No change, huh?" she asked softly.

Carlie swallowed. Her eyes were bloodshot. She shook her head.

The newcomer took something out of her pocket and removed Carlie's hand, just for a few seconds, long enough to press a small braided circle with a cross inside into Carson's palm.

"What is it?" Carlie asked in a whisper. "It looks like a prayer wheel…and those are Lakota colors…"

"You know that?" the visitor asked, and the smile grew bigger. "It is a prayer wheel. Those are our colors," she added. "Red and yellow, black and white, the colors of the four directions."

"It may be just what he needs," Carlie replied, folding his hand back inside both of hers, with the prayer circle inside it. "Are you a *wicasa wakan?*" she added, her eyes wide with curiosity as she referenced a holy person in the tribe who could heal the sick.

"A *wasichu,* and you know that?" she laughed, using the Lakota word that referred to anyone outside the tribe. She grinned from ear to ear. "No. I'm not. But my grandfather is. He still lives on the rez in Wapiti Ridge Sioux Reservation. It's where I'm from. Somebody called the rez to find a relative who knew him, so my cousin answered their questions and then he called me. We've got family all over," she added with a twinkle in her eyes. "Even in South Texas."

Carlie smiled. "Nice to know. It's like where I live, in Comanche Wells. I know everybody, and everybody knows my family for generations."

She nodded. "It's that way back home, too." She looked at Carson. "Cousin Bob Tail is praying for him. Now he is a *wicasa wakan,*" she added.

"I believe in prayer," Carlie replied, looking back at Carson. "I think God comes in all colors and races and belief systems."

The visitor laid a hand on her shoulder and leaned down. "Cousin Bob Tail says he's going to wake up soon." She stood up and chuckled. "Don't you tell a soul I said that. They'll take back my medical degree!"

"You're a doctor," Carlie guessed, smiling.

"Neurologist," she said. "And I believe in modern medicine. I just think no technology is so perfect that it won't be helped by a few prayers." She winked, glanced at Carson again, smiled, and went out.

"You hear that?" she asked Carson. "Now you have to get better so people won't think Cousin Bob Tail is a fraud."

EVEN SHE, WITH no medical training, could tell that Carson was getting worse. She got up and bent over him, brushing back the unruly long black hair that had escaped the neat ponytail he usually wore it in.

She leaned close to brush her mouth over his. She stopped. Frowned. There was a fleeting wisp of memory. Garlic. He smelled of garlic. She knew he hated it because he'd once told Rourke he couldn't abide it in Italian dishes and Rourke had told her, just in passing conversation.

Another flash of memory. Wyoming. Merissa Kirk. She'd been poisoned with the pesticide malathion disguised in capsules by Richard Martin, who'd substituted it in her migraine headache capsules. A cohort of Martin's, a woman, had tried again to poison Merissa when she was in the hospital. The woman, on Martin's orders, had put malathion in a beef dish that Merissa had for supper. It had smelled of overpowering garlic! Cash Grier had told her all about it. She let go of Carson's hand and rushed out the door. The doctor, the Lakota neurologist, was standing at the desk.

"Please, may I speak with you?" she asked hurriedly.

"Yes…"

Carlie pulled her into Carson's cubicle. While she was walking, she was relaying the memories that had gone through her head. "Smell his breath," she asked softly.

Dr. Beaulieu caught her breath. "Poison?" She was thinking out loud. "It would account for the deterioration better than the slight head injury…"

"The woman who did it, she answered the phone when I called Carson. She said I'd get to watch him die slowly, over days!"

"Poison," the doctor agreed, black eyes narrowed. "That could explain it."

SHE WENT OUT. They came and took Carson out of the cubicle and wheeled him quickly back to the emergency surgical suite.

"It will be all right," Dr. Beaulieu assured her as she went by. "We're running a blood screen for poison right now, and I have a phone call in to the doctor whose name you gave me in Wyoming." She pressed Carlie's arm with her hand. "I think you may have saved his life."

"Cousin Bob Tail will be happy," Carlie said with just a hint of a smile.

"Oh, yes."

It seemed to take forever. Carlie sat in the waiting room this time, as close to the door as she could get, her legs pressed tightly together, her hands clenched in her lap, praying. She didn't have the presence of mind to call anyone. She was too involved in the moment.

She remembered Carson being so hostile to her in the beginning, antagonizing her with every breath, flaunting Lanette in front of her, insulting her. Then he'd frightened her, and with incredible skill, he'd treated her, taken her to the emergency room and then to have lunch by a flowing stream in the woods.

Afterward, in his arms, she'd felt things she'd never known in her young life. They'd fed the birds together and he'd told her the Brulé legend of the crow and how it became black. At the end, he'd told her it would never work out for the two of them and he was going to have to leave.

Now, there was the danger. She knew he wasn't tame. He would never be tame. He wouldn't marry her and settle down in Comanche Wells, Texas, and have children with her. He was like her father. Jake Blair had overcome his own past to change and transform himself into a man of God, into a minister. But Carson was different.

She looked at her hands, tightly clenched in her lap. Ringless. They'd be that way forever. She was never going to get married. She would have married Carson, if he'd asked. But nobody else. She'd be an old maid and fuss in her garden. She smiled sadly. Maybe one day Carson would marry someone and bring his children to visit her. Maybe they could at least remain friends. She hoped so.

The door to the surgical suite opened and Dr. Beaulieu came out. She sat beside Carlie and held her cold hands.

"We were in time," she said. "They've just finished washing out his stomach. They're giving him drugs to neutralize the effects of the poison. Your quick thinking saved his life."

Tears, hot and wet, rolled down Carlie's pale face. "Thank you."

"Oh, it wasn't me, honey," she laughed. "I just relayed the message to the right people. I only do head injuries, although I've put in my time in emergency rooms." She smiled sadly.

"Back home, there are so many sick people with no money, no way to afford decent health care. I tried to go back and work there, but I was just overwhelmed by the sheer volume of people. I decided I needed more training, so I specialized and came here to do my residency. This is where my life is now. But one day, I'll go back to the rez and open a free clinic." She smiled, showing white teeth. "That's my dream."

"You're a nice person."

"You really love that man, don't you?" she asked with a piercing gaze.

Carlie smiled sadly. "It doesn't help much. He's a wolf. He isn't tameable."

"You know, that's what I said about my husband." She chuckled. "But he was. I have three kids."

"Lucky you."

"I am, truly." She cocked her head. "You know, Carson's great-great-grandfather rode with Crazy Horse. His family dates back far beyond the Little Big Horn."

The knowledge was surprising. Delightful. "Like mine in Comanche Wells," Carlie said softly.

"Yes. You both come from villages where families grow together. We aren't so very different, you know."

"He doesn't...love me," Carlie replied sadly. "If he did, I'd follow him around the world on my knees through broken glass."

"How do you know he doesn't?"

"He was leaving when this happened. He said it would never work out."

"I see." The other woman's face was sad. "I am truly sorry."

"I'm happy that he'll live," Carlie replied. "Even if he marries someone else and has ten kids and grows old, I'll still be happy."

Dr. Beaulieu nodded slowly. "And that is how love should be. To wish only the best for those we love, even if they choose someone else."

"When can I see him?"

"They'll take him out to a room very soon," she said, smiling. "We had him in ICU because he wasn't improving. But while they still had the tube down his throat he woke up and began cursing the technician." She chuckled. "I think they'll be very happy to release him to the poor nurses on the ward."

Carlie grinned. "He's conscious?"

"Oh, yes." She stood up. "Now will you relax?"

"I'll try." She stood up, too. *"Pilamaya ye,"* she said softly in Lakota. The feminine form of *thank you.*

Dr. Beaulieu's eyes widened. "You speak Lakota?"

"Only a few words. Those are my best ones, and I imagine my accent is atrocious."

"I've been here for two years and not one person has ever spoken even one word of Lakota to me," the other woman said with pursed lips. "However few, I appreciate the effort it took to learn them." She nodded toward the emergency suite. "Does he know you speak them?"

Carlie hesitated and then shook her head. "I was afraid he'd think I was, well, doing it just to impress him. I learned it when I was still in school. I loved reading about Crazy Horse. Of course, his mother was Miniconjou Lakota and his father was part Miniconjou, but he was raised Oglala Lakota…"

Dr. Beaulieu put her hand on Carlie's shoulder. "Okay, now you have to marry him," she said firmly. "Even on the rez, there are some people who don't know all that about Crazy Horse." And she laughed.

CARSON WAS MOVED into a room. Carlie had phoned her father and her boss to tell them Carson was out of danger.

She was allowed in when they got him settled in the bed and hooked up to a saline drip. He was sitting up, glaring, like a wolf in a trap.

"You look better," she said, hesitating in the doorway.

"Better," he scoffed. He was hoarse, from the tube. "If you agree that having your stomach pumped with a tube down your throat is better!"

"At least you're alive," she pointed out.

He glared at her. "What are you doing here?"

She froze in place. Flushed. She wasn't certain what to say. "I phoned you for Rourke and Lanette answered…"

"Lanette." He blinked. "We were having coffee. I was about to tell her that I'd never tasted worse coffee when she came up behind me and hit me in the head. A gun went off." He shifted uncomfortably. "She shot me!" He glanced at Carlie. "Where is she?"

"They have a BOLO for her," she replied, using the abbreviation for a "Be on the lookout." "She hasn't surfaced yet. Fred Baldwin, who kidnapped me, is in custody in Jacobsville, along with the watch that Richard Martin stole from the assistant prosecutor he killed. He's turned state's evidence against Matthew Helm. They should be at his door pretty soon."

Carson was staring at her. "That doesn't answer the question. Why are you here?"

"Nobody else could be spared," she lied. "My father came by earlier. The others will be along soon, I'm sure."

His black eyes narrowed. He didn't speak. He didn't offer her a chair or ask her to sit down.

"There's a neurosurgeon here. A Dr. Beaulieu. She's Lakota. She said your cousin Bob Tail was praying for you, and that he said you'd live."

"Cousin Bob Tail usually can't even predict the weather," he scoffed.

"Well, he was right this time," she said, feeling uncomfortable. She twisted her small purse in her hands.

"Was there anything else?" he asked, his eyes unblinking and steady on her face.

She shook her head.

"Then I imagine visiting hours are over and you should go home before it gets dark."

"It's already dark," she murmured.

"All the more reason."

She nodded.

"They'll have someone watching you," he said.

"I guess."

"Don't go down any back roads and keep your phone with you."

"It's in my purse."

"Put it in your coat pocket so that you can get to it in a hurry if you have to," he continued curtly.

She grimaced, but she took it out and slid it into her coat pocket.

"Good night," he said.

She managed a faint smile. "Good night. I'm glad you're okay."

He didn't answer her.

She walked out, hesitated at the door. But she didn't look back when she left. She didn't want him to see the tears.

THEY'D GIVEN HIM something for pain. The gunshot wound, while nonfatal, was painful. So was his throat, where the tube had gone down. He was irritated that Carlie had come to see him out of some sort of obligation. Nobody else was available, she'd said. It was a chore. She hadn't come because she was terrified that he was going to die, because she cared. She'd come because nobody else was available.

Yet he was still concerned that she was driving home alone in the dark, when there had been attempts on her life. He'd wanted to phone Cash and ask him to watch out for her. Then he laughed inwardly at his own folly. Of course Cash would have her watched. He probably had somebody in the hospital the whole time, somebody who would keep her under surveillance even when she drove home.

He fell asleep, only to wake much later, feeling as if he had concrete in his side where the bullet had hit.

"Hurts, huh?"

He looked up into a face he knew. "Sunflower," he said,

chuckling as he used the nickname he'd hung on her years ago. Dr. Beaulieu had been a childhood playmate. He knew her very well, knew her family for generations.

She grinned. "You're looking better."

"I feel as if a truck ran through my side," he said, grimacing. "They pumped my stomach."

"Yes. Apparently the woman who shot you also hit you on the head to show us an obvious head injury. But she poisoned you first. The poison was killing you. If it hadn't been for your friend from Comanche Wells, you'd be dead. We were treating the obvious injuries. None of us looked for poison because we didn't expect to see it." She hesitated. "We did blood work, but it was routine stuff."

"My friend?" He still felt foggy.

"Yes. The dark-headed girl who speaks Lakota," she replied. "She smelled garlic on your breath and recalled that you hated it and would never ingest it willingly. Then she remembered a poisoning case in Wyoming in a hospital there, a woman who was given malathion in a beef dish…"

"Merissa Kirk," Carson said heavily. "Yes."

"So we checked with the attending physician there for verification. I was involved only peripherally, of course, since my specialty is neurology. We thought you were unconscious because of the head wound."

"The coffee," Carson recalled. "The coffee tasted funny."

She nodded. "She told the dark-haired girl that she would get to watch you die slowly. When she smelled your breath, she remembered what the woman told her."

"Lanette." His face tautened. "I hope they hang her. If they'll let me out, I'll track her down, wherever she goes."

Dr. Beaulieu was smiling. "She said you were like a wolf, that you could never be tame. She said it didn't matter, that she only wanted you to be happy, even if it was with some other woman." She shook her head. "She thanked me in Lakota. It was a shock. Most *wasicus* can't speak a word of our language."

"I know."

"She even knew that Crazy Horse's mother was Miniconjou," she said.

"Where's my cell phone?" he asked.

She raised both eyebrows. "Cell phone?"

"Yes. Wasn't it brought in with me?" he asked.

"Let me check." She phoned the clerk at the emergency room where he was brought in. They checked the records. She thanked them and hung up. "There was no cell phone with you when you were admitted," she said.

He grimaced. All his private numbers were there, including Carlie's, her father's and Rourke's. If Lanette had taken it…

"Will you hand me the phone, please? And tell me how to get an outside line…"

CARLIE WAS NO sooner back home than her phone rang while she was opening the front door. She answered it.

There was nobody there. Only silence.

"Hello?" she persisted. "Look, tell me who you are or I'm calling the police."

There was a dial tone.

It worried her. She went inside to talk to her father. But he wasn't there. A note on the hall table said that he'd been called to a meeting of the finance committee at the church. He wouldn't be long.

Carlie hung up her old coat. She started upstairs when she remembered that she'd left her cell phone in her coat. She went to get it just as there was a knock on the door.

CHAPTER FOURTEEN

"WHAT DO YOU MEAN, you can't get her on the phone?" Carson raged at Cash Grier. "Get somebody over there, for God's sake! Lanette has my cell phone. It has Carlie's number and Rourke's real number on it!"

"Will you slow down and calm down?" Cash asked softly. "I've got people watching Carlie's house. Believe me, nobody's touching her."

"Okay. How about her father?"

"At a church meeting. We have someone outside."

"Rourke?"

Cash laughed. "I arrested Rourke two hours ago in the act of placing cocaine in the glove compartment of Calhoun Ballenger's son's truck."

"Arrested?"

"You've been out of the loop," Cash told him. "Blake Kemp, our district attorney, was on the scene, along with agents from the DEA, ICE and several other agencies. We had to make it look good, in case Helm slips through our fingers and Rourke has to go undercover again."

"All right." Carson's head was throbbing. His wound hurt. "Carlie said she came because nobody else was available to sit with me—"

"Really? You should talk to the staff. She sat in the corridor outside the E.R. and refused to budge. When they got you to ICU, she did the same thing. They even called security. She sat where she was and cried. Finally, the neurosurgeon on your case took pity on her and let her in."

"Dr. Beaulieu?" he asked.

"No, it was a man. Anyway, she smelled garlic on your breath. She connected you with the Wyoming case, told Dr. Beaulieu, and the rest is history. Saved your life, son," he added. "You were dying and they didn't know why. I assume your blond friend hit you on the head and shot you so that they wouldn't think of looking for poison until it was too late."

"I don't remember any of this."

"I guess not. I had Carlie call you at your apartment because Rourke couldn't risk having his number show up on your phone, assuming that it was bugged by Helm's men. Lanette answered it. She told Carlie that you'd be a long time dying and she'd have to watch you suffer. Almost came true."

"Almost." His heart lifted like a bird. Carlie had lied. She'd been with him all the way, all the time. She did care. Cared a lot.

"So just get well, will you? We've got everything covered down here."

"Okay." He drew in a breath. "Thanks, Cash."

"You'd do it for me."

"In a heartbeat."

He hung up the phone and closed his eyes. He should call Carlie. He wanted to. But that was when the pain meds they'd been shoveling into him took effect. He went to sleep.

CARLIE OPENED THE DOOR. Just as she did it, she realized that she shouldn't have done it. She had no weapon, her phone was in her coat, she was vulnerable. Just like when she'd answered the door and Fred Baldwin had carried her off.

Her father stared back at her with set lips. "How many times do I have to tell you to make sure who's at the door before you answer it?" he asked.

She smiled sheepishly. "Sorry, Dad." She stared at him. "Why did you knock?"

He grimaced. "Forgot my keys."

"See? It's genetic," she told him. "You lose your keys, I lose my phone. It's catching, and I got it from you!"

He chuckled. "Heard from Carson?"

"He's sitting up in bed yelling at people," she said.

He let out a relieved whistle. "I wouldn't have given a nickel for his chances when I saw him," he replied. He smiled. "I wouldn't have told you that. You still had hope. I guess they've got some super neurosurgeons in that hospital."

"It wasn't the head injury," she said. "Or the gunshot wound. It was poison. She put malathion in his coffee."

"Good Lord!" he exclaimed. "That's diabolical!"

"Yes. I hope they catch her," she said doggedly. "I hope they lock her up for a hundred years!"

He hugged Carlie. "I can appreciate how you must feel."

She hugged him back. "Carson sent me home," she said, giving way to tears. "I think I made him mad by just going up there."

He grimaced. "Maybe he's trying to be kind, in his way, Carlie. You know he's probably never going to be able to settle in some small town."

"I know. It doesn't help."

She drew back and wiped her eyes. "How about some coffee and cake?"

"That sounds nice."

"Did you just try to call me?" she added on the way.

"Me? No. Why?"

"Just a wrong number, I guess. Somebody phoned and hung up." She laughed. "I'm probably just getting paranoid, is all. I'll make a pot of coffee."

TWO DAYS LATER, Carson was out of the hospital. He was a little weak, but he felt well enough to drive. He went to his apartment first, looking for the missing cell phone. He knew he wouldn't find it. He hoped they could catch Lanette before she managed to get out of the country. She probably had several aliases that she could refer to if she was as competent at her job as he now believed she was.

A contract killer, and he'd been dating her. All the while she'd been hell-bent on killing Carlie's father. He felt like an idiot.

He drove down to Jacobsville to Cash Grier's office. As soon as he opened the door, he looked for Carlie, but she wasn't at her desk. He went on in and knocked at Cash's door.

"Come in."

He opened the door, expecting Carlie to be taking dictation or discussing the mail. She wasn't there, either.

"You look like hell," Cash said. "But at least you're still alive. Welcome back."

"Thanks. Where's Carlie?" he asked.

"Bahamas," he replied easily.

He frowned. "What's she doing in the Bahamas?"

"Haven't a clue," Cash said heavily. "She and Robin took off early yesterday on a red-eye flight out of San Antonio. She asked off for a couple of days and I told her to go ahead. She's had a rough time of it."

"I tried to call her. I didn't get an answer."

"Same here. I don't think her cell phone is working. Her father's still looking for it. She said she left it in her coat pocket, but then they noticed there's a hole in the pocket. Probably fell out somewhere and she didn't notice. She was pretty upset over you."

"I heard." He was feeling insecure. He thought Carlie cared. But she'd gone to the Bahamas with another man. He'd heard her speak of Robin with affection. Had he chased her into the arms of another man with his belligerent attitude? He should have called her father when he couldn't reach her, called the house phone. The damned drugs had kept him under for the better part of two days!

"Why did she go to the Bahamas with a man?" he asked shortly.

Cash frowned. "I don't know. She and Robin have always been close, from what I've heard. And he took her to the Valentine's Day dance." He hesitated. "It didn't seem like a love match to me. But…"

"Yes. But."

Cash could see the pain in the other man's face. "I'm sorry."

"So am I." He managed a smile. "I'm leaving."

"Today?"

He nodded. "I'm going home. I have some ghosts to lay."

Cash got up, went around the desk and extended his hand. "If you ever need help, you've got my number," he told the younger man.

Carson returned the pressure. He smiled. "Thanks."

"Keep in touch."

"I'll do that, too." He glanced out at the empty desk where Carlie usually sat.

"What do you want me to tell her?" Cash asked.

Carson's face set into hard lines. "Nothing. Nothing at all."

CARLIE STOOD UP with Robin and his fiancée, Lucy Tims, at their secret wedding in Nassau.

"I hope you'll be very happy," she told them, kissing both radiant faces.

"We will until we have to go home and face the music," Robin chuckled. "But that's not for a few days. We're going to live in paradise until then. Thanks so much for coming with us, Carlie."

"It was my pleasure. Thanks for my plane ticket," she added gently. "I sort of needed to get away for a little while."

"Stay for a couple of days anyway," Robin coaxed.

She shook her head. "Overnight was all I can manage. The

chief won't even be able to deal with the mail without me," she joked. "I'm going back tonight. You two be happy, okay?"

"Okay." They kissed her again.

She didn't want to say, but she was hoping that Carson might come to see her when he was out of the hospital. It was a long shot, after his antagonistic behavior, but hope died hard. She went home and wished for the best.

SHE MISSED HER cell phone. She knew it had probably fallen through the hole in her pocket and it was gone forever. It was no great loss. It was a cheap phone and it only had a couple of numbers in it, one was her father and the other was Cash Grier.

But it was like losing a friend, because Carson had carried it around with him before he brought it to her. It had echoes of his touch. Pathetic, she told herself, cherishing objects because they'd been held.

It had been several days. She was getting used to the idea that Carson was gone for good. Chief Grier had told her that Carson had come by the office on his way out of town. But he hadn't had a message for Carlie. That was all right. She hadn't really expected one.

She disguised the hurt on the job, but she went home and cried herself to sleep. Wolves couldn't be tamed, she reminded herself. It was useless to hope for a future that included Carson. Just useless.

ROURKE WAS BAILED out by Jake Blair. They had a good laugh about his imminent prosecution for breaking and entering, possession of narcotics and possible conspiracy.

They laughed because Rick Marquez and the San Antonio assistant D.A. working the case finally had enough evidence to arrest Matthew Helm. It made headlines all over the country, especially when Rourke gave a statement to the effect that Mr. Helm had ordered him to plant narcotics on Calhoun Ballenger's son Terry and that Charro Mendez had supplied them.

There was an attempt to extradite Mendez to stand trial in the U.S. on drug charges, but he mysteriously vanished.

Helm wasn't so fortunate. He, his senior campaign staff and at least one San Antonio police officer were arrested and charged with crimes ranging from attempted murder to theft of police evidence and narcotics distribution.

It came as a shock when Marquez released a statement heralding Fred Baldwin as a material witness in the case. Fred, who was turning state's evidence, was being given a pardon by the governor of the state in return for his cooperation.

That news was pleasing to Eb Scott, whose kids had become great playmates of the big, gentle man who lived with them while Helm was under investigation. Eb wanted to give Fred a job, in fact, but Cash Grier beat him to it. Fred was wearing a uniform again, having been cleared of all charges against him in Chicago, his record restored, his reputation unstained, his former partner now under investigation for police corruption.

He was Jacobsville's newest patrol officer, and his first assignment was speaking to children in grammar school about the dangers of drugs. He was in his element. Children seemed to love him.

Carlie went about her business, working diligently, keeping up with correspondence for the chief. But the sadness in her was visible. She'd lost that impish spark that had made her so much fun to be around. Her father grieved for her, with her. He understood what she was going through as she tried to adjust to life without Carson, without even the occasional glimpse of him in town. He was long gone, now.

AUTUMN CAME TO Jacobs County. The maples were beautiful and bright, and Carlie was filling her bird feeders for the second time, as the migrating birds came from the north on their way to warmer climates. Cardinals and blue jays were everywhere. The male goldfinches were losing their bright gold color and turning a dull green, donning their winter coats.

Carlie was still wearing her threadbare one with the hole in
the pocket sewn up. Her phone had miraculously reappeared,
brought in by a street person who found it and traded it to a
soup kitchen worker for a sandwich. The worker had turned
it in to police, who returned it to Carlie. She had the phone in
her pocket even now. It was safe enough with the hole mended.

The birds usually stayed nearby while she filled the feeders, but they suddenly took off as if a predator was approaching. It was an odd thing, but she'd observed it over the years
many times. Sometimes, for no apparent reason, birds just did
that. Flew up all together into the trees, when Carlie saw nothing threatening.

This time, however, there was a threat. It was standing just
behind her.

She turned, slowly, and there he was.

She tried valiantly not to let her joy show. But tears stung her
eyes. It had been months. A lifetime. She stood very still, the
container of birdseed held tight in her hands, her eyes misting
as she looked at him.

He seemed taller than ever. His hair wasn't in a ponytail. It
was loose around his shoulders, long and thick and as black as
a grackle's wing. He had something in a bag under one arm.
He was wearing that exquisite beaded jacket that was so familiar to her.

"Hello," he said.

"Hello," she said back.

He gave her coat a speaking look. "Same coat."

She managed a smile. "I was going to say the same thing."

He moved closer. He took the seed canister out of her hands
and placed it on the ground. He handed her the bag and nodded.

She opened it. Inside was the most exquisite coat she'd ever
seen in her life, white buckskin with beading, Oglala Lakota
colors of the four directions, in yellow, red, white and black
patterns on it. She gasped as she pulled it out of the bag and
just stared at it.

He held out his hand. She took off her ratty coat and gave it to him to hold while she tried on the new jacket. It was a perfect fit.

"It's the most beautiful thing in the world," she whispered, tears running down her cheeks.

"No, Carlie," he replied, dropping her old coat on top of the birdseed canister. "You're the most beautiful thing in the world. And I've missed you like hell! Come here...!"

He wrapped her up against him, half lifting her so that he could find her lips with his hard, cold mouth. He kissed her without a thought for whoever might see them. He didn't care.

He was home.

She held on for dear life and kissed him back with all the fear and sorrow and grief she'd felt in the months between when she thought she'd never see him again. Everything she felt was in that long, slow, sweet kiss.

"I love you," she choked.

"I know," he whispered into her mouth, the words almost a groan. "I've always known."

She gave up trying to talk. It was so sweet, to be in his arms. She was probably hallucinating and it wasn't real. She didn't care. If her mind had snapped, it could stay snapped. She'd never been so happy.

Eventually, he stood her back on her feet and held her away from him. "You've lost weight."

She nodded. She studied him. "You look...different."

He smiled slowly. "At peace," he explained. "I had to go home and face my demons. It wasn't easy."

She touched his hard face. "There was nothing you could have done to stop it," she said softly.

"That's what his own brother said. I made peace with his family, with her family."

"I'm glad."

"I had my cousin make the jacket. I'm glad it fits."

She smiled. "It's beautiful. I'll never take it off."

He pursed his lips. "Oh, I think you might want to do that in a week or so."

"I will? Why?"

He framed her face in his big, warm hands. "I'm not wearing clothes on my honeymoon. And neither are you."

"How do you know what I'll be wearing?" she asked, brightening.

"Because we'll be together." The smile faded. "Always. As long as we live. As long as the grass grows, and the wind blows, and the sun sets."

Tears rolled down her cheeks. "For so long?" she whispered brokenly.

"Longer." He bent and kissed away the tears. "I would have been here sooner, but I stopped by to talk to Micah Steele."

"Micah?"

He nodded. "I still have to do an internship. I'm arranging to do it here. Afterward, a year or two of residency in internal medicine, here if possible, San Antonio if not. Then I'll move into practice with Lou and Micah."

She was standing very still. She didn't understand. "You're going to medical school?"

He laughed softly. "I've already been to medical school. I got my medical license. But I never did an internship so I couldn't, technically, practice medicine." He smoothed her hand over his chest. "I did keep my medical license current. I guess I realized that I'd go back to it one day. I have some catching up to do, and I'll have to work late hours, but—"

"But you want to live here?" she asked, aghast.

"Of course," he said simply. "This is where your tribe lives, isn't it?" he teased.

Tears were falling hot and heavy now. "We're going to get married?"

He nodded. "I'm not asking, by the way," he said with pursed lips. "We're just doing it."

"Oh."

"And I don't have a ring yet. I thought we'd go together to pick them out. A set for you, and a band for me."

"You're going to wear a ring?" she asked.

"It seems to go with the position." He grinned.

She hesitated, just for a second.

"You're thinking of my reputation with women. I took them home, kissed them at the door and said good-night," he said, reading her apprehension. "It was a nice fiction, to keep home-bodies like you from getting too interested in me." He shrugged. "I haven't had anybody since I was widowed."

She pressed close into his arms, held on for dear life. "I would have married you anyway."

"I know that."

"But it's nice that you don't know a lot more than I do…"

"And that's where you're wrong," he whispered into her ear. "I'm a doctor. I know where ALL the nerve endings are."

"Gosh!"

"And the minute your father pronounces us man and wife, I'll prove it to you. When we're alone, of course. We wouldn't want to embarrass your father."

"No. We wouldn't want to do that." She pressed close into his arms, felt them fold around her, comforting and loving and safe. She closed her eyes. "You didn't say goodbye."

His arms contracted. "You went to the Bahamas with an-other man."

She jerked back, lifting horrified eyes. "No! I went to be a witness at his wedding to Lucy Tims!" she exclaimed.

He grimaced. "I know that, now. I didn't at the time. I tried to call you, but I never got an answer."

"I lost my phone. Some kind person turned it in at a soup kitchen in San Antonio."

He sighed, tracing her mouth with a long forefinger. "A com-edy of errors. I felt guilty, too. I'd sent you packing without re-alizing that you'd saved my life. I was still confused from the blow on the head and the drugs. I was worried that you'd be on the road alone in the dark." He leaned his forehead against hers. "Lanette was still on the loose. I was afraid for you. I should never have let you leave the hospital in the first place—"

"I was okay," she interrupted. "Cash Grier had people watching me all the time. Dad, too. Just in case."

"I hurt you. I never meant to." He closed his eyes as he rocked her in his arms. "I wasn't sure, Carlie. I had to be sure that I could settle down, that I could give up the wild ways. Until I was sure, I wasn't going to make promises."

She drew away. "And are you? Sure, I mean?"

He nodded. "That's why I went home." He smiled. "Cousin Bob Tail says we're going to have three sons. We have to name one for him."

"Okay," she said, without hesitation and with a big grin.

He laughed. "He wants us to name him Bob. Just Bob."

"I wouldn't mind." She searched his black eyes. "Our sons. Wow."

"Just what I was thinking. Wow." He chuckled.

"I haven't been playing online for a while."

"Neither have I," he confessed. "I missed you so much that I really wanted to. But I had to be sure, first." He sighed. "I guess if push comes to shove I can make an Alliance toon and we can run battlegrounds on the same side."

"Funny, I was just thinking I could make a Horde toon for the same reason."

He smiled. "We're on the same side in real life. That's enough."

"So," she asked, her green eyes twinkling, "when are we getting married?"

"Let's go and ask your father when he's free," he said.

She slid her hand into his and walked back into the house with him. Her father didn't even have to ask. He just grinned.

THEY WENT TO Tangier for their honeymoon. Carlie was horrified at the expense, but Carson just laughed.

"Honey, I've got enough in foreign banks to keep us going into our nineties," he said complacently. "I work because I enjoy working. I could retire tomorrow if I felt like it. But I think practicing medicine will occupy me for many years to come. That, and our children."

"You told Rourke you wanted to be an attorney," she recalled.

"Yes, well, if you tell somebody you gave up law they don't care. If you tell them you gave up medicine, that's a whole other set of explanations I didn't want to make. As it happens, I did a double major in undergraduate school in biology and chemistry, but I minored in history and anatomy. History and law do go together."

"I wouldn't know. Will it matter to you that I haven't been to college?"

"You're kidding, right?" he teased. "You can speak Lakota and you know who Crazy Horse's mother was. That's higher education enough to suit me."

"Okay. Just so you're sure," she laughed. "And you don't mind if I go on working for the chief?"

"He'd skin me if I tried to take you away," he said with a sigh. "He'd never find a stamp or a potato chip, and some new girl would surely find out about the alien files he's got locked up in his office and call the Air Force. So, no, you can go on working. I intend to."

She smiled. "Dr. Farwalker. Sounds very nice."

"I thought so myself."

TANGIER WAS AN amazing blend of old and new. There were high-rise apartment buildings near the centuries-old walled marketplace. Carlie found it fascinating as they drove through the city at night in the back of a taxicab.

It had been a very long flight, from San Antonio to Atlanta, Atlanta to Brussels, Brussels to Casablanca, Casablanca to Tangier. They'd arrived in the dead of night and Carlie was worried sick about being able to find a way to get into the city as they waited endlessly to get through passport control and customs. But there were cabs sitting outside the main building.

"Told you so," he chuckled.

"Is there any foreign city you haven't been to?" she wondered.

"Not many," he confessed. "You'll love this one. I'll take you around town tomorrow and show you where the pirates used to hang out."

"That's a deal."

CARLIE WAS SO tired by the time they got into the hotel, registered and were shown to their room that she almost wept.

"Now, now," he said softly. "We have our whole lives for what you're upset about missing. Sleep first. Then, we explore."

She smiled shyly. "Okay."

He watched her undress, with black eyes that appreciated every stitch that came off. But when she was down to her underwear, he moved close, pulled out a gown and handed it to her.

"First times are hard," he said gently. "Go put on your gown. I'll get into my pajamas while you're gone. Then we'll get some sleep before we do anything else. Deal?"

She smiled with relief. "Deal. I'm sorry," she started to add.

He put his fingers across her lips. "I like you just the way you are," he told her.

"Hang-ups and all?"

He smiled. "Hang-ups and all."

She let out the breath she'd been holding and darted into the bathroom, chiding herself for her wedding night nerves. It was natural, she supposed, despite the fact that most people had the wedding night long before the wedding. She and Carson must be throwbacks, she decided, because he'd wanted to wait as much as she had.

The lights were out when she came back into the room. The shutters were open, and moonlight filtered across the bed, where Carson was sprawled under the sheet. He held out his arm. She darted into bed and went close, pillowing her cheek on his hard, warm chest.

"Oh, that feels good," she whispered.

"I was about to say the same thing. Happy?"

"I could die of it."

"I know exactly what you mean." He closed his eyes, tucked her close and fell asleep almost at once. So did she. It had been a very long trip.

SHE WOKE THE next morning to the smell of coffee. She opened her eyes. Carson was sitting on the side of the bed in his pajama bottoms holding the cup just over her head.

"What a wonderful smell," she moaned.

"Sit up and have a sip. They serve a nice buffet breakfast downstairs, but I thought you might like coffee first."

"I would." She sat up, noticing at once how much of her small breasts were visible under the thin gown. He was looking at them with real interest, his eyes soft and hungry.

The way he looked at her made her feel beautiful. Exciting. Exotic.

"Tangier," she murmured, putting the cup down on the side table. "It makes me feel like I should be wearing a trenchcoat or something." Breathlessly, she slid the straps of the gown down her arms and let them fall.

Carson's expression was eloquent. He didn't even hesitate. He moved across the bed, putting her down on it, while his mouth opened and fed on her firm, soft breasts.

She arched up, shyness vanishing in the heat of sudden passion. She felt his hands go down her back, sliding fabric out of the way. She felt him move and then his body was moving on hers, bare and exciting.

He eased between her legs, his mouth poised over hers. He teased her lips while his body teased hers. He was smiling, but there was heat and passion in the smile. "Lift up," he whispered. "Seduce me."

"Gosh, I don't have…the slightest idea… I'm sorry… I…!" A tiny, helpless moan escaped her as his hand moved between them. "Carson, oh, gosh!"

"Yes, right there," he murmured at her lips. He chuckled softly. "It feels good, doesn't it? And this is just the beginning."

"Just the…?" She cried out again. Her body arched, shivering. What he was doing was shocking, invasive, she should be protesting or something, she should be… "Carson," she sobbed against his mouth. "Please…don't stop!"

"Never," he breathed against her lips. "Move this leg. Yes. Here. And that one. Now lift. Lift up, baby. Lift up…that's it… yes!"

There was a rhythm. She'd never known. In all her reading and covert watching of shocking movies, she'd never experienced anything like this.

It was one thing to read about it, quite another to do it. He knew more about her body than she did, apparently, and used that knowledge to take her to places she'd never dreamed about. The sensations piled upon themselves, growing and multiplying, until she felt as if she had the sun inside her and it was going to explode any second. The tension was so high that it was like being pulled apart in the sweetest sort of way.

She dug her nails into his hips as he strained down toward her, his powerful body arched above her as he drove down one last time.

She heard herself sobbing as she fell and fell, into layers of sweet heat that burned and burned and burned. It was like tides, rippling and falling, overwhelming and falling, crushing and falling, until finally she burst like fireworks and shuddered endlessly under the heavy, hard thrust of his body.

She heard him cry out at her ear, a husky sound that was so erotic, she shivered again when she felt his body cord and ripple and then, quite suddenly, relax.

He was heavy. His skin was hot, damp. She held him, smoothed the long, thick hair at his back, loving him.

"Everybody says it hurts the first time," she murmured.

"Oh? Did it?"

She laughed secretly. "I don't know."

He chuckled, the sound rippling against her hard-tipped breasts. He moved on her, feeling her instant response. He lifted his head and looked into her wide, soft eyes. "You will never get away," he promised her. "No matter how far, how fast you run, I will find you."

"I will never run," she said with a sigh. "Everything I want or love in all the world is right here, in my arms."

He bent and kissed her eyes shut as he began to move. She shivered gently.

"How long do you want to wait?" he whispered at her mouth.

"How...long? For...what?" she gasped, moving with him.

"To make a baby," he whispered back.

Her eyes opened. She shivered again. The look on her face was all the answer he needed. He held her gaze as he moved, tenderly, enclosing her in his legs, bending them beside her, so that they were locked together in the most intimate position she'd ever experienced.

"Oh...my...goodness," she said, looking straight into his eyes.

His hands framed her face. His was strained, taut, as he moved expertly on her body.

"I can't bear it," she managed to say.

"Yes, you can," he whispered. His eyes held hers. "I love you. This is how much..."

He shifted, and she cried out. The pleasure was beyond words, beyond description. She held on and sobbed with each slow, deep, torturous movement of his hips as he built the tension and built it and built it until she exploded into a million tiny hot pieces of sheer joy.

He groaned, almost convulsing, as the pleasure bit into him. "Never," he whispered hoarsely. "Never, never like this!"

She couldn't even manage a word. She just clung to him, enjoying the sight of the pleasure in his face, in the corded muscles of his body, in the sweet agony that echoed in the helpless movements of his hips.

Long after they felt the last ripple of pleasure, they clung to each other in the bright stillness of the morning, unable to let go.

"I think I dreamed you," he whispered finally.

"I know I dreamed you," she replied at his ear, still holding tight.

He rolled over so that she was beside him, but still joined to his body.

"I didn't know it felt like this," she confessed shyly. "I feel hungry now in a way I didn't before."

He smiled, brushing his mouth over hers. "You can't miss what you've never had."

"I guess so." She drew in a breath and looked down.

He smiled to himself and pulled away, letting her look. Her eyes were as wide as saucers when he moved away.

"Show-and-tell," he teased.

She blushed. "Men in racy magazines don't look like that," she whispered. "I only saw one and he was, well, he was..." She cleared her throat. "He wasn't that impressive."

He chuckled. He pulled her to her feet, enjoying her nudity. "I have an idea."

"You do? What?" she asked, looking up at him with a smile.

"Let's have a shower, and then breakfast and go look for pirates."

"I would like that very much."

He led her toward the bathroom.

She hesitated at the door.

He raised an eyebrow.

"What you said." She indicated the bed. "Was it just, I mean, did you really mean it?"

He pulled her close. "I want children very much, Carlie," he said softly. "They'll come when it's time for them to come." He smiled. "If it's this year, I don't mind at all. Do you?"

She laughed and hugged him close. "Oh, no, I don't mind!"

"Then let's have a shower and go eat. I'm starving!"

LIFE WITH CARSON was fascinating. They found more in common every day. They moved into a house of their own and Carson went to work at Jacobsville General as an intern. It was long hours and hard work. He never complained and when he got home, he told Carlie all the interesting things he'd learned that day. She never tired of listening.

Fred Baldwin had coffee with her when he started out on his patrols. He'd turned into a very good cop, and he'd have done anything for Cash Grier. He'd have done anything for Carlie, too. He told her that her father was going to have to share her with him because he didn't have a daughter of his own. She'd almost cried at the tenderness in his big brown eyes.

Lanette had been found, but not in a condition that would lead to trial. She took a flight to a small South American country that had no extradition treaty with the United States, but had the misfortune to run into the brother of a man she'd killed for money. Since she had no living family, they buried her in an unmarked grave in South America.

Matthew Helm was arrested, prosecuted and convicted on so many felony counts that he'd only get out of prison when he was around 185 years old. Or so the jury decided.

His cohorts went with him. The wife of the murdered assistant district attorney was in the courtroom when the sentence was pronounced.

Calhoun Ballenger won the special election and went to Washington, D.C., with his wife, Abby, as the junior United States senator from the grand state of Texas. Terry, having just graduated from high school, was off to college with his two brothers, Ed and Matt.

Calhoun had given Fred Baldwin a musical watch that played an Italian folk song when he learned about Fred's role in preventing the potential criminalization of his son Terry. Fred wore the watch to work every day.

Charro Mendez was still on the run. But people across the border were watching and waiting for his return.

Two months after Carlie and Carson were married, she was waiting for him at the front door when he came home from a long day at the hospital. She was holding a small plastic device in her hands. She handed it to him with an impish grin.

He looked at it, read it, picked her up and swung her around in his arms, kissing her the whole while and looking as if he'd won the lottery.

Seven months later, a little boy was born at Jacobsville General Hospital. They named him Jacob Allen Cassius Fred Farwalker, for his father, his grandfather and his two godfathers. Officer Fred Baldwin held him while he was baptized. He cried.

* * * * *

Sutton's Way

Visit her Author Profile page
on millsandboon.com.au, or
dianapalmer.com, for more titles!

To Barry Call
of Charbons in Gainesville, GA
Many thanks

CHAPTER ONE

THE NOISE OUTSIDE the cabin was there again, and Amanda shifted restlessly with the novel in her lap, curled up in a big armchair by the open fireplace in a rug. Until now, the cabin had been paradise. There was three feet of new snow outside, she had all the supplies she needed to get her through the next few wintery weeks of Wyoming weather, and there wasn't a telephone in the place. Best of all, there wasn't a neighbor.

Well, there was, actually. But nobody in their right mind would refer to that man on the mountain as a neighbor. Amanda had only seen him once and once was enough.

She'd met him, if their head-on encounter could be referred to as a meeting, on a snowy Saturday last week. Quinn Sutton's majestic ranch house overlooked this cabin nestled against the mountainside. He'd been out in the snow on a horse-drawn sled that contained huge square bales of hay, and he was heaving them like feather pillows to a small herd of red-and-white cattle. The sight had touched Amanda, because it indicated concern. The tall, wiry rancher out in a blizzard feeding his starving cattle. She'd even smiled at the tender picture it made.

And then she'd stopped her four-wheel-drive vehicle and stuck her blond head out the window to ask directions to the Blalock Durning place, which was the cabin one of her aunt's friends was loaning her. And the tender picture dissolved into stark hostility.

The tall rancher turned toward her with the coldest black eyes and the hardest face she'd ever seen in her life. He had a day's growth of stubble, but the stubble didn't begin to cover up the frank homeliness of his lean face. He had amazingly high cheekbones, a broad forehead and a jutting chin, and he looked as if someone had taken a straight razor to one side of his face, which had a wide scratch. None of that bothered Amanda because Hank Shoeman and the other three men who made music with her group were even uglier than Quinn Sutton. But at least Hank and the boys could smile. This man looked as if he invented the black scowl.

"I said," she'd repeated with growing nervousness, "can you tell me how to get to Blalock Durning's cabin?"

Above the sheepskin coat, under the battered gray ranch hat, Quinn Sutton's tanned face didn't move a muscle. "Follow the road, turn left at the lodgepoles," he'd said tersely, his voice as deep as a rumble of thunder.

"Lodgepoles?" she'd faltered. "You mean Indian lodgepoles? What do they look like?"

"Lady," he said with exaggerated patience, "a lodgepole is a pine. It's tall and piney, and there are a stand of them at the next fork in the road."

"You don't need to be rude, Mr...?"

"Sutton," he said tersely. "Quinn Sutton."

"Nice to meet you," she murmured politely. "I'm Amanda." She wondered if anyone might accidentally recognize her here in the back of beyond, and on the off chance, she gave her mother's maiden name instead of her own last name. "Amanda Corrie," she added untruthfully. "I'm going to stay in the cabin for a few weeks."

"This isn't the tourist season," he'd said without the slightest pretense at friendliness. His black eyes cut her like swords.

"Good, because I'm not a tourist," she said.

"Don't look to me for help if you run out of wood or start hearing things in the dark," he added coldly. "Somebody will tell you eventually that I have no use whatsoever for women."

While she was thinking up a reply to that, a young boy of about twelve had come running up behind the sled.

"Dad!" he called, amazingly enough to Quinn Sutton. "There's a cow in calf down in the next pasture. I think it's a breech!"

"Okay, son, hop on," he told the boy, and his voice had become fleetingly soft, almost tender. He looked back at Amanda, though, and the softness left him. "Keep your door locked at night," he'd said. "Unless you're expecting Durning to join you," he added with a mocking smile.

She'd stared at him from eyes as black as his own and started to tell him that she didn't even know Mr. Durning, who was her aunt's friend, not hers. But she bit her tongue. It wouldn't do to give this man an opening. "I'll do that little thing," she agreed. She glanced at the boy, who was eyeing her curiously from his perch on the sled. "And it seems that you do have at least one use for women," she added with a vacant smile. "My condolences to your wife, Mr. Sutton."

She'd rolled up the window before he could speak and she'd whipped the four-wheel-drive down the road with little regard for safety, sliding all over the place on the slick and rutted country road.

She glared into the flames, consigning Quinn Sutton to them with all her angry heart. She hoped and prayed that there wouldn't ever be an accident or a reason she'd have to seek out his company. She'd rather have asked help from a passing timber wolf. His son hadn't seemed at all like him, she recalled. Sutton was as dangerous looking as a timber wolf, with a face like the side of a bombed mountain and eyes that were coal-black and cruel. In the sheepskin coat he'd been wearing with that raunchy Stetson that day, he'd looked like one of the old mountain men might have back in Wyoming's early days. He'd given Amanda some bad moments and she'd hated him after that uncomfortable confrontation. But the boy had been kind. He was redheaded and blue-eyed, nothing like his father, not a bit of resemblance.

She knew the rancher's name only because her aunt had mentioned him, and cautioned Amanda about going near the Sutton ranch. The ranch was called Ricochet, and Amanda had immediately thought of a bullet going awry. Probably one of Sutton's ancestors had thrown some lead now and again. Mr. Sutton looked a lot more like a bandit than he did a rancher, with his face unshaven, that wide, awful scrape on his cheek and his crooked nose. It was an unforgettable face all around, especially those eyes....

She pulled the rug closer and gave the book in her slender hand a careless glance. She wasn't really in the mood to read. Memories kept tearing her heart. She leaned her blond head back against the chair and her dark eyes studied the flames with idle appreciation of their beauty.

The nightmare of the past few weeks had finally caught up with her. She'd stood onstage, with the lights beating down on her long blond hair and outlining the beige leather dress that was her trademark, and her voice had simply refused to cooperate. The shock of being unable to produce a single note had caused her to faint, to the shock and horror of the audience.

She came to in a hospital, where she'd been given what seemed to be every test known to medical science. But nothing would produce her singing voice, even though she could talk. It was, the doctor told her, purely a psychological problem, caused by the trauma of what had happened. She needed rest.

So Hank, who was the leader of the group, had called her Aunt Bess and convinced her to arrange for Amanda to get away from it all. Her aunt's rich boyfriend had this holiday cabin in Wyoming's Grand Teton Mountains and was more than willing to let Amanda recuperate there. Amanda had protested, but Hank and the boys and her aunt had insisted. So here she was, in the middle of winter, in several feet of snow, with no television, no telephone and facilities that barely worked. Roughing it, the big, bearded bandleader had told her, would do her good.

She smiled when she remembered how caring and kind the guys had been. Her group was called Desperado, and her leather costume was its trademark. The four men who made up the rest of it were fine musicians, but they looked like the Hell's Angels on stage in denim and leather with thick black beards and mustaches and untrimmed hair. They were really pussycats under that rough exterior, but nobody had ever been game enough to try to find out if they were.

Hank and Deke and Jack and Johnson had been trying to get work at a Virginia night spot when they'd run into Amanda Corrie Callaway, who was also trying to get work there. The club needed a singer and a band, so it was a match made in heaven, although Amanda with her sheltered upbringing had been a little afraid of her new backup band. They, on the other hand, had been nervous around her because she was such a far cry from the usual singers they'd worked with. The shy, introverted young blonde made them self-conscious about their appearance. But their first performance together had been a phenomenal hit, and they'd been together four years now.

They were famous, now. Desperado had been on the music videos for two years, they'd done television shows and magazine interviews, and they were recognized everywhere they went. Especially Amanda, who went by the stage name of Mandy Callaway. It wasn't a bad life, and it was making them rich. But there wasn't much rest or time for a personal life. None of the group was married except Hank, and he was already getting a divorce. It was hard for a homebound spouse to accept the frequent absences that road tours required.

She still shivered from the look Quinn Sutton had given her, and now she was worried about her Aunt Bess, though the woman was more liberal minded and should know the score. But Sutton had convinced Amanda that she wasn't the first woman to be at Blalock's cabin. She should have told that arrogant rancher what her real relationship with Blalock Durning was, but he probably wouldn't have believed her.

Of course, she could have put him in touch with Jerry and proved it. Jerry Allen, their road manager, was one of the best in the business. He'd kept them from starving during the beginning, and they had an expert crew of electricians and carpenters who made up the rest of the retinue. It took a huge bus to carry the people and equipment, appropriately called the "Outlaw Express."

Amanda had pleaded with Jerry to give them a few weeks rest after the tragedy that had cost her her nerve, but he'd refused. Get back on the horse, he'd advised. And she'd tried. But the memories were just too horrible.

So finally he'd agreed to Hank's suggestion and she was officially on hiatus, as were the other members of the group, for a month. Maybe in that length of time she could come to grips with it, face it.

It had been a week and she felt better already. Or she would, if those strange noises outside the cabin would just stop! She had horrible visions of wolves breaking in and eating her.

"Hello?"

The small voice startled her. It sounded like a boy's. She got up, clutching the fire poker in her hand and went to the front door. "Who's there?" she called out tersely.

"It's just me. Elliot," he said. "Elliot Sutton."

She let out a breath between her teeth. Oh, no, she thought miserably, what was he doing here? His father would come looking for him, and she couldn't bear to have that...that savage anywhere around!

"What do you want?" she groaned.

"I brought you something."

It would be discourteous to refuse the gift, she guessed, especially since he'd apparently come through several feet of snow to bring it. Which brought to mind a really interesting question: where was his father?

She opened the door. He grinned at her from under a thick cap that covered his red hair.

"Hi," he said. "I thought you might like to have some roasted peanuts. I did them myself. They're nice on a cold night."

Her eyes went past him to a sled hitched to a sturdy draft horse. "Did you come in that?" she asked, recognizing the sled he and his father had been riding the day she'd met them.

"Sure," he said. "That's how we get around in winter, what with the snow and all. We take hay out to the livestock on it. You remember, you saw us. Well, we usually take hay out on it, that is. When Dad's not laid up," he added pointedly, and his blue eyes said more than his voice did.

She knew she was going to regret asking the question before she opened her mouth. She didn't want to ask. But no young boy came to a stranger's house in the middle of a snowy night just to deliver a bag of roasted peanuts.

"What's wrong?" she asked with resigned perception.

He blinked. "What?"

"I said, what's wrong?" She made her tone gentler. He couldn't help it that his father was a savage, and he was worried under that false grin. "Come on, you might as well tell me."

He bit his lower lip and looked down at his snow-covered boots. "It's my dad," he said. "He's bad sick and he won't let me get the doctor."

So there it was. She knew she shouldn't have asked. "Can't your mother do something?" she asked hopefully.

"My mom ran off with Mr. Jackson from the livestock association when I was just a little feller," he replied, registering Amanda's shocked expression. "She and Dad got divorced and she died some years ago, but Dad doesn't talk about her. Will you come, miss?"

"I'm not a doctor," she said, hesitating.

"Oh, sure, I know that," he agreed eagerly, "but you're a girl.

And girls know how to take care of sick folks, don't they?" The confidence slid away and he looked like what he was—a terrified little boy with nobody to turn to. "Please, lady," he added. "I'm scared. He's hot and shaking all over and—!"

"I'll get my boots on," she said. She gathered them from beside the fireplace and tugged them on, and then she went for a coat and stuffed her long blond hair under a stocking cap. "Do you have cough syrup, aspirins, throat lozenges—that sort of thing?"

"Yes, ma'am," he said eagerly, then sighed. "Dad won't take them, but we have them."

"Is he suicidal?" Amanda asked angrily as she went out the door behind him and locked the cabin before she climbed on the sled with the boy.

"Well sometimes things get to him," he ventured. "But he doesn't ever get sick, and he won't admit that he is. But he's out of his head and I'm scared. He's all I got."

"We'll take care of him," she promised, and hoped she could deliver on the promise. "Let's go."

"Do you know Mr. Durning well?" he asked as he called to the draft horse and started him back down the road and up the mountain toward the Sutton house.

"He's sort of a friend of a relative of mine," she said evasively. The sled ride was fun, and she was enjoying the cold wind and snow in her face, the delicious mountain air. "I'm only staying at the cabin for a few weeks. Just time to…get over something."

"Have you been sick, too?" he asked curiously.

"In a way," she said noncommittally.

The sled went jerkily up the road, around the steep hill. She held on tight and hoped the big draft horse had steady feet. It was a harrowing ride at the last, and then they were up, and the huge redwood ranch house came into sight, blazing with light from its long, wide front porch to the gabled roof.

"It's a beautiful house," Amanda said.

"My dad added on to it for my mom, before they married," he

told her. He shrugged. "I don't remember much about her, except she was redheaded. Dad sure hates women." He glanced at her apologetically. "He's not going to like me bringing you...."

"I can take care of myself," she returned, and smiled reassuringly. "Let's go see how bad it is."

"I'll get Harry to put up the horse and sled," he said, yelling toward the lighted barn until a grizzled old man appeared. After a brief introduction to Amanda, Harry left and took the horse away.

"Harry's been here since Dad was a boy," Elliot told her as he led her down a bare-wood hall and up a steep staircase to the second storey of the house. "He does most everything, even cooks for the men." He paused outside a closed door, and gave Amanda a worried look. "He'll yell for sure."

"Let's get it over with, then."

She let Elliot open the door and look in first, to make sure his father had something on.

"He's still in his jeans," he told her, smiling as she blushed. "It's okay."

She cleared her throat. So much for pretended sophistication, she thought, and here she was twenty-four years old. She avoided Elliot's grin and walked into the room.

Quinn Sutton was sprawled on his stomach, his bare muscular arms stretched toward the headboard. His back gleamed with sweat, and his thick, black hair was damp with moisture. Since it wasn't hot in the room, Amanda decided that he must have a high fever. He was moaning and talking unintelligibly.

"Elliot, can you get me a basin and some hot water?" she asked. She took off her coat and rolled up the sleeves of her cotton blouse.

"Sure thing," Elliot told her, and rushed out of the room.

"Mr. Sutton, can you hear me?" Amanda asked softly. She sat down beside him on the bed, and lightly touched his bare shoulder. He was hot, all right—burning up. "Mr. Sutton," she called again.

"No," he moaned. "No, you can't do it…!"

"Mr. Sutton…"

He rolled over and his black eyes opened, glazed with fever, but Amanda barely noticed. Her eyes were on the rest of him, male perfection from shoulder to narrow hips. He was darkly tanned, too, and thick, black hair wedged from his chest down his flat stomach to the wide belt at his hips. Amanda, who was remarkably innocent not only for her age, but for her profession as well, stared like a star-struck girl. He was beautiful, she thought, amazed at the elegant lines of his body, at the ripple of muscle and the smooth, glistening skin.

"What the hell do you want?" he rasped.

So much for hero worship, she thought dryly. She lifted her eyes back to his. "Elliot was worried," she said quietly. "He came and got me. Please don't fuss at him. You're raging with fever."

"Damn the fever, get out," he said in a tone that might have stopped a charging wolf.

"I can't do that," she said. She turned her head toward the door where Elliot appeared with a basin full of hot water and a towel and washcloth over one arm.

"Here you are, lady," he said. "Hi, Dad," he added with a wan smile at his furious father. "You can beat me when you're able again."

"Don't think I won't," Quinn growled.

"There, there, you're just feverish and sick, Mr. Sutton," Amanda soothed.

"Get Harry and have him throw her off my land," Quinn told Elliot in a furious voice.

"How about some aspirin, Elliot, and something for him to drink? A small whiskey and something hot—"

"I don't drink whiskey," Quinn said harshly.

"He has a glass of wine now and then," Elliot ventured.

"Wine, then." She soaked the cloth in the basin. "And you

might turn up the heat. We don't want him to catch a chill when I sponge him down."

"You damned well aren't sponging me down!" Quinn raged.

She ignored him. "Go and get those things, please, Elliot, and the cough syrup, too."

"You bet, lady!" he said, grinning.

"My name is Amanda," she said absently.

"Amanda," the boy repeated, and went back downstairs.

"God help you when I get back on my feet," Quinn said with fury. He laid back on the pillow, shivering when she touched him with the cloth. "Don't…!"

"I could fry an egg on you. I have to get the fever down. Elliot said you were delirious."

"Elliot's delirious to let you in here," he shuddered. Her fingers accidentally brushed his flat stomach and he arched, shivering. "For God's sake, don't," he groaned.

"Does your stomach hurt?" she asked, concerned. "I'm sorry." She soaked the cloth again and rubbed it against his shoulders, his arms, his face.

His black eyes opened. He was breathing roughly, and his face was taut. The fever, she imagined. She brushed back her long hair, and wished she'd tied it up. It kept flowing down onto his damp chest.

"Damn you," he growled.

"Damn you, too, Mr. Sutton." She smiled sweetly. She finished bathing his face and put the cloth and basin aside. "Do you have a long-sleeved shirt?"

"Get out!"

Elliot came back with the medicine and a small glass of wine. "Harry's making hot chocolate," he said with a smile. "He'll bring it up. Here's the other stuff."

"Good," she said. "Does your father have a pajama jacket or something long-sleeved?"

"Sure!"

"Traitor," Quinn groaned at his son.

"Here you go." Elliot handed her a flannel top, which she proceeded to put on the protesting and very angry Mr. Sutton.

"I hate you," Quinn snapped at her with his last ounce of venom.

"I hate you, too," she agreed. She had to reach around him to get the jacket on, and it brought her into much too close proximity to him. She could feel the hair on his chest rubbing against her soft cheek, she could feel her own hair smoothing over his bare shoulder and chest. Odd, that shivery feeling she got from contact with him. She ignored it forcibly and got his other arm into the pajama jacket. She fastened it, trying to keep her fingers from touching his chest any more than necessary because the feel of that pelt of hair disturbed her. He shivered violently at the touch of her hands and her long, silky hair, and she assumed it was because of his fever.

"Are you finished?" Quinn asked harshly.

"Almost." She pulled the covers over him, found the electric-blanket control and turned it on. Then she ladled cough syrup into him, gave him aspirin and had him take a sip of wine, hoping that she wasn't overdosing him in the process. But the caffeine in the hot chocolate would probably counteract the wine and keep it from doing any damage in combination with the medicine. A sip of wine wasn't likely to be that dangerous anyway, and it might help the sore throat she was sure he had.

"Here's the cocoa," Harry said, joining them with a tray of mugs filled with hot chocolate and topped with whipped cream.

"That looks delicious. Thank you so much," Amanda said, and smiled shyly at the old man.

He grinned back. "Nice to be appreciated." He glared at Quinn. "Nobody else ever says so much as a thank-you!"

"It's hard to thank a man for food poisoning," Quinn rejoined weakly.

"He ain't going to die," Harry said as he left. "He's too damned mean."

"That's a fact," Quinn said and closed his eyes.

He was asleep almost instantly. Amanda drew up a chair and sat down beside him. He'd still need looking after, and presumably the boy went to school. It was past the Christmas holidays.

"You go to school, don't you?" she asked Elliot.

He nodded. "I ride the horse out to catch the bus and then turn him loose. He comes to the barn by himself. You're staying?"

"I'd better, I guess," she said. "I'll sit with him. He may get worse in the night. He's got to see a doctor tomorrow. Is there one around here?"

"There's Dr. James in town, in Holman that is," he said. "He'll come out if Dad's bad enough. He has a cancer patient down the road and he comes to check on her every few days. He could stop by then."

"We'll see how your father is feeling. You'd better get to bed," she said and smiled at him.

"Thank you for coming, Miss... Amanda," Elliot said. He sighed. "I don't think I've ever been so scared."

"It's okay," she said. "I didn't mind. Good night, Elliot."

He smiled at her. "Good night."

He went out and closed the door. Amanda sat back in her chair and looked at the sleeping face of the wild man. He seemed vulnerable like this, with his black eyes closed. He had the thickest lashes she'd ever seen, and his eyebrows were thick and well shaped above his deep-set eyes. His mouth was rather thin, but it was perfectly shaped, and the full lower lip was sensuous. She liked that jutting chin, with its hint of stubbornness. His nose was formidable and straight, and he wasn't that bad looking... asleep. Perhaps it was the coldness of his eyes that made him seem so much rougher when he was awake. Not that he looked that unintimidating even now. He had so many coarse edges....

She waited a few minutes and touched his forehead. It was a little cooler, thank God, so maybe he was going to be better by morning. She went into the bathroom and washed her face and went back to sit by him. Somewhere in the night, she fell asleep with her blond head pillowed on the big arm of the chair. Voices woke her.

"Has she been there all night, Harry?" Quinn was asking.

"Looks like. Poor little critter, she's worn out."

"I'll shoot Elliot!"

"Now, boss, that's no way to treat the kid. He got scared, and I didn't know what to do. Women know things about illness. Why, my mama could doctor people and she never had no medical training. She used herbs and things."

Amanda blinked, feeling eyes on her. She found Quinn Sutton gazing steadily at her from a sitting position on the bed.

"How do you feel?" she asked without lifting her sleepy head.

"Like hell," he replied. "But I'm a bit better."

"Would you like some breakfast, ma'am?" Harry asked with a smile. "And some coffee?"

"Coffee. Heavenly. But no breakfast, thanks, I won't impose," she said drowsily, yawning and stretching uninhibitedly as she sat up, her full breasts beautifully outlined against the cotton blouse in the process.

Quinn felt his body tautening again, as it had the night before so unexpectedly and painfully when her hands had touched him. He could still feel them, and the brush of her long, silky soft hair against his skin. She smelled of gardenias and the whole outdoors, and he hated her more than ever because he'd been briefly vulnerable.

"Why did you come with Elliot?" Quinn asked her when Harry had gone.

She pushed back her disheveled hair and tried not to think how bad she must look without makeup and with her hair uncombed. She usually kept it in a tight braid on top of her head when she wasn't performing. It made her feel vulnerable to have its unusual length on display for a man like Quinn Sutton.

"Your son is only twelve," she answered him belatedly. "That's too much responsibility for a kid," she added. "I know. I had my dad to look after at that age, and no mother. My dad drank," she added with a bitter smile. "Excessively. When he drank he got into trouble. I can remember knowing how to call a bail bondsman at the age of thirteen. I never dated, I never took friends home with me. When I was eighteen, I ran away from home. I don't even know if he's still alive, and I don't care."

"That's one problem Elliot won't ever have," he replied quietly. "Tough girl, aren't you?" he added, and his black eyes were frankly curious.

She hadn't meant to tell him so much. It embarrassed her, so she gave him her most belligerent glare. "Tough enough, thanks," she said. She got out of the chair. "If you're well enough to argue, you ought to be able to take care of yourself. But if that fever goes up again, you'll need to see the doctor."

"I'll decide that," he said tersely. "Go home."

"Thanks, I'll do that little thing." She got her coat and put it on without taking time to button it. She pushed her hair up under the stocking cap, aware of his eyes on her the whole time.

"You don't fit the image of a typical hanger-on," he said unexpectedly.

She glanced at him, blinking with surprise. "I beg your pardon?"

"A hanger-on," he repeated. He lifted his chin and studied her with mocking thoroughness. "You're Durning's latest lover, I gather. Well, if it's money you're after, he's the perfect choice. A pretty little tramp could go far with him... Damn!"

She stood over him with the remains of his cup of hot chocolate all over his chest, shivering with rage.

"I'm sorry," she said curtly. "That was a despicable thing to do to a sick man, but what you said to me was inexcusable."

She turned and went to the door, ignoring his muffled curses as he threw off the cover and sat up.

"I'd cuss, too," she said agreeably as she glanced back at him one last time, her eyes running helplessly over the broad expanse of hair-roughened skin. "All that sticky hot chocolate in that thicket on your chest," she mused. "It will probably take steam cleaning to remove it. Too bad you can't attract a 'hanger-on' to help you bathe it out. But, then, you aren't as rich as Mr. Durning, are you?" And she walked out, her nose in the air. As she went toward the stairs, she imagined that she heard laughter. But of course, that couldn't have been possible.

CHAPTER TWO

AMANDA REGRETTED THE hot-chocolate incident once she was back in the cabin, even though Quinn Sutton had deserved every drop of it. How dare he call her such a name!

Amanda was old-fashioned in her ideas. A real country girl from Mississippi who'd had no example to follow except a liberated aunt and an alcoholic parent, and she was like neither of them. She hardly even dated these days. Her working gear wasn't the kind of clothing that told men how conventional her ideals were. They saw the glitter and sexy outfit and figured that Amanda, or just "Mandy" as she was known onstage, lived like her alter ego looked. There were times when she rued the day she'd ever signed on with Desperado, but she was too famous and making too much money to quit now.

She put her hair in its usual braid and kept it there for the rest of the week, wondering from time to time about Quinn Sutton and whether or not he'd survived his illness. Not that she cared, she kept telling herself. It didn't matter to her if he turned up his toes.

There was no phone in the cabin, and no piano. She couldn't play solitaire, she didn't have a television. There was only the radio and the cassette player for company, and Mr. Durning's taste in music was really extreme. He liked opera and nothing else. She'd have died for some soft rock, or just an instrument to practice on. She could play drums as well as the synthesizer and piano, and she wound up in the kitchen banging on the counter with two stainless-steel knives out of sheer boredom.

When the electricity went haywire in the wake of two inches of freezing rain on Sunday night, it was almost a relief. She sat in the darkness laughing. She was trapped in a house without heat, without light, and the only thing she knew about fireplaces was that they required wood. The logs that were cut outside were frozen solid under the sleet and there were none in the house. There wasn't even a pack of matches.

She wrapped up in her coat and shivered, hating the solitude and the weather and feeling the nightmares coming back in the icy night. She didn't want to think about the reason her voice had quit on her, but if she spent enough time alone, she was surely going to go crazy reliving that night onstage.

Lost in thought, in nightmarish memories of screams and her own loss of consciousness, she didn't hear the first knock on the door until it came again.

"Miss Corrie!" a familiar angry voice shouted above the wind.

She got up, feeling her way to the door. "Keep your shirt on," she muttered as she threw it open.

Quinn Sutton glared down at her. "Get whatever you'll need for a couple of days and come on. The power's out. If you stay here you'll freeze to death. It's going below zero tonight. My ranch has an extra generator, so we've still got the power going."

She glared back. "I'd rather freeze to death than go anywhere with you, thanks just the same."

He took a slow breath. "Look, your morals are your own business. I just thought—"

She slammed the door in his face and turned, just in time to have him kick in the door and come after her.

"I said you're coming with me, lady," he said shortly. He bent and picked her up bodily and started out the door. "And to hell with what you'll need for a couple of days."

"Mr....Sutton!" she gasped, stunned by the unexpected contact with his hard, fit body as he carried her easily out the door and closed it behind them.

"Hold on," he said tautly and without looking at her. "The snow's pretty heavy right through this drift."

In fact, it was almost waist deep. She hadn't been outside in two days, so she hadn't noticed how high it had gotten. Her hands clung to the old sheepskin coat he was wearing. It smelled of leather and tobacco and whatever soap he used, and the furry collar was warm against her cold cheek. He made her feel small and helpless, and she wasn't sure she liked it.

"I don't like your tactics," she said through her teeth as the wind howled around them and sleet bit into her face like tiny nails.

"They get results. Hop on." He put her up on the sled, climbed beside her, grasped the reins and turned the horse back toward the mountain.

She wanted to protest, to tell him to take his offer and go to hell. But it was bitterly cold and she was shivering too badly to argue. He was right, and that was the hell of it. She could freeze to death in that cabin easily enough, and nobody would have found her until spring came or until her aunt persuaded Mr. Durning to come and see about her.

"I don't want to impose," she said curtly.

"We're past that now," he replied. "It's either this or bury you."

"I'm sure I know which you'd prefer," she muttered, huddling in her heavy coat.

"Do you?" he asked, turning his head. In the daylight glare of snow and sleet, she saw an odd twinkle in his black eyes. "Try digging a hole out there."

She gave him a speaking glance and resigned herself to going with him.

He drove the sled right into the barn and left her to wander through the aisle, looking at the horses and the two new calves in the various stalls while he dealt with unhitching and stalling the horse.

"What's wrong with these little things?" she asked, her hands in her pockets and her ears freezing as she nodded toward the two calves.

"Their mamas starved out in the pasture," he said quietly. "I couldn't get to them in time."

He sounded as if that mattered to him. She looked up at his dark face, seeing new character in it. "I didn't think a cow or two would matter," she said absently.

"I lost everything I had a few months back," he said matter-of-factly. "I'm trying to pull out of bankruptcy, and right now it's a toss-up as to whether I'll even come close. Every cow counts." He looked down at her. "But it isn't just the money. It disturbs me to see anything die from lack of attention. Even a cow."

"Or a mere woman?" she said with a faint smile. "Don't worry, I know you don't want me here. I'm...grateful to you for coming to my rescue. Most of the firewood was frozen and Mr. Durning apparently doesn't smoke, because there weren't a lot of matches around."

He scowled faintly. "No, Durning doesn't smoke. Didn't you know?"

She shrugged. "I never had reason to ask," she said, without telling him that it was her aunt, not herself, who would know about Mr. Durning's habits. Let him enjoy his disgusting opinion of her.

"Elliot said you'd been sick."

She lifted a face carefully kept blank. "Sort of," she replied.

"Didn't Durning care enough to come with you?"

"Mr. Sutton, my personal life is none of your business," she said firmly. "You can think whatever you want to about me. I don't care. But for what it's worth, I hate men probably as much as you hate women, so you won't have to hold me off with a stick."

His face went hard at the remark, but he didn't say anything. He searched her eyes for one long moment and then turned toward the house, gesturing her to follow.

Elliot was overjoyed with their new house guest. Quinn Sutton had a television and all sorts of tapes, and there was, surprisingly enough, a brand-new keyboard on a living-room table.

She touched it lovingly, and Elliot grinned at her. "Like it?" he asked proudly. "Dad gave it to me for Christmas. It's not an expensive one, you know, but it's nice to practice on. Listen."

He turned it on and flipped switches, and gave a pretty decent rendition of a tune by Genesis.

Amanda, who was formally taught in piano, smiled at his efforts. "Very good," she praised. "But try a B-flat instead of a B at the end of that last measure and see if it doesn't give you a better sound."

Elliot cocked his head. "I play by ear," he faltered.

"Sorry." She reached over and touched the key she wanted. "That one." She fingered the whole chord. "You have a very good ear."

"But I can't read music," he sighed. His blue eyes searched her face. "You can, can't you?"

She nodded, smiling wistfully. "I used to long for piano lessons. I took them in spurts and then begged a...friend to let me use her piano to practice on. It took me a long time to learn just the basics, but I do all right."

"All right" meant that she and the boys had won a Grammy award for their last album and it had been one of her own songs that had headlined it. But she couldn't tell Elliot that. She was convinced that Quinn Sutton would have thrown her out the front door if he'd known what she did for a living. He didn't seem like a rock fan, and once he got a look at her stage costume and her group, he'd probably accuse her of a lot worse than being his neighbor's live-in lover. She shivered. Well, at least she didn't like Quinn Sutton, and that was a good thing. She might get out of here without having him find out who she really was, but just in case, it wouldn't do to let herself become interested in him.

"I don't suppose you'd consider teaching me how to read music?" Elliot asked. "For something to do, you know, since we're going to be snowed in for a while, the way it looks."

"Sure, I'll teach you," she murmured, smiling at him. "If you dad doesn't mind," she added with a quick glance at the doorway.

Quinn Sutton was standing there, in jeans and red-checked flannel shirt with a cup of black coffee in one hand, watching them.

"None of that rock stuff," he said shortly. "That's a bad influence on kids."

"Bad influence?" Amanda was almost shocked, despite the fact that she'd gauged his tastes very well.

"Those raucous lyrics and suggestive costumes, and satanism," he muttered. "I confiscated his tapes and put them away. It's indecent."

"Some of it is, yes," she agreed quietly. "But you can't lump it all into one category, Mr. Sutton. And these days, a lot of the groups are even encouraging chastity and going to war on drug use..."

"You don't really believe that bull, do you?" he asked coldly.

"It's true, Dad," Elliot piped up.

"You can shut up," he told his son. He turned. "I've got a lot of paperwork to get through. Don't turn that thing on high, will you? Harry will show you to your room when you're ready to bed down, Miss Corrie," he added, and looked as if he'd like to have shown her to a room underwater. "Or Elliot can."

"Thanks again," she said, but she didn't look up. He made her feel totally inadequate and guilty. In a small way, it was like going back to that night...

"Don't stay up past nine, Elliot," Quinn told his son.

"Okay, Dad."

Amanda looked after the tall man with her jaw hanging loose. "What did he say?" she asked.

"He said not to stay up past nine," Elliot replied. "We all go to bed at nine," he added with a grin at her expression. "There, there, you'll get used to it. Ranch life, you know. Here, now, what was that about a B-flat? What's a B-flat?"

She was obviously expected to go to bed with the chickens and probably get up with them, too. Absently she picked up the keyboard and began to explain the basics of music to Elliot.

"Did he really hide all your tapes?" she asked curiously.

"Yes, he did," Elliot chuckled, glancing toward the stairs. "But I know where he hid them." He studied her with pursed lips. "You know, you look awfully familiar somehow."

Amanda managed to keep a calm expression on her face, despite her twinge of fear. Her picture, along with that of the men in the group, was on all their albums and tapes. God forbid that Elliot should be a fan and have one of them, but they were popular with young people his age. "They say we all have a counterpart, don't they?" she asked and smiled. "Maybe you saw somebody who looked like me. Here, this is how you run a C scale...."

She successfully changed the subject and Elliot didn't bring it up again. They went upstairs a half hour later, and she breathed a sigh of relief. Since the autocratic Mr. Sutton hadn't given her time to pack, she wound up sleeping in her clothes under the spotless white sheets. She only hoped that she wasn't going to have the nightmares here. She couldn't bear the thought of having Quinn Sutton ask her about them. He'd probably say that she'd gotten just what she deserved.

But the nightmares didn't come. She slept with delicious abandon and didn't dream at all. She woke up the next morning oddly refreshed just as the sun was coming up, even before Elliot knocked on her door to tell her that Harry had breakfast ready downstairs.

She combed out her hair and rebraided it, wrapping it around the crown of her head and pinning it there as she'd had it last night. She tidied herself after she'd washed up, and went downstairs with a lively step.

Quinn Sutton and Elliot were already making great inroads into huge, fluffy pancakes smothered in syrup when she joined them.

Harry brought in a fresh pot of coffee and grinned at her. "How about some hotcakes and sausage?" he asked.

"Just a hotcake and a sausage, please," she said and grinned back. "I'm not much of a breakfast person."

"You'll learn if you stay in these mountains long," Quinn said, sparing her a speaking glance. "You need more meat on those bones. Fix her three, Harry."

"Now, listen…" she began.

"No, you listen," Quinn said imperturbably, sipping black coffee. "My house, my rules."

She sighed. It was just like old times at the orphanage, during one of her father's binges when she'd had to live with Mrs. Brim's rules. "Yes, sir," she said absently.

He glared at her. "I'm thirty-four, and you aren't young enough to call me 'sir.'"

She lifted startled dark eyes to his. "I'm twenty-four," she said. "Are you really just thirty-four?" She flushed even as she said it. He did look so much older, but she hadn't meant to say anything. "I'm sorry. That sounded terrible."

"I look older than I am," he said easily. "I've got a friend down in Texas who thought I was in my late thirties, and he's known me for years. No need to apologize." He didn't add that he had a lot of mileage on him, thanks to his ex-wife. "You look younger than twenty-four," he did add.

He pushed away his empty plate and sipped coffee, staring at her through the steam rising from it. He was wearing a blue-checked flannel shirt this morning, buttoned up to his throat, with jeans that were well fitting but not overly tight. He didn't dress like the men in Amanda's world, but then, the men she knew weren't the same breed as this Teton man.

"Amanda taught me all about scales last night," Elliot said excitedly. "She really knows music."

"How did you manage to learn?" Quinn asked her, and she saw in his eyes that he was remembering what she'd told him about her alcoholic father.

She lifted her eyes from her plate. "During my dad's binges, I stayed at the local orphanage. There was a lady there who played for her church. She taught me."

"No sisters or brothers?" he asked quietly.

She shook her head. "Nobody in the world, except an aunt." She lifted her coffee cup. "She's an artist, and she's been living with her latest lover—"

"You'd better get to school, son," Quinn interrupted tersely, nodding at Elliot.

"I sure had, or I'll be late. See you!"

He grabbed his books and his coat and was gone in a flash, and Harry gathered the plates with a smile and vanished into the kitchen.

"Don't talk about things like that around Elliot," Quinn said shortly. "He understands more than you think. I don't want him corrupted."

"Don't you realize that most twelve-year-old boys know more about life than grown-ups these days?" she asked with a faint smile.

"In your world, maybe. Not in mine."

She could have told him that she was discussing the way things were, not the way she preferred them, but she knew it would be useless. He was so certain that she was wildly liberated. She sighed. "Maybe so," she murmured.

"I'm old-fashioned," he added. His dark eyes narrowed on her face. "I don't want Elliot exposed to the liberated outlook of the so-called modern world until he's old enough to understand that he has a choice. I don't like a society that ridicules honor and fidelity and innocence. So I fight back in the only way I can. I go to church on Sunday, Miss Corrie," he mused, smiling at her curious expression. "Elliot goes, too. You might not know it from watching television or going to movies, but there are still a few people in America who also go to church on Sunday, who work hard all week and find their relaxation in ways that don't involve drugs, booze or casual sex. How's that for a shocking revelation?"

"Nobody ever accused Hollywood of portraying real life," she replied with a smile. "But if you want my honest opinion, I'm pretty sick of gratuitous sex, filthy language and graphic violence in the newer movies. In fact, I'm so sick of it that I've gone back to watching the old-time movies from the 1940s." She laughed at his expression. "Let me tell you, these old movies had real handicaps—the actors all had to keep their clothes on and they couldn't swear. The writers were equally limited, so they created some of the most gripping dramas ever produced. I love them. And best of all, you can even watch them with kids."

He pursed his lips, his dark eyes holding hers. "I like George Brent, George Sanders, Humphrey Bogart, Bette Davis and Cary Grant best," he confessed. "Yes, I watch them, too."

"I'm not really all that modern myself," she confessed, toying with the tablecloth. "I live in the city, but not in the fast lane." She put down her coffee cup. "I can understand why you feel the way you do, about taking Elliot to church and all. Elliot told me a little about his mother…"

He closed up like a plant. "I don't talk to outsiders about my personal life," he said without apology and got up, towering over her. "If you'd like to watch television or listen to music, you're welcome. I've got work to do."

"Can I help?" she asked.

His heavy eyebrows lifted. "This isn't the city."

"I know how to cut open a bale of hay," she said. "The orphanage was on a big farm. I grew up doing chores. I can even milk a cow."

"You won't milk the kind of cows I keep," he returned. His dark eyes narrowed. "You can feed those calves in the barn, if you like. Harry can show you where the bottle is."

Which meant that he wasn't going to waste his time on her. She nodded, trying not to feel like an unwanted guest. Just for a few minutes she'd managed to get under that hard reserve. Maybe that was good enough for a start. "Okay."

His black eyes glanced over her hair. "You haven't worn it down since the night Elliot brought you here," he said absently.

"I don't ever wear it down at home, as a rule," she said quietly. "It…gets in my way." It got recognized, too, she thought, which was why she didn't dare let it loose around Elliot too often.

His eyes narrowed for an instant before he turned and shouldered into his jacket.

"Don't leave the perimeter of the yard," he said as he stuck his weather-beaten Stetson on his dark, thick hair. "This is wild country. We have bears and wolves, and a neighbor who still sets traps."

"I know my limitations, thanks," she said. "Do you have help, besides yourself?"

He turned, thrusting his big, lean hands into work gloves. "Yes, I have four cowboys who work around the place. They're all married."

She blushed. "Thank you for your sterling assessment of my character."

"You may like old movies," he said with a penetrating stare. "But no woman with your kind of looks is a virgin at twenty-four," he said quietly, mindful of Harry's sharp ears. "And I'm a backcountry man, but I've been married and I'm not stupid about women. You won't play me for a fool."

She wondered what he'd say if he knew the whole truth about her. But it didn't make her smile to reflect on that. She lowered her eyes to the thick white mug. "Think what you like, Mr. Sutton. You will anyway."

"Damned straight."

He walked out without looking back, and Amanda felt a vicious chill even before he opened the door and went out into the cold white yard.

She waited for Harry to finish his chores and then went with him to the barn, where the little calves were curled up in their stalls of hay.

"They're only days old," Harry said, smiling as he brought the enormous bottles they were fed from. In fact, the nipples were stretched across the top of buckets and filled with warm mash and milk. "But they'll grow. Sit down, now. You may get a bit dirty…"

"Clothes wash," Amanda said easily, smiling. But this outfit was all she had. She was going to have to get the elusive Mr. Sutton to take her back to the cabin to get more clothes, or she'd be washing out her things in the sink tonight.

She knelt down in a clean patch of hay and coaxed the calf to take the nipple into its mouth. Once it got a taste of the warm liquid, it wasn't difficult to get it to drink. Amanda loved the feel of its silky red-and-white coat under her fingers as she stroked it. The animal was a Hereford, and its big eyes were pink rimmed and soulful. The calf watched her while it nursed.

"Poor little thing," she murmured softly, rubbing between its eyes. "Poor little orphan."

"They're tough critters, for all that," Harry said as he fed the other calf. "Like the boss."

"How did he lose everything, if you don't mind me asking?"

He glanced at her and read the sincerity in her expression. "I don't guess he'd mind if I told you. He was accused of selling contaminated beef."

"Contaminated…how?"

"It's a long story. The herd came to us from down in the Southwest. They had measles. Not," he added when he saw her puzzled expression, "the kind humans get. Cattle don't break out in spots, but they do develop cysts in the muscle tissue and if it's bad enough, it means that the carcasses have to be destroyed." He shrugged. "You can't spot it, because there are no definite symptoms, and you can't treat it because there isn't a drug that cures it. These cattle had it and contaminated the rest of our herd. It was like the end of the world. Quinn had sold the beef cattle to the packing-plant operator. When the meat was ordered destroyed, he came back on Quinn to recover his money, but Quinn had already spent it to buy new cattle. We went to court... Anyway, to make a long story short, they cleared Quinn of any criminal charges and gave him the opportunity to make restitution. In turn, he sued the people who sold him the contaminated herd in the first place." He smiled ruefully. "We just about broke even, but it meant starting over from scratch. That was last year. Things are still rough, but Quinn's a tough customer and he's got a good business head. He'll get through it. I'd bet on him."

Amanda pondered that, thinking that Quinn's recent life had been as difficult as her own. At least he had Elliot. That must have been a comfort to him. She said as much to Harry.

He gave her a strange look. "Well, yes, Elliot's special to him," he said, as if there were things she didn't know. Probably there were.

"Will these little guys make it?" she asked when the calf had finished his bottle.

"I think so," Harry said. "Here, give me that bottle and I'll take care of it for you."

She sighed, petting the calf gently. She liked farms and ranches. They were so real, compared to the artificial life she'd known since she was old enough to leave home. She loved her work and she'd always enjoyed performing, but it seemed sometimes as if she lived in another world. Values were nebulous, if they even existed, in the world where she worked. Old-fashioned ideas like morality, honor, chastity were laughed at or ignored. Amanda kept hers to herself, just as she kept her privacy intact. She didn't discuss her inner feelings with anyone. Probably her friends and associates would have died laughing if they'd known just how many hang-ups she had, and how distant her outlook on life was from theirs.

"Here's another one," Quinn said from the front of the barn.

Amanda turned her head, surprised to see him because he'd ridden out minutes ago. He was carrying another small calf, but this one looked worse than the younger ones did.

"He's very thin," she commented.

"He's got scours." He laid the calf down next to her. "Harry, fix another bottle."

"Coming up, boss."

Amanda touched the wiry little head with its rough hide. "He's not in good shape," she murmured quietly.

Quinn saw the concern on her face and was surprised by it. He shouldn't have been, he reasoned. Why would she have come with Elliot in the middle of the night to nurse a man she didn't even like, if she wasn't a kind woman?

"He probably won't make it," he agreed, his dark eyes searching hers. "He'd been out there by himself for a long time. It's a big property, and he's a very small calf," he defended when she gave him a meaningful look. "It wouldn't be the first time we missed one, I'm sorry to say."

"I know." She looked up as Harry produced a third bottle, and her hand reached for it just as Quinn's did. She released it, feeling odd little tingles at the brief contact with his lean, sure hand.

"Here goes," he murmured curtly. He reached under the calf's chin and pulled its mouth up to slide the nipple in. The calf could barely nurse, but after a minute it seemed to rally and then it fed hungrily.

"Thank goodness," Amanda murmured. She smiled at Quinn, and his eyes flashed as they met hers, searching, dark, full of secrets. They narrowed and then abruptly fell to her soft mouth, where they lingered with a kind of questioning irritation, as if he wanted very much to kiss her and hated himself for it. Her heart leaped at the knowledge. She seemed to have a new, built-in insight about this standoffish man, and she didn't understand either it or her attitude toward him. He was domineering and hardheaded and unpredictable and she should have disliked him. But she sensed a sensitivity in him that touched her heart. She wanted to get to know him.

"I can do this," he said curtly. "Why don't you go inside?"

She was getting to him, she thought with fascination. He was interested in her, but he didn't want to be. She watched the way he avoided looking directly at her again, the angry glance of his eyes.

Well, it certainly wouldn't do any good to make him furious at her, especially when she was going to be his unwanted houseguest for several more days, from the look of the weather.

"Okay," she said, giving in. She got to her feet slowly. "I'll see if I can find something to do."

"Harry might like some company while he works in the kitchen. Wouldn't you, Harry?" he added, giving the older man a look that said he'd damned sure better like some company.

"Of course I would, boss," Harry agreed instantly.

Amanda pushed her hands into her pockets with a last glance at the calves. She smiled down at them. "Can I help feed them while I'm here?" she asked gently.

"If you want to," Quinn said readily, but without looking up.

"Thanks." She hesitated, but he made her feel shy and tongue-tied. She turned away nervously and walked back to the house.

Since Harry had the kitchen well in hand, she volunteered to iron some of Quinn's cotton shirts. Harry had the ironing board set up, but not the iron, so she went into the closet and produced one. It looked old, but maybe it would do, except that it seemed to have a lot of something caked on it.

She'd just started to plug it in when Harry came into the room and gasped.

"Not that one!" he exclaimed, gently taking it away from her. "That's Quinn's!"

She opened her mouth to make a remark, when Harry started chuckling.

"It's for his skis," he explained patiently.

She nodded. "Right. He irons his skis. I can see that."

"He does. Don't you know anything about skiing?"

"Well, you get behind a speedboat with them on..."

"Not waterskiing. *Snow* skiing," he emphasized.

She shrugged. "I come from southern Mississippi." She grinned at him. "We don't do much business in snow, you see."

"Sorry. Well, Quinn was an Olympic contender in giant slalom when he was in his late teens and early twenties. He would have made the team, but he got married and Elliot was on the way, so he gave it up. He still gets in plenty of practice," he added, shuddering. "On old Ironside peak, too. Nobody, but nobody, skis it except Quinn and a couple of other experts from Larry's Lodge over in Jackson Hole."

"I haven't seen that one on a map..." she began, because she'd done plenty of map reading before she came here.

"Oh, that isn't its official name, it's what Quinn calls it." He grinned. "Anyway, Quinn uses this iron to put wax on the bottom of his skis. Don't feel bad, I didn't know any better, either, at first, and I waxed a couple of shirts. Here's the right iron."

He handed it to her, and she plugged it in and got started. The elusive Mr. Sutton had hidden qualities, it seemed. She'd watched the winter Olympics every four years on television, and downhill skiing fascinated her. But it seemed to Amanda that giant slalom called for a kind of reckless skill and speed that would require ruthlessness and single-minded determination. Considering that, it wasn't at all surprising to her that Quinn Sutton had been good at it.

CHAPTER THREE

AMANDA HELPED HARRY do dishes and start a load of clothes in the washer. But when she took them out of the dryer, she discovered that several of Quinn's shirts were missing buttons and had loose seams.

Harry produced a needle and some thread, and Amanda set to work mending them. It gave her something to do while she watched a years-old police drama on television.

Quinn came in with Elliot a few hours later.

"Boy, the snow's bad," Elliot remarked as he rubbed his hands in front of the fire Harry had lit in the big stone fireplace. "Dad had to bring the sled out to get me, because the bus couldn't get off the main highway."

"Speaking of the sled," Amanda said, glancing at Quinn, "I've got to have a few things from the cabin. I'm really sorry, but I'm limited to what I'm wearing...."

"I'll run you down right now, before I go out again."

She put the mending aside. "I'll get my coat."

"Elliot, you can come, too. Put your coat back on," Quinn said unexpectedly, ignoring his son's surprised glance.

Amanda didn't look at him, but she understood why he wanted Elliot along. She made Quinn nervous. He was attracted to her and he was going to fight it to the bitter end. She wondered why he considered her such a threat.

He paused to pick up the shirt she'd been working on, and his expression got even harder as he glared at her. "You don't need to do that kind of thing," he said curtly.

"I've got to earn my keep somehow." She sighed. "I can feed the calves and help with the housework, at least. I'm not used to sitting around doing nothing," she added. "It makes me nervous."

He hesitated. An odd look rippled over his face as he studied the neat stitches in his shirtsleeve where the rip had been. He held it for a minute before he laid it gently back on the sofa. He didn't look at Amanda as he led the way out the door.

It didn't take her long to get her things together. Elliot wandered around the cabin. "There are knives all over the counter," he remarked. "Want me to put them in the sink?"

"Go ahead. I was using them for drumsticks," she called as she closed her suitcase.

"They don't look like they'd taste very good." Elliot chuckled.

She came out of the bedroom and gave him an amused glance. "Not that kind of drumsticks, you turkey. Here." She put down the suitcase and took the blunt stainless-steel knives from him. She glanced around to make sure Quinn hadn't come into the house and then she broke into an impromptu drum routine that made Elliot grin even more.

"Say, you're pretty good," he said.

She bowed. "Just one of my minor talents," she said. "But I'm better with a keyboard. Ready to go?"

"Whenever you are."

She started to pick up her suitcase, but Elliot reached down and got it before she could, a big grin on his freckled face. She wondered again why he looked so little like his father. She knew that his mother had been a redhead, too, but it was odd that he didn't resemble Quinn in any way at all.

Quinn was waiting on the sled, his expression unreadable,

impatiently smoking his cigarette. He let them get on and turned the draft horse back toward his own house. It was snowing lightly and the wind was blowing, not fiercely but with a nip in it. Amanda sighed, lifting her face to the snow, not caring that her hood had fallen back to reveal the coiled softness of her blond hair. She felt alive out here as she never had in the city, or even back East. There was something about the wilderness that made her feel at peace with herself for the first time since the tragedy that had sent her retreating here.

"Enjoying yourself?" Quinn asked unexpectedly.

"More than I can tell you," she replied. "It's like no other place on earth."

He nodded. His dark eyes slid over her face, her cheeks flushed with cold and excitement, and they lingered there for one long moment before he forced his gaze back to the trail. Amanda saw that look and it brought a sense of foreboding. He seemed almost angry.

In fact, he was. Before the day was out, it was pretty apparent that he'd withdrawn somewhere inside himself and had no intention of coming out again. He barely said two words to Amanda before bedtime.

"He's gone broody," Elliot mused before he and Amanda called it a night. "He doesn't do it often, and not for a long time, but when he's got something on his mind, it's best not to get on his nerves."

"Oh, I'll do my best," Amanda promised, and crossed her heart.

But that apparently didn't do much good, in her case, because he glared at her over breakfast the next morning and over lunch, and by the time she finished mending a window curtain in the kitchen and helped Harry bake a cake for dessert, she was feeling like a very unwelcome guest.

She went out to feed the calves, the nicest of her daily chores, just before Quinn was due home for supper. Elliot had lessons and he was holed up in his room trying to get them done in time for a science-fiction movie he wanted to watch after sup-per. Quinn insisted that homework came first.

She fed two of the three calves and Harry volunteered to feed the third, the little one that Quinn had brought home with scours, while she cut the cake and laid the table. She was just finishing the place settings when she heard the sled draw up outside the door.

Her heart quickened at the sound of Quinn's firm, measured stride on the porch. The door opened and he came in, along with a few snowflakes.

He stopped short at the sight of her in an old white apron with wisps of blond hair hanging around her flushed face, a bowl of whipped potatoes in her hands.

"Don't you look domestic?" he asked with sudden, bitter sarcasm.

The attack was unexpected, although it shouldn't have been. He'd been irritable ever since the day before, when he'd noticed her mending his shirt.

"I'm just helping Harry," she said. "He's feeding the calves while I do this."

"So I noticed."

She put down the potatoes, watching him hang up his hat and coat with eyes that approved his tall, fit physique, the way the red-checked flannel shirt clung to his muscular torso and long back. He was such a lonely man, she thought, watching him. So alone, even with Elliot and Harry here. He turned un-expectedly, catching her staring and his dark eyes glittered.

He went to the sink to wash his hands, almost vibrating with pent-up anger. She sensed it, but it only piqued her curiosity. He was reacting to her. She felt it, knew it, as she picked up a dish towel and went close to him to wrap it gently over his wet hands. Her big black eyes searched his, and she let her fingers linger on his while time seemed to end in the warm kitchen.

His dark eyes narrowed, and he seemed to have stopped breathing. He was aware of so many sensations. Hunger. Anger.

Loneliness. Lust. His head spun with them, and the scent of her was pure, soft woman, drifting up into his nostrils, cocooning him in the smell of cologne and shampoo. His gaze fell helplessly to her soft bow of a mouth and he wondered how it would feel to bend those few inches and take it roughly under his own. It had been so long since he'd kissed a woman, held a woman. Amanda was particularly feminine, and she appealed to everything that was masculine in him. He almost vibrated with the need to reach out to her.

But that way lay disaster, he told himself firmly. She was just another treacherous woman, probably bored with confinement, just keeping her hand in with attracting men. He probably seemed like a pushover, and she was going to use her charms to make a fool of him. He took a deep, slow breath and the glitter in his eyes became even more pronounced as he jerked the towel out of her hands and moved away.

"Sorry," she mumbled. She felt her cheeks go hot, because there had been a cold kind of violence in the action that warned her his emotions weren't quite under control. She moved away from him. Violence was the one thing she did expect from men. She'd lived with it for most of her life until she'd run away from home.

She went back to the stove, stirring the sauce she'd made to go with the boiled dumpling.

"Don't get too comfortable in the kitchen," he warned her. "This is Harry's private domain and he doesn't like trespassers. You're just passing through."

"I haven't forgotten that, Mr. Sutton," she replied, and her eyes kindled with dark fire as she looked at him. There was no reason to make her feel so unwelcome. "Just as soon as the thaw comes, I'll be out of your way for good."

"I can hardly wait," he said, biting off the words.

Amanda sighed wearily. It wasn't her idea of the perfect rest spot. She'd come away from the concert stage needing healing, and all she'd found was another battle to fight.

"You make me feel so at home, Mr. Sutton," she said wistfully. "Like part of the family. Thanks so much for your gracious hospitality, and do you happen to have a jar of rat poison...?"

Quinn had to bite hard to keep from laughing. He turned and went out of the kitchen as if he were being chased.

After supper, Amanda volunteered to wash dishes, but Harry shooed her off. Quinn apparently did book work every night, because he went into his study and closed the door, leaving Elliot with Amanda for company. They'd watched the science-fiction movie Elliot had been so eager to see and now they were working on the keyboard.

"I think I've got the hang of C major," Elliot announced, and ran the scale, complete with turned under thumb on the key of F.

"Very good," she enthused. "Okay, let's go on to G major."

She taught him the scale and watched him play it, her mind on Quinn Sutton's antagonism.

"Something bothering you?" Elliot asked suspiciously.

She shrugged. "Your dad doesn't want me here."

"He hates women," he said. "You knew that, didn't you?"

"Yes. But why?"

He shook his head. "It's because of my mother. She did something really terrible to him, and he never talks about her. He never has. I've got one picture of her, in my room."

"I guess you look like her," she said speculatively.

He handed her the keyboard. "I've got red hair and freckles like she had," he confessed. "I'm just sorry that I...well, that I don't look anything like Dad. I'm glad he cares about me, though, in spite of everything. Isn't it great that he likes me?"

What an odd way to talk about his father, Amanda thought as she studied him. She wanted to say something else, to ask about that wording, but it was too soon. She hid her curiosity in humor.

"'There are more things in heaven and earth, Horatio, than are dreamt of in your philosophy,'" she intoned deeply.

He chuckled. "Hamlet," he said. "Shakespeare. We did that in English class last month."

"Culture in the high country." She applauded. "Very good, Elliot."

"I like rock culture best," he said in a stage whisper. "Play something."

She glanced toward Quinn's closed study door with a grimace. "Something soft."

"No!" he protested, and grinned. "Come on, give him hell."

"Elliot!" she chided.

"He needs shaking up, I tell you, he's going to die an old maid. He gets all funny and red when unmarried ladies talk to him at church, and just look at how grumpy he's been since you've been around. We've got to save him, Amanda," he said solemnly.

She sighed. "Okay. It's your funeral." She flicked switches, turning on the auto rhythm, the auto chords, and moved the volume to maximum. With a mischievous glance at Elliot, she swung into one of the newest rock songs, by a rival group, instantly recognizable by the reggae rhythm and sweet harmony.

"Good God!" came a muffled roar from the study.

Amanda cut off the keyboard and handed it to Elliot.

"No!" Elliot gasped.

But it was too late. His father came out of the study and saw Elliot holding the keyboard and started smoldering.

"It was her!" Elliot accused, pointing his finger at her.

She peered at Quinn over her drawn-up knees. "Would I play a keyboard that loud in your house, after you warned me not to?" she asked in her best meek voice.

Quinn's eyes narrowed. They went back to Elliot.

"She's lying," Elliot said. "Just like the guy in those truck commercials on TV...!"

"Keep it down," Quinn said without cracking a smile. "Or I'll give that thing the decent burial it really needs. And no more damned rock music in my house! That thing has earphones. Use them!"

"Yes, sir," Elliot groaned.

Amanda saluted him. "We hear and obey, excellency!" she said with a deplorable Spanish accent. "Your wish is our command. We live only to serve…!"

The slamming of the study door cut her off. She burst into laughter while Elliot hit her with a sofa cushion.

"You animal," he accused mirthfully. "Lying to Dad, accusing me of doing something I never did! How could you?"

"Temporary insanity," she gasped for breath. "I couldn't help myself."

"We're both going to die," he assured her. "He'll lie awake all night thinking of ways to get even and when we least expect it, pow!"

"He's welcome. Here. Run that G major scale again."

He let her turn the keyboard back on, but he was careful to move the volume switch down as far as it would go.

It was almost nine when Quinn came out of the study and turned out the light.

"Time for bed," he said.

Amanda had wanted to watch a movie that was coming on, but she knew better than to ask. Presumably they did occasionally watch television at night. She'd have to ask one of these days.

"Good night, Dad. Amanda," Elliot said, grinning as he went upstairs with a bound.

"Did you do your homework?" Quinn called up after him.

"Almost."

"What the hell does that mean?" he demanded.

"It means I'll do it first thing in the morning! 'Night, Dad!"

A door closed.

Quinn glared at Amanda. "That won't do," he said tersely. "His homework comes first. Music is a nice hobby, but it's not going to make a living for him."

Why not, she almost retorted, it makes a six-figure annual income for me, but she kept her mouth shut.

"I'll make sure he's done his homework before I offer to show him anything else on the keyboard. Okay?"

He sighed angrily. "All right. Come on. Let's go to bed."

She put her hands over her chest and gasped, her eyes wide and astonished. "Together? Mr. Sutton, really!"

His dark eyes narrowed in a veiled threat. "Hell will freeze over before I wind up in bed with you," he said icily. "I told you, I don't want used goods."

"Your loss," she sighed, ignoring the impulse to lay a lamp across his thick skull. "Experience is a valuable commodity in my world." She deliberately smoothed her hands down her waist and over her hips, her eyes faintly coquettish as she watched him watching her movements. "And I'm very experienced," she drawled. In music, she was.

His jaw tautened. "Yes, it does show," he said. "Kindly keep your attitudes to yourself. I don't want my son corrupted."

"If you really meant that, you'd let him watch movies and listen to rock music and trust him to make up his own mind about things."

"He's only twelve."

"You aren't preparing him to live in the real world," she protested.

"This," he said, "is the real world for him. Not some fancy apartment in a city where women like you lounge around in bars picking up men."

"Now you wait just a minute," she said. "I don't lounge around in bars to pick up men." She shifted her stance. "I hang out in zoos and flash elderly men in my trench coat."

He threw up his hands. "I give up."

"Good! Your room or mine?"

He whirled, his dark eyes flashing. Her smile was purely provocative and she was deliberately baiting him, he could sense it. His jaw tautened and he wanted to pick her up and shake her for the effect her teasing was having on him.

"Okay, I quit," Amanda said, because she could see that he'd reached the limits of his control and she wasn't quite brave enough to test the other side of it. "Good night. Sweet dreams."

He didn't answer her. He followed her up the stairs and watched her go into her room and close the door. After a minute, he went into his own room and locked the door. He laughed mirthlessly at his own rash action, but he hoped she could hear the bolt being thrown.

She could. It shocked her, until she realized that he'd done it deliberately, probably trying to hurt her. She laid back on her bed with a long sigh. She didn't know what to do about Mr. Sutton. He was beginning to get to her in a very real way. She had to keep her perspective. This was only temporary. It would help to keep it in mind.

Quinn was thinking the same thing. But when he turned out the light and closed his eyes, he kept feeling Amanda's loosened hair brushing down his chest, over his flat stomach, his loins. He shuddered and woke up sweating in the middle of the night. It was the worst and longest night of his life.

The next morning, Quinn glared at Amanda across the breakfast table after Elliot had left for school.

"Leave my shirts alone," he said curtly. "If you find any more tears, Harry can mend them."

Her eyebrows lifted. "I don't have germs," she pointed out. "I couldn't contaminate them just by stitching them up."

"Leave them alone," he said harshly.

"Okay. Suit yourself." She sighed. "I'll just busy myself making lacy pillows for your bed."

He said something expressive and obscene; her lips fell open and she gaped at him. She'd never heard him use language like that.

It seemed to bother him that he had. He put down his fork, left his eggs and went out the door as if leopards were stalking him.

Amanda stirred her eggs around on the plate, feeling vaguely guilty that she'd given him such a hard time that he'd gone without half his breakfast. She didn't know why she needled him. It seemed to be a new habit, maybe to keep him at bay, to keep him from noticing how attracted she was to him.

"I'm going out to feed the calves, Harry," she said after a minute.

"Dress warm. It's snowing again," he called from upstairs.

"Okay."

She put on her coat and hat and wandered out to the barn through the path Quinn had made in the deep snow. She'd never again grumble at little two- and three-foot drifts in the city, she promised herself. Now that she knew what real snow was, she felt guilty for all her past complaints.

The barn was warmer than the great outdoors. She pushed snowflakes out of her eyes and face and went to fix the bottles as Harry had shown her, but Quinn was already there and had it done.

"No need to follow me around trying to get my attention," Amanda murmured with a wicked smile. "I've already noticed how sexy and handsome you are."

He drew in a furious breath, but just as he was about to speak she moved closer and put her fingers against his cold mouth.

"You'll break my heart if you use ungentlemanly language, Mr. Sutton," she told him firmly. "I'll just feed the calves and admire you from afar, if you don't mind. It seems safer than trying to throw myself at you."

He looked torn between shaking her and kissing her. She stood very still where he towered above her, even bigger than usual in that thick shepherd's coat and his tall, gray Stetson. He looked down at her quietly, his narrowed eyes lingering on her flushed cheeks and her soft, parted mouth.

Her hands were resting against the coat, and his were on her arms, pulling. She could hardly breathe as she realized that he'd actually touched her voluntarily. He jerked her face up under his, and she could see anger and something like bitterness in the dark eyes that held hers until she blushed.

"Just what are you after, city girl?" he asked coldly.

"A smile, a kind word and, dare I say it, a round of hearty laughter?" she essayed with wide eyes, trying not to let him see how powerfully he affected her.

His dark eyes fell to her mouth. "Is that right? And nothing more?"

Her breath came jerkily through her lips. "I...have to feed the calves."

His eyes narrowed. "Yes, you do." His fingers on her arms contracted, so that she could feel them even through the sleeves of her coat. "Be careful what you offer me," he said in a voice as light and cold as the snow outside the barn. "I've been without a woman for one hell of a long time, and I'm alone up here. If you're not what you're making yourself out to be, you could be letting yourself in for some trouble."

She stared up at him only half comprehending what he was saying. As his meaning began to filter into her consciousness, her cheeks heated and her breath caught in her throat.

"You...make it sound like a threat," she breathed.

"It is a threat, Amanda," he replied, using her name for the first time. "You could start something you might not want to finish with me, even with Elliot and Harry around."

She bit her lower lip nervously. She hadn't considered that. He looked more mature and formidable than he ever had before, and she could feel the banked-down fires in him kindling even as he held her.

"Okay," she said after a minute.

He let her go and moved away from her to get the bottles. He handed them to her with a long, speculative look.

"It's all right," she muttered, embarrassed. "I won't attack you while your back is turned. I almost never rape men."

He lifted an eyebrow, but he didn't smile. "You crazed female sex maniac," he murmured.

"Goody Two Shoes," she shot back.

A corner of his mouth actually turned up. "You've got that one right," he agreed. "Stay close to the house while it's snowing like this. We wouldn't want to lose you."

"I'll just bet we wouldn't," she muttered and stuck her tongue out at his retreating back.

She knelt down to feed the calves, still shaken by her confrontation with Quinn. He was an enigma. She was almost certain that he'd been joking with her at the end of the exchange, but it was hard to tell from his poker face. He didn't look like a man who'd laughed often or enough.

The littlest calf wasn't responding as well as he had earlier. She cuddled him and coaxed him to drink, but he did it without any spirit. She laid him back down with a sigh. He didn't look good at all. She worried about him for the rest of the evening, and she didn't argue when the television was cut off at nine o'clock. She went straight to bed, with Quinn and Elliot giving her odd looks.

CHAPTER FOUR

AMANDA WAS SUBDUED at the breakfast table, more so when Quinn started watching her with dark, accusing eyes. She knew she'd deliberately needled him for the past two days, and now she was sorry. He'd hinted that her behavior was about to start something, and she was anxious not to make things any worse than they already were.

The problem was that she was attracted to him. The more she saw of him, the more she liked him. He was different from the superficial, materialistic men in her own world. He was hardheaded and stubborn. He had values, and he spoke out for them. He lived by a rigid code of ethics, and *honor* was a word that had great meaning for him. Under all that, he was sensitive and caring. Amanda couldn't help the way she was beginning to feel about him. She only wished that she hadn't started off on the wrong foot with him.

She set out to win him over, acting more like her real self. She was polite and courteous and caring, but without the rough edges she'd had in the beginning. She still did the mending, despite his grumbling, and she made cushions for the sofa out of some cloth Harry had put away. But all her domestic actions only made things worse. Quinn glared at her openly now, and his lack of politeness raised even Harry's eyebrows.

Amanda had a sneaking hunch that it was attraction to her that was making him so ill-humored. He didn't act at all like an experienced man, despite his marriage, and the way he looked at her was intense. If she could bring him out into the open, she thought, it might ease the tension a little.

She did her chores, including feeding the calves, worrying even more about the littlest one because he wasn't responding as well today as he had the day before. When Elliot came home, she refused to help him with the keyboard until he did his homework. With a rueful smile and a knowing glance at his dad, he went up to his room to get it over with.

Meanwhile, Harry went out to get more firewood and Amanda was left in the living room with Quinn watching an early newscast.

The news was, as usual, all bad. Quinn put out his cigarette half angrily, his dark eyes lingering on Amanda's soft face.

"Don't you miss the city?" he asked.

She smiled. "Sure. I miss the excitement and my friends. But it's nice here, too." She moved toward the big armchair he was sitting in, nervously contemplating her next move. "You don't mind all that much, do you? Having me around, I mean?"

He glared up at her. He was wearing a blue-checked flannel shirt, buttoned up to the throat, and the hard muscles of his chest strained against it. He looked twice as big as usual, his dark hair unruly on his broad forehead as he stared up into her eyes.

"I'm getting used to you, I guess," he said stiffly. "Just don't get too comfortable."

"You really don't want me here, do you?" she asked quietly.

He sighed angrily. "I don't like women," he muttered.

"I know." She sat down on the arm of his chair, facing him. "Why not?" she asked gently.

His body went taut at the proximity. She was too close. Too female. The scent of her got into his nostrils and made him shift restlessly in the chair. "It's none of your damned business why not," he said evasively. "Will you get up from there?"

She warmed at the tone of his voice. So she did disturb him! Amanda smiled gently as she leaned forward. "Are you sure you want me to?" she asked and suddenly threw caution to the wind and slid down into his lap, putting her soft mouth hungrily on his.

He stiffened. He jerked. His big hands bit into her arms so hard they bruised. But for just one long, sweet moment, his hard mouth gave in to hers and he gave her back the kiss, his lips rough and warm, the pressure bruising, and he groaned as if all his dreams had come true at once.

He tasted of smoke for the brief second that he allowed the kiss. Then he was all bristling indignation and cold fury. He slammed to his feet, taking her with him, and literally threw her away, so hard that she fell against and onto the sofa.

"Damn you," he ground out. His fists clenched at his sides. His big body vibrated with outrage. "You cheap little tart!"

She lay trembling, frightened of the violence in his now white face and blazing dark eyes. "I'm not," she defended feebly.

"Can't you live without it for a few days, or are you desperate enough to try to seduce me?" he hissed. His eyes slid over her with icy contempt. "It won't work. I've told you already, I don't want something that any man can have! I don't want any part of you, least of all your overused body!"

She got to her feet on legs that threatened to give way under her, backing away from his anger. She couldn't even speak. Her father had been like that when he drank too much, white-faced, icy hot, totally out of control. And when he got that way, he hit. She cringed away from Quinn as he moved toward her and suddenly, she whirled and ran out of the room.

He checked his instinctive move to go after her. So she was scared, was she? He frowned, trying to understand why. He'd only spoken the truth; did she not like hearing what she was? The possibility that he'd been wrong, that she wasn't a cheap little tart, he wouldn't admit even to himself.

He sat back down and concentrated on the television without

any real interest. When Elliot came downstairs, Quinn barely looked up.

"Where's Amanda going?" he asked his father.

Quinn raised an eyebrow. "What?"

"Where's Amanda going in such a rush?" Elliot asked again. "I saw her out the window, tramping through waist-deep snow. Doesn't she remember what you told her about old McNaber's traps? She's headed straight for them if she keeps on the way she's headed... Where are you going?"

Quinn was already on his feet and headed for the back door. He got into his shepherd's coat and hat without speaking, his face pale, his eyes blazing with mingled fear and anger.

"She was crying," Harry muttered, sparing him a glance. "I don't know what you said to her, but—"

"Shut up," Quinn said coldly. He stared the older man down and went out the back door and around the house, following in the wake Amanda's body had made. She was already out of sight, and those traps would be buried under several feet of snow. Bear traps, and she wouldn't see them until she felt them. The thought of that merciless metal biting her soft flesh didn't bear thinking about, and it would be his fault because he'd hurt her.

Several meters ahead, into the woods now, Amanda was cursing silently as she plowed through the snowdrifts, her black eyes fierce even through the tears. Damn Quinn Sutton, she panted. She hoped he got eaten by moths during the winter, she hoped his horse stood on his foot, she hoped the sled ran over him and packed him into the snow and nobody found him until spring. It was only a kiss, after all, and he'd kissed her back just for a few seconds.

She felt the tears burning coldly down her cheeks as they started again. Damn him. He hadn't had to make her feel like such an animal, just because she'd kissed him. She cared about him. She'd only wanted to get on a friendlier footing with him. But now she'd done it. He hated her for sure, she'd seen it in his eyes, in his face, when he'd called her those names. Cheap little tart, indeed! Well, Goody Two Shoes Sutton could just hold his breath until she kissed him again, so there!

She stopped to catch her breath and then plowed on. The cabin was somewhere down here. She'd stay in it even if she did freeze to death. She'd shack up with a grizzly bear before she'd spend one more night under Quinn Sutton's roof. She frowned. Were there grizzly bears in this part of the country?

"Amanda, stop!"

She paused, wondering if she'd heard someone call her name, or if it had just been the wind. She was in a break of lodgepole pines now, and a cabin was just below in the valley. But it wasn't Mr. Durning's cabin. Could that be McNaber's...?

"Amanda!"

That was definitely her name. She glanced over her shoulder and saw the familiar shepherd's coat and dark worn Stetson atop that arrogant head.

"Eat snow, Goody Two Shoes!" she yelled back. "I'm going home!"

She started ahead, pushing hard now. But he had the edge, because he was walking in the path she'd made. He was bigger and faster, and he had twice her stamina. Before she got five more feet, he had her by the waist.

She fought him, kicking and hitting, but he simply wrapped both arms around her and held on until she finally ran out of strength.

"I hate you," she panted, shivering as the cold and the exertion got to her. "I hate you!"

"You'd hate me more if I hadn't stopped you," he said, breathing hard. "McNaber lives down there. He's got bear traps all over the place. Just a few more steps, and you'd have been up to your knees in them, you little fool! You can't even see them in snow this deep!"

"What would you care?" she groaned. "You don't want me

around. I don't want to stay with you anymore. I'll take my chances at the cabin!"

"No, you won't, Amanda," he said. His embrace didn't even loosen. He whipped her around, his big hands rough on her sleeves as he shook her. "You're coming back with me, if I have to carry you!"

She flinched, the violence in him frightening her. She swallowed, her lower lip trembling and pulled feebly against his hands.

"Let go of me," she whispered. Her voice shook, and she hated her own cowardice.

He scowled. She was paper white. Belatedly he realized what was wrong and his hands released her. She backed away as far as the snow would allow and stood like a young doe at bay, her eyes dark and frightened.

"Did he hit you?" he asked quietly.

She didn't have to ask who. She shivered. "Only when he drank," she said, her voice faltering. "But he always drank." She laughed bitterly. "Just…don't come any closer until you cool down, if you please."

He took a slow, steadying breath. "I'm sorry," he said, shocking her. "No, I mean it. I'm really sorry. I wouldn't have hit you, if that's what you're thinking. Only a coward would raise his hand to a woman," he said with cold conviction.

She wrapped her arms around herself and stood, just breathing, shivering in the cold.

"We'd better get back before you freeze," he said tautly. Her very defensiveness disarmed him. He felt guilty and protective all at once. He wanted to take her to his heart and comfort her, but even as he stepped toward her, she backed away. He hadn't imagined how much that would hurt until it happened. He stopped and stood where he was, raising his hands in an odd gesture of helplessness. "I won't touch you," he promised. "Come on, honey. You can go first."

Tears filmed her dark eyes. It was the first endearment she'd ever heard from him and it touched her deeply. But she knew it was only casual. Her behavior had shocked him and he didn't know what to do. She let out a long breath.

Without a quip or comeback, she eased past him warily and started back the way they'd come. He followed her, giving thanks that he'd been in time, that she hadn't run afoul of old McNaber's traps. But now he'd really done it. He'd managed to make her afraid of him.

She went ahead of him into the house. Elliot and Harry took one look at her face and Quinn's and didn't ask a single question.

She sat at the supper table like a statue. She didn't speak, even when Elliot tried to bring her into the conversation. And afterward, she curled up in a chair in the living room and sat like a mouse watching television.

Quinn couldn't know the memories he'd brought back, the searing fear of her childhood. Her father had been a big man, and he was always violent when he drank. He was sorry afterward, sometimes he even cried when he saw the bruises he'd put on her. But it never stopped him. She'd run away because it was more than she could bear, and fortunately there'd been a place for runaways that took her in. She'd learned volumes about human kindness from those people. But the memories were bitter and Quinn's bridled violence had brought them sweeping in like storm clouds.

Elliot didn't ask her about music lessons. He excused himself a half hour early and went up to bed. Harry had long since gone to his own room.

Quinn sat in his big chair, smoking his cigarette, but he started when Amanda put her feet on the floor and glanced warily at him.

"Don't go yet," he said quietly. "I want to talk to you."

"We don't have anything to say to each other," she said quietly. "I'm very sorry for what I did this afternoon. It was impulsive and stupid, and I promise I'll never do it again. If you can just put up with me until it thaws a little, you'll never have to see me again."

He sighed wearily. "Is that what you think I want?" he asked, searching her face.

"Of course it is," she replied simply. "You've hated having me here ever since I came."

"Maybe I have. I've got more reason to hate and distrust women than you'll ever know. But that isn't what I want to talk about," he said, averting his gaze from her wan face. He didn't like thinking about that kiss and how disturbing it had been. "I want to know why you thought I might hit you."

She dropped her eyes to her lap. "You're big, like my father," she said. "When he lost his temper, he always hit."

"I'm not your father," Quinn pointed out, his dark eyes narrowing. "And I've never hit anyone in a temper, except maybe another man from time to time when it was called for. I never raised my hand to Elliot's mother, although I felt like it a time or two, in all honesty. I never lifted a hand to her even when she told me she was pregnant with Elliot."

"Why should you have?" she asked absently. "He's your son."

He laughed coldly. "No, he isn't."

She stared at him openly. "Elliot isn't yours?" she asked softly.

He shook his head. "His mother was having an affair with a married man and she got caught out." He shrugged. "I was twenty-two and grass green and she mounted a campaign to marry me. I guess I was pretty much a sitting duck. She was beautiful and stacked and she had me eating out of her hand in no time. We got married and right after the ceremony, she told me what she'd done. She laughed at how clumsy I'd been during the courtship, how she'd had to steel herself not to be sick when I'd kissed her. She told me about Elliot's father and how much she loved him, then she dared me to tell people the truth about how easy it had been to make me marry her." He blew out a cloud of smoke, his eyes cold with memory. "She had me over a barrel. I was twice as proud back then as I am now. I couldn't bear to have the whole community laughing at me. So I stuck it out. Until Elliot was born, and she and his father took off for parts unknown for a weekend of love. Unfortunately for them, he wrecked the car in his haste to get to a motel and killed both of them outright."

"Does Elliot know?" she asked, her voice quiet as she glanced toward the staircase.

"Sure," he said. "I couldn't lie to him about it. But I took care of him from the time he was a baby, and I raised him. That makes me his father just as surely as if I'd put the seed he grew from into his mother's body. He's my son, and I'm his father. I love him."

She studied his hard face, seeing behind it to the pain he must have suffered. "You loved her, didn't you?"

"Calf love," he said. "She came up on my blind side and I needed somebody to love. I'd always been shy and clumsy around girls. I couldn't even get a date when I was in school because I was so rough-edged. She paid me a lot of attention. I was lonely." His big shoulders shrugged. "Like I said, a sitting duck. She taught me some hard lessons about your sex," he added, his narrowed eyes on her face. "I've never forgotten them. And nobody's had a second chance at me."

Her breath came out as a sigh. "That's what you thought this afternoon, when I kissed you," she murmured, reddening at her own forwardness. "I'm sorry. I didn't realize you might think I was playing you for a sucker."

He frowned. "Why did you kiss me, Amanda?"

"Would you believe, because I wanted to?" she asked with a quiet smile. "You're a very attractive man, and something about you makes me weak in the knees. But you don't have to worry about me coming on to you again," she added, getting to her feet. "You teach a pretty tough lesson yourself. Good night, Mr. Sutton. I appreciate your telling me about Elliot. You needn't worry that I'll say anything to him or to anybody else. I don't carry tales, and I don't gossip."

She turned toward the staircase, and Quinn's dark eyes followed her. She had an elegance of carriage that touched him, full of pride and grace. He was sorry now that he'd slapped her down so hard with cruel words. He really hadn't meant to. He'd been afraid that she was going to let him down, that she was playing. It hadn't occurred to him that she found him attractive or that she'd kissed him because she'd really wanted to.

He'd made a bad mistake with Amanda. He'd hurt her and sent her running, and now he wished he could take back the things he'd said. She wasn't like any woman he'd ever been exposed to. She actually seemed unaware of her beauty, as if she didn't think much of it. Maybe he'd gotten it all wrong and she wasn't much more experienced than he was. He wished he could ask her. She disturbed him very much, and now he wondered if it wasn't mutual.

Amanda was lying in bed, crying. The day had been horrible, and she hated Quinn for the way he'd treated her. It wasn't until she remembered what he'd told her that she stopped crying and started thinking. He'd said that he'd never slept with Elliot's mother, and that he hadn't been able to get dates in high school. Presumably that meant that his only experience with women had been after Elliot's mother died. She frowned. There hadn't been many women, she was willing to bet. He seemed to know relatively nothing about her sex. She frowned. If he still hated women, how had he gotten any experience? Finally her mind grew tired of trying to work it out and she went to sleep.

AMANDA WAS UP helping Harry in the kitchen the next morning when Quinn came downstairs after a wild, erotic dream that left him sweating and swearing when he woke up. Amanda had figured largely in it, with her blond hair loose and down to her lower spine, his hands twined in it while he made love to her in the stillness of his own bedroom. The dream had been so vivid that he could almost see the pink perfection of her breasts through the bulky, white-knit sweater she was wearing, and he almost groaned as his eyes fell to the rise and fall of her chest under it.

She glanced at Quinn and actually flushed before she dragged her eyes back down to the pan of biscuits she was putting into the oven.

"I didn't know you could make biscuits," Quinn murmured.

"Harry taught me," she said evasively. Her eyes went back to him again and flitted away.

He frowned at that shy look until he realized why he was getting it. He usually kept his shirts buttoned up to his throat, but this morning he'd left it open halfway down his chest because he was still sweating from that dream. He pursed his lips and gave her a speculative stare. He wondered if it were possible that he disturbed her as much as she disturbed him. He was going to make it his business to find out before she left here. If for no other reason than to salve his bruised ego.

He went out behind Elliot, pausing in the doorway. "How's the calf?" he asked Amanda.

"He wasn't doing very well yesterday," she said with a sigh. "Maybe he's better this morning."

"I'll have a look at him before I go out." He glanced out at the snow. "Don't try to get back to the cabin again, will you? You can't get through McNaber's traps without knowing where they are."

He actually sounded worried. She studied his hard face quietly. That was nice. Unless, of course, he was only worried that she might get laid up and he'd have to put up with her for even longer.

"Is the snow ever going to stop?" she asked.

"Hard to say," he told her. "I've seen it worse than this even earlier in the year. But we'll manage, I suppose."

"I suppose." She glared at him.

He pulled on his coat and buttoned it, propping his hat over one eye. "In a temper this morning, are we?" he mused.

His eyes were actually twinkling. She shifted back against the counter, grateful that Harry had gone off to clean the bedrooms. "I'm not in a temper. Cheap little tarts don't have tempers."

One eyebrow went up. "I called you that, didn't I?" He let his eyes run slowly down her body. "You shouldn't have kissed me like that. I'm not used to aggressive women."

"Rest assured that I'll never attack you again, Goody Two Shoes."

He chuckled softly. "Won't you? Well, disappointment is a man's lot, I suppose."

Her eyes widened. She wasn't sure she'd even heard him. "You were horrible to me!"

"I guess I was." His dark eyes held hers, making little chills up and down her spine at the intensity of the gaze. "I thought you were playing games. You know, a little harmless fun at the hick's expense."

"I don't know how to play games with men," she said stiffly, "and nobody, anywhere, could call you a hick with a straight face. You're a very masculine man with a keen mind and an overworked sense of responsibility. I wouldn't make fun of you even if I could."

His dark eyes smiled into hers. "In that case, we might call a truce for the time being."

"Do you think you could stand being nice to me?" she asked sourly. "I mean, it would be a strain, I'm sure."

"I'm not a bad man," he pointed out. "I just don't know much about women, or hadn't that thought occurred?"

She searched his eyes. "No."

"We'll have to have a long talk about it one of these days." He pulled the hat down over his eyes. "I'll check on the calves for you."

"Thanks." She watched him go, her heart racing at the look

in his eyes just before he closed the door. She was more nervous of him now than ever, but she didn't know what to do about it. She was hoping that the chinook would come before she had to start worrying too much. She was too confused to know what to do anymore.

CHAPTER FIVE

AMANDA FINISHED THE breakfast dishes before she went out to the barn. Quinn was still there, his dark eyes quiet on the smallest of the three calves. It didn't take a fortune teller to see that something was badly wrong. The small animal lay on its side, its dull, lackluster red-and-white coat showing its ribs, its eyes glazed and unseeing while it fought to breathe.

She knelt beside Quinn and he glanced at her with concern. "You'd better go back in the house, honey," he said.

Her eyes slid over the small calf. She'd seen pets die over the years, and now she knew the signs. The calf was dying. Quinn knew it, too, and was trying to shield her.

That touched her, oddly, more than anything he'd said or done since she'd been on Ricochet. She looked up at him. "You're a nice man, Quinn Sutton," she said softly.

He drew in a slow breath. "When I'm not taking bites out of you, you mean?" he replied. "It hurts like hell when you back away from me. You'll never know how sorry I am for what happened yesterday."

One shock after another. At least it took her mind off the poor, laboring creature beside them. "I'm sorry, too," she said. "I shouldn't have been so..." She stopped, averting her eyes. "I don't know much about men, Quinn," she said finally. "I've spent my whole adult life backing away from involvement, emotional or physical. I know how to flirt, but not much more." She risked a glance at him, and relaxed when she saw his face. "My aunt is Mr. Durning's lover, you know. She's an artist. A little flighty, but nice. I've…never had a lover."

He nodded quietly. "I've been getting that idea since we wound up near McNaber's cabin yesterday. You reacted pretty violently for an experienced woman." He looked away from her. That vulnerability in her pretty face was working on him again. "Go inside now. I can deal with this."

"I'm not afraid of death," she returned. "I saw my mother die. It wasn't scary at all. She just closed her eyes."

His dark eyes met hers and locked. "My father went the same way." He looked back down at the calf. "It won't be long now."

She sat down in the hay beside him and slid her small hand into his big one. He held it for a long moment. Finally his voice broke the silence. "It's over. Go have a cup of coffee. I'll take care of him."

She hadn't meant to cry, but the calf had been so little and helpless. Quinn pulled her close, holding her with quiet comfort, while she cried. Then he wiped the tears away with his thumbs and smiled gently. "You'll do," he murmured, thinking that sensitivity and courage was a nice combination in a woman.

She was thinking the exact same thing about him. She managed a watery smile and with one last, pitying look at the calf, she went into the house.

Elliot would miss it, as she would, she thought. Even Quinn had seemed to care about it, because she saw him occasionally sitting by it, petting it, talking to it. He loved little things. It was evident in all the kittens and puppies around the place, and in the tender care he took of all his cattle and calves. And although Quinn cursed old man McNaber's traps, Elliot had told her that he stopped by every week to check on the dour old man and make sure he had enough chopped wood and supplies. For a taciturn iceman, he had a surprisingly warm center.

She told Harry what had happened and sniffed a little while she drank black coffee. "Is there anything I can do?" she asked.

He smiled. "You do enough," he murmured. "Nice to have some help around the place."

"Quinn hasn't exactly thought so," she said dryly.

"Oh, yes he has," he said firmly as he cleared away the dishes they'd eaten his homemade soup and corn bread in. "Quinn could have taken you to Mrs. Pearson down the mountain if he'd had a mind to. He doesn't have to let you stay here. Mrs. Pearson would be glad of the company." He glanced at her and grinned at her perplexed expression. "He's been watching you lately. Sees the way you sew up his shirts and make curtains and patch pillows. It's new to him, having a woman about. He has a hard time with change."

"Don't we all?" Amanda said softly, remembering how clear her own life had been until that tragic night. But it was nice to know that Quinn had been watching her. Certainly she'd been watching him. And this morning, everything seemed to have changed between them. "When will it thaw?" she asked, and now she was dreading it, not anticipating it. She didn't want to leave Ricochet. Or Quinn.

Harry shrugged. "Hard to tell. Days. Weeks. This is raw mountain country. Can't predict a chinook. Plenty think they can, though," he added, and proceeded to tell her about a Blackfoot who predicted the weather with jars of bear grease.

She was much calmer, but still sad when Quinn finally came back inside.

He spared her a glance before he shucked his coat, washed his hands and brawny forearms and dried them on a towel.

He didn't say anything to her, and Harry, sensing the atmosphere, made himself scarce after he'd poured two cups of coffee for them.

"Are you all right?" he asked her after a minute, staring down at her bent head.

"Sure." She forced a smile. "He was so little, Quinn." She

stopped when her voice broke and lowered her eyes to the table. "I guess you think I'm a wimp."

"Not really." Without taking time to think about the consequences, his lean hands pulled her up by the arms, holding her in front of him so that her eyes were on a level with his deep blue, plaid flannel shirt. The sleeves were rolled up, and it was open at the throat, where thick, dark hair curled out of it. He looked and smelled fiercely masculine and Amanda's knees weakened at the unexpected proximity. His big hands bit into her soft flesh, and she wondered absently if he realized just how strong he was.

The feel of him so close was new and terribly exciting, especially since he'd reached for her for the first time. She didn't know what to expect, and her heart was going wild. She lowered her eyes to his throat. His pulse was jumping and she stared at it curiously, only half aware of his hold and the sudden increase of his breathing.

He was having hell just getting a breath. The scent of her was in his nostrils, drowning him. Woman smell. Sweet and warm. His teeth clenched. It was bad enough having to look at her, but this close, she made his blood run hot and wild as it hadn't since he was a young man. He didn't know what he was doing, but the need for her had haunted him for days. He wanted so badly to kiss her, the way she'd kissed him the day before, but in a different way. He wasn't quite sure how to go about it.

"You smell of flowers," he said roughly.

That was an interesting comment from a nonpoetic man. She smiled a little to herself. "It's my shampoo," she murmured.

He drew in a steadying breath. "You don't wear your hair down at all, do you?"

"Just at night," she replied, aware that his face was closer than it had been, because she could feel his breath on her forehead. He was so tall and overwhelming this close. He made her feel tiny and very feminine.

"I'm sorry about the calf, Amanda," he said. "We lose a few every winter. It's part of ranching."

The shock of her name on his lips made her lift her head. She stared up at him curiously, searching his dark, quiet eyes. "I suppose so. I shouldn't have gotten so upset, though. I guess men don't react to things the way women do."

"You don't know what kind of man I am," he replied. His hands felt vaguely tremulous. He wondered if she knew the effect she had on him. "As it happens, I get attached to the damned things, too." He sighed heavily. "Little things don't have much choice in this world. They're at the mercy of everything and everybody."

Her eyes softened as they searched his. He sounded different when he spoke that way. Vulnerable. Almost tender. And so alone.

"You aren't really afraid of me, are you?" he asked, as if the thought was actually painful.

She grimaced. "No. Of course not. I was ashamed of what I'd done, and a little nervous of the way you reacted to it, that's all. I know you wouldn't hurt me." She drew in a soft breath. "I know you resent having me here," she confessed. "I resented having to depend on you for shelter. But the snow will melt soon, and I'll leave."

"I thought you'd had lovers," he confessed quietly. "The way you acted...well, it just made all those suspicions worse. I took you at face value."

Amanda smiled. "It was all put-on. I don't even know why I did it. I guess I was trying to live down to your image of me."

He loved the sensation her sultry black eyes aroused in him. Unconsciously his hands tightened on her arms. "You haven't had a man, ever?" he asked huskily.

The odd shadow of dusky color along his cheekbones fascinated her. She wondered about the embarrassment asking the question had caused. "No. Not ever," she stammered.

"The way you look?" he asked, his eyes eloquent.

"What do you mean, the way I look?" she said, bristling.

"You know you're beautiful," he returned. His eyes darkened. "A woman who looks like you do could have her pick of men."

"Maybe," she agreed without conceit. "But I've never wanted a man in my life, to be dominated by a man. I've made my own way in the world. I'm a musician," she told him, because that didn't give away very much. "I support myself by playing a keyboard."

"Yes, Elliot told me. I've heard you play for him. You're good." He felt his heartbeat increasing as he looked at her. She smelled so good. He looked down at her mouth and remembered how it had felt for those few seconds when he'd given in to her playful kiss. Would she let him do it? He knew so little about those subtle messages women were supposed to send out when they wanted a man's lovemaking. He couldn't read Amanda's eyes. But her lips were parted and her breath was coming rather fast from between them. Her face was flushed, but that could have been from the cold.

She gazed up into his eyes and couldn't look away. He wasn't handsome. His face really seemed as if it had been chipped away from the side of the Rockies, all craggy angles and hard lines. His mouth was thin and faintly cruel looking. She wondered if it would feel as hard as it looked if he was in control, dominating her lips. It had been different when she'd kissed him....

"What are you thinking?" he asked huskily, because her eyes were quite frankly on his mouth.

"I...was wondering," she whispered hesitantly, "how hard your mouth would be if you kissed me."

His heart stopped and then began to slam against his chest. "Don't you know already?" he asked, his voice deeper, harsher. "You kissed me."

"Not...properly."

He wondered what she meant by properly. His wife had only kissed him when she had to, and only in the very beginning of their courtship. She always pushed him away and murmured something about mussing her makeup. He couldn't remember one time when he'd kissed anyone with passion, or when he'd ever been kissed by anyone else like that.

His warm, rough hands let go of her arms and came up to frame her soft oval face. His breath shuddered out of his chest when she didn't protest as he bent his dark head.

"Show me what you mean...by properly," he whispered.

He had to know, she thought dizzily. But his lips touched hers and she tasted the wind and the sun on them. Her hands clenched the thick flannel shirt and she resisted searching for buttons, because she wanted very much to touch that thicket of black, curling hair that covered his broad chest. She went on her tiptoes and pushed her mouth against his, the force of the action parting his lips as well as her own, and she felt him stiffen and heard him groan as their open mouths met.

She dropped back onto her feet, her wide, curious eyes meeting his stormy ones.

"Like that?" he whispered gruffly, bending to repeat the action with his own mouth. "I've never done it...with my mouth open," he said, biting off the words against her open lips.

She couldn't believe he'd said that. She couldn't believe, either, the sensations rippling down to her toes when she gave in to the force of his ardor and let him kiss her that way, his mouth rough and demanding as one big hand slid to the back of her head to press her even closer.

A soft sound passed her lips, a faint moan, because she couldn't get close enough to him. Her breasts were flattened against his hard chest, and she felt his heartbeat against them. But she wanted to be closer than that, enveloped, crushed to him.

"Did I hurt you?" he asked in a shaky whisper that touched her lips.

"What?" she whispered back dizzily.

"You made a sound."

Her eyes searched his, her own misty and half closed and

rapt. "I moaned," she whispered. Her nails stroked him through the shirt and she liked the faint tautness of his body as he reacted to it. "I like being kissed like that." She rubbed her forehead against him, smelling soap and detergent and pure man. "Could we take your shirt off?" she whispered.

Her hands were driving him nuts, and he was wondering the same thing himself. But somewhere in the back of his mind he remembered that Harry was around, and that it might look compromising if he let her touch him that way. In fact, it might get compromising, because he felt his body harden in a way it hadn't since his marriage. And because it made him vulnerable and he didn't want her to feel it, he took her gently by the arms and moved her away from him with a muffled curse.

"Harry," he said, his breath coming deep and rough.

She colored. "Oh, yes." She moved back, her eyes a little wild.

"You don't have to look so threatened. I won't do it again," he said, misunderstanding her retreat. Had he frightened her again?

"Oh, it's not that. You didn't frighten me." She lowered her eyes to the floor. "I'm just wondering if you'll think I'm easy...."

He scowled. "Easy?"

"I don't usually come on to men," she said softly. "And I've never asked anybody to take his shirt off before." She glanced up at him, fascinated by the expression on his face. "Well, I haven't," she said belligerently. "And you don't have to worry; I won't throw myself at you anymore, either. I just got carried away in the heat of the moment...."

His eyebrows arched. None of what she was saying made sense. "Like you did yesterday?" he mused, liking the color that came and went in her face. "I did accuse you of throwing yourself at me," he said on a long sigh.

"Yes. You seem to think I'm some sort of liberated sex maniac."

His lips curled involuntarily. "Are you?" he asked, and sounded interested.

She stamped her foot. "Stop that. I don't want to stay here anymore!"

"I'm not sure it's a good idea myself," he mused, watching her eyes glitter with rage. God, she was pretty! "I mean, if you tried to seduce me, things could get sticky."

The red in her cheeks got darker. "I don't have any plans to seduce you."

"Well, if you get any, you'd better tell me in advance," he said, pulling a cigarette from his shirt pocket. "Just so I can be prepared to fight you off."

That dry drawl confused her. Suddenly he was a different man, full of male arrogance and amusement. Things had shifted between them during that long, hard kiss. The distance had shortened, and he was looking at her with an expression she couldn't quite understand.

"How did you get to the age you are without winding up in someone's bed?" Quinn asked then. He'd wondered at her shyness with him and then at the way she blushed all the time. He didn't know much about women, but he wanted to know everything about her.

Amanda wrapped her arms around herself and shrugged. When he lit his cigarette and still stood there waiting for an answer, she gave in and replied. "I couldn't give up control," she said simply. "All my life I'd been dominated and pushed around by my father. Giving in to a man seemed like throwing away my rights as a person. Especially giving in to a man in bed," she stammered, averting her gaze. "I don't think there's anyplace in the world where a man is more the master than in a bedroom, despite all the liberation and freedom of modern life."

"And you think that women should dominate there."

She looked up. "Well, not dominate." She hesitated. "But a woman shouldn't be used just because she's a woman."

His thin mouth curled slightly. "Neither should a man."

"I wasn't using you," she shot back.

"Did I accuse you?" he returned innocently.

She swallowed. "No, I guess not." She folded her arms over her breasts, wincing because the tips were hard and unexpectedly tender.

"That hardness means you feel desire," he said, grinning when she gaped and then glared at him. She made him feel about ten feet tall. "I read this book about sex," he continued. "It didn't make much sense to me at the time, but it's beginning to."

"I am not available as a living model for sex education!"

He shrugged. "Suit yourself. But it's a hell of a loss to my education."

"You don't need educating," she muttered. "You were married."

He nodded. "Sure I was." He pursed his lips and let his eyes run lazily over her body. "Except that she never wanted me, before or after I married her."

Amanda's lips parted. "Oh, Quinn," she said softly. "I'm sorry."

"So was I, at the time." He shook his head. "I used to wonder at first why she pulled back every time I kissed her. I guess she was suffering it until she could get me to put the ring on her finger. Up until then, I thought it was her scruples that kept me at arm's length. But she never had many morals." He stared at Amanda curiously, surprised at how easy it was to tell her things he'd never shared with another human being. "After I found out what she really was, I couldn't have cared less about sharing her bed."

"No, I don't suppose so," she agreed.

He lifted the cigarette to his lips and his eyes narrowed as he studied her. "Elliot's almost thirteen," he said. "He's been my whole life. I've taken care of him and done for him. He knows there's no blood tie between us, but I love him and he loves me. In all the important ways, I'm his father and he's my son."

"He loves you very much," she said with a smile. "He talks about you all the time."

"He's a good boy." He moved a little closer, noticing how

she tensed when he came close. He liked that reaction a lot. It told him that she was aware of him, but shy and reticent. "You don't have men," he said softly. "Well, I don't have women."

"Not for…a few months?" she stammered, because she couldn't imagine that he was telling the truth.

He shrugged his powerful shoulders. "Well, not for a bit longer than that. Not much opportunity up here. And I can't go off and leave Elliot while I tomcat around town. It's been a bit longer than thirteen years."

"A bit?"

He looked down at her with a curious, mocking smile. "When I was a boy, I didn't know how to get girls. I was big and clumsy and shy, so it was the other boys who scored." He took another draw, a slightly jerky one, from his cigarette. "I still have the same problem around most women. It's not so much hatred as a lack of ability, and shyness. I don't know how to come on to a woman," he confessed with a faint smile.

Amanda felt as if the sun had just come out. She smiled back. "Don't you, really?" she asked softly. "I thought it was just that you found me lacking, or that I wasn't woman enough to interest you."

He could have laughed out loud at that assumption. "Is that why you called me Goody Two Shoes?" he asked pleasantly.

She laughed softly. "Well, that was sort of sour grapes." She lowered her eyes to his chest. "It hurt my feelings that you thought I didn't have any morals, when I'd never made one single move toward any other man in my whole life."

He felt warm all over from that shy confession. It took down the final brick in his wall of reserve. She wasn't like any woman he'd ever known. "I'm glad to know that. But you and I have more in common than a lack of technique," he said, hesitating.

"We do?" she asked. Her soft eyes held his. "What do you mean?"

He turned and deliberately put out his cigarette in the ashtray on the table beside them. He straightened and looked down at her speculatively for a few seconds before he went for broke. "Well, what I mean, Amanda," he replied finally, "is that you aren't the only virgin on the place."

CHAPTER SIX

"I DIDN'T HEAR THAT," Amanda said, because she knew she hadn't. Quinn Sutton couldn't have told her that he was a virgin.

"Yes, you did," he replied. "And it's not all that far-fetched. Old McNaber down the hill's never had a woman, and he's in his seventies. There are all sorts of reasons why men don't get experience. Morals, scruples, isolation, or even plain shyness. Just like women," he added with a meaningful look at Amanda. "I couldn't go to bed with somebody just to say I'd had sex. I'd have to care about her, want her, and I'd want her to care about me. There are idealistic people all over the world who never find that particular combination, so they stay celibate. And really, I think that people who sleep around indiscriminately are in the minority even in these liberated times. Only a fool takes that sort of risk with the health dangers what they are."

"Yes, I know." She watched him with fascinated eyes. "Haven't you ever...wanted to?" she asked.

"Well, that's the problem, you see," he replied, his dark eyes steady on her face.

"What is?"

"I have...wanted to. With you."

She leaned back against the counter, just to make sure she didn't fall down. "With me?"

"That first night you came here, when I was so sick, and your hair drifted down over my naked chest. I shivered, and you thought it was with fever," he mused. "It was a fever, all right, but it didn't have anything to do with the virus."

Her fingers clenched the counter. She'd wondered about his violent reaction at the time, but it seemed so unlikely that a cold man like Quinn Sutton would feel that way about a woman. He was human, she thought absently, watching him.

"That's why I've given you such a hard time," he confessed with narrowed, quiet eyes. "I don't know how to handle desire. I can't throw you over my shoulder and carry you upstairs, not with Elliot and Harry around, even if you were the kind of woman I thought at first you were. The fact that you're as innocent as I am only makes it more complicated."

She looked at him with new understanding, as fascinated by him as he seemed to be by her. He wasn't that bad looking, she mused. And he was terribly strong, and sexy in an earthy kind of way. She especially liked his eyes. They were much more expressive than that poker face.

"Fortunately for you, I'm kind of shy, too," she murmured.

"Except when you're asking men to take their clothes off," Quinn said, nodding.

Harry froze in the doorway with one foot lifted while Amanda gaped at him and turned red.

"Put your foot down and get busy," Quinn muttered irritably. "Why were you standing there?"

"I was getting educated." Harry chuckled. "I didn't know Amanda asked people to take their clothes off!"

"Only me," Quinn said, defending her. "And just my shirt. She's not a bad girl."

"Will you stop!" Amanda buried her face in her hands. "Go away!"

"I can't. I live here," Quinn pointed out. "Did I smell brandy on your breath?" he asked suddenly.

Harry grimaced even as Amanda's eyes widened. "Well, yes you do," he confessed. "She was upset and crying and all…"

"How much did you give her?" Quinn persisted.

"Only a few drops," Harry promised. "In her coffee, to calm her."

"Harry, how could you!" Amanda laughed. The coffee had tasted funny, but she'd been too upset to wonder why.

"Sorry," Harry murmured dryly. "But it seemed the thing to do."

"It backfired," Quinn murmured and actually smiled.

"You stop that!" Amanda told him. She sat down at the table. "I'm not tipsy. Harry, I'll peel those apples for the pie if I can have a knife."

"Let me get out of the room first, if you please," Quinn said, glancing at her dryly. "I saw her measuring my back for a place to put it."

"I almost never stab men with knives," she promised impishly.

He chuckled. He reached for his hat and slanted it over his brow, buttoning his old shepherd's coat because it was snowing outside again.

Amanda looked past him, the reason for all the upset coming back now as she calmed down. Her expression became sad.

"If you stay busy, you won't think about it so much," Quinn said quietly. "It's part of life, you know."

"I know." She managed a smile. "I'm fine. Despite Harry," she added with a chuckle, watching Harry squirm before he grinned back.

Quinn's dark eyes met hers warmly for longer than he meant, so that she blushed. He tore his eyes away finally, and went outside.

Harry didn't say anything, but his smile was speculative.

Elliot came home from school and persuaded Amanda to get out the keyboard and give him some more pointers. He admitted that he'd been bragging about her to his classmates and that she was a professional musician.

"Where do you play, Amanda?" Elliot asked curiously, and he stared at her with open puzzlement. "You look so familiar somehow."

She sat very still on the sofa and tried to stay calm. Elliot had already told her that he liked rock music and she knew Quinn had hidden his tapes. If there was a tape in his collection by Desperado, it would have her picture on the cover along with that of her group.

"Do I really look familiar?" she asked with a smile. "Maybe I just have that kind of face."

"Have you played with orchestras?" he persisted.

"No. Just by myself, sort of. In nightclubs," she improvised. Well, she had once sang in a nightclub, to fill in for a friend. "Mostly I do backup. You know, I play with groups for people who make tapes and records."

"Wow!" he exclaimed. "I guess you know a lot of famous singers and musicians?"

"A few," she agreed.

"Where do you work?"

"In New York City, in Nashville," she told him. "All over. Wherever I can find work."

He ran his fingers up and down the keyboard. "How did you ever wind up here?"

"I needed a rest," she said. "My aunt is…a friend of Mr. Durning. She asked him if I could borrow the cabin, and he said it was all right. I had to get away from work for a while."

"This doesn't bother you, does it? Teaching me to play, I mean?" he asked and looked concerned.

"No, Elliot, it doesn't bother me. I'm enjoying it." She ran a scale and taught it to him, then showed him the cadences of the chords that went with it.

"It's so complicated," he moaned.

"Of course it is. Music is an art form, and it's complex. But once you learn these basics, you can do anything with a chord. For instance..."

She played a tonic chord, then made an impromptu song from its subdominant and seventh chords and the second inversion of them. Elliot watched, fascinated.

"I guess you've studied for years," he said with a sigh.

"Yes, I have, and I'm still learning," she said. "But I love it more than anything. Music has been my whole life."

"No wonder you're so good at it."

She smiled. "Thanks, Elliot."

"Well, I'd better get my chores done before supper," he said, sighing. He handed Amanda the keyboard. "See you later."

She nodded. He went out. Harry was feeding the two calves that were still alive, so presumably he'd tell Elliot about the one that had died. Amanda hadn't had the heart to talk about it.

Her fingers ran over the keyboard lovingly and she began to play a song that her group had recorded two years back, a sad, dreamy ballad about hopeless love that had won them a Grammy. She sang it softly, her pure, sweet voice haunting in the silence of the room as she tried to sing for the first time in weeks.

"Elliot, for Pete's sake, turn that radio down, I'm on the telephone!" came a pleading voice from the back of the house.

She stopped immediately, flushing. She hadn't realized that Harry had come back inside. Thank God he hadn't seen her, or he might have asked some pertinent questions. She put the keyboard down and went to the kitchen, relieved that her singing voice was back to normal again.

Elliot was morose at the supper table. He'd heard about the calf and he'd been as depressed as Amanda had. Quinn didn't look all that happy himself. They all picked at the delicious chili Harry had whipped up; nobody had much of an appetite.

After they finished, Elliot did his homework while Amanda put the last stitches into a chair cover she was making for the living room. Quinn had gone off to do his paperwork and Harry was making bread for the next day.

It was a long, lazy night. Elliot went to bed at eight-thirty and not much later Harry went to his room.

Amanda wanted to wait for Quinn to come back, but something in her was afraid of the new way he looked at her. He was much more a threat now than he had been before, because she was looking at him with new and interested eyes. She was drawn to him more than ever. But he didn't know who she really was, and she couldn't tell him. If she were persuaded into any kind of close relationship with him, it could lead to disaster.

So when Elliot went to bed, so did Amanda. She sat at the dresser and let down her long hair, brushing it with slow, lazy strokes, when there was a knock at the door.

She was afraid that it might be Quinn, and she hesitated. But surely he wouldn't make any advances toward her unless she showed that she wanted them. Of course he wouldn't.

She opened the door, but it wasn't Quinn. It was Elliot. And as he stared at her, wheels moved and gears clicked in his young mind. She was wearing a long granny gown in a deep beige, a shade that was too much like the color of the leather dress she wore onstage. With her hair loose and the color of the gown, Elliot made the connection he hadn't made the first time he saw her hair down.

"Yes?" she prompted, puzzled by the way he was looking at her. "Is something wrong, Elliot?"

"Uh, no," he stammered. "Uh, I forgot to say good-night. Good night!" He grinned.

He turned, red faced, and beat a hasty retreat, but not to his own room. He went to his father's and searched quickly through the hidden tapes until he found the one he wanted. He held it up, staring blankly at the cover. There were four men who looked like vicious bikers surrounding a beautiful woman in buckskin with long, elegant, blond hair. The group was one of his favorites—Desperado. And the woman was Mandy. Amanda. His Amanda. He caught his breath. Boy, would she be in for it if his dad found out who she was! He put the tape into his pocket, feeling guilty for taking it when Quinn had told him not to. But these were desperate circumstances. He had to protect Amanda until he could figure out how to tell her that he knew the truth. Meanwhile, having her in the same house with him was sheer undiluted heaven! Imagine, a singing star that famous in his house. If only he could tell the guys! But that was too risky, because it might get back to Dad. He sighed. Just his luck, to find a rare jewel and have to hide it to keep someone from stealing it. He closed the door to Quinn's bedroom and went quickly back to his own.

Amanda slept soundly, almost missing breakfast. Outside, the sky looked blue for the first time in days, and she noticed that the snow had stopped.

"Chinook's coming," Harry said with a grin. "I knew it would."

Quinn's dark eyes studied Amanda's face. "Well, it will be a few days before they get the power lines back up again," he muttered. "So don't get in an uproar about it."

"I'm not in an uproar," Harry returned with a frown. "I just thought it was nice that we'll be able to get off the mountain and lay in some more supplies. I'm getting tired of beef. I want a chicken."

"So do I!" Elliot said fervently. "Or bear, or beaver or moose, anything but beef!"

Quinn glared at both of them. "Beef pays the bills around here," he reminded them.

They looked so guilty that Amanda almost laughed out loud.

"I'm sorry, Dad," Elliot sighed. "I'll tell my stomach to shut up about it."

Quinn's hard face relaxed. "It's all right. I wouldn't mind a chicken stew, myself."

"That's the spirit," Elliot said. "What are we going to do today? It's Saturday," he pointed out. "No school."

"You could go out with me and help me feed cattle," Quinn said.

"I'll stay here and help Harry," Amanda said, too quickly.

Quinn's dark eyes searched hers. "Harry can manage by himself. You can come with me and Elliot."

"You'll enjoy it," Elliot assured her. "It's a lot of fun. The cattle see us and come running. Well, as well as they can run in several feet of snow," he amended.

It was fun, too. Amanda sat on the back of the sled with Elliot and helped push the bales of hay off. Quinn cut the strings so the cattle could get to the hay. They did come running, reminding Amanda so vividly of women at a sale that she laughed helplessly until the others had to be told why she was laughing.

They came back from the outing in a new kind of harmony, and for the first time, Amanda understood what it felt like to be part of a family. She looked at Quinn and wondered how it would be if she never had to leave here, if she could stay with him and Elliot and Harry forever.

But she couldn't, she told herself firmly. She had to remember that this was a vacation, with the real world just outside the door.

Elliot was allowed to stay up later on Saturday night, so they watched a science-fiction movie together while Quinn grumbled over paperwork. The next morning they went to church on the sled, Amanda in the one skirt and blouse she'd packed, trying not to look too conspicuous as Quinn's few neighbors carefully scrutinized her.

When they got back home, she was all but shaking. She felt uncomfortable living with him, as if she really was a fallen woman now. He cornered her in the kitchen while she was washing dishes to find out why she was so quiet.

"I didn't think about the way people would react if you went with us this morning," he said quietly. "I wouldn't have subjected you to that if I'd just thought."

"It's okay," she said, touched by his concern. "Really. It was just a little uncomfortable."

He sighed, searching her face with narrowed eyes. "Most people around here know how I feel about women," he said bluntly. "That was why you attracted so much attention. People get funny ideas about woman haters who take in beautiful blondes."

"I'm not beautiful," she stammered shyly.

He stepped toward her, towering over her in his dress slacks and good white shirt and sedate gray tie. He looked handsome and strong and very masculine. She liked the spicy cologne he wore. "You're beautiful, all right," he murmured. His big hand touched her cheek, sliding down it slowly, his thumb brushing with soft abrasion over her full mouth.

Her breath caught as she looked up into his dark, soft eyes. "Quinn?" she whispered.

He drew her hands out of the warm, soapy water, still holding her gaze, and dried them on a dishcloth. Then he guided them, first one, then the other, up to his shoulders.

"Hold me," he whispered as his hands smoothed over her waist and brought her gently to him. "I want to kiss you."

She shivered from the sensuality in that soft whisper, lifting her face willingly.

He bent, brushing his mouth lazily over hers. "Isn't this how we did it before?" he breathed, parting his lips as they touched hers. "I like the way it feels to kiss you like this. My spine tingles."

"So...does mine." She slid her hands hesitantly into the thick, cool strands of hair at his nape and she went on tiptoe to give him better access to her mouth.

He accepted the invitation with quiet satisfaction, his mouth growing slowly rougher and hungrier as it fed on hers. He made a sound under his breath and all at once he bent, lifting her clear off the floor in a bearish embrace. His mouth bit hers, parting her lips, and she clung to him, moaning as the fever burned in her, too.

He let her go at once when Elliot called, "What?" from the living room. "Amanda, did you say something?"

"No... No, Elliot," she managed in a tone pitched a little higher than normal. Her answer appeared to satisfy him, because he didn't ask again. Harry was outside, but he probably wouldn't stay there long.

She looked up at Quinn, surprised by the intent stare he was giving her. He liked the way she looked, her face flushed, her mouth swollen from his kisses, her eyes wide and soft and faintly misty with emotion.

"I'd better get out of here," he said hesitantly.

"Yes." She touched her lips with her fingers and he watched the movement closely.

"Did I hurt your mouth?" he asked quietly.

She shook her head. "No. Oh, no, not at all," she said huskily.

Quinn nodded and sighed heavily. He smiled faintly and then turned and went back into the living room without another word.

It was a long afternoon, made longer by the strain Amanda felt being close to him. She found her eyes meeting his across the room and every time she flushed from the intensity of the look. Her body was hungry for him, and she imagined the reverse was equally true. He watched her openly now, with smoldering hunger in his eyes. They had a light supper and watched a little more television. But when Harry went to his room and Elliot called good-night and went up to bed, Amanda weakly stayed behind.

Quinn finished his cigarette with the air of a man who had all night, and then got up and reached for Amanda, lifting her into his arms.

"There's nothing to be afraid of," he said quietly, searching her wide, apprehensive eyes as he turned and carried her into his study and closed the door behind them.

It was a fiercely masculine room. The furniture was dark

wood with leather seats, the remnants of more prosperous times. He sat down in a big leather armchair with Amanda in his lap.

"It's private here," he explained. His hand moved one of hers to his shirt and pressed it there, over the tie. "Even Elliot doesn't come in when the door's shut. Do you still want to take my shirt off?" he asked with a warm smile.

Amanda sighed. "Well, yes," she stammered. "I haven't done this sort of thing before...."

"Neither have I, honey," he murmured dryly. "I guess we'll learn it together, won't we?"

She smiled into his dark eyes. "That sounds nice." She lowered her eyes to the tie and frowned when she saw how it was knotted.

"Here, I'll do it." He whipped it off with the ease of long practice and unlooped the collar button. "Now. You do the rest," he said deeply, and looked like a man anticipating heaven.

Her fingers, so adept on a keyboard, fumbled like two left feet while she worried buttons out of buttonholes. He was heavily muscled, tanned skin under a mass of thick, curling black hair. She remembered how it had looked that first night she'd been here, and how her hands had longed to touch it. Odd, because she'd never cared what was under a man's shirt before.

She pressed her hands flat against him, fascinated by the quick thunder of his heartbeat under them. She looked up into dark, quiet eyes.

"Shy?" he murmured dryly.

"A little. I always used to run a mile when men got this close."

The smile faded. His big hand covered hers, pressing them closer against him. "Wasn't there ever anyone you wanted?"

She shook her head. "The men I'm used to aren't like you. They're mostly rounders with a line a mile long. Everything is just casual to them, like eating mints." She flushed a little. "Intimacy isn't a casual thing to me."

"Or to me." His chest rose and fell heavily. He touched her

bright head. "Now will you take your hair down, Amanda?" he asked gently. "I've dreamed about it for days."

Amanda smiled softly. "Have you, really? It's something of a nuisance to wash and dry, but I've gotten sort of used to it." She unbraided it and let it down, enchanted by Quinn's rapt fascination with it. His big hands tangled in it, as if he loved the feel of it. He brought his face down and kissed her neck through it, drawing her against his bare chest.

"It smells like flowers," he whispered.

"I washed it before church this morning," she replied. "Elliot loaned me his blow-dryer but it still took all of thirty minutes to get the dampness out." She relaxed with a sigh, nuzzling against his shoulder while her fingers tugged at the thick hair on his chest. "You feel furry. Like a bear," she murmured.

"You feel silky," he said against her hair. With his hand, Quinn tilted her face up to his and slid his mouth onto hers in the silent room. He groaned softly as her lips parted under his. His arms lifted and turned her, wrapped her up, so that her breasts were lying on his chest and her cheek was pressed against his shoulder by the force of the kiss.

He tasted of smoke and coffee, and if his mouth wasn't expert, it was certainly ardent. She loved kissing him. She curled her arms around his neck and turned a little more, hesitating when she felt the sudden stark arousal of his body.

Her eyes opened, looking straight into his, and she colored.

"I'm sorry," he murmured, starting to shift her, as if his physical reaction to her embarrassed him.

"No, Quinn," she said, resisting gently, holding his gaze as she relaxed into him, shivering a little. "There's nothing to apologize for. I...like knowing you want me," she whispered, lowering her eyes to his mouth. "It just takes a little getting used to. I've never let anyone hold me like this."

His chest swelled with that confession. His cheek rested on her hair as he settled into the chair and relaxed himself, taking her weight easily. "I'm glad about that," he said. "But it isn't just physical with me. I wanted you to know."

She smiled against his shoulder. "It isn't just physical with me, either." She touched his hard face, her fingers moving over his mouth, loving the feel of it, the smell of his body, the warmth and strength of it. "Isn't it incredible?" She laughed softly. "I mean, at our ages, to be so green…"

He laughed, too. It would have stung to have heard that from any other woman, but Amanda was different. "I've never minded less being inexperienced," he murmured.

"Oh, neither have I." She sighed contentedly.

His big hand smoothed over her shoulder and down her back to her waist and onto her rib cage. He wanted very much to run it over her soft breast, but that might be too much too soon, so he hesitated.

Amanda smiled to herself. She caught his fingers and, lifting her face to his eyes, deliberately pulled them onto her breast, her lips parting at the sensation that steely warmth imparted. The nipple hardened and she caught her breath as Quinn's thumb rubbed against it.

"Have you ever seen a woman…without her top on?" she whispered, her long hair gloriously tangled around her face and shoulders.

"No," he replied softly. "Only in pictures." His dark eyes watched the softness his fingers were tracing. "I want to see you that way. I want to touch your skin…like this."

She drew his hand to the buttons of her blouse and lay quietly against him, watching his hard face as he loosened the buttons and pulled the fabric aside. The bra seemed to fascinate him. He frowned, trying to decide how it opened.

"It's a front catch," she whispered. She shifted a little, and found the catch. Her fingers trembled as she loosened it. Then, watching him, she carefully peeled it away from the high, taut throb of her breasts and watched him catch his breath.

"My God," he breathed reverently. He touched her with trembling fingers, his eyes on the deep mauve of her nipples against the soft pink thrust of flesh, his body taut with sudden aching longing. "My God, I've never seen anything so beautiful."

He made her feel incredibly feminine. She closed her eyes and arched back against his encircling arm, moaning softly.

"Kiss me...there," she whispered huskily, aching for his mouth.

"Amanda..." He bent, delighting in her femininity, the obvious rapt fascination of the first time in her actions so that even if he hadn't suspected her innocence he would have now. His lips brushed over the silky flesh, and his hands lifted her to him, arched her even more. She tasted of flower petals, softly trembling under his warm, ardent mouth, her breath jerking past her parted lips as she lay with her eyes closed, lost in him.

"It's so sweet, Quinn," she whispered brokenly.

His lips brushed up her body to her throat, her chin, and then they locked against her mouth. He turned her slowly, so that her soft breasts lay against the muted thunder of his hair-roughened chest. He felt her shiver before her arms slid around his neck and she deliberately pressed closer, drawing herself against him and moaning.

"Am I hurting you?" he asked huskily, his mouth poised just above hers, a faint tremor in his arms. "Amanda, am I hurting you?"

"No." She opened her eyes and they were like black pools, soft and deep and quiet. With her blond hair waving at her temples, her cheeks, her shoulders, she was so beautiful that Quinn's breath caught.

He sat just looking at her, indulging his hunger for the sight of her soft breasts, her lovely face. She lay quietly in his arms without a protest, barely breathing as the spell worked on them.

"I'll live on this the rest of my life," he said roughly, his voice deep and soft in the room, with only an occasional crackle from the burning fire in the potbellied stove to break the silence.

"So will I," she whispered. She reached up to his face, touching it in silence, adoring its strength. "We shouldn't have done this," she said miserably. "It will make it…so much more difficult, when I have to leave. The thaw…!"

His fingers pressed against her lips. "One day at a time," he said. "Even if you leave, you aren't getting away from me completely. I won't let go. Not ever."

Tears stung her eyes. The surplus of emotion sent them streaming down her cheeks and Quinn caught his breath, brushing them away with his long fingers.

"Why?" he whispered.

"Nobody ever wanted to keep me before," she explained with a watery smile. "I've always felt like an extra person in the world."

He found that hard to imagine, as beautiful as she was. Perhaps her reticence made her of less value to sophisticated men, but not to him. He found her a pearl beyond price.

"You're not an extra person in my world," he replied. "You fit."

She sighed and nuzzled against him, closing her eyes as she drank in the exquisite pleasure of skin against skin, feeling his heart beat against her breasts. She shivered.

"Are you cold?" he asked.

"No. It's…so wonderful, feeling you like this," she whispered. "Quinn?"

He eased her back in his arm and watched her, understanding as she didn't seem to understand what was wrong.

His big, warm hand covered her breast, gently caressing it. "It's desire," he whispered softly. "You want me."

"Yes," she whispered.

"You can't have me. Not like this. Not in any honorable way." He sighed heavily and lifted her against him to hold her, very hard. "Now hold on, real tight. It will pass."

She shivered helplessly, drowning in the warmth of his body, in its heat against her breasts. But he was right. Slowly the ache began to ease away and her body stilled with a huge sigh.

"How do you know so much when you've...when you've never...?"

"I told you, I read a book. Several books." He chuckled, the laughter rippling over her sensitive breasts. "But, my God, reading was never like this!"

She laughed, too, and impishly bit his shoulder right through the cloth.

Then he shivered. "Don't," he said huskily.

She lifted her head, fascinated by the expression on his face. "Do you like it?" she asked hesitantly.

"Yes, I like it," he said with a rueful smile. "All too much." He gazed down at her bareness and his eyes darkened. "I like looking at your breasts, too, but I think we'd better stop this while we can."

He tugged the bra back around her with a grimace and hooked the complicated catch. He deftly buttoned her blouse up to her throat, his eyes twinkling as they met hers.

"Disappointed?" he murmured. "So am I. I have these dreams every night of pillowing you on your delicious hair while we make love until you cry out."

She could picture that, too, and her breath lodged in her throat as she searched his dark eyes. His body, bare and moving softly over hers on white sheets, his face above her...

She moaned.

"Oh, I want it, too," he whispered, touching his mouth with exquisite tenderness to hers. "You in my bed, your arms around me, the mattress moving under us." He lifted his head, breathing unsteadily. "I might have to hurt you a little at first," he said gruffly. "You understand?"

"Yes." She smoothed his shirt, absently drawing it back together and fastening the buttons with a sense of possession. "But only a little, and I could bear it for what would come afterward," she said, looking up. "Because you'd pleasure me then."

"My God, would I," he whispered. "Pleasure you until you were exhausted." He framed her face in his hands and kissed her gently. "Please go to bed, Amanda, before I double over and start screaming."

She smiled against his mouth and let him put her on her feet. She laughed when she swayed and he had to catch her.

"See what you do to me?" she mused. "Make me dizzy."

"Not half as dizzy as you make me." He smoothed down her long hair, his eyes adoring it. "Pretty little thing," he murmured.

"I'm glad you like me," she replied. "I'll do my best to stay this way for the next fifty years or so, with a few minor wrinkles."

"You'll be beautiful to me when you're an old lady. Good night."

She moved away from him with flattering reluctance, her dark eyes teasing his. "Are you sure you haven't done this before?" she asked with a narrow gaze. "You're awfully good at it for a beginner."

"That makes two of us," he returned dryly.

She liked the way he looked, with his hair mussed and his thin mouth swollen from her kisses, and his shirt disheveled. It made her feel a new kind of pride that she could disarrange him so nicely. After one long glance, she opened the door and went out.

"Lock your door," he whispered.

She laughed delightedly. "No, you lock yours the way you did the other night."

He shifted uncomfortably. "That was a low blow. I'm sorry."

"Oh, I was flattered," she corrected. "I've never felt so dangerous in all my life. I wish I had one of those long, black silk negligees…"

"Will you get out of here?" he asked pleasantly. "I think I did mention the urge to throw you on the floor and ravish you?"

"With Elliot right upstairs? Fie, sir, think of my reputation."

"I'm trying to, if you'll just go to bed!"

"Very well, if I must." She started up the staircase, her black eyes dancing as they met his. She tossed her hair back and smiled at him. "Good night, Quinn."

"Good night, Amanda. Sweet dreams."

"They'll be sweet from now on," she agreed. She turned reluctantly and went up the staircase. He watched her until she went into her room and closed the door.

It wasn't until she was in her own room that she realized just what she'd done.

She wasn't some nice domestic little thing who could fit into Quinn's world without any effort. She was Amanda Corrie Callaway, who belonged to a rock group with a worldwide reputation. On most streets in most cities, her face was instantly recognizable. How was Quinn going to take the knowledge of who she really was—and the fact that she'd deceived him by leading him to think she was just a vacationing keyboard player? She groaned as she put on her gown. It didn't bear thinking about. From sweet heaven to nightmare in one hour was too much.

CHAPTER SEVEN

AMANDA HARDLY SLEPT from the combined shock of Quinn's ardor and her own guilt. How could she tell him the truth now? What could she say that would take away the sting of her deceit?

She dressed in jeans and the same button-up pink blouse she'd worn the night before and went down to breakfast.

Quinn looked up as she entered the room, his eyes warm and quiet.

"Good morning," she said brightly.

"Good morning yourself," Quinn murmured with a smile. "Sleep well?"

"Barely a wink," she said, sighing, her own eyes holding his.

He chuckled, averting his gaze before Elliot became suspicious. "Harry's out feeding your calves," he said, "and I'm on my way over to Eagle Pass to help one of my neighbors feed some stranded cattle. You'll have to stay with Elliot—it's teacher workday."

"I forgot," Elliot wailed, head in hands. "Can you imagine that I actually forgot? I could have slept until noon!"

"There, there," Amanda said, patting his shoulder. "Don't you want to learn some more chords?"

"Is that what you do?" Quinn asked curiously, because now every scrap of information he learned about her was precious.

"You said you played a keyboard for a living. Do you teach music?"

"Not really," she said gently. "I play backup for various groups," she explained. "That rock music you hate…" she began uneasily.

"That's all right," Quinn replied, his face open and kind. "I was just trying to get a rise out of you. I don't mind it all that much, I guess. And playing backup isn't the same thing as putting on those god-awful costumes and singing suggestive lyrics. Well, I'm gone. Stay out of trouble, you two," he said as he got to his feet in the middle of Amanda's instinctive move to speak, to correct his assumption that all she did was play backup. She wanted to tell him the truth, but he winked at her and Elliot and got into his outdoor clothes before she could find a way to break the news. By the time her mind was working again, he was gone.

She sat back down, sighing. "Oh, Elliot, what a mess," she murmured, her chin in her hands.

"Is that what you call it?" he asked with a wicked smile. "Dad's actually grinning, and when he looked at you, you blushed. I'm not blind, you know. Do you like him, even if he isn't Mr. America?"

"Yes, I like him," she said with a shy smile, lowering her eyes. "He's a pretty special guy."

"I think so, myself. Eat your breakfast. I want to ask you about some new chords."

"Okay."

They were working on the keyboard when the sound of an approaching vehicle caught Amanda's attention. Quinn hadn't driven anything motorized since the snow had gotten so high.

"That's odd," Elliot said, peering out the window curtain. "It's a four-wheel drive… Oh, boy." He glanced at Amanda. "You aren't gonna like this."

She lifted her eyebrows. "I'm not?" she asked, puzzled.

The knock at the back door had Harry moving toward it before Amanda and Elliot could. Harry opened it and looked up and up and up. He stood there staring while Elliot gaped at the grizzly-looking man who loomed over him in a black Western costume, complete with hat.

"I'm looking for Mandy Callaway," he boomed.

"Hank!"

Amanda ran to the big man without thinking, to be lifted high in the air while he chuckled and kissed her warmly on one cheek, his whiskers scratching.

"Hello, peanut!" he grinned. "What are you doing up here? The old trapper down the hill said you hadn't been in Durning's cabin since the heavy snow came."

"Mr. Sutton took me in and gave me a roof over my head. Put me down," she fussed, wiggling.

He put her back on her feet while Harry and Elliot still gaped.

"This is Hank," she said, holding his enormous hand as she turned to face the others. "He's a good friend, and a terrific musician, and I'd really appreciate it if you wouldn't tell Quinn he was here just yet. I'll tell him myself. Okay?"

"Sure," Harry murmured. He shook his head. "You for real, or do you have stilts in them boots?"

"I used to be a linebacker for the Dallas Cowboys." Hank grinned.

"That would explain it," Harry chuckled. "Your secret's safe with me, Amanda." He excused himself and went to do the washing.

"Me, too," Elliot said, grinning, "as long as I get Mr. Shoeman's autograph before he leaves."

Amanda let out a long breath, her eyes frightened as they met Elliot's.

"That's right," Elliot said. "I already knew you were Mandy Callaway. I've got a Desperado tape. I took it out of Dad's drawer and hid it as soon as I recognized you. You'll tell him when the time's right. Won't you?"

"Yes, I will, Elliot," she agreed. "I'd have done it already except that...well, things have gotten a little complicated."

"You can say that again." Elliot led the way into the living room, watching Hank sit gingerly on a sofa that he dwarfed. "I'll just go make sure that tape's hidden," he said, leaving them alone.

"Complicated, huh?" Hank said. "I hear this Sutton man's a real woman hater."

"He was until just recently." She folded her hands in her lap. "And he doesn't approve of rock music." She sighed and changed the subject. "What's up, Hank?"

"We've got a gig at Larry's Lodge," he said. "I know, you don't want to. Listen for a minute. It's to benefit cystic fibrosis, and a lot of other stars are going to be in town for it, including a few pretty well-known singers." He named some of them and Amanda whistled. "See what I mean? It's strictly charity, or I wouldn't have come up here bothering you. The boys and I want to do it." His dark eyes narrowed. "Are you up to it?"

"I don't know. I tried to sing here a couple of times, and my voice seems to be good enough. No more lapses. But in front of a crowd..." She spread her hands. "I don't know, Hank."

"Here." He handed her three tickets to the benefit. "You think about it. If you can, come on up. Sutton might like the singers even if he doesn't care for our kind of music." He studied her. "You haven't told him, have you?"

She shook her head, smiling wistfully. "Haven't found the right way yet. If I leave it much longer, it may be too late."

"The girl's family sent you a letter," he said. "Thanking you for what you tried to do. They said you were her heroine...aw, now, Mandy, stop it!"

She collapsed in tears. He held her, rocking her, his face red with mingled embarrassment and guilt.

"Mandy, come on, stop that," he muttered. "It's all over and done with. You've got to get yourself together. You can't hide out here in the Tetons for the rest of your life."

"Can't I?" she wailed.

"No, you can't. Hiding isn't your style. You have to face the stage again, or you'll never get over it." He tilted her wet face. "Look, would you want somebody eating her guts out over you if you'd been Wendy that night? It wasn't your fault, damn it! It wasn't anybody's fault; it was an accident, pure and simple."

"If she hadn't been at the concert…"

"If, if, if," he said curtly. "You can't go back and change things to suit you. It was her time. At the concert, on a plane, in a car, however, it would still have been her time. Are you listening to me, Mandy?"

She dabbed her eyes with the hem of her blouse. "Yes, I'm listening."

"Come on, girl. Buck up. You can get over this if you set your mind to it. Me and the guys miss you, Mandy. It's not the same with just the four of us. People are scared of us when you aren't around."

That made her smile. "I guess they are. You do look scruffy, Hank," she murmured.

"You ought to see Johnson." He sighed. "He's let his beard go and he looks like a scrub brush. And Deke says he won't change clothes until you come back."

"Oh, my God," Amanda said, shuddering, "tell him I'll think hard about this concert, okay? You poor guys. Stay upwind of him."

"We're trying." He got up, smiling down at her. "Everything's okay. You can see the letter when you come to the lodge. It's real nice. Now stop beating yourself. Nobody else blames you. After all, babe, you risked your life trying to save her. Nobody's forgotten that, either."

She leaned against him for a minute, drawing on his strength. "Thanks, Hank."

"Anytime. Hey, kid, you still want that autograph?" he asked.

Elliot came back into the room with a pad and pen. "Do I!" he said, chuckling.

Hank scribbled his name and Desperado's curly-Q logo underneath. "There you go."

"He's a budding musician," Amanda said, putting an arm around Elliot. "I'm teaching him the keyboard. One of these days, if we can get around Quinn, we'll have him playing backup for me."

"You bet." Hank chuckled, and ruffled Elliot's red hair. "Keep at it. Mandy's the very best. If she teaches you, you're taught."

"Thanks, Mr. Shoeman."

"Just Hank. See you at the concert. So long, Mandy."

"So long, pal."

"What concert?" Elliot asked excitedly when Hank had driven away.

Amanda handed him the three tickets. "To a benefit in Jackson Hole. The group's going to play there. Maybe. If I can get up enough nerve to get back onstage again."

"What happened, Amanda?" he asked gently.

She searched his face, seeing compassion along with the curiosity, so she told him, fighting tears all the way.

"Gosh, no wonder you came up here to get away," Elliot said with more than his twelve years worth of wisdom. He shrugged. "But like he said, you have to go back someday. The longer you wait, the harder it's going to be."

"I know that," she groaned. "But Elliot, I…" She took a deep breath and looked down at the floor. "I love your father," she said, admitting it at last. "I love him very much, and the minute he finds out who I am, my life is over."

"Maybe not," he said. "You've got another week until the concert. Surely in all that time you can manage to tell him the truth. Can't you?"

"I hope so," she said with a sad smile. "You don't mind who I am, do you?" she asked worriedly.

"Don't be silly." He hugged her warmly. "I think you're super, keyboard or not."

She laughed and hugged him back. "Well, that's half the battle."

"Just out of curiosity," Harry asked from the doorway, "who was the bearded giant?"

"That was Hank Shoeman," Elliot told him. "He's the drummer for Desperado. It's a rock group. And Amanda—"

"—plays backup for him," she volunteered, afraid to give too much away to Harry.

"Well, I'll be. He's a musician?" Harry shook his head. "Would have took him for a bank robber," he mumbled.

"Most people do, and you should see the rest of the group." She grinned. "Don't give me away, Harry, okay? I promise I'll tell Quinn, but I've got to do it the right way."

"I can see that," he agreed easily. "Be something of a shock to him to meet your friend after dark, I imagine."

"I imagine so," she said, chuckling. "Thanks, Harry."

"My pleasure. Desperado, huh? Suits it, if the rest of the group looks like he does."

"Worse," she said, and shuddered.

"Strains the mind, don't it?" Harry went off into the kitchen and Amanda got up after a minute to help him get lunch.

Quinn wasn't back until late that afternoon. Nobody mentioned Hank's visit, but Amanda was nervous and her manner was strained as she tried not to show her fears.

"What's wrong with you?" he asked gently during a lull in the evening while Elliot did homework and Harry washed up. "You don't seem like yourself tonight."

She moved close to him, her fingers idly touching the sleeve of his red flannel shirt. "It's thawing outside," she said, watching her fingers move on the fabric. "It won't be long before I'll be gone."

He sighed heavily. His fingers captured hers and held them. "I've been thinking about that. Do you really have to get back?"

She felt her heart jump. Whatever he was offering, she wanted to say yes and let the future take care of itself. But she couldn't. She grimaced. "Yes, I have to get back," she said miserably. "I have commitments to people. Things I promised to do." Her fingers clenched his. "Quinn, I have to meet some people at Larry's Lodge in Jackson Hole next Friday night." She looked up. "It's at a concert and I have tickets. I know you don't like rock, but there's going to be all kinds of music." Her eyes searched his. "Would you go with me? Elliot can come, too. I…want you to see what I do for a living."

"You and your keyboard?" he mused gently.

"Sort of," she agreed, hoping she could find the nerve to tell him everything before next Friday night.

"Okay," he replied. "A friend of mine works there—I used to be with the Ski Patrol there, too. Sure, I'll go with you." The smile vanished, and his eyes glittered down at her. "I'll go damned near anywhere with you."

Amanda slid her arms around him and pressed close, shutting her eyes as she held on for dear life. "That goes double for me, mountain man," she said half under her breath.

He bent his head, searching for her soft mouth. She gave it to him without a protest, without a thought for the future, gave it to him with interest, with devotion, with ardor. Her lips opened invitingly, and she felt his hands on her hips with a sense of sweet inevitability, lifting her into intimate contact with the aroused contours of his body.

"Frightened?" he whispered unsteadily just over her mouth when he felt her stiffen involuntarily.

"Of you?" she whispered back. "Don't be absurd. Hold me any way you want. I adore you…!"

He actually groaned as his mouth pressed down hard on hers. His arms contracted hungrily and he gave in to the pleasure of possession for one long moment.

Her eyes opened and she watched him, feeding on the slight contortion of his features, his heavy brows drawn over his crooked nose, his long, thick lashes on his cheek as he kissed her. She did adore him, she thought dizzily. Adored him, loved him, worshiped him. If only she could stay with him forever like this.

Quinn lifted his head and paused as he saw her watching him. He frowned slightly, then bent again. This time his eyes stayed open, too, and she went under as he deepened the kiss. Her eyes closed in self-defense and she moaned, letting him see the same vulnerability she'd seen in him. It was breathlessly sweet.

"This is an education," he said, laughing huskily, when he drew slightly away from her.

"Isn't it, though?" she murmured, moving his hands from her hips up to her waist and moving back a step from the blatant urgency of his body. "Elliot and Harry might come in," she whispered.

"I wouldn't mind," he said unexpectedly, searching her flushed face. "I'm not ashamed of what I feel for you, or embarrassed by it."

"This from a confirmed woman hater?" she asked with twinkling eyes.

"Well, not exactly confirmed anymore," he confessed. He lifted her by the waist and searched her eyes at point-blank range until she trembled from the intensity of the look. "I couldn't hate you if I tried, Amanda," he said quietly.

"Oh, I hope not," she said fervently, thinking ahead to when she would have to tell him the truth about herself.

He brushed a lazy kiss across her lips. "I think I'm getting the hang of this," he murmured.

"I think you are, too," she whispered. She slid her arms around his neck and put her warm mouth hungrily against his, sighing when he caught fire and answered the kiss with feverish abandon.

A slight, deliberate cough brought them apart, both staring blankly at the small redheaded intruder.

"Not that I mind," Elliot said, grinning, "but you're blocking the pan of brownies Harry made."

"You can think of brownies at a time like this?" Amanda groaned. "Elliot!"

"Listen, he can think of brownies with a fever of a hundred and two," Quinn told her, still holding her on a level with his eyes. "I've seen him get out of a sickbed to pinch a brownie from the kitchen."

"I like brownies, too," Amanda confessed with a warm smile, delighted that Quinn didn't seem to mind at all that Elliot had seen them in a compromising position. That made her feel lighter than air.

"Do you?" Quinn smiled and brushed his mouth gently against hers, mindless of Elliot's blatant interest, before he put her back on her feet. "Harry makes his from scratch, with real baker's chocolate. They're something special."

"I'll bet they are. Here. I'll get the saucers," she volunteered, still catching her breath.

Elliot looked like the cat with the canary as she dished up brownies. It very obviously didn't bother him that Amanda and his dad were beginning to notice each other.

"Isn't this cozy?" he remarked as they went back into the living room and Amanda curled up on the sofa beside his dad, who never sat there.

"Cozy, indeed," Quinn murmured with a warm smile for Amanda.

She smiled back and laid her cheek against Quinn's broad chest while they watched television and ate brownies. She didn't move even when Harry joined them. And she knew she'd never been closer to heaven.

That night they were left discreetly alone, and she lay in Quinn's strong arms on the long leather couch in his office while wood burned with occasional hisses and sparks in the potbellied stove.

"I've had a raw deal with this place," he said eventually between kisses. "But it's good land, and I'm building a respectable herd of cattle. I can't offer you wealth or position, and we've got a ready-made family. But I can take care of you," he said solemnly, looking down into her soft eyes. "And you won't want for any of the essentials."

Her fingers touched his lean cheek hesitantly. "You don't know anything about me," she said. "When you know my background, you may not want me as much as you think you do." She put her fingers against his mouth. "You have to be sure."

"Damn it, I'm already sure," he muttered.

But was he? She was the first woman he'd ever been intimate with. Couldn't that blind him to her real suitability? What if it was just infatuation or desire? She was afraid to take a chance on his feelings, when she didn't really know what they were.

"Let's wait just a little while longer before we make any plans, Quinn. Okay?" she asked softly, turning in his hard arms so that her body was lying against his. "Make love to me," she whispered, moving her mouth up to his. "Please…"

He gave in with a rough groan, gathering her to him, crushing her against his aroused body. He wanted her beyond rational thought. Maybe she had cold feet, but he didn't. He knew what he wanted, and Amanda was it.

His hands smoothed the blouse and bra away with growing expertise and he fought out of his shirt so that he could feel her soft skin against his. But it wasn't enough. He felt her tremble and knew that it was reflected in his own arms and legs. He moved against her with a new kind of sensuousness, lifting his head to hold her eyes while he levered her onto her back and eased over her, his legs between both of hers in their first real intimacy.

She caught her breath, but she didn't push him to try to get away.

"It's just that new for you, isn't it?" he whispered huskily as his hips moved lazily over hers and he groaned. "God, it burns me to…feel you like this."

"I know." She arched her back, loving his weight, loving the fierce maleness of his body. Her arms slid closer around him and she felt his mouth open on hers, his tongue softly searching as it slid inside, into an intimacy that made her moan. She began to tremble.

His lean hand slid under her, getting a firm grip, and he brought her suddenly into a shocking, shattering position that made her mindless with sudden need. She clutched him desperately, shuddering, her nails digging into him as the contact racked her like a jolt of raw electricity.

He pulled away from her without a word, shuddering as he lay on his back, trying to get hold of himself.

"I'm sorry," he whispered. "I didn't mean to let it go so far with us."

She was trembling, too, trying to breathe while great hot tears rolled down her cheeks. "Gosh, I wanted you," she whispered tearfully. "Wanted you so badly, Quinn!"

"As badly as I wanted you, honey," he said heavily. "We can't let things get that hot again. It was a close call. Closer than you realize."

"Oh, Quinn, couldn't we make love?" she asked softly, rolling over to look down into his tormented face. "Just once…?"

He framed his face in his hands and brought her closed eyes to his lips. "No. I won't compromise you."

She hit his big, hair-roughened chest. "Goody Two Shoes…!"

"Thank your lucky stars that I am," he chuckled. His eyes dropped to her bare breasts and lingered there before he caught the edges of her blouse and tugged them together. "You sex-crazed female, haven't you ever heard about pregnancy?"

"That condition where I get to have little Quinns?"

"Stop it, you're making it impossible for me," he said huskily. "Here, get up before I lose my mind."

She sat up with a grimace. "Spoilsport."

"Listen to you," he muttered, putting her back into her clothes with a wry grin. "I'll give you ten to one that you'd be yelling your head off if I started taking off your jeans."

She went red. "My jeans…!"

His eyebrows arched. "Amanda, would you like me to explain that book I read to you? The part about how men and women…"

She cleared her throat. "No, thanks, I think I've got the hang of it now," she murmured evasively.

"We might as well add a word about birth control," he added with a chuckle when he was buttoning up his own shirt. "You don't take the pill, I assume?"

She shook her head. The whole thing was getting to be really embarrassing!

"Well, that leaves prevention up to me," he explained. "And that would mean a trip into town to the drugstore, since I never indulged, I never needed to worry about prevention. *Now* do you get the picture?"

"Boy, do I get the picture." She grimaced, avoiding his knowing gaze.

"Good girl. That's why we aren't lying down anymore."

She sighed loudly. "I guess you don't want children."

"Sure I do. Elliot would love brothers and sisters, and I'm crazy about kids." He took her slender hands in his and smoothed them over with his thumbs. "But kids should be born inside marriage, not outside it. Don't you think so?"

She took a deep breath, and her dark eyes met his. "Yes."

"Then we'll spend a lot of time together until you have to meet your friends at this concert," he said softly. "And afterward, you and I will come in here again and I'll ask you a question."

"Oh, Quinn," she whispered with aching softness.

"Oh, Amanda," he murmured, smiling as his lips softly touched hers. "But right now, we go to bed. Separately. Quick!"

"Yes, sir, Mr. Sutton." She got up and let him lead her to the staircase.

"I'll get the lights," he said. "You go on up. In the morning after we get Elliot off to school you can come out with me, if you want to."

"I want to," she said simply. She could hardly bear to be

parted from him even overnight. It was like an addiction, she
thought as she went up the staircase. Now if only she could
make it last until she had the nerve to tell Quinn the truth....

The next few days went by in a haze. The snow began to
melt and the skies cleared as the long-awaited chinook blew in.
In no time at all it was Friday night and Amanda was getting
into what Elliot would recognize as her stage costume. She'd
brought it, with her other things, from the Durning cabin. She
put it on, staring at herself in the mirror. Her hair hung long
and loose, in soft waves below her waist, in the beige leather
dress with the buckskin boots that matched, she was the very
picture of a sensuous woman. She left off the headband. There
would be time for that if she could summon enough courage
to get onstage. She still hadn't told Quinn. She hadn't had the
heart to destroy the dream she'd been living. But tonight he'd
know. And she'd know if they had a future. She took a deep
breath and went downstairs.

CHAPTER EIGHT

AMANDA SAT IN the audience with Quinn and Elliot at a far table while the crowded hall rang with excited whispers. Elliot was tense, like Amanda, his eyes darting around nervously. Quinn was frowning. He hadn't been quite himself since Amanda came down the staircase in her leather dress and boots, looking expensive and faintly alien. He hadn't asked any questions, but he seemed as uptight as she felt.

Her eyes slid over him lovingly, taking in his dark suit. He looked out of place in fancy clothes. She missed the sight of him in denim and his old shepherd's coat, and wondered fleetingly if she'd ever get to see him that way again after tonight—if she'd ever lie in his arms on the big sofa and warm to his kisses while the fire burned in the stove. She almost groaned. Oh, Quinn, she thought, I love you.

Elliot looked uncomfortable in his blue suit. He was watching for the rest of Desperado while a well-known Las Vegas entertainer warmed up the crowd and sang his own famous theme song.

"What are you looking for, son?" Quinn asked.

Elliot shifted. "Nothing. I'm just seeing who I know."

Quinn's eyebrows arched. "How would you know anybody

in this crowd?" he muttered, glancing around. "My God, these are show people. Entertainers. Not people from our world."

That was a fact. But hearing it made Amanda heartsick. She reached out and put her hand over Quinn's.

"Your fingers are like ice," he said softly. He searched her worried eyes. "Are you okay, honey?"

The endearment made her warm all over. She smiled sadly and slid her fingers into his, looking down at the contrast between his callused, work-hardened hand and her soft, pale one. His was a strong hand, hers was artistic. But despite the differences, they fit together perfectly. She squeezed her fingers. "I'm fine," she said. "Quinn…"

"And now I want to introduce a familiar face," the Las Vegas performer's voice boomed. "Most of you know the genius of Desperado. The group has won countless awards for its topical, hard-hitting songs. Last year, Desperado was given a Grammy for 'Changes in the Wind,' and Hank Shoeman's song 'Outlaw Love' won him a country music award and a gold record. But their fame isn't the reason we're honoring them tonight."

To Amanda's surprise, he produced a gold plaque. "As some of you may remember, a little over a month ago, a teenage girl died at a Desperado concert. The group's lead singer leaped into the crowd, disregarding her own safety, and was very nearly trampled trying to protect the fan. Because of that tragedy, Desperado went into seclusion. We're proud to tell you tonight that they're back and they're in better form than ever. This plaque is a token of respect from the rest of us in the performing arts to a very special young woman whose compassion and selflessness have won the respect of all."

He looked out toward the audience where Amanda sat frozen. "This is for you—Amanda Corrie Callaway. Will you come up and join the group, please? Come on, Mandy!"

She bit her lower lip. The plaque was a shock. The boys seemed to know about it, too, because they went to their instruments grinning and began to play the downbeat that Desperado was known for, the deep throbbing counter rhythm that was their trademark.

"Come on, babe!" Hank called out in his booming voice, he and Johnson and Deke and Jack looking much more like backwoods robbers than musicians with their huge bulk and outlaw gear.

Amanda glanced at Elliot's rapt, adoring face, and then looked at Quinn. He was frowning, his dark eyes searching the crowd. She said a silent goodbye as she got to her feet. She reached into her pocket for her headband and put it on her head. She couldn't look at him, but she felt his shocked stare as she walked down the room toward the stage, her steps bouncing as the rhythm got into her feet and her blood.

"Thank you," she said huskily, kissing the entertainer's cheek as she accepted the plaque. She moved in between Johnson and Deke, taking the microphone. She looked past Elliot's proud, adoring face to Quinn's. He seemed to be in a state of dark shock. "Thank you all. I've had a hard few weeks. But I'm okay now, and I'm looking forward to better times. God bless, people. This one is for a special man and a special boy, with all my love." She turned to Hank, nodded, and he began the throbbing drumbeat of "Love Singer."

It was a song that touched the heart, for all its mad beat. The words, in her soft, sultry, clear voice caught every ear in the room. She sang from the heart, with the heart, the words fierce with meaning as she sang them to Quinn. "Love you, never loved anybody but you, never leave me lonely, love…singer."

But Quinn didn't seem to be listening to the words. He got to his feet and jerked Elliot to his. He walked out in the middle of the song and never looked back once.

Amanda managed to finish, with every ounce of willpower she had keeping her onstage. She let the last few notes hang in the air and then she bowed to a standing ovation. By the time she and the band did an encore and she got out of the hall, the truck they'd come in was long gone. There was no note, no message. Quinn had said it all with his eloquent back when he walked out of the hall. He knew who she was now, and he wanted no part of her. He couldn't have said it more clearly if he'd written it in blood.

She kept hoping that he might reconsider. Even after she went backstage with the boys, she kept hoping for a phone call or a glimpse of Quinn. But nothing happened.

"I guess I'm going to need a place to stay," Amanda said with a rueful smile, her expression telling her group all they needed to know.

"He couldn't handle it, huh?" Hank asked quietly. "I'm sorry, babe. We've got a suite, there's plenty of room for one more. I'll go up and get your gear tomorrow."

"Thanks, Hank." She took a deep breath and clutched the plaque to her chest. "Where's the next gig?"

"That's my girl," he said gently, sliding a protective arm around her. "San Francisco's our next stop. The boys and I are taking a late bus tomorrow." He grimaced at her knowing smile. "Well, you know how I feel about airplanes."

"Chicken Little," she accused. "Well, I'm not going to sit on a bus all day. I'll take the first charter out and meet you guys at the hotel."

"Whatever turns you on," Hank chuckled. "Come on. Let's get out of here and get some rest."

"You did good, Amanda," Johnson said from behind her. "We were proud."

"You bet," Deke and Jack seconded.

She smiled at them all. "Thanks, group. I shocked myself, but at least I didn't go dry the way I did last time." Her heart was breaking in two, but she managed to hide it. Quinn, she moaned inwardly. Oh, Quinn, was I just an interlude, an infatuation?

She didn't sleep very much. The next morning Amanda watched Hank start out for Ricochet then went down to a breakfast that she didn't even eat while she waited for him to return.

He came back three hours later, looking ruffled.

"Did you get my things?" she asked when he came into the suite.

"I got them." He put her suitcase down on the floor. "Part at Sutton's place, part at the Durning cabin. Elliot sent you a note." He produced it.

"And... Quinn?"

"I never saw him," he replied tersely. "The boy and the old man were there. They didn't mention Sutton and I didn't ask. I wasn't feeling too keen on him at the time."

"Thanks, Hank."

He shrugged. "That's the breaks, kid. It would have been a rough combination at best. You're a bright-lights girl."

"Am I?" she asked, thinking how easily she'd fit into Quinn's world. But she didn't push it. She sat down on the couch and opened Elliot's scribbled note.

Amanda,
I thought you were great. Dad didn't say anything all the way home and last night he went into his study and didn't come out until this morning. He went hunting, he said, but he didn't take any bullets. I hope you are okay. Write me when you can. I love you.
Your friend, Elliot.

She bit her lip to keep from crying. Dear Elliot. At least he still cared about her. But her fall from grace in Quinn's eyes had been final, she thought bitterly. He'd never forgive her for deceiving him. Or maybe it was just that he'd gotten over his brief infatuation with her when he found out who she really was. She didn't know what to do. She couldn't remember ever feeling so miserable. To have discovered something that precious, only to lose it forever. She folded Elliot's letter and put it into her purse. At least it would be something to remember from her brief taste of heaven.

For the rest of the day, the band and Jerry, the road manager, got the arrangements made for the San Francisco concert, and final travel plans were laid. The boys were to board the San Francisco bus the next morning. Amanda was to fly out on a special air charter that specialized in flights for business executives. They'd managed to fit her in at the last minute when a computer-company executive had canceled his flight.

"I wish you'd come with us," Hank said hesitantly. "I guess I'm overreacting and all, but I hate airplanes."

"I'll be fine," she told him firmly. "You and the boys have a nice trip and stop worrying about me. I'll be fine."

"If you say so," Hank mumbled.

"I do say so." She patted him on the shoulder. "Trust me."

He shrugged and left, but he didn't look any less worried. Amanda, who'd gotten used to his morose predictions, didn't pay them any mind.

She went to the suite and into her bedroom early that night. Her fingers dialed the number at Ricochet. She had to try one last time, she told herself. There was at least the hope that Quinn might care enough to listen to her explanation. She had to try.

The phone rang once, twice, and she held her breath, but on the third ring the receiver was lifted.

"Sutton," came a deep weary-sounding voice.

Her heart lifted. "Oh, Quinn," she burst out. "Quinn, please let me try to explain—"

"You don't have to explain anything to me, Amanda," he said stiffly. "I saw it all on the stage."

"I know it looks bad," she began.

"You lied to me," he said. "You let me think you were just a shy little innocent who played a keyboard, when you were some fancy big-time entertainer with a countrywide following."

"I knew you wouldn't want me if you knew who I was," she said miserably.

"You knew I'd see right through you if I knew," he corrected, his voice growing angrier. "You played me for a fool."

"I didn't!"

"All of it was a lie. Nothing but a lie! Well, you can go back to your public, Miss Callaway, and your outlaw buddies, and make some more records or tapes or whatever the hell they are. I never wanted you in the first place except in bed, so it's no great loss to me." He was grimacing, and she couldn't see the agony in his eyes as he forced the words out. Now that he knew who and what she was, he didn't dare let himself weaken. He had to make her go back to her own life, and stay out of his. He had nothing to give her, nothing that could take the place of fame and fortune and the world at her feet. He'd never been more aware of his own inadequacies as he had been when he'd seen Amanda on that stage and heard the applause of the audience. It ranked as the worst waking nightmare of his life, putting her forever out of his reach.

"Quinn!" she moaned. "Quinn, you don't mean that!"

"I mean it," he said through his teeth. He closed his eyes. "Every word. Don't call here again, don't come by, don't write. You're a bad influence on Elliot now that he knows who you are. I don't want you. You've worn out your welcome at Ricochet." He hung up without another word.

Amanda stared at the telephone receiver as if it had sprouted wings. Slowly she put it back in the cradle just as the room splintered into wet crystal around her.

She put on her gown mechanically and got into bed, turning out the bedside light. She lay in the dark and Quinn's words echoed in her head with merciless coolness. *Bad influence. Don't want you. Worn out your welcome. Never wanted you anyway except in bed.*

She moaned and buried her face in her pillow. She didn't know how she was going to go on, with Quinn's cold contempt dogging her footsteps. He hated her now. He thought she'd been playing a game, enjoying herself while she made a fool out of him. The tears burned her eyes. How quickly it had all ended, how finally. She'd hoped to keep in touch with Elliot, but that wouldn't be possible anymore. She was a bad influence on

Elliot, so he wouldn't be allowed to contact her. She sobbed her hurt into the cool linen. Somehow, being denied contact with Elliot was the last straw. She'd grown so fond of the boy during those days she'd spent at Ricochet, and he cared about her, too. Quinn was being unnecessarily harsh. But perhaps he was right, and it was for the best. Maybe she could learn to think that way eventually. Right now she had a concert to get to, a sold-out one from what the boys and Jerry had said. She couldn't let the fans down.

Amanda got up the next morning, looking and feeling as if it were the end of the world. The boys took her suitcase downstairs, not looking too closely at her face without makeup, her long hair arranged in a thick, haphazard bun. She was wearing a dark pantsuit with a cream-colored blouse, and she looked miserable.

"We'll see you in San Francisco," Jerry told her with a smile. "I have to go nursemaid these big, tough guys, so you make sure the pilot of your plane has all his marbles, okay?"

"I'll check him out myself," she promised. "Take care of yourselves, guys. I'll see you in California."

"Okay. Be good, babe," Hank called. He and the others filed into the bus Jerry had chartered and Jerry hugged her impulsively and went in behind them.

She watched the bus pull away, feeling lost and alone, not for the first time. It was cold and snowy, but she hadn't wanted her coat. It was packed in her suitcase, and had already been put on the light aircraft. With a long sigh, she went back to the cab and sat disinterestedly in it as it wound over the snowy roads to the airport.

Fortunately the chinook had thawed the runways so that the planes were coming and going easily. She got out at the air charter service hangar and shook hands with the pilot.

"Don't worry, we're in great shape," he promised Amanda with a grin. "In fact, the mechanics just gave us another once-over to be sure. Nothing to worry about."

DIANA PALMER 363

"Oh, I wasn't worried," she said absently and allowed herself to be shepherded inside. She slid into an empty aisle seat on the right side and buckled up. Usually she preferred to sit by the window, but today she wasn't in the mood for sight-seeing. One snow-covered mountain looked pretty much like another to her, and her heart wasn't in this flight or the gig that would follow it. She leaned back and closed her eyes.

It seemed to take forever for all the businessmen to get aboard. Fortunately there had been one more cancellation, so she had her seat and the window seat as well. She didn't feel like talking to anyone, and was hoping she wouldn't have to sit by some chatterbox all the way to California.

She listened to the engines rev up and made sure that her seat belt was properly fastened. They would be off as soon as the tower cleared them, the pilot announced. Amanda sighed. She called a silent goodbye to Quinn Sutton, and Elliot and Harry, knowing that once this plane lifted off, she'd never see any of them again. She winced at the thought. Oh, Quinn, she moaned inwardly, why wouldn't you *listen?*

The plane got clearance and a minute later, it shot down the runway and lifted off. But it seemed oddly sluggish. Amanda was used to air travel, even to charter flights, and she opened her eyes and peered forward worriedly as she listened to the whine become a roar.

She was strapped in, but a groan from behind took her mind off the engine. The elderly man behind her was clutching his chest and groaning.

"What's wrong?" she asked the worried businessman in the seat beside the older man.

"Heart attack, I think." He grimaced. "What can we do?"

"I know a little CPR," she said. She unfastened her seat belt; so did the groaning man's seat companion. But just as they started to lay him on the floor, someone shouted something. Smoke began to pour out of the cockpit, and the pilot called for everyone to assume crash positions. Amanda turned, almost in slow motion. She could feel the force of gravity increase as the plane started down. The floor went out from under her and her last conscious thought was that she'd never see Quinn again....

Elliot was watching television without much interest, wishing that his father had listened when Amanda had phoned the night before. He couldn't believe that he was going to be forbidden to even speak to her again, but Quinn had insisted, his cold voice giving nothing away as he'd made Elliot promise to make no attempt to contact her.

It seemed so unfair, he thought. Amanda was no wild party girl, surely his father knew that? He sighed heavily and munched on another potato chip.

The movie he was watching was suddenly interrupted as the local station broke in with a news bulletin. Elliot listened for a minute, gasped and jumped up to get his father.

Quinn was in the office, not really concentrating on what he was doing, when Elliot burst in. The boy looked odd, his freckles standing out in an unnaturally pale face.

"Dad, you'd better come here," he said uneasily. "Quick!"

Quinn's first thought was that something had happened to Harry, but Elliot stopped in front of the television. Quinn frowned as his dark eyes watched the screen. They were showing the airport.

"What's this all—" he began, then stopped to listen.

"...plane went down about ten minutes ago, according to our best information," the man, probably the airport manager, was saying. "We've got helicopters flying in to look for the wreckage, but the wind is up, and the area the plane went down in is almost inaccessible by road."

"What plane?" Quinn asked absently.

"To repeat our earlier bulletin," the man on television seemed to oblige, "a private charter plane has been reported lost somewhere in the Grand Teton Mountains just out of Jackson Hole. One eyewitness interviewed by KWJC-TV newsman Bill Donovan stated that he saw flames shooting out of the cockpit of the twin-engine aircraft and that he watched it plummet into the mountains and vanish. Aboard the craft were prominent San Francisco businessmen Bob Doyle and Harry Brown, and the lead singer of the rock group Desperado, Mandy Callaway."

Quinn sat down in his chair hard enough to shake it. He knew his face was as white as Elliot's. In his mind, he could hear his own voice telling Mandy he didn't want her anymore, daring her to ever contact him again. Now she was dead, and he felt her loss as surely as if one of his arms had been severed from his body.

That was when he realized how desperately he loved her. When it was too late to take back the harsh words, to go after her and bring her home where she belonged. He thought of her soft body lying in the cold snow, and a sound broke from his throat. He'd sent her away because he loved her, not because he'd wanted to hurt her, but she wouldn't have known that. Her last memory of him would have been a painful, hateful one. She'd have died thinking he didn't care.

"I don't believe it," Elliot said huskily. He was shaking his head. "I just don't believe it. She was onstage Friday night, singing again—" His voice broke and he put his face in his hands.

Quinn couldn't bear it. He got up and went past a startled Harry and out the back door in his shirtsleeves, so upset that he didn't even feel the cold. His eyes went to the barn, where he'd watched Amanda feed the calves, and around the back where she'd run from him that snowy afternoon and he'd had to save her from McNaber's bear traps. His big fists clenched by his sides and he shuddered with the force of the grief he felt, his face contorting.

"Amanda!" He bit off the name.

A long time later, he was aware of someone standing nearby. He didn't turn because his face would have said too much.

"Elliot told me," Harry said hesitantly. He stuck his hands into his pockets. "They say where she is, they may not be able to get her out."

Quinn's teeth clenched. "I'll get her out," he said huskily. "I won't leave her out there in the cold." He swallowed. "Get my skis and my boots out of the storeroom, and my insulated ski suit out of the closet. I'm going to call the lodge and talk to Terry Meade."

"He manages Larry's Lodge, doesn't he?" Harry recalled.

"Yes. He can get a chopper to take me up."

"Good thing you've kept up your practice," Harry muttered. "Never thought you'd need the skis for something this awful, though."

"Neither did I." He turned and went back inside. He might have to give up Amanda forever, but he wasn't giving her up to that damned mountain. He'd get her out somehow.

He grabbed the phone, ignoring Elliot's questions, and called the lodge, asking for Terry Meade in a tone that got instant action.

"Quinn!" Terry exclaimed. "Just the man I need. Look, we've got a crash—"

"I know," Quinn said tightly. "I know the singer. Can you get me a topo map of the area and a chopper? I'll need a first-aid kit, too, and some flares—"

"No sooner said than done," Terry replied tersely. "Although I don't think that first-aid kit will be needed, Quinn, I'm sorry."

"Well, pack it anyway, will you?" He fought down nausea. "I'll be up there in less than thirty minutes."

"We'll be waiting."

Quinn got into the ski suit under Elliot's fascinated gaze.

"You don't usually wear that suit when we ski together," he told his father.

"We don't stay out that long," Quinn explained. "This suit is a relatively new innovation. It's such a tight weave that it keeps out moisture, but it's made in such a way that it allows sweat to get out. It's like having your own heater along."

"I like the boots, too," Elliot remarked. They were blue, and they had a knob on the heel that allowed them to be tightened to fit the skier's foot exactly. Boots had to fit tight to work properly. And the skis themselves were equally fascinating. They had special brakes that unlocked when the skier fell, which stopped the ski from sliding down the hill.

"Those sure are long skis," Elliot remarked as his father took precious time to apply hot wax to them.

"Longer than yours, for sure. They fit my height," Quinn said tersely. "And they're short compared to jumping skis."

"Did you ever jump, Dad, or did you just do downhill?"

"Giant slalom," he replied. "Strictly Alpine skiing. That's going to come in handy today."

Elliot sighed. "I don't guess you'll let me come along?"

"No chance. This is no place for you." His eyes darkened. "God knows what I'll find when I get to the plane."

Elliot bit his lower lip. "She's dead, isn't she, Dad?" he asked in a choked tone.

Quinn's expression closed. "You stay here with Harry, and don't tie up the telephone. I'll call home as soon as I know anything."

"Take care of yourself up there, okay?" Elliot murmured as Quinn picked up the skis and the rest of his equipment, including gloves and ski cap. "I don't say it a lot, but I love you, Dad."

"I love you, too, son." Quinn pulled him close and gave him a quick, rough hug. "I know what I'm doing. I'll be okay."

"Good luck," Harry said as Quinn went out the back door to get into his pickup truck.

"I'll need it," Quinn muttered. He waved, started the truck, and pulled out into the driveway.

Terry Meade was waiting with the Ski Patrol, the helicopter pilot, assorted law enforcement officials and the civil defense director and trying to field the news media gathered at Larry's Lodge.

"This is the area where we think they are," Terry said grimly, showing Quinn the map. "What you call Ironside peak, right? It's not in our patrol area, so we don't have anything to do with it officially. The helicopter tried and failed to get into the valley below it because of the wind. The trees are dense down there and visibility is limited by blowing snow. Our teams are going to start here," he pointed at various places on the map. "But this hill is a killer." He grinned at Quinn. "You cut your teeth on it when you were practicing for the Olympics all those years ago, and you've kept up your practice there. If anyone can ski it, you can."

"I'll get in. What then?"

"Send up a flare. I'm packing a cellular phone in with the other stuff you asked for. It's got a better range than our walkie-talkies. Everybody know what to do? Right. Let's go."

He led them out of the lodge. Quinn put on his goggles, tugged his ski cap over his head and thrust his hands into his gloves. He didn't even want to think about what he might have to look at if he was lucky enough to find the downed plane. He was having enough trouble living with what he'd said to Amanda the last time he'd talked to her.

He could still hear her voice, hear the hurt in it when he'd told her he didn't want her. Remembering that was like cutting open his heart. For her sake, he'd sent her away. He was a poor man. He had so little to offer such a famous, beautiful woman. At first, at the lodge, his pride had been cut to ribbons when he discovered who she was, and how she'd fooled him, how she'd deceived him. But her adoration had been real, and when his mind was functioning again, he realized that. He'd almost phoned her back, he'd even dialed the number. But her world was so different from his. He couldn't let her give up everything she'd worked all her life for, just to live in the middle of nowhere. She deserved so much more. He sighed wearily. If she died, the last conversation would haunt him until the day he died. He didn't think he could live with it. He didn't want to have to try. She had to be alive. Oh, dear God, she had to be!

CHAPTER NINE

THE SUN WAS bright, and Quinn felt its warmth on his face as the helicopter set him down at the top of the mountain peak where the plane had last been sighted.

He was alone in the world when the chopper lifted off again. He checked his bindings one last time, adjusted the lightweight backpack and stared down the long mountainside with his ski poles restless in his hands. This particular slope wasn't skied as a rule. It wasn't even connected with the resort, which meant that the Ski Patrol didn't come here, and that the usual rescue toboggan posted on most slopes wouldn't be in evidence. He was totally on his own until he could find the downed plane. And he knew that while he was searching this untamed area, the Ski Patrol would be out in force on the regular slopes looking for the aircraft.

He sighed heavily as he stared down at the rugged, untouched terrain, which would be a beginning skier's nightmare. Well, it was now or never. Amanda was down there somewhere. He had to find her. He couldn't leave her there in the cold snow for all eternity.

He pulled down his goggles, suppressed his feelings and shoved the ski poles deep as he propelled himself down the slope. The first couple of minutes were tricky as he had to allow for the slight added weight of the backpack. But it took scant time to adjust, to balance his weight on the skis to compensate.

The wind bit his face, the snow flew over his dark ski suit as he wound down the slopes, his skis throwing up powdered snow in his wake. It brought back memories of the days when he'd maneuvered through the giant slalom in Alpine skiing competition. He'd been in the top one percent of his class, a daredevil skier with cold nerve and expert control on the slopes. This mountain was a killer, but it was one he knew like the back of his hand. He'd trained on this peak back in his early days of competition, loving the danger of skiing a slope where no one else came. Even for the past ten years or so, he'd honed his skill here every chance he got.

Quinn smiled to himself, his body leaning into the turns, not too far, the cutting edge of his skis breaking his speed as he maneuvered over boulders, down the fall line, around trees and broken branches or over them, whichever seemed more expedient.

His dark eyes narrowed as he defeated the obstacles. At least, thank God, he was able to do something instead of going through hell sitting at home waiting for word. That in itself was a blessing, even if it ended in the tragedy everyone seemed to think it would. He couldn't bear to imagine Amanda dead. He had to think positively. There were people who walked away from airplane crashes. He had to believe that she could be one of them. He had to keep thinking that or go mad.

He'd hoped against hope that when he got near the bottom of the hill, under those tall pines and the deadly updrafts and downdrafts that had defeated the helicopter's reconnoitering, that he'd find the airplane. But it wasn't there. He turned his skis sideways and skidded to a stop, looking around him. Maybe the observer had gotten his sighting wrong. Maybe it was another peak, maybe it was miles away. He bit his lower lip raw, tasting the lip balm he'd applied before he came onto the slope. If anyone on that plane was alive, time was going to make the difference. He had to find it quickly, or Amanda wouldn't have a prayer if she'd managed to survive the initial impact.

He started downhill again, his heartbeat increasing as the worry began to eat at him. On an impulse, he shot across the fall line, parallel to it for a little while before he maneuvered back and went down again in lazy *S* patterns. Something caught his attention. A sound. Voices!

He stopped to listen, turning his head. There was wind, and the sound of pines touching. But beyond it was a voice, carrying in the silence of nature. Snow blanketed most sound, making graveyard peace out of the mountain's spring noises.

Quinn adjusted his weight on the skis and lifted his hands to his mouth, the ski poles dangling from his wrists. "Hello! Where are you?" he shouted, taking a chance that the vibration of his voice wouldn't dislodge snow above him and bring a sheet of it down on him.

"Help!" voices called back. "We're here! We're here!"

He followed the sound, praying that he wasn't following an echo. But no, there, below the trees, he saw a glint of metal in the lowering sun. The plane! Thank God, there were survivors! Now if only Amanda was one of them…

He went the rest of the way down. As he drew closer, he saw men standing near the almost intact wreckage of the aircraft. One had a bandage around his head, another was nursing what looked like a broken arm. He saw one woman, but she wasn't blond. On the ground were two still forms, covered with coats. Covered up.

Please, God, no, he thought blindly. He drew to a stop.

"I'm Sutton. How many dead?" he asked the man who'd called to him, a burly man in a gray suit and white shirt and tie.

"Two," the man replied. "I'm Jeff Coleman, and I sure am glad to see you." He shook hands with Quinn. "I'm the pilot. We had a fire in the cockpit and it was all I could do to set her down at all. God, I feel bad! For some reason, three of the passengers had their seat belts off when we hit." He shook his head. "No hope for two of them. The third's concussed and looks comatose."

Quinn felt himself shaking inside as he asked the question he had to ask. "There was a singer aboard," he said. "Amanda Callaway."

"Yeah." The pilot shook his head and Quinn wanted to die, he wanted to stop breathing right there... "She's the concussion."

Quinn knew his hand shook as he pushed his goggles up over the black ski cap. "Where is she?" he asked huskily.

The pilot didn't ask questions or argue. He led Quinn past the two bodies and the dazed businessmen who were standing or sitting on fabric they'd taken from the plane, trying to keep warm.

"She's here," the pilot told him, indicating a makeshift stretcher constructed of branches and pillows from the cabin, and coats that covered the still body.

"Amanda," Quinn managed unsteadily. He knelt beside her. Her hair was in a coiled bun on her head. Her face was alabaster white, her eyes closed, long black lashes lying still on her cheekbones. Her mouth was as pale as the rest of her face, and there was a bruise high on her forehead at the right temple. He stripped off his glove and felt the artery at her neck. Her heart was still beating, but slowly and not very firmly. Unconscious. Dying, perhaps. "Oh, God," he breathed.

He got to his feet and unloaded the backpack as the pilot and two of the other men gathered around him.

"I've got a modular phone," Quinn said, "which I hope to God will work." He punched buttons and waited, his dark eyes narrowed, holding his breath.

It seemed to take forever. Then a voice, a recognizable voice, came over the wire. "Hello."

"Terry!" Quinn called. "It's Sutton. I've found them."

"Thank God!" Terry replied. "Okay, give me your position."

Quinn did, spreading out his laminated map to verify it, and then gave the report on casualties.

"Only one unconscious?" Terry asked again.

"Only one," Quinn replied heavily.

"We'll have to airlift you out, but we can't do it until the wind dies down. You understand, Quinn, the same downdrafts and updrafts that kept the chopper out this morning are going to keep it out now."

"Yes, I know, damn it," Quinn yelled. "But I've got to get her to a hospital. She's failing already."

Terry sighed. "And there you are without a rescue toboggan. Listen, what if I get Larry Hale down there?" he asked excitedly. "You know Larry; he was national champ in downhill a few years back, and he's a senior member of the Ski Patrol now. We could airdrop you the toboggan and some supplies for the rest of the survivors by plane. The two of you could tow her to a point accessible by chopper. Do you want to risk it, Quinn?"

"I don't know if she'll be alive in the morning, Terry," Quinn said somberly. "I'm more afraid to risk doing nothing than I am of towing her out. It's fairly level, if I remember right, all the way to the pass that leads from Caraway Ridge into Jackson Hole. The chopper might be able to fly down Jackson Hole and come in that way, without having to navigate the peaks. What do you think?"

"I think it's a good idea," Terry said. "If I remember right, they cleared that pass from the Ridge into Jackson Hole in the fall. It should still be accessible."

"No problem," Quinn said, his jaw grim. "If it isn't cleared, I'll clear it, by hand if necessary."

Terry chuckled softly. "Hale says he's already on the way. We'll get the plane up—hell of a pity he can't land where you are, but it's just too tricky. How about the other survivors?"

Quinn told him their conditions, along with the two bodies that would have to be airlifted out.

"Too bad," he replied. He paused for a minute to talk to somebody. "Listen, Quinn, if you can get the woman to Caraway Ridge, the chopper pilot thinks he can safely put down there. About the others, can they manage until morning if we drop the supplies?"

Quinn looked at the pilot. "Can you?"

"I ate snakes in Nam and Bill over there served in Antarctica." He grinned. "Between us, we can keep these pilgrims warm and even feed them. Sure, we'll be okay. Get that little lady out if you can."

"Amen," the man named Bill added, glancing at Amanda's still form. "I've heard her sing. It would be a crime against art to let her die."

Quinn lifted the cellular phone to his ear. "They say they can manage, Terry. Are you sure you can get them out in the morning?"

"If we have to send the snowplow in through the valley or send in a squad of snowmobiles and a horse-drawn sled, you'd better believe we'll get them out. The Ski Patrol is already working out the details."

"Okay."

Quinn unloaded his backpack. He had flares and matches, packets of high-protein dehydrated food, the first-aid kit and some cans of sterno.

"Paradise," the pilot said, looking at the stores. "With that, I can prepare a seven-course meal, build a bonfire and make a house. But those supplies they're going to drop will come in handy, just the same."

Quinn smiled in spite of himself. "Okay."

"We can sure use this first-aid kit, but I've already set a broken arm and patched a few cuts. Before I became a pilot, I worked in the medical corps."

"I had rescue training when I was in the Ski Patrol," Quinn replied. He grinned at the pilot. "But if I ever come down in a plane, I hope you're on it."

"Thanks. I hope none of us ever come down again." He glanced at the two bodies. "God, I'm sorry about them." He glanced at Amanda. "I hope she makes it."

Quinn's jaw hardened. "She's a fighter," he said. "Let's hope she cares enough to try." He alone knew how defeated she'd probably felt when she left the lodge. He'd inflicted some terrible damage with his coldness. Pride had forced him to send her away, to deny his own happiness. Once he knew how famous and wealthy she was in her own right, he hadn't felt that he had the right to ask her to give it all up to live with him and Elliot in the wilds of Wyoming. He'd been doing what he thought was best for her. Now he only wanted her to live.

He took a deep breath. "Watch for the plane and Hale, will you? I'm going to sit with her."

"Sure." The pilot gave him a long look that he didn't see before he went back to talk to the other survivors.

Quinn sat down beside Amanda, reaching for one cold little hand under the coats that covered her. It was going to be a rough ride for her, and she didn't need any more jarring. But if they waited until morning, without medical help, she could die. It was much riskier to do nothing than it was to risk moving her. And down here in the valley, the snow was deep and fairly level. It would be like Nordic skiing; cross-country skiing. With luck, it would feel like a nice lazy sleigh ride to her.

"Listen to me, honey," he said softly. "We've got a long way to go before we get you out of here and to a hospital. You're going to have to hold on for a long time." His hand tightened around hers, warming it. "I'll be right with you every step of the way. I won't leave you for a second. But you have to do your part, Amanda. You have to fight to stay alive. I hope that you still want to live. If you don't, there's something I need to tell you. I sent you away not because I hated you, Amanda, but because I loved you so much. I loved you enough to let you go back to the life you needed. You've got to stay alive so that I can tell you that," he added, stopping because his voice broke.

He looked away, getting control back breath by breath. He thought he felt her fingers move, but he couldn't be sure. "I'm going to get you out of here, honey, one way or the other, even if I have to walk out with you in my arms. Try to hold on, for me." He brought her hand to his mouth and kissed the palm hungrily. "Try to hold on, because if you die, so do I. I can't keep going unless you're somewhere in the world, even if I never see you again. Even if you hate me forever."

He swallowed hard and put down her hand. The sound of an airplane in the distance indicated that supplies were on the way. Quinn put Amanda's hand back under the cover and bent to brush his mouth against her cold, still one.

"I love you," he whispered roughly. "You've got to hold on until I can get you out of here."

He stood, his face like the stony crags above them, his eyes glittering as he joined the others.

The plane circled and seconds later, a white parachute appeared. Quinn held his breath as it descended, hoping against hope that the chute wouldn't hang up in the tall trees and that the toboggan would soft-land so that it was usable. A drop in this kind of wind was risky at best.

But luck was with them. The supplies and the sled made it in one piece. Quinn and the pilot and a couple of the sturdier survivors unfastened the chute and brought the contents back to the wreckage of the commuter plane. The sled was even equipped with blankets and a pillow and straps to keep Amanda secured.

Minutes later, the drone of a helicopter whispered on the wind, and not long after that, Hale started down the mountainside.

It took several minutes. Quinn saw the flash of rust that denoted the distinctive jacket and white waist pack of the Ski Patrol above, and when Hale came closer, he could see the gold cross on the right pocket of the jacket—a duplicate of the big one stenciled on the jacket's back. He smiled, remembering when he'd worn that same type of jacket during a brief stint as a ski patrolman. It was a special kind of occupation, and countless skiers owed their lives to those brave men and women. The National Ski Patrol had only existed since 1938. It was created by Charles Dole of Connecticut, after a skiing accident that took the life of one of his friends. Today, the Ski Patrol had over 10,000 members nationally, of whom ninety-eight percent were volunteers. They were the first on the slopes and the last off, patroling for dangerous areas and rescuing injured people. Quinn had once been part of that elite group and he still had the greatest respect for them.

Hale was the only color against the whiteness of the snow. The sun was out, and thank God it hadn't snowed all day. It had done enough of that last night.

Quinn's nerves were stretched. He hadn't had a cigarette since he'd arrived at the lodge, and he didn't dare have one now. Nicotine and caffeine tended to constrict blood vessels, and the cold was dangerous enough without giving it any help. Experienced skiers knew better than to stack the odds against themselves.

"Well, I made it." Hale grinned, getting his breath. "How are you, Quinn?" He extended a hand and Quinn shook it.

The man in the Ski Patrol jacket nodded to the others, accepted their thanks for the supplies he'd brought with him, which included a makeshift shelter and plenty of food and water and even a bottle of cognac. But he didn't waste time. "We'd better get moving if we hope to get Miss Callaway out of here by dark."

"She's over here," Quinn said. "God, I hate doing this," he added heavily when he and Hale were standing over the unconscious woman. "If there was any hope, any at all, that the chopper could get in here..."

"You can feel the wind for yourself," Hale replied, his eyes solemn. "We're the only chance she has. We'll get her to the chopper. Piece of cake," he added with a reassuring smile.

"I hope so," Quinn said somberly. He bent and nodded to Hale. They lifted her very gently onto the long sled containing the litter. It had handles on both ends, because it was designed to be towed. They attached the towlines, covered Amanda carefully and set out, with reassurances from the stranded survivors.

There was no time to talk. The track was fairly straightforward, but it worried Quinn, all the same, because there were crusts that jarred the woman on the litter. He towed, Hale guided, their rhythms matching perfectly as they made their way down the snow-covered valley. Around them, the wind sang through the tall firs and lodgepole pines, and Quinn thought about the old trappers and mountain men who must have come through this valley a hundred, two hundred years before. In those days of poor sanitation and even poorer medicine, Amanda wouldn't have stood a chance.

He forced himself not to look back. He had to concentrate on getting her to the Ridge. All that was important now, was that she get medical help while it could still do her some good. He hadn't come all this way to find her alive, only to lose her.

It seemed to take forever. Once Quinn was certain that they'd lost their way as they navigated through the narrow pass that led to the fifty-mile valley between the Grand Tetons and the Wind River Range, an area known as Jackson Hole. But he recognized landmarks as they went along, and eventually they wound their way around the trees and along the sparkling river until they reached the flats below Caraway Ridge.

Quinn and Hale were both breathing hard by now. They'd changed places several times, so that neither got too tired of towing the toboggan, and they were both in peak condition. But it was still a difficult thing to do.

They rested, and Quinn reached down to check Amanda's pulse. It was still there, and even seemed to be, incredibly, a little stronger than it had been. But she was pale and still and Quinn felt his spirits sink as he looked down at her.

"There it is," Hale called, sweeping his arm over the ridge. "The chopper."

"Now if only it can land," Quinn said quietly, and he began to pray.

The chopper came lower and lower, then it seemed to shoot up again and Quinn bit off a hard word. But the pilot corrected for the wind, which was dying down, and eased the helicopter toward the ground. It seemed to settle inch by inch until it landed safe. The pilot was out of it before the blades stopped.

"Let's get out of here," he called to the men. "If that wind catches up again, I wouldn't give us a chance in hell of getting out. It was a miracle that I even got in!"

Quinn released his bindings in a flash, leaving his skis and poles for Hale to carry, along with his own. He got one side of the stretcher while the pilot, fortunately no lightweight himself, got the other. They put the stretcher in the back of the broad helicopter, on the floor, and Quinn and Hale piled in—Hale in the passenger seat up front, Quinn behind with Amanda, carefully laying ski equipment beside her.

"Let's go!" the pilot called as he revved up the engine.

It was touch and go. The wind decided to play tag with them, and they almost went into a lodgepole pine on the way up. But the pilot was a tenacious man with good nerves. He eased down and then up, down and up until he caught the wind off guard and shot up out of the valley and over the mountain.

Quinn reached down and clasped Amanda's cold hand in his. Only a little longer, honey, he thought, watching her with his heart in his eyes. Only a little longer, for God's sake, hold on!

It was the longest ride of his entire life. He spared one thought for the people who'd stayed behind to give Amanda her chance and he prayed that they'd be rescued without any further injuries. Then his eyes settled on her pale face and stayed there until the helicopter landed on the hospital lawn.

The reporters, local, state and national, had gotten word of the rescue mission. They were waiting. Police kept them back just long enough for Amanda to be carried into the hospital, but Quinn and Hale were caught. Quinn volunteered Hale to give an account of the rescue and then he ducked out, leaving the other man to field the enthusiastic audience while he trailed quickly behind the men who'd taken Amanda into the emergency room.

He drank coffee and smoked cigarettes and glared at walls for over an hour until someone came out to talk to him. Hale had to go back to the lodge, to help plan the rescue of the rest of the survivors, but he promised to keep in touch. After he'd gone, Quinn felt even more alone. But at last a doctor came into the waiting room, and approached him.

"Are you related to Miss Callaway?" the doctor asked with narrowed eyes.

Quinn knew that if he said no, he'd have to wait for news of her condition until he could find somebody who was related to her, and he had no idea how to find her aunt.

"I'm her fiancé," he said without moving a muscle in his face. "How is she?"

"Not good," the doctor, a small wiry man, said bluntly. "But I believe in miracles. We have her in intensive care, where she'll stay until she regains consciousness. She's badly concussed. I gather she hasn't regained consciousness since the crash?" Quinn shook his head. "That sleigh ride and helicopter lift didn't do any good, either," he added firmly, adding when he saw the expression on Quinn's tormented face, "but I can understand the necessity for it. Go get some sleep. Come back in the morning. We won't know anything until then. Maybe not until much later. Concussion is tricky. We can't predict the outcome, as much as we'd like to."

"I can't rest," Quinn said quietly. "I'll sit out here and drink coffee, if you don't mind. If this is as close to her as I can get, it'll have to do."

The doctor took a slow breath. "We keep spare beds in cases like this," he said. "I'll have one made up for you when you can't stay awake any longer." He smiled faintly. "Try to think positively. It isn't medical, exactly, but sometimes it works wonders. Prayer doesn't hurt, either."

"Thank you," Quinn said.

The doctor shrugged. "Wait until she wakes up. Good night."

Quinn watched him go and sighed. He didn't know what to do next. He phoned Terry at the lodge to see if Amanda's band had called. Someone named Jerry and a man called Hank had been phoning every few minutes, he was told. Quinn asked for a phone number and Terry gave it to him.

He dialed the area code. California, he figured as he waited for it to ring.

"Hello?"

"This is Quinn Sutton," he began.

"Yes, I recognize your voice. It's Hank here. How is she?"

"Concussion. Coma, I guess. She's in intensive care and she's still alive. That's about all I know."

There was a long pause. "I'd hoped for a little more than that."

"So had I," Quinn replied. He hesitated. "I'll phone you in the morning. The minute I know anything. Is there anybody we should notify...her aunt?"

"Her aunt is a scatterbrain and no help at all. Anyway, she's off with Blalock Durning in the Bahamas on one of those incommunicado islands. We couldn't reach her if we tried."

"Is there anybody else?" Quinn asked.

"Not that I know of." There was a brief pause. "I feel bad about the way things happened. I hate planes, you know. That's why the rest of us went by bus. We stopped here in some hick town to make sure Amanda got her plane, and Terry told us what happened. We got a motel room and we're waiting for a bus back to Jackson. It will probably be late tomorrow before we get there. We've already canceled the gig. We can't do it without Amanda."

"I'll book a room for you," Quinn said.

"Make it a suite," Hank replied, "and if you need anything, you know, anything, you just tell us."

"I've got plenty of cigarettes and the coffee machine's working. I'm fine."

"We'll see you when we get there. And Sutton—thanks. She really cares about you, you know?"

"I care about her," he said stiffly. "That's why I sent her away. My God, how could she give all that up to live on a mountain in Wyoming?"

"Amanda's not a city girl, though," Hank said slowly. "And she changed after those days she spent with you. Her heart wasn't with us anymore. She cried all last night…"

"Oh, God, don't," Quinn said.

"Sorry, man," Hank said quietly. "I'm really sorry, that's the last thing I should have said. Look, go smoke a cigarette. I think I'll tie one on royally and have the boys put me to bed. Tomorrow we'll talk. Take care."

"You, too."

Quinn hung up. He couldn't bear to think of Amanda crying because of what he'd done to her. He might lose her even yet, and he didn't know how he was going to go on living. He felt so alone.

He was out of change after he called the lodge and booked the suite for Hank and the others, but he still had to talk to Elliot and Harry. He dialed the operator and called collect. Elliot answered the phone immediately.

"How is she?" he asked quickly.

Quinn went over it again, feeling numb. "I wish I knew more," he concluded. "But that's all there is."

"She can't die," Elliot said miserably. "Dad, she just can't!"

"Say a prayer, son," he replied. "And don't let Harry teach you any bad habits while I'm gone."

"No, sir, I won't," Elliot said with a feeble attempt at humor. "You're going to stay, I guess?"

"I have to," Quinn said huskily. He hesitated. "I love her."

"So do I," Elliot said softly. "Bring her back when you come."

"If I can. If she'll even speak to me when she wakes up," Quinn said with a total lack of confidence.

"She will," Elliot told him. "You should have listened to

some of those songs you thought were so horrible. One of hers won a Grammy. It was all about having to give up things we love to keep from hurting them. She always seemed to feel it when somebody was sad or hurt, you know. And she risked her own life trying to save that girl at the concert. She's not some-one who thinks about getting even with people. She's got too much heart."

Quinn drew deeply from his cigarette. "I hope so, son," he said. "You get to bed. I'll call you tomorrow."

"Okay. Take care of yourself. Love you, Dad."

"Me, too, son," Quinn replied. He hung up. The waiting area was deserted now, and the hospital seemed to have gone to sleep. He sat down with his Styrofoam cup of black coffee and finished his cigarette. The room looked like he felt—empty.

CHAPTER TEN

IT WAS LATE morning when the nurse came to shake Quinn gently awake. Apparently around dawn he'd gone to sleep sitting up, with an empty coffee cup in his hand. He thought he'd never sleep at all.

He sat up, drowsy and disheveled. "How is Amanda?" he asked immediately.

The nurse, a young blonde, smiled at him. "She's awake and asking for you."

"Oh, thank God," he said heavily. He got quickly to his feet, still a little groggy, and followed her down to the intensive-care unit, where patients in tiny rooms were monitored from a central nurses' station and the hum and click and whir of life-supporting machinery filled the air. If she was asking for him, she must not hate him too much. That thought sustained him as he followed the nurse into one of the small cubicles where Amanda lay.

Amanda looked thinner than ever in the light, her face pinched, her eyes hollow, her lips chapped. They'd taken her hair down somewhere along the way and tied it back with a pink ribbon. She was propped up in bed, still with the IV in position, but she'd been taken off all the other machines.

She looked up and saw Quinn and all the weariness and pain

went out of her face. She brightened, became beautiful despite her injuries, her eyes sparkling. Her last thought when she'd realized in the plane what was going to happen had been of Quinn. Her first thought when she'd regained consciousness had been of him. The pain, the grief of having him turn away from her was forgotten. He was here, now, and that meant he had to care about her.

"Oh, Quinn!" she whispered tearfully, and held out her arms.

He went to her without hesitation, ignoring the nurses, the aides, the whole world. His arms folded gently around her, careful of the tubes attached to her hand, and his head bent over hers, his cheek on her soft hair, his eyes closed as he shivered with reaction. She was alive. She was going to live. He felt as if he were going to choke to death on his own rush of feeling.

"My God," he whispered shakily. "I thought I'd lost you."

That was worth it all, she thought, dazed from the emotion in his voice, at the tremor in his powerful body as he held her. She clung to him, her slender arms around his neck, drowning in pleasure. She'd wondered if he hadn't sent her away in a misguided belief that it was for her own good. Now she was sure of it. He couldn't have looked that haggard, that terrible, unless she mattered very much to him. Her aching heart soared. "They said you brought me out."

"Hale and I did," he said huskily. He lifted his head, searching her bright eyes slowly. "It's been the longest night of my life. They said you might die."

"Oh, we Callaways are tough birds," she said, wiping away a tear. She was still weak and sore and her headache hadn't completely gone away. "You look terrible, my darling," she whispered on a choked laugh.

The endearment fired his blood. He had to take a deep breath before he could even speak. His fingers linked with hers. "I felt pretty terrible when we listened to the news report, especially when I remembered the things I said to you." He took a deep breath. "I didn't know if you'd hate me for the rest of your life, but even if you did, I couldn't just sit on my mountain and let other people look for you." His thumb gently stroked the back of her pale hand. "How do you feel, honey?"

"Pretty bad. But considering it all, I'll do. I'm sorry about the men who died. One of them was having a heart attack," she explained. "The other gentleman who was sitting with him alerted me. We both unfastened our seat belts to try and give CPR. Just after I got up, the plane started down," she said. "Quinn, do you believe in predestination?"

"You mean, that things happen the way they're meant to in spite of us?" He smiled. "I guess I do." His dark eyes slid over her face hungrily. "I'm so glad it wasn't your time, Amanda."

"So am I." She reached up and touched his thin mouth with just the tips of her fingers. "Where is it?" she asked with an impish smile as a sudden delicious thought occurred to her.

He frowned. "Where's what?"

"My engagement ring," she said. "And don't try to back out of it," she added firmly when he stood there looking shocked. "You told the doctor and the whole medical staff that I was your fiancée, and you're not ducking out of it now. You're going to marry me."

His eyebrows shot up. "I'm what?" he said blankly.

"You're going to marry me. Where's Hank? Has anybody phoned him?"

"I did. I was supposed to call him back." He checked his watch and grimaced. "I guess it's too late now. He and the band are on the way back here."

"Good. They're twice your size and at least as mean." Her eyes narrowed. "I'll tell them you seduced me. I could be pregnant." She nodded, thinking up lies fast while Quinn's face mirrored his stark astonishment. "That's right, I could."

"You could not," he said shortly. "I never…!"

"But you're going to," she said with a husky laugh. "Just wait until I get out of here and get you alone. I'll wrestle you down and start kissing you, and you'll never get away in time."

"Oh, God," he groaned, because he knew she was right. He couldn't resist her that way, it was part of the problem.

"So you'll have to marry me first," she continued. "Because I'm not that kind of girl. Not to mention that you aren't that kind of guy. Harry likes me and Elliot and I are already friends, and I could even get used to McNaber if he'll move those traps." She pursed her lips, thinking. "The concert tour is going to be a real drag, but once it's over, I'll retire from the stage and just make records and tapes and CDs with the guys. Maybe a video now and again. They'll like that, too. We're all basically shy and we don't like live shows. I'll compose songs. I can do that at the house, in between helping Harry with the cooking and looking after sick calves, and having babies," she added with a shy smile.

He wanted to sit down. He hadn't counted on this. All that had mattered at the time was getting her away from the wreckage and into a hospital where she could be cared for. He hadn't let himself think ahead. But she obviously had. His head spun with her plans.

"Listen, you're an entertainer," he began. His fingers curled around hers and he looked down at them with a hard, grim sigh. "Amanda, I'm a poor man. All I've got is a broken-down ranch in the middle of nowhere. You'd have a lot of hardships, because I won't live on your money. I've got a son, even if he isn't mine, and…"

She brought his hand to her cheek and held it there, nuzzling her cheek against it as she looked up at him with dark, soft, adoring eyes. "I love you," she whispered.

He faltered. His cheeks went ruddy as the words penetrated, touched him, excited him. Except for his mother and Elliot, nobody had ever said that to him before Amanda had. "Do you?" he asked huskily. "Still? Even after the way I walked off and left you there at the lodge that night? After what I said to you on the phone?" he added, because he'd had too much time to agonize over his behavior, even if it had been for what he thought was her own good.

"Even after that," she said gently. "With all my heart. I just want to live with you, Quinn. In the wilds of Wyoming, in a grass shack on some island, in a mansion in Beverly Hills—it would all be the same to me—as long as you loved me back and we could be together for the rest of our lives."

He felt a ripple of pure delight go through him. "Is that what you really want?" he asked, searching her dark eyes with his own.

"More than anything else in the world," she confessed. "That's why I couldn't tell you who and what I really was. I loved you so much, and I knew you wouldn't want me…" Her voice trailed off.

"I want you, all right," he said curtly. "I never stopped. Damn it, woman, I was trying to do what was best for you!"

"By turning me out in the cold and leaving me to starve to death for love?" she asked icily. "Thanks a bunch!"

He looked away uncomfortably. "It wasn't that way and you know it. I thought maybe it was the novelty. You know, a lonely man in the backwoods," he began.

"You thought I was having the time of my life playing you for a fool," she said. Her head was beginning to hurt, but she had to wrap it all up before she gave in and asked for some more medication. "Well, you listen to me, Quinn Sutton, I'm not the type to go around deliberately trying to hurt people. All I ever wanted was somebody to care about me—just me, not the pretty girl on the stage."

"Yes, I know that now," he replied. He brought her hand to his mouth and softly kissed the palm. The look on his face weakened her. "So you want a ring, do you? It will have to be something sensible. No flashy diamonds, even if I could give you something you'd need sunglasses to look at."

"I'll settle for the paper band on a King Edward cigar if you'll just marry me," she replied.

"I think I can do a little better than that," he murmured dryly. He bent over her, his lips hovering just above hers. "And no long engagement," he whispered.

"It takes three days, doesn't it?" she whispered back. "That *is* a long engagement. Get busy!"

He stifled a laugh as he brushed his hard mouth gently over her dry one. "Get well," he whispered. "I'll read some books real fast."

She colored when she realized what kind of books he was referring to, and then smiled under his tender kiss. "You do that," she breathed. "Oh, Quinn, get me out of here!"

"At the earliest possible minute," he promised.

The band showed up later in the day while Quinn was out buying an engagement ring for Amanda. He'd already called and laughingly told Elliot and Harry what she'd done to him, and was delighted with Elliot's pleasure in the news and Harry's teasing. He did buy her a diamond, even if it was a moderate one, and a gold band for each of them. It gave him the greatest kind of thrill to know that he was finally marrying for all the right reasons.

When he got back to the hospital, the rest of the survivors had been airlifted out and all but one of them had been treated and released. The news media had tried to get to Amanda, but the band arrived shortly after Quinn left and ran interference. Hank gave out a statement and stopped them. The road manager, as Quinn found out, had gone on to San Francisco to make arrangements for canceling the concert.

The boys were gathered around Amanda, who'd been moved into a nice private room. She was sitting up in bed, looking much better, and her laughing dark eyes met Quinn's the minute he came in the door.

"Hank brought a shotgun," she informed him. "And Deke and Johnson and Jack are going to help you down the aisle. Jerry's found a minister, and Hank's already arranged a blood test for you right down the hall. The license—"

"Is already applied for," Quinn said with a chuckle. "I did that myself. Hello, boys," he greeted them, shaking hands as he was introduced to the rest of the band. "And you can unload the shotgun. I'd planned to hold it on Amanda, if she tried to back out."

"Me, back out? Heaven forbid!" she exclaimed, smiling as Quinn bent to kiss her. "Where's my ring?" she whispered against his hard mouth. "I want it on, so these nurses won't make eyes at you. There's this gorgeous redhead…"

"I can't see past you, pretty thing," he murmured, his eyes soft and quiet in a still-gaunt face. "Here it is." Quinn produced it and slid it on her finger. He'd measured the size with a small piece of paper he'd wrapped around her finger, and he hoped that the method worked. He needn't have worried, because the ring was a perfect fit, and she acted as if it were the three-carat monster he'd wanted to get her. Her face lit up, like her pretty eyes, and she beamed as she showed it to the band.

"Did you sleep at all?" Hank asked him while the others gathered around Amanda.

"About an hour, I think," Quinn murmured dryly. "You?"

"I couldn't even get properly drunk," Hank said, sighing, "so the boys and I played cards until we caught the bus. We slept most of the way in. It was a long ride. From what I hear," he added with a level look, "you and that Hale fellow had an even longer one, bringing Amanda out of the mountains."

"You'll never know." Quinn looked past him to Amanda, his dark eyes full of remembered pain. "I had to decide whether or not to move her. I thought it was riskier to leave her there until the next morning. If we'd waited, we had no guarantee that the helicopter would have been able to land even then. She could have died. It's a miracle she didn't."

"Miracles come in all shapes and sizes," Hank mused, staring at her. "She's been ours. Without her, we'd never have gotten anywhere. But being on the road has worn her out. The boys and I were talking on the way back about cutting out personal appearances and concentrating on videos and albums. I think Amanda might like that. She'll have enough to do from now on, I imagine, taking care of you and your boy," he added with a grin. "Not to mention all those new brothers and sisters you'll be adding. I grew up on a ranch," he said surprisingly. "I have five brothers."

Quinn's eyebrows lifted. "Are they all runts like you?" he asked with a smile.

"I'm the runt," Hank corrected.

Quinn just shook his head.

AMANDA WAS RELEASED from the hospital two days later. Every conceivable test had been done, and fortunately there were no complications. The doctor had been cautiously optimistic at first, but her recovery was rapid—probably due, the doctor said with a smile, to her incentive. He gave Amanda away at the brief ceremony, held in the hospital's chapel just before she was discharged, and one of the nurses was her matron of honor. There were a record four best men; the band. But for all its brevity and informality, it was a ceremony that Amanda would never forget. The Methodist minister who performed it had a way with words, and Amanda and Quinn felt just as married as if they'd had the service performed in a huge church with a large crowd present.

The only mishap was that the press found out about the wedding, and Amanda and Quinn and the band were mobbed as they made their way out of the hospital afterward. The size of the band members made them keep well back. Hank gave them his best wildman glare while Jack whispered something about the bandleader becoming homicidal if he was pushed too far. They escaped in two separate cars. The driver of the one taking Quinn and Amanda to the lodge managed to get them there over back roads, so that nobody knew where they were.

Terry had given them the bridal suite, on the top floor of the lodge, and the view of the snowcapped mountains was exquisite. Amanda, still a little shaky and very nervous, stared out at them with mixed feelings.

"I don't know if I'll ever think of them as postcards again," she remarked to Quinn, who was trying to find places to put everything from their suitcase. He'd had to go to Ricochet for his suit and a change of clothing.

"What, the mountains?" he asked, smiling at her. "Well, it's not a bad thing to respect them. But airplanes don't crash that often, and when you're well enough, I'm going to teach you to ski."

She turned and looked at him for a long time. Her wedding outfit was an off-white, a very simple shirtwaist dress with a soft collar and no frills. But with her long hair around her shoulders and down to her waist, framed in the light coming through the window, she looked the picture of a bride. Quinn watched her back and sighed, his eyes lingering on the small sprig of lily of the valley she was wearing in her hair—a present from a member of the hospital staff.

"One of the nurses brought me a newspaper," Amanda said. "It told all about how you and Mr. Hale got me out." She hesitated. "They said that only a few men could ski that particular mountain without killing themselves."

"I've been skiing it for years," he said simply. He took off the dark jacket of his suit and loosened his tie with a long sigh. "I knew that the Ski Patrol would get you out, but they usually only work the lodge slopes—you know, the ones with normal ski runs. The peak the plane landed on was off the lodge property and out-of-the-way. It hadn't even been inspected. There are all sorts of dangers on slopes like that—fallen trees, boulders, stumps, debris, not to mention the threat of avalanche. The Ski Patrol marks dangerous runs where they work. They're the first out in the morning and the last off the slopes in the afternoon."

"You seem to know a lot about it," Amanda said.

"I used to be one of them," he replied with a grin. "In my younger days. It's pretty rewarding."

"There was a jacket Harry showed me," she frowned. "A rust-colored one with a big gold cross on the back…"

"My old patrol jacket." He chuckled. "I wouldn't part with it for the world. If I'd thought of it, I'd have worn it that day." His eyes darkened as he looked at her. "Thank God I knew that slope," he said huskily. "Because I'd bet money that you wouldn't have lasted on that mountain overnight."

"I was thinking about you when the plane went down," she confessed. "I wasn't sure that I'd ever see you again."

"Neither was I when I finally got to you." He took off his tie and threw it aside. His hand absently unfastened the top buttons of his white shirt as he moved toward her. "I was trying so hard to do the right thing," he murmured. "I didn't think I could give you what you needed, what you were used to."

"I'm used to you, Mr. Sutton," she murmured with a smile. Amanda slid her arms under his and around him, looking up at him with her whole heart in her dark eyes. "Bad temper, irritable scowl and all. Anything you can't give me, I don't want. Will that do?"

His broad chest rose and fell slowly. "I can't give you much. I've lost damned near everything."

"You have Elliot and Harry and me," she pointed out. "And some fat, healthy calves, and in a few years, Elliot will have a lot of little brothers and sisters to help him on the ranch."

A faint dusky color stained his high cheekbones. "Yes."

"Why, Mr. Sutton, honey, you aren't shy, are you?" she whispered dryly as she moved her hands back around to his shirt and finished unbuttoning it down his tanned, hair-roughened chest.

"Of course I'm shy," he muttered, heating up at the feel of her slender hands on his skin. He caught his breath and shuddered when she kissed him there. His big hands slid into her long, silky hair and brought her even closer. "I like that," he breathed roughly. "Oh, God, I love it!"

She drew back after a minute, her eyes sultry, drowsy.

"Wouldn't you like to do that to me?" she whispered. "I like it, too."

He fumbled with buttons until he had the dress out of the way and she was standing in nothing except a satin teddy. He'd never seen one before, except in movies, and he stared at her with his breath stuck somewhere in his chest. It was such a sexy garment low on her lace-covered breasts, nipped at her slender waist, hugging her full hips. Below it were her elegant silk-clad legs, although he didn't see anything holding up her hose.

"It's a teddy," she whispered. "If you want to slide it down," she added shyly, lowering her eyes to his pulsating chest, "I could step out of it."

He didn't know if he could do that and stay on his feet. The thought of Amanda unclothed made his knees weak. But he slid the straps down her arms and slowly, slowly, peeled it away from her firm, hard-tipped breasts, over her flat stomach, and then over the panty hose she was wearing. He caught them as well and eased the whole silky mass down to the floor.

She stepped out of it, so much in love with him that all her earlier shyness was evaporating. It was as new for him as it was for her, and that made it beautiful. A true act of love.

She let him look at her, fascinated by the awe in his hard face, in the eyes that went over her like an artist's brush, capturing every line, every soft curve before he even touched her.

"Amanda, you're the most beautiful creature I've ever seen," he said finally. "You look like a drawing of a fairy I saw in an old-time storybook…all gold and ivory."

She reached up and leaned close against him, shivering a little when her breasts touched his bare chest. The hair was faintly abrasive and very arousing. She moved involuntarily and gasped at the sensation.

"Do you want to help me?" he whispered as he stripped off his shirt and his hands went to his belt.

"I…" She hesitated, her nerve retreating suddenly at the intimacy of it. She grimaced. "Oh, Quinn, I'm such a coward!" She hid her face against his chest and felt his laughter.

"Well, you're not alone," he murmured. "I'm not exactly an exhibitionist myself. Look, why don't you get under the covers and close your eyes, and we'll pretend it's dark."

She looked up at him and laughed. "This is silly."

"Yes, I know." He sighed. "Well, honey, we're married. I guess it's time to face all the implications of sharing a bed."

He sat down, took off his boots and socks, stood to unbuckle his belt, holding her eyes, and slid the zip down. Everything came off, and seconds later, she saw for herself all the differences between men and women.

"You've gone scarlet, Mrs. Sutton," he observed.

"You aren't much whiter yourself, Mr. Sutton," she replied.

He laughed and reached for her and she felt him press against her. It was incredible, the feel of skin against skin, hair-rough flesh against silky softness. He bent and found her mouth and began to kiss her lazily, while his big, rough hands slid down her back and around to her hips. His mouth opened at the same time that his fingers pulled her thighs against his, and she felt for the first time the stark reality of arousal.

He felt her gasp and lifted his head, searching her flushed face. "That has to happen before anything else can," he whispered. "Don't be afraid. I think I know enough to make it easy for you."

"I love you, Quinn," she whispered back, forcing her taut muscles to relax, to give in to him. She leaned her body into his with a tiny shiver and lifted her mouth. "However it happens between us, it will be all right."

He searched her eyes and nodded. His mouth lowered to hers. He kissed her with exquisite tenderness while his hands found the softness of her breasts. Minutes later, his mouth traced them, covered the hard tips in a warm, moist suction that drew new sounds from her. He liked that, so he lifted her and put her on the big bed, and found other places to kiss her that made the sounds louder and more tormented.

The book had been very thorough and quite explicit, so he knew what to do in theory. Practice was very different. He hadn't known that women could lose control, too. That their bodies were so soft, or so strong. That their eyes grew wild and their faces contorted as the pleasure built in them, that they wept with it. Her pleasure became his only goal in the long, exquisite oblivion that followed.

By the time he moved over her, she was more than ready for him, she was desperate for him. He whispered to her, gently guided her body to his as he fought for control of his own raging need so that he could satisfy hers first.

There was one instant when she stiffened and tried to pull away, but he stopped then and looked down into her frightened eyes.

"It will only hurt for a few seconds," he whispered huskily. "Link your hands in mine and hold on. I'll do it quickly."

"All...all right." She felt the strength in his hands and her eyes met his. She swallowed.

He pushed, hard. She moaned a little, but her body accepted him instantly and without any further difficulty.

Her eyes brightened. Her lips parted and she breathed quickly and began to smile. "It's gone," she whispered. "Quinn, I'm a woman now...."

"My woman," he whispered back. The darkness grew in his eyes. He bent to her mouth and captured it, held it as he began to move, his body dancing above hers, teaching it the rhythm. She followed where he led, gasping as the cadence increased, as the music began to grow in her mind and filtered through her arms and legs. She held on to him with the last of her strength, proud of his stamina, of the power in his body that was taking hers from reality and into a place she'd never dreamed existed.

She felt the first tremors begin, and work into her like fiery pins, holding her body in a painful arch as she felt the tension build. It grew to unbearable levels. Her head thrashed on the pillow and she wanted to push him away, to make him stop, because she didn't think she could live through what was happening to her. But just as she began to push him the tension broke and she fell, crying out, into a hot, wild satisfaction that convulsed her. Above her, Quinn saw it happen and finally gave in to the desperate fever of his own need. He drove for his own satisfaction and felt it take him, his voice breaking on Amanda's name as he went into the fiery depths with her.

Afterward, he started to draw away, but her arms went around him and refused to let go. He felt her tears against his hot throat.

"Are you all right?" he asked huskily.

"I died," she whispered brokenly. Her arms contracted. "Don't go away, please don't. I don't want to let you go," she moaned.

He let his body relax, giving her his full weight. "I'll crush you, honey," he whispered in her ear.

"No, you won't." She sighed, feeling his body pulse with every heartbeat, feeling the dampness of his skin on her own, the glory of his flesh touching hers. "This is nice."

He laughed despite his exhaustion. "There's a new word for it," he murmured. He growled and bit her shoulder gently. "Wildcat," he whispered proudly. "You bit me. Do you remember? You bit me and dug your nails into my hips and screamed."

"So did you," she accused, flushing. "I'll have bruises on my thighs…"

"Little ones," he agreed. He lifted his head and searched her dark, quiet eyes. "I couldn't help that, at the last. I lost it. Really lost it. Are you as sated as I am?" he mused. "I feel like I've been walking around like half a person all my life, and I've just become whole."

"So do I." Her eyes searched his, and she lifted a lazy hand to trace his hard, thin lips. After a few seconds, she lifted her hips where they were still joined to his and watched his eyes kindle. She drew in a shaky breath and did it again, delighting in the sudden helpless response of his body.

"That's impossible," he joked. "The book said so."

Amanda pulled his mouth down to hers. "Damn the book," she said and held on as he answered her hunger with his own.

They slept and finally woke just in time to go down to dinner. But since neither of them wanted to face having to get dressed, they had room service send up a tray. They drank champagne and ate thick steaks and went back to bed. Eventually they even slept.

The next morning, they set out for Ricochet, holding hands all the way home.

CHAPTER ELEVEN

ELLIOT AND HARRY were waiting at the door when Quinn brought Amanda home. There was a big wedding cake on the table that Harry had made, and a special present that Elliot had made Harry drive him to town in the sleigh to get—a new Desperado album with a picture of Amanda on the cover.

"What a present," Quinn murmured, smiling at Amanda over the beautiful photograph. "I guess I'll have to listen to it now, won't I?"

"I even got Hank Shoeman's autograph," Elliot enthused. "Finally I can tell the guys at school! I've been going nuts ever since I realized who Amanda was...."

"You knew?" Quinn burst out. "And you didn't tell me? So that's why that tape disappeared."

"You were looking for it?" Elliot echoed.

"Sure, just after we got home from the lodge that night I deserted Amanda," Quinn said with a rueful glance at her. "I was feeling pretty low. I just wanted to hear her voice, but the tape was missing."

"Sorry, Dad," Elliot said gently. "I'll never do it again, but I was afraid you'd toss her out if you knew she was a rock singer. She's really terrific, you know, and that song that won a Grammy was one of hers."

"Stop, you'll make me blush," Amanda groaned.

"I can do that," Quinn murmured dryly and the look he gave Amanda brought scarlet color into her hot cheeks.

"You were in the paper, Dad," Elliot continued excitedly. "And on the six o'clock news, too! They told all about your skiing days and the Olympic team. Dad, why didn't you keep going? They said you were one of the best giant slalom skiers this country ever produced, but that you quit with a place on the Olympic team in your pocket."

"It's a long story, Elliot," he replied.

"It was because of my mother, wasn't it?" the boy asked gravely.

"Well, you were on the way and I didn't feel right about deserting her at such a time."

"Even though she'd been so terrible to you?" he probed.

Quinn put his hands on his son's shoulders. "I'll tell you for a fact, Elliot, you were mine from the day I knew about your existence. I waited for you like a kid waiting for a Christmas present. I bought stuff and read books about babies and learned all the things I'd need to know to help your mother raise you. I'd figured, you see, that she might eventually decide that having you was pretty special. I'm sorry that she didn't."

"That's okay," Elliot said with a smile. "You did."

"You bet I did. And do."

"Since you like kids so much, you and Amanda might have a few of your own," Elliot decided. "I can help. Me and Harry can wash diapers and make formula…"

Amanda laughed delightedly. "Oh, you doll, you!" She hugged Elliot. "Would you really not mind other kids around?"

"Heck, no," Elliot said with genuine feeling. "All the other guys have little brothers and sisters. It gets sort of lonely, being the only one." He looked up at her admiringly. "And they'd be awful pretty, if some of them were girls."

She grinned. "Maybe we'll get lucky and have another redhead, too. My mother was redheaded. So was my grandmother. It runs in the family."

Elliot liked that, and said so.

"Hank Shoeman has a present for you, by the way," she told Elliot. "No, there's no use looking in the truck, he ordered it."

Elliot's eyes lit up. "What is it? An autographed photo of the group?"

"It's a keyboard," Amanda corrected gently, smiling at his awe. "A real one, a Moog like I play when we do instrumentals."

"Oh, my gosh!" Elliot sat down. "I've died and gone to heaven. First I get a great new mother and now I get a Moog. Maybe I'm real sick and have a high fever," he frowned, feeling his forehead.

"No, you're perfectly well," Quinn told him. "And I guess it's all right if you play some rock songs," he added with a grimace. "I got used to turnips, after all, that time when Harry refused to cook any more greens. I guess I can get used to loud music."

"I refused to cook greens because we had a blizzard and canned turnips was all I had," Harry reminded him, glowering. "Now that Amanda's here, we won't run out of beans and peas and such, because she'll remember to tell me we're out so I can get some more."

"I didn't forget to remind you," Quinn muttered.

"You did so," Elliot began. "I remember—"

"That's it, gang up on me," Quinn glowered at them.

"Don't you worry, sweet man, I'll protect you from ghastly turnips and peas and beans," she said with a quick glance at Harry and Elliot. "I like asparagus, so I'll make sure that's all we keep here. Don't you guys like asparagus?"

"Yes!" they chorused, having been the culprits who told Amanda once that Quinn hated asparagus above all food in the world.

Quinn groaned.

"And I'll make liver and onions every night," Amanda added. "We love that, don't we, gang?"

"We sure do!" they chorused again, because they knew it was the only meat Quinn wouldn't eat.

"I'll go live with McNaber," he threatened.

Amanda laughed and slid her arms around him. "Only if we get to come, too." She looked up at him. "It's all right. We all really hate asparagus and liver and onions."

"That's a fact, we do," Elliot replied. "Amanda, are you going to go on tour with the band?"

"No," she said quietly. "We'd all gotten tired of the pace. We're going to take a well-earned rest and concentrate on videos and albums."

"I've got this great idea for a video," Elliot volunteered.

She grinned. "Okay, tiger, you can share it with us when Hank and the others come for a visit."

His eyes lit up. "They're all coming? The whole group?"

"My aunt is marrying Mr. Durning," she told him, having found out that tidbit from Hank. "They're going to live in Hawaii, and the band has permission to use the cabin whenever they like. They've decided that if I like the mountains so much, there must be something special about them. Our next album is going to be built around a mountain theme."

"Wow." Elliot sighed. "Wait'll I tell the guys."

"You and the guys can be in the video," Amanda promised. "We'll find some way to fit you into a scene or two." She studied Harry. "We'll put Harry in, too."

"Oh, no, you won't!" he said. "I'll run away from home first."

"If you do, we'll starve to death." Amanda sighed. "I can't do cakes and roasts. We'll have to live on potatoes and fried eggs."

"Then you just make a movie star out of old Elliot and I'll stick around," he promised.

"Okay," Amanda said, "but what a loss to women everywhere. You'd have been super, Harry."

He grinned and went back to the kitchen to cook. Elliot eventually wandered off, too, and Quinn took Amanda into the study and closed the door.

They sat together in his big leather armchair, listening to the crackling of the fire in the potbellied stove.

"Remember the last time we were in here together?" he asked lazily between kisses.

"Indeed, I do," she murmured with a smile against his throat. "We almost didn't stop in time."

"I'm glad we did." He linked her fingers with his. "We had a very special first time. A real wedding night. That's marriage the way it was meant to be; a feast of first times."

She touched his cheek lightly and searched his dark eyes. "I'm glad we waited, too. I wanted so much to go to my husband untouched. I just want you to know that it was worth the wait. I love you, really love you, you know?" She sighed shakily. "That made it much more than my first intimate experience."

He brought his mouth down gently on hers. "I felt just that way about it," he breathed against her lips. "I never asked if you wanted me to use anything...?"

"So I wouldn't get pregnant?" She smiled gently. "I love kids."

"So do I." He eased back and pulled her cheek onto his chest, smoothing her long, soft hair as he smiled down into her eyes. "I never dreamed I'd find anyone like you. I'd given up on women. On life, too, I guess. I've been bitter and alone for such a long time, Amanda. I feel like I was just feverish and dreaming it all."

"You aren't dreaming." She pulled him closer to her and kissed him with warm, slow passion. "We're married and I'm going to love you for the rest of my life, body and soul. So don't get any ideas about trying to get away. I've caught you fair and square and you're all mine."

He chuckled. "Really? If you've caught me, what are you going to do with me?"

"Have I got an answer for that," she whispered with a sultry smile. "You did lock the door, didn't you?" she murmured, her voice husky as she lifted and turned so that she was facing him, her knees beside him on the chair. His heart began to race violently.

"Yes, I locked the door. What are you... Amanda!"

She smiled against his mouth while her hands worked at fastenings. "That's my name, all right," she whispered. She nipped his lower lip gently and laughed delightedly when she felt him helping her. "Life is short. We'd better start living it right now."

"I couldn't possibly agree more," he whispered back, and his husky laugh mingled with hers in the tense silence of the room.

Beside them, the burning wood crackled and popped in the stove while the snow began to fall again outside the window. Amanda had started it, but almost immediately Quinn took control and she gave in with a warm laugh. She knew already that things were done Sutton's way around Ricochet. And this time, she didn't really mind at all.

* * * * *

NEW RELEASES!

Four sisters. One surprise will. One year to wed.

Don't miss these two volumes of *Wed In The Outback*!

When Holt Waverly leaves his flourishing outback estate to his four daughters, it comes to pass that without an eldest son to inherit, the farm will be entailed to someone else…unless all his daughters are married within the year!

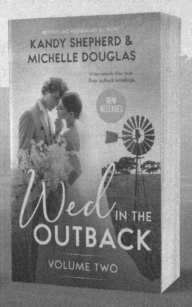

May 2024

July 2024

MILLS & BOON

Subscribe and fall in love with a Mills & Boon series today!

You'll be among the first to read stories delivered to your door monthly and enjoy great savings.

WE SIMPLY LOVE ROMANCE

Keep reading for an excerpt of
Texas On My Mind
by Delores Fossen.
Find it in the
The McCords: Riley & Lucky anthology,
out now!

CHAPTER ONE

THERE WERE TWO women in Captain Riley McCord's bed. Women wearing cutoff shorts, skinny tops and flip-flops.

Riley blinked a couple of times to make sure they weren't by-products of his pain meds and bone-deep exhaustion. *Nope.* They were real enough because he could hear them breathing.

See them breathing, too.

The lamp on the nightstand was on, the milky-yellow light spilling over them. Their tops holding in those C-cups were doing plenty of moving with each breath they took.

He caught a glimpse of a nipple.

If he'd still been a teenager, Riley might have considered having two women in his bed a dream come true. Especially in this room. He'd grown up in this house, had had plenty of fantasies in that very bed. But he was thirty-one now, and with his shoulder throbbing like an abscessed tooth, taking on two women didn't fall into fantasy territory. More like suicide.

Besides, man-rule number two applied here: don't do anything half-assed. Anything he attempted right now would be significantly less than half and would make an ass out of him.

Who the hell were they?

And why were they there in his house, in his bed?

The place was supposed to be empty since he'd called ahead

and given the cook and housekeeper the week off. The sisters, Della and Stella, had pretty much run the house since Riley's folks had been killed in a car wreck thirteen years ago. Clearing out the pair hadn't been easy, but he'd used his captain's I'm-giving-the-orders-here voice.

For once it had worked.

His kid sister was away at college. His older brother Lucky was God knew where. Lucky's twin, Logan, was on a business trip and wouldn't be back for at least another week. Even when Logan returned, he'd be spending far more time running the family's cattle brokerage company than actually in the house. That lure of emptiness was the only reason Riley had decided to come here for some peace and quiet.

And so that nobody would see him wincing and grunting in pain.

Riley glanced around to try to figure out who the women were and why they were there. When he checked the family room, he saw a clue by the fireplace. A banner. Well, sort of. He flicked on the lights to get a better look. It was a ten-foot strip of white crepe paper.

Welcome Home, Riley, Our Hero, was written on it.

The black ink had bled, and the tape on one side had given way, and now it dangled and coiled like a soy-sauced ramen noodle.

There were bowls of chips, salsa and other food on the coffee table next to a picture of him in his uniform. Someone had tossed flag confetti all around the snacks, and some of the red, white and blue sparkles had landed on the floor and sofa. In the salsa, too.

Apparently, this was supposed to be the makings of a homecoming party for him.

Whoever had done this probably hadn't counted on his flight from the base in Germany being delayed nine hours. Riley hadn't counted on it, either. Now, it was three in the morning, and he darn sure didn't want to celebrate.

Or have women in his bed.

And he hoped it didn't lower his testosterone a couple of notches to have an unmanly thought like that.

Riley put his duffel bag on the floor. Not quietly, but the women didn't stir even an eyelash. He considered just waking them, but heck, that would require talking to them, and the only thing he wanted right now was another hit of pain meds and a place to collapse.

He went to the bedroom next to his. A guest room. No covers or pillows, which would mean a hunt to find some. That sent him to Lucky's room on the other side of the hall. Covers, yes, but there was another woman asleep facedown with her sleeve-tattooed arm dangling off the side. There was also a saddle on the foot of the bed. Thankfully, Riley's mind was too clouded to even want to consider why it was there.

Getting desperate now and feeling a little like Goldilocks in search of a "just right" place to crash, he went to Logan's suite, the only other bedroom downstairs. Definitely covers there. He didn't waste the energy to turn on the light to have a closer look; since this was Logan's space, it would no doubt be clean enough to pass a military inspection.

No saddles or women, thank God, and he wouldn't have to climb the stairs that he wasn't sure he could climb anyway.

Riley popped a couple of pain meds and dropped down on the bed, his eyes already closing before his head landed against something soft and crumbly. He considered investigating it. *Briefly* considered it. But when it didn't bite, shoot or scald him, he passed on the notion of an investigation.

Whatever was soft and crumbly would just have to wait.

RILEY JACKKNIFED IN Logan's bed, the pain knocking the breath right out of him. Without any kind of warning, the nightmare that he'd been having had morphed into a full-fledged flashback.

Sometimes he could catch the flashback just as it was bubbling to the surface, and he could stomp it back down with his mental steel-toed combat boots. Sometimes humming "Jingle Bells" helped.

Not this time, though.

The flashback had him by the throat before Riley could even get out a single note of that stupid song he hated. Why had his brain chosen that little Christmas ditty to blur out the images anyway?

The smell came first. Always the fucking smell. The dust and debris whipped up by the chopper. The Pave Hawk blades slicing through the dirt-colored smoke. But not drowning out the sounds.

He wasn't sure how sounds like that could make it through the thump of the blades, the shouts, screams and the chaos. But they did. The sounds always did.

Someone was calling for help in a dialect Riley barely understood. But you didn't need to know the words to hear the fear.

Or smell it.

The images came with a vengeance. Like a chopped-up snake crawling and coiling together to form a neat picture of hell. A handful of buildings on fire, others ripped apart from the explosion. Blood on the bleached-out sand. The screams for help. The kids.

Why the hell were there kids?

Riley had been trained to rescue military and civilians after the fight, after all hell had broken loose. Had been conditioned to deal with fires, blood, IEDs, gunfire, and being dropped into the middle of it so he could do his job and save lives.

But nobody had ever been able to tell him how to deal with the kids.

PTSD. Such a tidy little label. A dialect that civilians understood, or thought they did anyway. But it was just another label for shit. Shit that Riley didn't want in his head.

He grabbed his pain meds from the pocket of his uniform and shoved one, then another into his parched mouth. Soon, very soon, he could start stomping the images back into that little shoe box he'd built in his head.

Soon.

He closed his eyes, the words finally coming that he needed to hear.

"Jingle bells, jingle bells…"

He really did need to come up with a more manly sounding song to kick some flashback ass.

